Shirley Jackson award-winner Kaaron Warren published her first short story in 1993 and has had fiction in print every year since. She was recently given the Peter McNamara Lifetime Achievement Award and was Guest of Honour at World Fantasy 2018, Stokercon 2019 and Geysercon 2019. Kaaron was a Fellow at the Museum for Australian Democracy, where she researched prime ministers, artists and serial killers. She's judged the World Fantasy Awards and the Shirley Jackson Awards.

She has published five multi-award winning novels (*Slights, Walking the Tree, Mistification, The Grief Hole* and *Tide of Stone*) and seven short story collections, including the multi-award winning *Through Splintered Walls*. She has won the ACT Writers and Publishers Award four times and twice been awarded the Canberra Critics Circle Award for Fiction. Her most recent novella, *Into Bones Like Oil* (Meerkat Press), was shortlisted for a Shirley Jackson Award and the Bram Stoker Award, winning the Aurealis Award.

Kaaron Warren Titles
Published By
IFWG Publishing Australia

The Grief Hole
The Gate Theory (short fiction collection)
Slights
Mistification
Walking the Trees (released 2022)
Morace's Story (released 2022)

Tool Tales (with Ellen Datlow) (released 2021)

Mistification

by
Kaaron Warren

Mistification

All Rights Reserved

ISBN-13: 978-1-922556-27-1

Copyright ©2021 Kaaron Warren

First published 2011

V.1.0

Printed in Palatino Linotype.

IFWG Publishing International
Gold Coast

www.ifwgpublishing.com

For Nana Mel, who helped me develop a love for reading.

"Of magic '…which, in almost every age *except the present*, has maintained its dominion over the mind of man.'"

—*Edward Gibbon*, Decline & Fall of the Roman Empire

"Another damned, thick, square book! Always scribble, scribble, scribble! Eh, Mr Gibbon?"

—William Henry, Duke of Gloucester (1743-1805), upon receiving Vol. II of *Decline & Fall of the Roman Empire*

Warning

Please do not accept as truth any data following. Much comes from opinions of those long dead or discredited. Much comes from invention and twisting. Much comes from seedy books bought in dusty bookshops for $1.00 per kilogram.

A single pail of water can produce enough fog to cover 231 km2 to a depth of 2405 metres.

Marvo the Magician does not need the pail.

Marvo could remember, first, the smell of hand lotion. To him it meant birth, strange birth, and the sound of people running. It was his grandmother's soft hand covering his mouth to silence his screams.

He appeared in an enormous house, amongst ant-like numbers of residents. He had no recollection of his birth; no record. He did not have a mother to tell him, "I spent twelve hours having you, twelve hours of agony. But when I held you in my arms it was all worth it."

He did not have a father to say, "You little rotter, you kept me up all night for weeks on end. You would not stop crying. But your mother was more beautiful than I've ever seen her, giving birth to you."

He did not have friends to compare growing up with; he could not remember growing up. His second memory was of the guns; guns and screams. It was his first image of the house; filled with running, screaming people. A house like a hotel, with a huge, dark lobby, floors covered with dark green linoleum. Two staircases, one up the west wall, one up the east. People running up and down the stairs, carrying things, baskets, bundles, children.

He was still; he did not run. He waited and watched with his grandmother's hand over his mouth. He watched men dressed in green like the lino, carrying guns and shooting the people.

Marvo was afraid of these men. He watched as they lined people up and shot them, watched the bodies fall onto the green floor (where the blood did not show, and there was no sun to shine on the puddles and make them glisten, where their belongings and their children fell).

Marvo was snatched up by his grandmother. She was very small, only slightly taller than him, and he was eight, or nine perhaps. She had black hair but it was a wig; Marvo knew because it fell off as she dragged him through a small door she had produced by pressing a panel in the wall of the kitchen.

They walked narrow corridors and passed through niches. The walls were so thin he could hear the shouts and screams and shots. He could hear people being dragged from cupboards, from under beds, where they must have imagined they were safe. He followed his grandmother, poor old thing using the last of her strength to make him safe. They came to a rope ladder dangling down and she climbed it. He could see up her dress to her underwear.

At the top of the ladder there was a landing and a trap door. His grandmother used her hands to tell him to keep back (they had not spoken or made a sound since the men in green burst in) and she lifted up the door. He helped her pull the ladder up and then they let it drop down through the trap door. She climbed down first, then he did, and he found himself in the room which was to be his home for the next four years. It was a long climb down.

The machine guns spat (the walls here, too, were thin. He could hear the men's words, listen to them). As each person was found, the machine guns spat. His grandmother stood in the middle of the room, listening, waiting. She counted on her fingers, counted as her friends (if that's what they were—Marvo didn't know) or her family were found and killed. He realised he must have known her for at least a while before the guns, because he heeded her, trusted her.

Half the roof consisted of the platform with the trap door they climbed through and the other half was skylight. Somebody planned well; the room was bright and warm. Marvo grew to love the sun through the roof, love the uncontrollable warmth of it.

There was a single bed. His grandmother slept there alone; he did not like the idea of sharing with her. He slept on the floor for four years and never got used to sleeping in a bed. In the future, with lovers, he rarely stayed over, or let them stay with him. He was embarrassed to be found on the floor each morning, sleeping soundly, the sleep he could never find in a bed.

There was a TV, which made him happy, though he didn't know what to watch, he couldn't remember watching before. His grandmother shook her finger at him. She turned the sound right down, then removed the knob.

The house remained full of men for the four years of their incarceration. Marvo grew very restless in the room with only his grandmother for company. They talked in whispers. She told him stories, taught him lessons through stories because there were no books. She told him the story of a cruel spell, of a woman who dared to stand up for her cause and not forget her lessons.

"You must never forget your lessons," she said. And he didn't, because what else was there to do but remember?

The Spell of Age

This witchy woman learnt when she was very young, that, while friends come and go, your family always remains. She was still young when she found that her mother was under attack.

Her dearest friend said, "Your mother is an old witch now. Her magic is no longer relevant. You must stop her from practising."

All of her learning had come from her mother, and the young woman did not believe her mother's magic was useless. She saw in a sudden moment of clarity that her friend was deeply jealous of that learning, and that she sought to cause a rift, to halve the magic.

The young woman said, "I can't stop my mother from practising magic. I still learn from her as I learn from you. A triangle is solid and powerful, when its lines meet. There are three in our triangle of learning."

But the friend disappeared, and the young woman began to get old very quickly. She realised the extent of her friend's jealousy. The hatred.

It was a spell of age her friend placed on her. The young woman's bones ached, riddled with rheumatism, and she went to her mother, the witch. Her mother could not change the spell. She could only provide another. Weeping, she said, "Take a potato and allow it to go black and hard in your pocket. This will cure your rheumatism. This may also keep you from bad luck, tough with a spell so heavy on your shoulders."

It was painful to be offered merely a lifting of symptoms, not her young life back, but it was something. The young woman carried that potato, fingering it with her pain-filled fingers until that pain faded.

"I wish we could find a place to be safe," her mother said.

The young woman felt the finality of the words. She left the village and did not return.

"She would not be seen in the world outside again," Marvo's grandmother said.

"Outside where?" asked Marvo. He knew only one outside; outside this room.

"Where the wind blows and the trees rustle. Where scent abounds and the texture beneath your feet is rough."

His grandmother clasped his arm with her strong fingers. So much power in those hands. "One day you will see outside, but don't wish it too soon. It will come."

The first few months passed. He slept a lot, and listened. He awakened from a cocoon, emerging to an unfamiliar world. He got to know the room very well and grew up quickly. It was vital, in order to stop his grandmother from leaving the room each night, risking her heart up and down the ladder to steal the food they needed to stay alive. He took over the job when he was nine; she had to let him, she was not fast enough anymore to do what was needed. She was close to discovery each time.

So Marvo began the trips, and slowly the room filled with things. He brought food, but he also brought found objects, things lost by the men, things left on the table at night, things dropped behind the couch. The room (so bare when they arrived:the bed and the TV, and a chair and a small table) began to fill with things: socks, condoms (used and unused—Marvo had no idea what they were and his grandmother didn't tell him. It was many years before he realised what the substance was and he laughed to remember he had kept them as special objects), stubs of pencils, half-empty pens, writing pads with three or four sheets of paper left, newspapers, slippers, underwear, bullets; a thousand little things people didn't miss and didn't care for. His room resembled a junkyard, though each item was noted and neatly placed in position. Marvo knew how many of everything there was. He was good with numbers.

Once he stole books. One of the men had been clearing out a child's room. In a rubbish pile by the door were six thin books, books of numbers and how to figure them. Marvo took them back with him and waited till his grandmother was asleep. He was not sure what she thought of books, whether she wanted to be the only one to tell him things. She had taught him to read using the TV instruction book. He never had trouble with equipment in his adult life.

He flicked through the books. Each had a different-coloured cover: purple, mauve, aqua, dark blue, red and green. He read them so he knew every word, every figure. He flicked through them for hours, trying to pick the one he knew the least. He flicked through them, wishing hard for something new, something exciting, he flicked through them and one changed colour. It was brown. Tan brown. It was a new book inside too. He didn't tell his grandmother. He put the books away and didn't look at them for a while. He thought he must have missed the brown one, thought there must have been seven from the start.

The tan book obsessed him, though. His mind's voice repeated the title, *How to Be a Magnificent Magician,* loud and soft, again and again, until he took the book to a corner and began to read.

What you need, it said:
- *a piece of black cloth*
- *a selection of small balls*
- *a magic wand*
- *a stuffed toy until a real animal would be safe*
- *some coins*
- *some cards*
- *a length of rope*
- *a collection of large handkerchiefs*
- *patience*
- *and plenty of time.*

Marvo collected all the things first. He improvised on his pieces.

The black cloth he found screwed up in a ball beside a toilet.

His grandmother said it belonged to a nun, and Marvo imagined that:

She came knocking on one of the doors of the large mansion, softly shaking her collection box. "For the orphans in the other wing." The other wing was a long way away, over the other side of the world.

"Come in," said the head man, the one who had watched from the top of the stairs, the one who did not shoot anyone himself but watched all the shooting. "Please, come in."

"We're collecting door to door," said the nun. "The orphans are in great need."

"Ah, but my money is here in an inside room. Surely you can bear my company for a few moments."

The nun entered the head man's room. He click-locked the door behind her.

"What do you look like beneath that black sweep?" he asked. "What body do you have?"

She was a young nun, unused to the ways of men. "The orphans, sir, they need the help of those in our fortunate positions."

The man laughed. "I have no love for the unfortunate. I feel no need to support their failure. However, if you were to agree to lie with me, an arrangement could be made."

The nun tried to leave the room, but the man grabbed the thick material of her black dress and, using his strength, tore it through the centre. The nun wept and whimpered, prayed and pleaded.

Marvo could not imagine the next scene. The television usually faded, and returned with:

The nun, naked and bleeding, holding her dress to her chest. The man gestured to the toilet and she went in there to clean herself.

The man, however, came behind her and caressed her skull with the brass nude statue. The nun collapsed, and her body was hidden in one of the rooms. The dress was forgotten, kicked behind the toilet and left to gather stench and dust.

This became Marvo's magic black cloth, and, eventually, his black cloak. The blood of the nun was never removed. You cannot see blood on dark cloth.

Marvo knew about the head man, listening to him mutter, alone regardless of who was in the room, drunk, incoherent:

"I was supposed to be the magician. That was what my dream meant. I was walking along a cliff top and a cat was leading me. It led me to a castle which reached into the clouds."

Marvo never had this dream, and he didn't place any faith in dreams. He didn't believe in them.

"I was waiting," the head man muttered, "for the magic to be bestowed upon me. Then I heard of the birth of that one, that strange birth, and it looked like he'd be it, he'd be the one. So I had him killed."

One of the men in the room laughed. "Killed them all," the man said. Marvo did not tell his grandmother of their glee in the slaughter. He told her how the men lived in the house like kings.

She said, "That man thinks you are dead, and he's waiting for his own magic to come." This made his grandmother laugh soundlessly.

"What's funny, Grandma? When will his magic come?" Marvo

thought of his magician book and wondered if the head man would like to read it.

"He will not come into magic. Even if he had killed you, your magic would not be his."

"Anyone can learn it, though. I'll show you."

Marvo jumped up to grab his magician's book. He opened it at the page which showed you how to make a ball disappear.

"It's only practice, the book says. Maybe if that man practised he'd be happier and not so mean to people."

"This is a different sort of magic, Marvo. You'll discover it when you're bigger. Stronger," she said. "But you have to wait until you're old enough. You're too young and brittle at the moment for real magic." She hugged him to her, squeezed him, to show him how much stronger she was than he. "I'll keep you a while longer," she said.

It was difficult for Marvo to find the small balls listed in the book. He wanted a lot of them. Eventually he realised the fruit they ate contained round stones. The cherries, apricots, plums, and the avocado, all taken from the rubbish, discarded as old, but very fresh. Was there someone helping them in the big house? His grandmother would not answer this question. Thus Marvo collected the second requirement.

The wand proved very hard. He could find no short, smooth stick. He sought each time he was out, looked for anything which may prove appropriate.

Then there was a terrible time amongst the men of the house, a raging screaming smashing which kept Marvo close to his grandmother, hungry but unwilling to go out for food, for three days. At the end of it, one man was left blind. Marvo listened with fascination as he progressed. Marvo remembered how the woman in his grandmother's story had paid so much for her belief in her mother, had paid with her youth, and wondered what cause this man had paid for. Marvo closed his eyes to imagine life without sight and felt a certain power. The blind man stumbled about the rooms of the house, tapping with a smooth white cane. Marvo watched through a ventilation shaft. He felt safe watching the blind man. The blind man could not see him.

He could tell that the blind man imagined people were in the room with him, that people entered and sat silently. He would guess who it was, and face a blank spot, talking.

"You can't hurt me like this," he said, "I know your face, I can see it in my mind. My mind is not blind."

He waved into space with his white cane. Marvo felt covetous for the first time. He wanted the cane. It rarely left the blind man's hand, though. Only as he slept.

The cane had led a very exciting life, Marvo knew. He was an eavesdropper, a listener-in. The blind man told the story of the cane and why such a beautiful thing was discarded.

He told it often. It was the only story his fellows loved to hear. They woke from lethargy and listened, leaned forward, breathed more quietly. Marvo never told his grandmother he listened to these stories. He thought she wanted her stories to be his only lessons.

The Cane

This came from a man who didn't need it anymore. Used it for years to beat his wife. He could see all right; everything working okay there. It was the downstairs department, the old one-two. Because he wanted to, his wife being not bad to look at, but he couldn't. He'd been okay with sluts and scrags, although he was often drunk then. So either the booze propped his prick up or it stole away the memory of his flops.

He'd try away and fail, and there under the bed sat the cane. He'd reach it out and give her a belt, swipe her with it, and pretend he hated her.

The wife got tired of this after a while. It wasn't like she deserved it, talked back or whatever. So she got some outside help.

I don't know if it was magic, or watching what she was doing, but it worked. First, she laid out two large rubber sheets on the lounge room floor. She poured jars of honey over one, wheat on the other.

Then she slowly removed her clothes. She bathed, soaping each crevice and nook, cleaning each strand of hair. She rinsed until her skin squeaked.

She walked naked to the room of honey and wheat, where her husband sat waiting and watching. She rolled over and over in the honey till her whole body was covered with it. Then she rolled in the wheat.

With his help, she removed the grains, rolling them off her skin and into a bowl. They ground the grains in a mill, four hands turning the handle anti-clockwise. The flour she mixed into a dough which she kneaded and kneaded and kneaded. Then she baked it into bread.

The man ate the bread and was very pleased with the results. So pleased he gave away his wife-beating cane and swore never to use it again.

"How did she knead the dough?" the men always asked. He was teasing them, making the most of their attention.

"Between her legs. On her cunt," he said.

Marvo would not use the cane to beat anybody. It was his magic wand.

Marvo did not tell his grandmother of his trip to the blind man's bedroom. With quiet in his blood, Marvo entered the room in the hour before dawn. He reached for the cane. Clasped it. It felt alien; it did not feel magical. Marvo was deeply disappointed. He expected a knowing, a familiarity and a rightness.

He silently carried his magic wand to the room.

The blind man was very upset with the disappearance of his cane. He blamed another member of the household who took great offence and shot the blind man. Marvo felt somewhat responsible for the blind man's death but knew he needed the wand. The wand was his.

The stuffed toys were not a difficult prospect. Marvo merely searched the rooms where children had slept; some of them had not been emptied. He took a selection of creatures: a blue rabbit, a pink bear, a small duck, a tiny hippopotamus. These he presented to his grandmother proudly.

"You have gone beyond childish things," she said, although he was only nine.

"I need these for my magic."

Coins he found beneath beds, behind cushions, scattered here and there. Marvo was wealthy with small change.

He wasn't sure about cards. There were many packs about, but they were kept very carefully and were in constant use. Marvo found stiff paper and had a collection of coloured pens. He borrowed a pack one night and copied each one, returning the cards before morning.

His grandmother was impressed with his talent.

Marvo had to create and invent to complete his task. Rope he made from twirling strings together, collecting fabric scraps (old underpants and socks, filthy towels and rags) and unravelling them. Then re-twirling, many hours of careful labour, his concentration on the magic of his rope. The only rope of its kind in the world. He made it far longer than requested. He wanted length and strength in the rope. He used the rope ladder as a gauge of strength.

The final physical item (patience and time he had no end of) were the handkerchiefs and these he stole and washed in their tiny basin. He felt no one would miss the vile things. Marvo and his grandmother used the rain water that filtered down through a hose system from the roof. Their toilet was a hole in the floor which led directly to a sewer pipe; the smell was terrible but at least they were never embarrassed about making smells themselves. Once the lid was shut, the smell was lessened.

Marvo spent months collecting his needs, then his training began. Having no distractions, he easily mastered every trick in the book. He then began to create his own, using the basic magic learnt. Soon, the book seemed foolish to him, too easy.

His grandmother lay on her bed, propped up with pillows and clothes rolled pillow-shape. She was his only audience, and a harsh critic.

"I see your hands moving," she said. "I know where the Ace of Hearts is." She taught him many more tricks and would not let him rest until they were right.

For three years Marvo played and played his tricks until the movements were as natural as scratching an itch.

His grandmother was patient with him. They talked in their whisper; he never learnt to talk much above it, in all his life. He needed the microphone even for the smallest audiences; his act was mostly demonstration. He did not talk much.

The house was all he knew. During his time there, he imagined it was the entire world; the places he saw on the television were other rooms of the house, some bigger than others, some vast, incredibly huge. He saw on the TV rivers and lakes, and the sea. He wondered why the water did not flow through their room. His grandmother did not know either.

His grandmother talked and talked (whispered and whispered) until she could talk no more. Then she slept.

She told him few tales about herself. They made her too sad. Once, when she made him sit quietly for many hours, sit and do nothing while she rested, he crawled to her bed and whispered, "I hate you." She had told him about hate and he had seen the faces hatred drew on people on TV. He had seen the faces of the men in green, on the blind man and on the head man.

He didn't understand how she could rest with her eyes open and if she was watching, why couldn't he do something interesting?

"I hate you," he said.

"Don't say that. You can't take back a word like hate. It's there forever. And it can only turn against you."

"How, Grandmother?" A story would be better than sitting in the corner.

"Hatred can eat you up. Like love, it is rarely reciprocated to the same degree. You love your tricks, Marvo. You must be careful to let people believe they *are* tricks, at all times. Let them think there is an answer, an explanation. If they think your magic is true, they will hate you. This has happened to me more than once."

The Barren Village

I lived in a village where there was much barrenness. The women were not falling pregnant, the cows were dry and the fields lay fallow.

This village had been in existence for many hundreds of years, each hardship dealt with and overcome. This generation, however, was weaker than the others. They had no sense of community, or history. They did not care what their parents had done, only what they could take from life.

But they were a good group at heart; kind to each other and loving of children born—though none were under three in this village. No child had been born for three years.

I was not the healer of the village. I made food, collected food. They decided the healer was powerless to do anything. She tried, with science, to undo the emptiness of the wombs, but she failed.

So, through connivance and magic, my mother and I caused an uproar. We sent this husband to that wife; that wife to that son; that daughter to that husband; that wife to that bachelor. I was only fifteen but I helped.

They enjoyed it, let me tell you. It was a cold and misty weekend, nothing to do but stay indoors.

And they did, let me tell you.

Every woman of childbearing age fell pregnant. In response the cows gave milk and the fields grew wheat.

I was the only one not pregnant; the only one who remembered the weekend.

"I don't remember my husband doing this," said one wife. "Did he do it while I was asleep? Disgusting."

I did not remind them of their adventures. Plans were made to marry the unmarried girls off.

My mother said, "Why bother? Let them live together with me and my daughter, in my home, and we will bring up the children that way." A reasonable suggestion, I thought, looking at the bachelors of the village.

There was Tom, who beat his dog. Adam, an idiot who stared directly into the sun for most of the day, hoping to sneeze and prove himself sane, because idiots can't sneeze. If you need to sneeze, looking into the sun dilates the eyes and triggers the sneeze process. Adam stared and stared, but no sneeze came.

John, bow-legged and bow-backed. And others, equally unattractive.

The girls thought my mother's idea was marvellous, but the villagers began to look at us strangely.

"Why is her daughter not pregnant?" they said.

I confessed I had helped the process, and they thanked me, gifted me, glorified me. Then a girl came of age but could not fall pregnant.

"Tell me the trick," she said. "Give us your ingredients."

"There is no trick," I said.

This was a mistake. The villagers were torn between fearing us, believing we had performed true magic, and hating us, thinking we were keeping it to ourselves. Either way, we became outcasts in that place.

No one would buy my food, or talk to me, or serve me. I had no food but that which I cooked. I had no companionship; the girls went to husbands foul.

I hated that loneliness. So I searched in books, dusty and old, to find a fertility recipe.

There is a mushroom called *Amanita muscaria*, shaped like an erect, fiery topped penis. I told them of this fungus, and they were happy to believe I was a ritual prostitute, that I danced over the mushrooms, squatted over them with naked genitals, that this crude dance sent good seed to womb.

Once I had provided this explanation, I became popular again. It had all been spoiled for my mother and I, though, and we moved from there soon after.

"Did you go to a better place?" Marvo asked

She closed her eyes. "That's a story you already know."

"Did you enjoy it, Grandmother? Did you have fun with all the other girls?" He couldn't imagine his old grandmother doing that thing they did on TV.

"I did not. I was not ready for pregnancy."

Marvo was barely shocked by this; they shared a lot, in their small prison.

Marvo listened to his grandmother, taking in every word whether he understood it or not. Each piece of information he used later in his life.

He learnt to lie about what he loved and feared. Every story he told had an element of deception about it. He learnt it from her, this carefulness of spirit. She taught him that to give it all is to surrender; that true emotions and thoughts are secrets to be kept forever. He practised on her; if he was feeling boredom and hatred towards her he would give her a hug. If she asked his opinion of a show they watched he would lie. He became very good at it; better than her.

He caught her weeping one day and the sight made him want to cry. But he said, "Shut up, will you? Your noise is painful."

She was not making a sound, but she snivelled the tears away.

"Pathetic," Marvo said, though he longed to hug her as she hugged him when he was sad.

He felt guilty, so when he saw chocolate in the kitchen he snatched it up from its place— slipped down between the stove and the sink. Marvo often found treasures there. As a free man, he sometimes hid small morsels in his own clean kitchen, to try to recapture that moment of discovery.

He described the scene to his grandmother and she said they had been making chocolate mousse. It was a fancy sounding dessert for such rough men, but Marvo had seen a woman around lately, a soft and gentle woman who spent her time in the head man's room. She did not stay for long, to Marvo's disappointment. She was so lovely to listen to.

He took the four squares of chocolate to his grandmother.

"Chocolate," she said. "Two bits each." Marvo was only ten, but he was already wary of addiction.

"I've never tried it before, so why start now? You have it all."

He watched as his grandmother dusted a square off and placed it on her tongue. She saved the other pieces, took one only every few days, and within a week her stash was gone.

"Chocolate," his grandmother told him, "is reward and taunt all in one. It gives you energy and gives you problems. It can make you fat." When they saw chocolate on TV, she would dig her fingers into his shoulders, lick her lips, suck her teeth as if to dredge a skerrick of flavour. They watched the chocolate unwrap itself and wait to be cracked.

Marvo became a great listener. It was his contact with the outer world, the world outside the room, listening to the conversations of the men and the women who lived out there. He heard what they said through the walls, he heard what they did. He knew when it was safe to travel to the countries on the other side of the wall. He knew who loved who, who lied to who, who was the boss and what problems they experienced. Listening was something he did well; and he would always use it to his advantage. He listened, questioned.

He discovered dissatisfaction, or at least the name for what he was feeling when he saw food on TV and wondered at its taste. He said, "Why can't we eat a plateful of food, like on TV, where they get whole bits of food?" He had returned from the kitchen, where he scraped plates for their night meal.

His grandmother said, "The scraping is part of the power of the food. Much great magic comes from scrapings. An old piece of flint used by our ancestors as a tool will calm a stomach ache or soothe inflamed eyes. Add a scraping to water, swallow it down (swallow scrapings many thousands of years old) or press it upon the aching part. Very powerful magic.

"In Wales, a tomb from the fourteenth century has been all but destroyed as people come and scrape, scrape, scrape, at the stone columns. Scraping, scraping, for their eyes or their tummies.

"Our scrapings are for our tummies, are they not? You must never despise any form of magic."

This is one lesson Marvo later chose to forget. He couldn't abide all magic. He learnt to despise the magic of illusionists, for their trickery and fakery; but he didn't believe they were magic, so didn't imagine he was disobeying his grandmother.

He didn't care about the history of scrapings. He was tired of scrappy food, of silence, of being still. He wanted to run, but he could only guess how it felt. He saw races on TV, wondered how they knew when to start, saw them racing, running, the sweat, the *heat* of them. Arms in the air for victory, arms dangling simian-like for loss. Throats pulsing, red-faced *excitement*.

Marvo tried to run from one end of the room to the other. He pushed himself off from the wall, took three or four lunging, thrilling steps, and his grandmother threw a pillow at his face. It was the closest she could go to hurting him. She would have hurt him, if she could be sure he wouldn't fall or scream, and she pinched his elbow, the punishment she gave instead of a belting or a yelling. Pinched hard so his mouth opened and his eyes watered, but he didn't cry. He never cried.

He practised in slow motion, long silent steps which stretched his muscles and made him strong. His arms swung perfectly. He moved from one end of the room to the other, for hours at a time.

His grandmother watched him, each lap her eyes getting tighter, squintier, until she had to face the wall to escape the repetition, her wig slipping to reveal her scalp. Marvo would learn that she had already lost her magic and could not protect herself from frustrations, irritations.

Marvo never got tired of repetition. It was one of the things which made him a magnificent magician. He took delight in practice, doing things one hundred or two hundred times, over and over.

Marvo always won his races. It was hard to picture opponents. He could only remember faces from TV. He ran against the fastest racers and always won.

One night his training saved his life.

For three years, Marvo had been tripping into the house. Never outside it—he was still unaware of a world outside the house. He found food and things nightly, each dusk heralding the chance of new adventure. Each time he reached the world outside, fear came momentarily. The unknown scared and thrilled him and as he climbed the ladder there was always the chance of something new. But for three years it was always the familiar he saw. Then one night, he felt dangerous and bad, he wanted his throat to throb, his face to go red. He wanted to find the room where the races were held.

• He collected their food and left it in the tunnel, then he ran up the stairs, the wind in his ears, hair ruffled. That was good. He ran up the hall, past dark doors (doors behind which islands slept, cars rested, crowds nestled silent) till he came upon a shaft of light. Here, perhaps, were the races. Regaining some sense, he slowed his pace and crept to the door.

There, he heard shouting voices, so loud his ears rang. And he saw flesh, true flesh. He had not even seen himself naked—there was no large mirror in the room and he would not appear that way with his grandmother around. He most certainly had not seen her naked. He did not mind the most horrific stories, graphic details, the cruellest sights on the television. But to see his grandmother naked, or to touch himself, was too shocking. He hated discussions about himself, any intimation of person. When his grandmother wanted to talk about what he would do when he left the room forever, he hated that.

He had seen TV flesh, but this was so soft, so...meaty. It looked like food, like something you would eat, and the thought made Marvo sick. He knew you did not eat human flesh. The sight horrified Marvo and he gave a half-shout, the greatest noise he had made in three years. A grunt.

The flesh stopped writhing. A voice demanded, "Who's there? Who is it?" and Marvo ran, fleet of foot and invisible, down the stairs and out of sight before the man could rise, wrap and follow.

Marvo sat behind the wall in the tunnel to catch his breath. The food was there, gathered earlier. But if his grandmother heard his breath, she would punish him.

When he was rested, Marvo returned to the room. He now knew the feeling of excitement.

His grandmother was not in a curious mood when he returned. She didn't ask about his red face, she didn't want to hear about the adventure. Marvo, forgetting about the trouble he might get into, began to whisper quickly, words describing each step.

"I want to run again, Grandmother. I loved how it felt."

"You will run plenty when you're older. Outside."

"Outside? When?"

"Not yet, Marvo. When you're older."

He pestered her for three days, desperate to know what she meant. The more he pestered, the quieter she became until, if he closed his eyes, he thought he was alone.

He learnt a lesson there: desperation is not the way to get what you want. People will give it to you if you pretend you don't want it. Because six months later, when Marvo was twelve, when they had spent four years in their room, his grandmother grew thinner and thinner. He brought more food, took risks to bring her treats, thin slices of cake, shaved off the sides of leftovers; soft bread when he stole out early in the morning rather than late at night; and, once more, chocolate. She nibbled at his offerings, then told him to eat the rest himself.

"My age is giving me a message of speed: *tell it all, tell it now*," she said.

She began to tell him something about the world outside the house. "The whole world is not in the house. The places on TV are outside it, they are far away. You can travel to them; you can find them. Seek sometimes with your eyes closed, sometimes shut your ears. You will catch things that way."

His grandmother told him that he must leave soon. She began to cry. She said, "I will be dying soon. You must not remember me; you must leave; carry my body into the passageway near the air vent; they will find me eventually and we will not give away this place. You will need it again. Go to the city," she said. "The biggest city you can find. There the magic will come." She gave him a large white envelope. "In here there is a message for you to read when you turn thirteen. You don't have to read it on your birthday. You read it when you are ready. Once you read it, you will no longer be a child. You will have the weight of the world on your shoulders. You will be a different person."

Marvo took the envelope, thinking that perhaps he would never choose to read it.

It was not until he was much older he considered how bored his grandmother must have been. He was able to potter and play and imagine; she lay on the bed and watched the TV, or told him stories. He hoped that she was never bored, that his magic saved her. She was happy, alone and quiet with her magical grandson.

One morning, she said, "I would like to go today," and he put his hands over her eyes and kissed her nose, something he didn't really like to do because she was so old, he only wanted to kiss a young woman, a woman from one of the other rooms of the world, one of the young women he saw on TV. But he kissed her nose and touched her eyes and felt her relax. She had told him all about death so he did not feel frightened of her dead body. He was frightened at the thought of leaving, but she had given him a parcel, with money and jewels to use, and a message he was not to read until he turned thirteen.

He carried her up the ladder; she was so light he climbed as easily as he did every night. He remembered he'd left the TV on, so rested her on the platform to go down again and turn it off.

He took one last look at his things, his bits and pieces, knowing he could not take them all with him. He took the sound knob his grandmother had removed from the TV; it would forever remind him of this room. He had known where it sat for two years now, and he considered it a sign of his maturity that he had never used it to turn up the sound. He left almost everything else behind. He left the wand which had never felt right, the toys, the fruit pits. All he took was the TV knob, the nun's habit, the note his grandmother had given him and the rope he had made himself.

If dying wishes are not fulfilled, the restless spirit will come back to haunt the living who failed in that promise. Marvo feared this so he did as his grandmother wished.

He placed her body near the air vent, the place she had designated for her final resting. He searched her pockets to find a memento, something with her smell. He found a small, black potato.

He listened until it was safe to leave, then he walked through the corridors of the house. Silently and quickly, he arrived at the door he believed led to the other side, to the world where there were beaches and caves and other people, animals and weather, books and places to eat, nuns and people who ran.

The small door was almost concealed beneath the stairs. Marvo had never opened it for fear of letting that world in.

He stood by the door. He felt excitement and what he identified as terror. He didn't know where the entrance to the other world would be. What if he appeared in a jail, opened up a door and walked straight into the exercise yard? Or into a bedroom, or a school room? He didn't know.

He closed his eyes, thinking of his grandmother.

"Goodbye, love," he whispered. He threw open the door and stepped inside.

It was dark. He was not there yet; another door, perhaps, on the wall, which needed to be opened. He walked forward, his hands outstretched.

With a noise so loud his ears numbed, he came to a collection of brooms and mops, tripped over a metal bucket on the floor. He clutched and grabbed to save himself from falling and clasped a small and perfect stick. With it he balanced and stood. This was a broom closet. Like in all the shows he had seen. It was not the door. It was a closet. And he had made enough noise to raise the house.

He listened for sounds of arousal. He heard a mutter, foot-fall, a door slamming open.

There was only one other door he had not tried. His grandmother called it the "front door" and told him it led to the Front, where the men waited with guns. Marvo now felt this was the door for his exit. But where would the men be?

Running now, he reached the door. He knew locks and keys. Here was a lock without a key.

He closed his eyes. He saw a hand removing a key and placing it in a pocket.

There were shouts now. He had been heard.

On either side of the door, windows, four panes, just big enough for his small body. Using his new cane he smashed a pane. He threw himself outside, feeling no cut, no pain.

The men were shouting now. Marvo landed running.

It was cold. It was dark. Marvo smelled leaves, the air, mud, grass. He did not falter as he breathed in these things. He knew what they were from TV, and from his grandmother's descriptions.

He ran.

The men were more used to running and Marvo heard guns, heard clicks. They could see him clearly. The moon was bright.

Marvo thought hard about concealment. If the men couldn't see him he would be safe. Marvo saw the first of his own true magic. A little magic of his own, a little mist.

The mist rose about him and quickly grew. He could not see his way, so he closed his eyes and ran with his cane before him, letting it lead him.

The voices faded. The smell of gun was gone. Marvo paused once to glimpse his home in its entirety. The place of his birth and childhood. It was so much smaller than he'd imagined, but then he'd imagined it was the whole world. It stood three storeys tall, with two dozen windows. The roof was steep and needed repair and it was built of grey stone. He knew that deep inside was his room and his grandmother's body. Ivy, healthy and wild, covered half the house. Someone had attempted to clean one corner and that section looked naked compared to the mossy rest of it.

He would seek throughout his life for other stories of strange births.

He ran.

The mist travelled with him as he ran over dirt, grass and macadam. The smells around him changed, assaulted him.

His surroundings became more complicated, and there were people, more and more people as he ran.

Night fell, but he didn't want to sleep. He ran through towns, through suburban streets, past wild yowling packs of dogs and incurious hunting cats. He rested sometimes, looking back to see where he came from. No men were in sight, no guns either.

He didn't know big city from small but when, as the sun rose, he had been running on hard ground for an hour he decided this was a big enough place. He saw people asleep in doorways. He found a doorway for himself, curled up away from the sun, and gave in to exhaustion.

The world outside the house was strange and terrifying. Loud. If it wasn't for the mist, Marvo would have been lost. It softened the noises and it cleared in certain directions, leading him.

He expected it to be like the world on TV, where you could find everything in careful compartments. In reality, food shops sat next to clothing shops next to bookshops. At least everything was labelled, large words he could read and understand.

People behaved differently than they did on TV. Some of them did stand and talk and smile at each other, but they didn't stand still for half an hour and talk and move from the kitchen to the lounge room, then back again. They walked past him and disappeared. He could not see the end of the world from where he stood. There was no familiar face, no rocks or rivers, no beach, no mountains to climb. Just a city, and he had seen those, though never so big; a city big and loud, hurting his ears. He walked up and down, sniffing the smells, waiting for magic to come.

He had only ever whispered in his grandmother's ear. He leant towards people and whispered into their ears. It took him a while to lose this disconcerting habit. As people rushed past him, he whispered, "Where is the beach? Where is the magic show?" but they didn't hear him. He wondered if he was speaking a different language, then he realised they couldn't hear him. His voice was too soft; he couldn't shout. The sound of his own voice was more frightening than anything else, because it was familiar and strange together. He wondered what his grandmother's voice would have sounded like, and he was sad because he would never know. He cried alone, ignored by everyone who passed.

The smells of the city astounded him. He had not smelled things before—hot chips and car fumes, other people (his grandmother did not smell), the road, the footpath, the feet upon it, the smell of babies, the smell of hair. The smell of flowers. His grandmother would draw a simple rose and tell him of its scent, but he was stunned to realise flowers had such a powerful smell.

He sat in a place where people could watch TV and drink coffee, and the coffee was hot and tasted bitter, and he was amazed to learn something about the TV shows he thought he knew so well.

There were songs on TV. It had always seemed strange; he did not know why the shows he watched had the same clippings for a minute or so every time; the rocking ship, the walk through the haunted house. The same thing every night. He didn't ask his grandmother because he didn't find it questionable, merely interesting. Now he realised they were songs telling the story of the show, telling it every night.

Marvo spent his first two nights alone, wandering the streets, sniffing and looking and being invisible. He found a man asleep on the footpath, his limbs curled up, his flesh half bare and covered with goosebumps. Marvo whispered to the man, "Are you cold? Would you like to use my cloak?"

"I haven't slept in half a year," the man said, and accepted the cloak as a pillow and a coverlet. He spoke very loudly. "You have lent me your cloak. I will lend you the story of my birth, but you must give it back when I have finished. It is not to be repeated."

Marvo agreed to the condition, though wondered how the man would know if he kept it.

"I hope you're mature enough to hear my story. I like my voices loud, my music, TV, my noise, I like it loud. I feel comforted by loudness, it takes me to my birth, though of course I don't remember that. I remember the hum of noise though, for sure. The hum and loudness of the riot."

Marvo had seen birth on TV. He knew what it looked like. It was people in sharp green clothes bending to obstruct the view. It was babies drawn from some secret place and held aloft, bloody and triumphant. It was women (never men) crying, baby placed in arms. He never knew the names of the babies he saw, so he christened them himself. They were Gilligan, Jim, Rolf, Jeannie, Barbara, Max. There was Bobby, Kirk, John, Marilyn, Bette, Sam. He named a hundred babies in that room. He knew about birth.

Marvo's head thudded, aching with the sound of the man's voice. He lay beside the man on the rough pavement, feeling its texture on his cheek, his palm. He felt the corner of the note his grandmother had given him dig into his hip and he shifted slightly.

Marvo remembered silence, and the lesson he learnt was that when he was sad, stressed, scared, he needed only to close himself up somewhere quiet like the room and he would be comforted.

"Are you ready to listen?" the man said.

Born Amongst Chaos

I don't have much left to me that's special, apart from the story of my birth. But my death will be of interest to an observer like you, a kindly boy like you. Stick around and watch me go if you like, but I can't tell you how long it'll be. By the time I finish the story, perhaps, or by the time you turn thirty. It'll be hunger or thirst that'll take me, nothing else.

It was one of those crazy things; no one ever traced its source. Some people thought the heat set it off, but that's no answer. People are hot all over the world and they don't riot like that. But there was cheap gin floating about, cheap as beer and they all drank it. They left it lying around and the kids drank it; my mum told me the phrase then was, "Keeps you cool at least." She didn't have any— she didn't want to hurt me in her womb. I've never forgotten that.

Another thing was the government had cut off the money going to poor people. Where I came from, that meant hunger. And so they were buying the cheap gin and no food, and when a big expensive car ran over one of us, the suburb erupted.

The car was destroyed by the people on the street. The two people inside (a driver and an owner, if you can believe the stories) were beaten, even though the person they ran over was saying, "I'm all right." The two rich people (well, the driver had a job so he was richer than most) were beaten to death, and soon the area was a war zone.

The noise began there. Thunder, screams, shots, sirens. My father wanted to get my mother away but a car was impossible—the people on the streets hated cars now and were tipping even the familiar ones over. So he bundled some things into our wheelbarrow and made Mum sit on top. She told me she had the giggles and so did Dad; her so pregnant, being wheeled like a child playing.

They didn't get very far. It was a bad choice Dad made, and years later, when Mum had lost her sense of humour, she was bitter about it.

"But look at me, Mum, I'm fine," I'd say to defend Dad. "Nothing wrong with me." But I said it in my loud voice, so she shook her head.

She had the pains right in the middle of the road, and there was no place to push her to privacy. She couldn't even lay on the road, because she would have been trampled on. I was born in a wheelbarrow in the middle of a riot.

The man smiled. He seemed very proud of this odd birth, and it was clear to Marvo that pride was a better feeling than shame. Marvo knew he would keep this story, not return it, and he didn't want the story for nothing.

"Wait here," he said. The man laughed in a dry-throated way.

Marvo had the coins he had collected in socks in his bag. He did not want to touch the treasures his grandmother had given him. Wary of everybody but the man with the unusual birth, he squatted in the alley to count the money in the dark.

He bought two hot dogs from a corner stand. Marvo had seen people buying and eating these a hundred times on the TV.

"Mustard? Sauce? Onions? Cheese?" Marvo nodded to the hot dog seller. He hadn't realised how wonderful the hot dogs would smell, how sweet the voice of the seller would be.

He took the hot dogs back to the alley and gave one to the man.

"What about a bottle?" he asked. "Where's the bottle?"

Marvo's grandmother had told him about alcohol. She said he would be allowed to have it when he was mature enough, but she didn't think he would need it.

"I'm not mature enough," Marvo told the man.

"Give me the money then, I'll go buy it."

"Tell me another story first, then you can have the whole bottle for yourself."

The man winked at Marvo, though it could have been a twitch. "I only have one story." Marvo gave him a sock full of coins and left to find a quiet place to spend the night.

As Marvo walked away, the man said, "It's all true. People don't lie when they're drunk. They may regret speaking the truth, because they weren't ready for it to be known. But they never lie."

It began to rain, and Marvo had never felt that cold water raining before. He stood staring upwards, the rain entering his eyes, cleansing his face, soaking him.

"Get inside, you silly boy," a lady said. She clutched his arm. "It's raining cats and dogs."†

---

† As his first foolish saying, Marvo investigated its meaning. He discovered that the saying came from Norse legend, where dogs were symbolic of wind, and cats were believed to be able to conjure up storms. Marvo, on discovering this, went out to the

Marvo could see that wasn't true.

"It's raining fresh water," he said.

"And if you stand in it and let yourself get wet you'll catch pneumonia. Come on, come into my house where it's warm." She covered him with an umbrella. He'd seen this on TV and in the house but the sound of being under it, with the rain pounding overhead, was surprisingly gentle.

Marvo waited in the lady's hall while she ran ahead to clean up. He played with the umbrella; open closed, up down, open closed.

"Stop it, silly boy. It's bad luck." He thought her the silly one, with her cats and dogs and her bad luck umbrella. His grandmother was the expert on bad luck. There were times every month when he was not allowed to look up at the sky through the skylight, because the moon was new, and his grandmother told him it was bad luck to look at a new moon through a window pane. Marvo took wishes of bad luck very seriously. He did not want bad luck; he wanted nothing bad. He wanted a good and happy life, without loss and sadness.

"Marvo Mee is my name. Not Silly Boy," he said.

Marvo used to read the titles on TV shows and saw that everyone had at least two names, if not three. There were no names in the room of his childhood, apart from Grandmother and Marvo.

"What's my name?" Marvo had said to his grandmother.

"Who am I?"

His grandmother said, "You Marvo, me Jane." Then she laughed, her silent rasp. It was a joke he didn't understand.

Now, when a second name seemed necessary, he remembered that one single joke his grandmother made.

"Marvo Mee," he said.

The lady made him take off his jumper and rubbed his arms. Her hands were even stronger than his grandmother's.

They stood in front of a heater. Marvo knew the names of most things.

"Heater," he whispered. He and his grandmother would sit in front of the TV and he would point at something and she would whisper, "Heater. Cat. Dog. Rain. Umbrella. Café. Coffee. Fur coat. Toasted sandwiches. Money. Car."

The lady's home had TV which made noise.

---

alleys of his city and found the right cat. Storm and mist, together. He also learnt that at times it had indeed rained some odd things: fish, coins, frozen faeces and frogs. He found out all sorts of odd things about frogs; he found a frog which gave birth from its back.

"You're not going to spend all night watching the box, are you? I've got plenty to show you," the lady said. Her voice was high and excited. Marvo followed her from room to room as she demonstrated a musical box which plunked away as the plastic couple adhered to the base had sex. Marvo had seen better on the subtitled movies on TV. Those were his favourite movies, of course, the ones with writing at the bottom. He could read the words and hear them whispered in his ear. He knew what they were saying. He loved any subtitled movies, even the boring ones.

She showed him her kitchen and opened up all sorts of containers and gave him tastes of things. Caviar and Stilton cheese, olives, many different flavoured foods. Marvo's tongue rejoiced. She brought him bread and honey, and though the sight of it made his mouth water, on thinking of the blind man's story—about the wife who kneaded the dough on her cunt—he could not take a bite. He did not want to be in the power of this lady.

She took him down to the dark cellar. Marvo had seen a show where the boy lived in a cellar with a mattress and a bowl of water. When the woman took his hand he clutched hers. If he did not let go her hand she could not leave him behind. He felt a sense of surrender. Of weakness.

There were many bottles there.

"Champagne," she said. She held the back of his head and poured some down his throat. It felt like it looked.

The woman began to giggle. He had not really heard the sound before, and he wanted her to stop. He wondered why the man with the loud birth had thought it good for his parents to giggle; the sound was foolish and uncontrolled. It frightened him. He put his hand over her mouth. She licked his fingers.

"Sweet little boy," she said. "Dear little boy."

She opened more champagne and poured it and took his hand again; he shook loose her hold. She wailed, "Dear little boy! Sweet little boy!" Marvo climbed the stairs and shut the door behind him. He sent mist under the door; it was all he had.

The lady would sleep, wake with a bad head and no memory of Marvo, just the scent of his hand on hers. She would sniff her hand, the alien smell entering her brain but not triggering an image which made her feel guilty.

Marvo wandered for many weeks, sleeping out or in, spending his coins carefully. He missed the room more than he could ever have guessed, missed its comfort, his grandmother always there, his things in place so he could walk about with his eyes closed and reach out to them.

On the street, if he closed his eyes for a moment, the sounds made him dizzy.

If he listened he could hear single voices rising above the others or single vehicles that he would follow. Or birds that he would watch.

The loudest voices were the sales people. They sold goods or services. For a while Marvo believed them when they said they held a magic duster, a magic cloth, a magic food, a magic drink. None of these were magic at all. He wished he could show them to his grandmother so they could laugh together at the nonsense.

He missed his grandmother powerfully and he spoke to people about their grandparents, wondering if his feelings were strange, out of place. He spoke to grandparents, too, once he found that some of them all lived together in small units. He took a ball and played in the driveway of "Sunshine Future Assisted Living".

They loved him, the grandparents there. They'd bring him out biscuits and lemonade. "Which one's your grandparent?" they'd ask and he'd wave his arm, smiling.

His favourite grandparent, who made soft chocolate biscuits with an explosion of honey in the middle, told him the story of her grandfather, a story of leaving the old to seek the new, cutting ties and using the string to strap your suitcase together.

The Child and the Tree

I don't know what my life would have been if my grandfather had not left in that way. His home was dark and he moved to the Great White Land for reasons I never understood. Adventure, he said, and the chance to do something unexpected, untraditional.

I did not like my grandfather. He left my grandmother and my mother behind to struggle alone; he came back to find only me alive, only me to listen to his tales of adventure. It was instinct and desire for comfort which brought him home to me. He told of his life. It was good, to hear the details of a life I knew so well. He told me how trapped he had felt, with everyone knowing his past, present and future. "I had to leave if I wanted to change the future," he said.

"You escaped nothing," I told him. "We know it all. At the age of twenty-four you felt great sorrow. At thirty, your life became suddenly larger. At thirty-seven, you became very ill."

He shook his head in disbelief. "Tell me more," he said. "Tell me my story."

"You were born to a very loving mother," I told him. "She nursed and cuddled you though, the other mothers said you were a newborn and should be left untouched, so your skin may settle around your flesh. They said by touching you so, your skin would be loose and wrinkles would come early."

My grandfather laughed. "I've learnt about birth in the other world. That's untrue, about the skin. Other people would laugh to hear it." He did not explain his own loose skin though. Old age, perhaps, but he was not that old.

"Your mother disobeyed and loved you all the more," I said. "When your navel cord fell off, a great ceremony was held. The cord was buried in a sacred place and a young sapling planted atop it. Then you were taken to the priest and named. Now your mother could hold you without words of admonishment from the other mothers.

"That tree and you grew well. From an early age you would sit beneath it and think. No one else would go to the tree but you."

"Is it still alive?" asked my grandfather.

"It is old and very sick. Its bark hangs in folds. You were ill once, a childhood disease many are able to throw off easily. You could not, and the tree bent its head to the ground in sorrow. When you recovered, so did the tree.

"You grew up, married. You deserted your home and your young wife and child, when you were twenty-one. You did not take anything but a pouch of coins. You left your wife and child to a life of suffering and shame.

"You did not tell your mother or wife where you were and you didn't care how they fared. You didn't know you had a granddaughter until you returned, and here I am, the last of your family."

"Where are they?" my grandfather asked me. "Where are my people?"

"All dead, gone," I told him. I took him to see his tree and showed him the history his wife, my grandmother, had written:

Age twenty-one: The tree has lost its leaves for the first time, then new branches sprout.

My grandfather said, "A thief stole my pouch when I arrived in the city."

Age twenty-four: A great storm. The tree absorbed the rain and now leaks water like tears.

"I married again. My wife died in childbirth. My child lived only three days."

Age thirty: A sudden growth spurt for this old tree.

"My business found great success. People knew my name."

Age thirty-seven: The tree sickens. Its leaves have dropped. Its bark is yellow.

"I travelled to another country and found a vicious disease."

"Age forty-two: New branches sprout.

"I became a father for the third time."

My grandfather was shocked to learn how shallow his escape had been. We knew his life without having seen it. We knew everything about him.

Marvo was startled and comforted that another person had a similar start in a new city carrying only a collection of coins.

"Did he meet a lady with an umbrella?" Marvo asked the woman.

"He met a lot of people." The woman wrinkled her face at him. "I didn't tell you the story to make you sympathise with my grandfather. You've heard the story wrong."

It was a lesson for Marvo that often a story is expected to elicit a particular reaction.

"He was a bad man to leave you all behind," Marvo said. "Did he stay with you then?"

The woman closed her eyes. "I left him. You understand I was only young, with my life ahead of me. I didn't want to act as nurse to an old man who I felt nothing for."

She shivered. Marvo knew from TV that when women shivered or cried you hugged them, or their crying would get worse.

"You did the right thing," he said, although he had no idea.

"You are such a kind boy. Your parents have done a good job." She blinked. Looked around. "Where are your parents? Which one is your grandparent? You're here so often but I've never seen you with an adult."

"I don't have any parents. I only had a grandmother and she died."

"But who is looking after you? Where are you living?"

Marvo was surprised. Did he have to live somewhere? That was a new lesson. He drew a small mist down around them. "I live in a big house with eight brothers and sisters. My mother is a nurse but only goes out to work a few hours a week because she likes to help us with our homework. My father is a builder and we all know how to fix anything. We never talk about my grandfather, Dad's dad, because he abandoned Dad when he was only five."

The mist worked well.

"Oh, you lucky boy to have such a loving family," she said.

He nodded, and gave her a plant that would never die.

As he walked away, he felt more sympathy for the grandfather and little desire for the family he had created for himself.

He thought that a sense of freedom, of individual choice, might be lost in a large family. He did not return to the place of assisted living. He sought elsewhere.

He enjoyed his search for magic, liked wandering from place to place, being treated like a child, or an adult, depending on how he felt. He liked running for the sake of it and he learned to wear running clothes to become invisible.

Marvo sought wisdom and magic in untraditional places because he didn't know where other people looked. He stood outside school buildings but could not enter. He had no papers, no certificates proving his existence. He learned that he needed a past and a family or there would be questions asked he couldn't answer.

He needed to use his storytelling skills in order to get by.

"My mother is buying some underwear," he said to the young hotel clerk. "The elastic broke on hers and she had to walk around without any." The clerk snickered and passed him the key to the hotel room. Knowing how to blind people with the promise of sexuality—this was a gift from the blind man in the big house.

There were many strange things in Marvo's world. He had seen things now that he did not think his grandmother had seen; he had seen men in ships going to space. He needed to know from them if it was different; if they had seen magic in space, and did they remember what it looked like?

He bought a ticket to the large lecture hall where they were speaking to the press and to the public. All the seats were taken so he folded his cape and sat on that.

"It was the perfect career move for all of us," the captain said. "The only way we'd become famous. None of us is any good at singing, we found out during the year. And none of us can draw and we're not too handsome. So all we had was our bravery.

"It was a long year out there, and the work, once you got used to the idea of being so far from earth, was pretty boring. Although the explosion was spectacular. And it ended our mission, not a bad thing really. Not a bad thing.

"We were sent to investigate the ship which had been sent to investigate Mars. It was spinning uselessly, spewing the world's money into the universe. The world and the media are fascinated with Mars—no true observation of the planet has been made, because equipment always fails. So we were sent to find the problem, but the problem exploded and we returned to earth.

"We landed safely, but had to lie flat in wheeled banana chairs for a week, get wheeled about the enormous lab until we adapted to gravity. We could not lift our arms to drink or smoke; even smiling was difficult."

"How does the moon look different from outer space, compared to how it looks from earth?" Marvo asked.

"It is quite ugly," said the captain. "It doesn't glow silver, or look like cheese. It is a large rock which is held in thrall by the earth."

"When did the moon begin to look ugly?" asked Marvo.

The reporters in the room were angry with him and wondered what such a young boy was doing there. They wanted to know how it felt to be back with wives (all three were men; the one woman on the programme remained behind to maintain ground control). How was it to see them, what did earth food taste like?

"It was a long way out before the moon grew ugly," said the captain. "We were headed towards it and for a moment our ship seemed to block the moon. We felt like we were causing a lunar eclipse."

The reporters muttered about minds being lost, the waste of it. Any of them would give their sanity to have ventured moonwards.

"The first noted lunar eclipse was in 721 BCE," said the third member of the crew. It was said he had kept the others entertained with ribald stories. Marvo wondered if perhaps he would tell one now, but did not ask.

"At this time, Shalmaneser V of Assyria took Hoshea, the king of Israel, prisoner, and besieged Sumaria. Once it fell, twenty-seven thousand Israelis were exiled to Medea and Mesopotamia. As they marched, the sky went dark, and the twenty-seven thousand waited in terror. They believed their God had deserted them; he didn't even love them enough to light their way in exile. This is how we felt on returning to earth. Like we were being plunged into darkness."

There was silence in the lecture hall. The three astronauts nodded like their heads sat on springs. Their audience was shocked. Some of the journalists had heard him to say, "They were exiled to Media," and were already framing the words which would destroy his career, for making such statements about their industry.

"Was the eclipse soon over?" said Marvo, and that was the last question of the night.

Marvo went backstage where his youth got him through the door. Marvo could ask all he liked of the astronauts; he was thirteen, young enough to be an obsessed fan. He learnt very well; he understood. They seemed happy to talk to Marvo. He was truly interested, and the third in command found himself talking of things they had agreed to keep silent about.

"What was it like to come back to the earth?" Marvo said. "Did you feel as if you didn't belong anymore?"

"When we were launched into society? We all found it strange. Don't tell anyone this. We'd been away, were used to our own company but it was more than that. The faces were ugly, greedy, selfish. The land burnt and poisonous, the water lifeless. It was like we had landed on a failed world."

Marvo understood how the familiar world could look so strange. What he saw on TV and what he saw in the real world were the same but so different. To him, the world was not flat and lifeless at all but so full of colour and depth it sometimes made him dizzy.

"How old are you, kid?" the astronaut asked him. They drank chocolate milk together.

"I turned thirteen last week," Marvo said. He didn't add, "I think." He had taken out the note his grandmother had given him many times in the last month. He was not ready to read it. Not ready to grow up.

"It's a big year for you. A lot of us figure out our destiny that year, you know."

"I will learn my destiny," Marvo said. "I have it written down in a note."

The astronaut didn't laugh. He took Marvo by the shoulders. "You read that note and you come and ask me anything, anything at all."

Marvo went to the motel room he was staying in and sat down with the note his grandmother had given him. He had been putting off the moment because he knew that after reading it everything would be different.

He opened it up and finally read of his destiny.

It gave him strength; gave him meaning and a need for more, for greater understanding.

I will call you son, though you may be daughter. I will never see your face or know your gender. Will you take my nose, my taste for spicy food, my lust for strength? All I know you have is what I give you now: my knowledge.

And this I received from my parent; many thousands of years these words have passed through to reach you; added to, taken from, changed. Up-dated. We are not afraid of change; unlike religion we embrace it, use it, make it happen. This is why we will never die.

There will always be someone who wants us to die.

Be careful, be silent, subtle; beware. Those in power hate our strength and will kill us for it; they have done so before. True cynics, true disbelievers, will not have children, because they can see the truth and know that to bring a child into this world is cruel and abusive.

We control the mist, we let it fall or we lift it as need be.

This is our tradition. Passed through life and death, dying without choice for the cause.

This is your inheritance.

You may be lucky; born into a time when there is a resurgence of belief in our art; when the ugliness of the world is so great that the magicians, the mist people, the veil droppers, the beautifiers, are in demand. You may need to work with the great leaders or against them.

Only you will know this. You must work the mist with a smile. You must not weaken, you must not fail. I sorrow for your great burden; only death will release you from it. I wish you love and health and a long life. You will know all with great sacrifice. I bid you farewell.

Marvo read these words and hoped one day they would make sense to him.

He was a part of the mist. The note, written in his grandmother's hand and to be re-written by him once it became battered, as it had been re-written for many hundreds of years, perhaps thousands, this note instructed without explaining; it told him his goal but did not tell him how to achieve it.

Marvo, even at thirteen, understood that the magicians were the protectors of humanity. Without the mist, the fantasy, the world might end. No one would want to live or bring children into the world. Humanity would die out. The message from his ancestors told him this, and even then he knew it to be true.

He visited the astronauts again to see how far away the mist had lasted.

He watched them, waiting for a lesson from these men who had been beyond the mist. Their description of the world when they returned showed him they had been away from the mist, out of its reach. He wondered if they would be protected by it again; he watched as it fell around their shoulders.

Another week or so and the magician's spell had done its work. At the celebratory dinners, they smiled and accepted and loved the faces staring lovingly up at them. The mist had once more descended.

Two years passed in Marvo's life. He spoke to people and became frustrated at their answers. He wanted understanding of his mission, his birth, the men in green. He couldn't find it.

He practised his magic and gathered more tricks. He studied leaders political and religious, following his instincts.

Many tried to sell him religion. Marvo had learnt about religion from his grandmother. She had taught him awareness, magic and superstition. All of this helped him understand religion. Marvo began to speak to these people, curious to hear their explanations. He wanted to see what sort of houses they had. Would they remind him of the room? Some did. These were large, high-ceilinged rooms, and when they were empty Marvo felt good. Then the people would come in, press close to him and stare at the front.

He began to notice flaws in the people he was with, similarities in their forms of belief. Later, he would identify these similarities as good magic. Using magical techniques for religious enlightenment. People called it theurgy and believed in it as a religion in its own right. Marvo saw it as illusion and it was the beginning of his realisation that religion would not explain his world to him. He wondered about the number of religions whose leader sits in a throne and is bathed in miraculous, magical shafts of sunlight. The followers gasp and sigh and sign up for another year; they never consider the possibility that maybe the throne had been placed in the path of the sun, rather than the sun following the exalted one wherever they be. This was one technique he saw. All religions were theurgical to one level or another, although many denied it.

It was the believers he met who had knowledge. He learnt more by talking to the people in the audience than by hearing the words of the leaders.

For two years after he learned of his birthright, Marvo sat in these rooms, the sun and the space making him feel at home. He learnt many things there.

He found a church group whose seventeen worshippers had come from around the world to be together. The church was small but beautiful, its details immaculate. Many hours of labour had carved the marble, polished the wood, created the stained glass windows. The people in the congregation were similar in build and colour, as if so much time spent exclusively in each other's company had made siblings of them. Marvo envied their closeness, their sense of family. He had no brother, no sister. He had never fought with another child. He never knew the pleasure of pulling someone's hair and having some of it come out at the roots.

He knew about families, though. He knew they lived in large houses and there were always a lot of them. They always faced the front so you could see their expressions. Marvo could never figure out which way was front, when he was talking.

The members of the church welcomed Marvo but were nervous of him; they did not know his morals, or his history. They did not know why such a young boy would come to them, what he had suffered, what they would have to heal. Still, they gave him tea, shared their ginger biscuits with him, and told him of their beliefs.

He asked them about birth, about strange births and strange lives.

They believed they were led by a great man who lived a strange life, a saint known as Chrysostom.

This man became known for many things. He was fervently against the use of superstition to protect and heal; he wanted people to turn to God for these. Marvo could not see the difference, though he did not say so. Asking God to help you, or helping yourself using accessories seemed to amount to the same thing. Marvo listened, all the same, to these people who believed so strongly in the teachings of this long-dead man. Their expert was an historian who loved to recite numbers. Marvo liked his information this way. It didn't need to be interpreted. The historian loved to talk and over great mounds of buttered vegetables he would do so.

"Our leader was born in the year 347, in Antioch, Syria. He was the son of Secundus, a commander of the Imperial troop. His mother, Anthusa, was widowed at twenty, but John lived beyond his father's years, not dying until the year 407. We celebrate his day on January 27th, the day his relics were transferred from the place of his death,

Comana, to Constantinople—now Istanbul. His skull is in the Vatopedi Monastery on Mount Athos. It is silver and jewel-encrusted.

"We worship him throughout the year. He was a great and learned man, both the archbishop of Constantinople and a Doctor of the Church. His name comes as a nickname, meaning 'golden mouth' because of his eloquence. He remains to this day one of history's greatest speakers.

"He became a hermit in 374, writing an account of his austerities and trials. He spent two years in a cave alone, as a 'solitary'. He became very sick.

"He was consecrated as archbishop on February 26th, 398. In that role he cut down his own expenses, taking all his perks and giving them to the poor and hospitals.

"He railed against immodest dress in women and spread Christianity to the Scythians and Goths, to Palestine and Persia. He preached against caul superstitions, which made him unpopular in some cities. He was very straight-laced, very careful. He was the one who said: 'I came naked into the world, and I can carry nothing out of it.'

"In 404 he was banished by Theophilus, the archbishop. The day he left, the Church and Senate House burnt down. His followers were blamed and tortured. He was made to walk hundreds of miles, and he died on the journey."

The followers gave all they had to the poor.

"It seems so clear," said the historian. "The saint was speaking out for the good, when in Greece at that time a new tax was imposed by Emperor Theodusius I to pay for war with Magnus Maximus: riots, statues broken, two officers sent to control people. Wrong versus right. Wrong is often so powerful and so filled with hatred for right. Wrong hates any sense of guilt."

The followers had few possessions and did not use cars or buses. They walked everywhere. They were fit and hungry. Marvo found small things they left behind: cherry pits, scraps of paper, shoelaces. He kept these things in a drawer with all his other found objects.

Marvo tried to be like them but could not sustain such selflessness. They didn't need or want his mist. They wanted to see the truth, and he left before he took that from them.

They made him curious about the power of money, the possession of it, the ability to give it away. He could have gathered money anywhere, lived anyhow, but Marvo found work, to see what it was like. He worked in a large hotel, where he was not allowed in the foyer: the guests should not see him.

"We don't like them to see the machinery behind the magic," said the manager, a tall man with dark eyes, eyes which saw all but didn't see Marvo's magic. Marvo got there hot and sweaty because he liked to run to work, then he'd shower and change. Marvo washed dishes, hundreds at a time. His partner at the sink would talk throughout the night, finding reasons for his position, excuses. Marvo's partner always wore gloves to wash the dishes. He was always well rugged up. His favourite tale involved the careless treatment of his most important possession.

An Early Loss

I was born in the hospital where my mother had no control over my birth or my first appearance into the world. Luckily, though, the nurse kept my navel cord safe for her.

My mother kept the cord for many years, hidden from my father because he didn't believe in those things. My life was good and happy; I was successful in school and I had many friends. My prospects were excellent. I wanted to be a police-man, but my mother wanted me to be a doctor. It was our only point of argument.

Then my dad started to turn into a real bastard. I don't know if he was jealous of me; I think he must have been because he seemed to hate me. He'd pick on me and call me names, yell at me if I didn't get perfect marks at school. My mother would protect me and that would make him madder.

"Can't he speak for himself?" my father shouted all the time. And no, I couldn't speak for myself, not very well. I was too scared of him. I thought he'd hit me if I said anything, and I've always hated the idea of pain.

One day, Dad was going through some drawers, looking for something, whatever, and he found the little box that Mum kept my navel cord in.

"This is disgusting," he said. He was really cruel. He said it was filthy and obscene, without realising he was talking to *me*, that his words were about me. He got a pair of scissors and, ignoring my mum's screams and shouts, my crying, he cut it into pieces and threw them away. I felt every cut, I felt suffocated when the cord was in the garbage bag. From that moment I've been a failure. That's why you see me here; that's why I'm doing this pathetic job.

It was a good story, so Marvo gave him a new umbilical cord as a gift. This was an error of judgement on Marvo's side, one he would not make again. The loss of the dishwasher's excuse for failure was the final straw. The loss was unbearable, and he took his life in one last attempt at bravery.

Marvo washed dishes for a few more weeks then gave up work for a while. He discovered magic shows, sitting in the dark, watching them, sneering at them.

At fifteen he believed himself to be the only true magician, regardless of what the note said. He watched the fumbling others pretending at magic, imagining that to fool the eye was magic. He would stare into the eyes of these people and see their falsity. He could ruin their magic with a word, a revelation. They could not touch his magic; his schooling was completed early. His magic was safe.

He went to see the matinee performance of *The Greatest Magician of All Time*, another fake.

He stayed for thirty bored minutes, rose to leave at the same time as an elderly man did. They rose from opposite sides of the aisle, stared into each other's eyes.

The old man winked and left with a speed unsuited to one of his age. Marvo was unable to blink or breathe with the shock of the other. He saw the truth and he knew he had been similarly recognised. The horror of the revelation made him feel vulnerable and he sat and watched the idiot magician complete his nonsense. By the end of the show he was completely terrified. His note had told him there were other magicians, but this was the first he'd seen. Marvo would be revealed as a failure, he would be held under scrutiny and found wanting, he would lose under any comparison with other real magicians. For the first time in his life, Marvo lacked confidence. But he knew he had to find the old man and speak to him. Imagine the truths they could tell! The help they could give!

He left the theatre ahead of the fidgeting children. The old man could not have gone far.

Outside, Marvo could see a thin trail of mist. It smelled faintly of peppermint. He followed the mist to the old man, selling truth on a street corner. *So few people see the truth*, the old man would tell them.

"This is your worst trait," Marvo saw him say to a large man in a patched business suit, "and this your best. Your biggest mistake was to do this. You have not yet done the best thing in your life, and you will not know until it is over that you have done it. I will not tell you your death; that is a truth better unknown." The old man had rejected his role as truth-hider and developed a new one.

The old man was raking it in; Marvo could see that money was to be made with truth, as much as fantasy. Marvo imagined himself as a preacher, very wealthy, dispensing the truth to adoring fans. But he knew it was not possible. The note told him that. To go beyond what the old man was doing would be too dangerous for him and for the profession. They could not be seen, not be known to many people. The old man's last customer walked away crying. Marvo watched, his face twisted.

The old man packed up his cards, his props. "You don't approve, young man?"

"I was told it was the job of the magician to keep the truth from the people; to show only the beauty."

"That is true. But you always have a choice. You are a true magician and filled with power." He led Marvo to a park bench in the sun. "There are many magicians, but few are true. We recognise each other easily because we see the truth. We do not acknowledge the false magicians. They are the ones who play tricks when the source is known. The point of magic to those types is the revelation. It is not real magic. Real magic is so amazing the idea of a solution is not even considered."

"You say those words, yet you don't help with the mist," Marvo said. "You are clearing the mist away for people."

The old man raised his fingertips, leaking peppermint-scented mist from them. "You do have a choice. I kept the mist for many years but I find I am losing my control of it. Around me, people forget things. Names and the fact they have children. I decided to tell the truth because I knew that every time a child is forgotten, left to die in a hot car, I was responsible. Me."

He turned his head away.

"I won't lose control," Marvo said.

"Most likely. I hope for your sake that is true. My way, I am in pain all the time. My bones grow against me."

"You could carry a potato in your pocket until it goes black. That helps with pain."

The old man smiled at him. "You are one of the strongest I've known. Seek the real as well as the fake. All knowledge makes you stronger." He slumped, almost asleep with exhaustion.

"Can I help you home?" Marvo said.

"No!" It was a snarl, a yellow-toothed, stink-breathed snarl. "We cannot meet beyond this. You can see already the interest we are causing."

It was true—children and their parents were gathered around the two expectantly.

"Children always know us, more so when we are together. Here, this will satisfy them."

The old man pulled out a handful of boiled lollies. Marvo tied his cape around his shoulders and handed them out. "No show today, no show."

Every parent let their child take the sweet from a stranger and Marvo said to the old man, "You should show them all the truth of what can happen to a child."

"They will learn it soon enough. They are all safe today."

The old man shook Marvo's hand. "You keep looking for answers. You look everywhere. Not just at the magic shows."

Marvo did not tell the old man this was old information. He knew how to look. He'd been doing it for three years.

Marvo sought out others, listening, hearing. The more he saw, the more he realised that he was one of few.

He knew how to spy and stalk, because he saw it all the time on TV. Spies wore black and they hardly ever got caught. Marvo dressed in black and walked on clouds. He followed those who called themselves witches, watched the circle of skyclad worshippers face north, south, east and west, to invoke the energies and the blessings of the elements. He saw no magic there, only ritual.

Marvo went to performances, séances and readings. He realised that not many true magicians lived off their magic. It made it harder for them to be found that way. He was determined that he would be easy to find, that the others could find him if they wanted.

He saw a lot of magic that wasn't true magic: he saw the pretence, the trickery. One magician who appeared on television would move a pen without touching it, and the audience would sigh and blow air through their teeth. Hypnosis, thought Marvo, because the magician moved the pen by blowing it, while pretending to move it with his mind.

This magician would bend a key simply by touching it gently, making the women and some of the men think, "I would bend too, if he touched me so gently." Marvo saw these looks and practised the touch himself, the gentle stroking, the magic of giving pleasure. He did not tell the people that the key had been bent in advance, had been pressed on the chair as the magician was standing, or against the table as he pushed himself back.

Another magician would read the minds of the audience, tell them what they were holding, the colour of it, how precious it was. Only Marvo could see the tiny mirror in his palm, only Marvo knew that good eyesight was magic all in itself.

His grandmother had told him he should accept all magic, but the illusionists stretched this beyond belief.

Marvo took to walking the streets and staring into people's eyes. They stared back or they looked away. He did not find recognition.

Then he saw an advert in the newspaper: "MAGICIANS WANTED", and he called the number.

"What can you do?" the man said. He sat on a dusty old couch, sunken in the middle. He seemed strangely short.

"Tricks of a varied nature. I am a master of concealment."

Marvo hid his face behind his cloak, holding it up like a bat's wing. The man laughed. Marvo's soft voice did not make him feel confident.

"How old are you?" he asked.

"Is that important?" asked Marvo. He closed his eyes and opened them again. The man suddenly saw an old fellow sitting opposite him, shaking and smiling, smoking a black cigarette.

Marvo, who had been pretending to smoke the wand he found on the desk, flicked it to full size. He pushed it up his nose. The man laughed in shock.

"You do kids' tricks. We're looking for adult magicians. Come back when your act has matured."

Marvo left, taking with him the list of names and phone numbers he had found on the desk and memorised. He saved the list of magicians for five years, making changes as he heard of them, keeping it ready to be used. He studied the names, knew them by heart, knew what magic they performed. El Dor played with fire; Shri Genfi the Shaman spoke hypnotic tongues.

Marvo went back to washing dishes. He was a popular workmate because he was so helpful in people's trouble. He was effective because he saw things others didn't see, like a shaman.

He had never been a sick child, recovered, though, as many ancient shamans were. Perhaps they had lain sick in their beds, hearing all. No one expected a sick child to be listening. They then knew the troubles before they were spoken. That was part of the cure. The people thought, "If he knows my trouble without me telling him, he must know the answer." They had faith, belief. That was the beginning of the solution.

Marvo was a shaman too. He listened behind the wall when he was in the room, desperate for sound to remind him he was alive. He heard everything.

At work, he helped and gave solutions. He was careful about this. In history people had feared and hated shamans, not understanding their power. People tried to prove that shamanism was a psychosis, brought on by epilepsy.

Marvo was selective about who he helped. But he was not so careful about some of the things he did. Things he'd seen on TV but not tried. A list he held in his head.

Things like sleeping overnight in a department store to see the dummies come to life. He collected many treasures the night he did that: old receipts, pieces of sharp plastic, packaging, discarded toys. The police didn't arrest him because he had no items of value and because they were susceptible to the mist.

He climbed a tower to hang a flag. He danced in steam on the hottest day ever when it rained on the footpath. Each time he was collected, spoken to. "People don't do these things. You need to think about your behaviour."

Finally, when he was seventeen, he took a mud bath in the foundations of a construction site. Naked. He had a bag of small things he'd found: parking tokens, the contents page of a book, a library card with the name *Jonas McCready*, a paint bottle lid. That was too much for the mist, even, so they sent him on a voyage of the mad. He was allocated a lawyer who helped him into a clinic.

He met some very interesting people in the psychiatric clinic. There, it would be easy to stop thinking, stop being. Sit and wait.

There was a man there who felt the weight of sin very greatly. Not his own sins; he did not commit any. The sins of the world. He spent most of his time weeding.

Marvo sat on the grass beside the flower bed and watched him.

"Would you like to hear a story?" he asked. The man nodded. "And then you will tell me one," said Marvo. The man nodded again, wiped his nose with his sleeve, his bare hands dripping with warm earth.

"Hands and noses, precious things. Do not take them for granted, especially if you are embarked on an adulterous affair. Your nose would once have been cut off, had you been caught, and for the remainder of your short life you would have been marked," said the man.

The pollen in the air was thick. Marvo sneezed; the nurse who watched over both of them sneezed too. She was the one nurse who made him smile, who watched his tricks without asking for explanation. Her name was Andra.

The gardener did not sneeze. Marvo later met an idiot on a bus who reminded him of this man. Idiots make more sense than doctors; they should not be disregarded, Marvo learned.

"I'll tell you the story while you work," Marvo said. The man nodded. Marvo told a story he'd learnt from Chrysostom's historian.

Caesar's Augurs

There are humans who can see the future and use the present; others who can't. My lawyer can't. Although I suppose I'm not doing a jail term for theft. He understood that I did not realise the removal of those little things mattered; people had not cared in the big house where I grew up.

The judge had me sent here.

As we left the court room, the lawyer placed his hand on my shoulder.

He said to me, "I'm sorry. It's the judge. She dislikes me." I shook my head. I told him that in ancient Rome, incompetent lawyers would purchase cauls from miscreant midwives.

Strapped to their chests, they believed it would make them win. "Perhaps that would work for you," I told him. Because the ancient Romans knew how to use the present.

In the year 44 BCE, though they did not call it that, a group of men sat sprawled around a marble room, wittily degrading servants and others lower than them. Many were lower: these men were augurs, and they sat next to Caesar and his officials. There were never thirteen; even then that number was considered unlucky. They needed to know everything that was happening. Have current information. They had a great interest in politics and the affairs of the people whose lives they may change in a moment. They watched and waited. One amongst them was quieter, yet it was to him that the others listened more often.

The augurs were happy to be talking and joking and not having to work. Thus, they did not welcome the messenger who came to them.

"There is a great wind to the north," spoke the messenger, hair tossed and clothes awry.

The augurs conferred for many hours to decide the good or bad signs innate in the wind. The city was settled after years of civil war. The augurs decided that the wind blew well for Caesar. Truthfully, it was easy to say so because for many months, the man had been sole ruler of the Roman world.

The augurs were right on that occasion: their ruler had a pleasant and successful day. They were not called upon again until one week later, when Caesar gathered them to him. They had helped him so greatly in the past with their apt and correct interpretation of the signs.

"Tell me," he said, "what of this mark?" His back was red with a raised rash.

"Your wife needs to cut her fingernails, perhaps?" snickered one. The others did not laugh. They conferred for many hours, until Caesar grew bored with waiting.

"Good or bad?" he shouted. "Answer me." The augurs, nodding to each other, agreed.

"The omen is good. You may walk without fear," they said. The quiet augur had not spoken. He saw something different than the others, yet he was bound to leave the change happen.

It was in his instructions; it was his birthright. Afterwards, he would need skill to bring cloud and mist.

The good reputation of the augurs could have been ruined, but they denied advising Caesar to go out. They claimed to have suggested he stay in and dine instead, and that he had insisted upon going out. Who were they to argue with the great leader?

After Caesar's death and the consequent battle for power, augurs became very much in demand. The leaders were unsure after years of disloyalty, murder, trickery. Sixteen augurs sat in the great room, chewing rich food and deciding the movements of the great.

Loyalty was not an important trait amongst the augurs. Nor, perhaps, was honesty — they would attempt to read the signs in a way attractive to Caesar; good news put the augurs in a powerful position.

If one was absent for reasons of illness or other, their lives were endangered, or at least their positions.

"To be ill on this day is not good," the remaining augurs would say.

"Perhaps ill luck for our great city to have such illness on this day."

The augurs could not help their arrogance. They were members of the patrician class. They were the aristocrats; they were men. They were constantly reminded of the superiority of these positions and they constantly reminded others. They married the empire's most beautiful women and slowly turned them to hags, they took younger and younger lovers.

Trabea, the traditional dress of their class, helped with the arrogance. Pure white, with a rich purple border, it set them apart from the grubby, grey crowd.

They would never wear secondhand clothes; they could be the

clothes of a man who died at sea before the journey was over. These clothes will dog the wearer with bad luck. Perhaps the man lost a bucket at sea. Whatever you do, don't lose that bucket at sea. A terrible portent of doom.

The augur who had been silent was found guilty and put to death. In that way, the augurs proved their worth.

<hr>

"Interesting theory," said the gardener.

"No, it's truth," said Marvo. "That quiet augur is an ancestor of mine."

Marvo learnt about trust when the historian told him this story. He learnt not to trust, and that everyone was more interested in self-preservation than helping others, especially when it could be presented as selflessness.

"It must be true then, if you know the person. Were there weeds in Rome? Perhaps there is another theory, there were too many weeds."

"Tell me that theory, or another one," Marvo said.

The gardener rubbed his face with dirt-covered hands and nodded. "The weeds are God's curse upon Adam, you see, as punishment for his behaviour. The weeds grow, and if there are too many then Man's actions can't be accounted for. I think perhaps that in Rome there were too many people listening to your relative and not pulling up the weeds. They let the weeds grow and their city collapsed. There's a story for you."

Marvo knelt and helped pull weeds. They worked in silence.

"Marvo, I'd like some help please," said the nurse, Andra.

He rose, dusted off his knees.

"You looked like you needed rescuing," Andra said. "Ten more weeds and you would have been there for good."

"Perhaps," Marvo said.

She was such an odd nurse. She wasn't cheery and friendly. She didn't make the patients feel better. She cleaned the bed pans and washed the patients. She was very quiet. She didn't talk to anyone. But she watched Marvo all the time. In his small, private room at the hospital he collected many things: little balls of hair, a plastic spoon from lunch. He had food hidden as well because he hated to be hungry. Packets of biscuits, of potato chips, of dried fruit and nuts.

Andra said, "Where did you find these things?" He was pleased she did not ask why. He thought she sounded envious, as if she wished she had found the things first and honestly wondered about their history.

He had small buttons and coins; in his drawer he had more secret things, jewellery hidden from its owners, wallets.

They walked together back to his room, Marvo wiping his dirty hands on his pants.

"Tell me a story," he said. She had given him a marvellous scrub in the morning. "Tell me a story," he said. "Tell me a story."

"That's not my thing."

"What is your thing?"

She winked at him. That afternoon, she slipped his night-pills into her pocket, leaving him drug-free, alert.

That night, when all the others in the ward were drugged and asleep, Andra came to him. He was sitting up, waiting, wide-eyed. She sat on his bed and spoke in a whisper which made him feel like home.

"I don't have a thing," she said. "I have nothing. But I love all your bits and pieces."

She looked through his collection of buttons, toe rings, ring pulls, string.

"Tell me a story," he said again.

"I only know stories about sex," she said. That was okay by Marvo. For the first time in his life he had an erection.

"You know how the only sound worse than your parents fighting is your parents fucking? That surreptitious grunting, the squeak, squeak as they quietly go for it. You think it's not possible, and they look the same the next morning, so you think you might have imagined it, but who would be sick enough to fantasise parents doing it? Who would be that depraved?"

"You," said Marvo. He had an idea what she meant. He had heard the bedsprings through the thin walls in the house. He grinned.

She offered to give him a sponge bath and he accepted, for the first time forgetting about getting a story. He remembered a long time later, only when he realised what she had done. He wanted all of her time but she couldn't give it to him. She would not even give him a story. She knew what great value there was in them. He wanted all of her trust.

Although Marvo didn't trust easily, he worked hard at gaining trust. Without trust he would not be believed.

Marvo gave a show in the clinic for patients who thought and accepted like children. They trusted him then, they told him stories.

"My son was desperate to reach the world," one woman said. She rubbed her hands with oil, her skin glistened with it. She was allowed to be naked; she could do what she liked so long as she didn't hurt anybody. In this place, they competed to be the most naked, the most crazy. Alone, they said, "I'm totally sane," but they enjoyed the insanity they invented.

She rubbed oil into her arms as she talked.

Helpful Old Lady

He was always a weak little thing. He wasn't finished when he came out. He didn't have strength yet, so he was sick and weak for his first three years.

I met an old woman in the park. She had been watching my son playing his gentle games in his slow and gentle way alone at my feet.

"The poor dear has weak limbs. That's all," she said. "All his illnesses stem from that."

She looked at me to see my reaction. I nodded. It had been my instinct, that once his legs and arms strengthened, his defences would too.

"What are you willing to do for your son?" she asked.

"Anything," I said. Truly. I never lie. So I agreed to her cure.

"Only human fat, rubbed into the skin daily, will strengthen his limbs. I have the knowledge to render the fat, but I do not have the raw materials. I'm too old and ugly. I look like a witch, and people don't trust me. I need your help to bring the material in."

"Do you have to kill them or can you just take the fat?" I wanted to be clear about what I was doing.

"There will be some death involved," she said. "That's why we will select people who will not be missed, and who deserve to die anyway. Like that fellow over there."

The park attendant leant on a rake and watched the children. He smiled and nodded at them, big brother and best friend.

"When he finds them alone, he takes them to his little office and molests them," said the old lady. "Each child he touches will be truly damaged."

My son could be next, I thought, and our partnership was struck. It was successful; my son is wonderfully strong and healthy, an athlete and father. But the old lady died and her house was cleaned up. They found all sorts of things and there was a photo of me and my baby. Not fair, really. My baby is lost to me anyway. They have locked me up here and he does not come to visit.

Marvo freed the lady from the home. He got her a job as a park attendant, where she could be with children, watch over them, protect them. And he helped her son to love her again. This was an action he would not regret. The son, now loved and wanted, became a movie maker, and spread the mist over the world.

Another time, Marvo met a very sleepy woman in the hospital.

"I can't seem to keep my eyes open," she said. "Sleep, that's my motto."

"Why are you so tired?" Marvo said.

"They always ask me that, but they don't want to know the answer. They want some story about my terrible childhood, how sleep was the only way to escape it."

"But your childhood was good."

"Oh, yes. Would you like to hear the story of my birth?"

Marvo nodded.

Born Without Waking Up

My mother was the Queen of Spades, a dark and serious woman, who taught me to respect the serious side of life. My father died when I was very young, and Mother never got out of the habit of wearing black. It suited her.

She would let me sleep as much as I wanted. She knew I needed it, because of my birth.

I was taken by caesarean section, not because of my mother, because of me. The doctors thought I was still—they thought I was dead, because I didn't move and struggle to leave the dark room.

So they lifted me from my mother and saw that I was merely sleeping. I was fast asleep! I received a nasty slap and woke up, and I've hated waking up ever since.

Marvo could see this woman was happy to be so sleepy so he did not want to take that away from her. Instead, he convinced the director of the clinic to change the rule that no patient was to remain in bed during the day. It made no sense they were allowed to be naked but not allowed to sleep. Patients began to sleep in, to have afternoon dozes, and, after a while, much recovered, to be released. The woman amongst them. Once she was allowed to sleep when she was tired, she wasn't tired when she was awake.

Marvo was seen as recovered also. They admired his problem-solving skills and his way with people. They packed his bag and sent him off within an hour, his paperwork done. He had no time to say goodbye to Andra. But he did not forget. He could find her when he wished.

Marvo did not ever go to school, though it was hard to tell. He was very knowledgeable. He was clever with figures; one of his tricks was to add large numbers in his head and give the answer as if surprised by it. He did not talk of his lack of education because he did not believe it existed. He swapped stories for his education. He learnt something from every story he heard.

He learnt from the stories he told as well as the ones he heard. He didn't always know how they would turn out; he didn't know how the person would react to the story. Telling the story changed it, every time.

On the bus to a lecture by his friend the Chrysostom historian, Marvo watched a woman eat a meat pie with such delight he had to talk to her. Marvo often found stories on the bus. He rarely drove; there were no stories in a car. There was no magic in a car. He caught the bus or he ran.

"Is that a special pie?" he asked. "Why are you eating it on the bus like that?" The woman didn't answer, so he told her a story.

The Tree of Knowledge, the Tree of Life

In the year we now call 4004 BCE, there was a great king. He was humble, as far as his intelligence went. But he did not believe in gaining knowledge; there was no learning in his kingdom. He believed you knew what you knew and that was good enough. Other places on the earth were creating jewellery and culture to go with it; glazed soapstone beads and communication. The priests of this king were the only communicators. They were the ones with knowledge.

But there was the evil of travel and salesmen. They came with their paper and tools. They spoke of ideas, of thought. They became wealthy by their addition and sums.

The king's citizens knew nothing of mathematics. They held out full palms and the priests and the travellers would take what they wanted.

The people began to wonder. They said, "What if?" and "Why?" It was a matter of great concern to the priests.

They took the people to the plain, where two trees rested side by side.

"These," said the priest of Voice, "these are all you seek. This tree is the Tree of Life. This the Tree of Knowledge. You may all choose, but let me say: Life is eternal, Knowledge destroys life as you know it. Choose."

First the king and queen, Master and She, had to choose. They knew nothing of the fruits of the tree—save from what they could see, that Life was small and brown, Knowledge red and large.

Master wanted to choose Life. His wife preferred Knowledge; she had long mistrusted the priests and wished to know what they knew.

"Take Knowledge with me," she said to her husband. "With Knowledge we can discover the secret of eternal life ourselves." The king loved and respected her deeply. It was one reason he was king. They turned to the Tree of Knowledge, watched by their people.

To try to convince them otherwise, a priest hurried forward to take a berry from the Tree of Life. He ate it, then leapt and leapt, laughing and shouting for joy.

"Oh, precious life," he said. The people saw the nut-brown berries, colour of their colour, flesh of their flesh, so comforting, so familiar. They watched Master and She.

Then She stepped forward and took two pieces of the red fruit. She gave one to Master.

"No," said the priests. The king was not to eat the fruit.

Where was fear?

Master and She placed the fruit between their lips.

"From ignorance to knowledge," said She, staring a priest right in the eye. He recoiled from her strength, from the force of her knowledge already existent.

She bit her fruit. She pressed her husband's chin up, his head down, crushing his mouthful between reluctant teeth.

The people waited; they did not choose.

The king and queen died within minutes of each other, six days later. There was no burial. Their unconsecrated bodies were kept as an example of what knowledge can do: destroy the soul.

Everybody else chose Life.

When the people eventually died, of old age or disease or accident, the priests said, "You destroyed the magic of everlasting life with your aberrant behaviour. It is not the fault of the Tree of Life."

Soon the Trees were lost, the plain forgotten, the people gone.

The story remained, though, Great Man and Woman, Master and She, Adam and Eve, lost to knowledge. The names changed slowly, lost letters and gained letters, as people with different tongues spoke them and the other players faded against the importance of the two long-dead rulers. The two trees became one.

The woman said, "You know it's not normal to tell stories to people on buses."

"I love stories. Hearing them and telling them."

"Why?"

"It's magic, mythology."

"But you said your story was true," the woman said. Her pie was finished but she still smelled of it.

"The Greeks said mythology meant a story telling—*mythos*, or story, and *logo*, or telling. Or a rationale of stories. So a story becomes true just by the telling of it."

She stared at him. She had gravy in the corner of her mouth.

"I tell you that story because it's about an ancestor of mine," he said.

"The king?" she asked.

"No, the priest," he said. Her face fell; she did not like the priest's role in the story.

"No, the priest was very important. He was protecting the people from knowledge, from truth. Nobody needs to know everything. You would prefer not to know, perhaps, that you have gravy in the corner of your mouth."

She wiped the gravy away with her fingers, rubbed them together to roll the gravy off. Taking on the formal tone of his storytelling, she said, "I have six children. The last time I ate a pie all to myself, without having to give away any pastry or a bite, was three months before I fell pregnant with the first one. We went to the football. After the match, my husband wiped the gravy from the corner of my mouth. He kissed me. He said, 'I really would like to marry you', because we had not yet decided—he had not yet agreed—to marry. As I was eating that pie I remembered the kiss. I don't often get to eat a pie on my own. And I was imagining I'd murdered my husband and cooked him in a pie."

Marvo laughed. He sent the woman a mist to thank her for showing him you could never guess what a person was thinking. The mist made her husband seem kind and loving again.

The woman did not feel silly telling her plain tale of pies and kisses in the same voice as his tale of kings and priests and creation. Marvo made her feel her story was vital.

Under other circumstances, he would not have told her this priest was his ancestor. He would have allowed her to discover it for herself, because that would make the knowledge stronger, more magical. Reputation grows through rumour, not self-advertisement, but sometimes you have to start the rumour yourself. He did not have time, on that bus trip, for anything else.

Marvo learnt from his grandmother that listening is very important in magic. You have to try to feel what your audience feels, sense what they want. They will tell you, by sighing or muttering, and if they forgot they said something and you remind them they think you're clever.

He never forgot this. He always listened, like a shaman.

Marvo felt more in control of his mist at a personal level. He still wasn't sure he could control a large mist, but he knew it leaked out anyway, sometimes while he slept. He would awake to news of a wealthy philanthropist setting up a fund so that every child would have a computer, and he would see smiling faces when he went to buy the milk. He would know the mist was thick.

His grandmother had told him the story of Master and She to teach him that eternal life is never easy. It was a prescient warning against what he would do in the future: he sought eternal life, fearing death. She hoped to persuade him to accept death as the natural and right process, but her message was not enough to change his mind, many years later.

Some stories he overheard on the bus and stole. He heard a man muttering this to his companion one day.

The Tick-Tock Man

Look, there's a watchmaker's shop. See in the window: all those watches. Always reminds me of a story I once heard, never forgotten it.

This was before the advent of television, when we had the radio. There was a show called *Five Minute Glimpses.*† You know, supposed to show how the other half lives.

---

† This story was taken from the radio show, which existed in Australia in the 1950s.

There was this one story which stuck in my mind, never forgotten it.

It was about a watchmaker, who worked alone in his shop all day. Being alone like that, all those clocks ticking incessantly drove him mad, so he sold his shop and bought a flat, I don't know where it was. But his neighbour upstairs had a pegleg, you see, tap tap with his wooden leg on the floor boards all day.

Drove the watchmaker mad, and he went up and murdered the fellow!

So they gave him life in jail, a cell of his own. But you wouldn't believe it—a tap outside his cell leaked, drip, drip.

So... He had a chair in his room, an old one, and he took a splinter of wood, the longest he could find, and pierced his eardrums so he couldn't hear a thing.

But it didn't work. He could hear his heart, thump, thump.

So he took another splinter and pierced his heart. Killed himself. Then he was free from it all, not bothered by clocks or taps or hearts or drips.

But I always wondered if he made it to the Pearly Gates, and there's Saint Peter, plucking away on his harp all day.

Pluck, pluck.

M arvo never left a story behind.

Sometimes he traded a trick for a story. If the story was good, it would be a good trick, a magic trick to help the storyteller. If it was not much of a story (he did not think the lady with the pie told much of a story, but she had surprised him) he would perform a trick of illusion and leave it at that, make the person think they were happy or make them forget one nasty memory. He took away one woman's memory of an abortion; it didn't happen.

Sometimes he realised later he already knew something. Sometimes he used a lesson before he learnt it.

He slept in odd places, with odd people. He was awoken by screams one night, screams of such intensity they entered Marvo's dreams. He dreamt he was cutting down a rain forest and the saws were squealing and screaming like banshees.

"I had a terrible dream," the man next to him said. His hair was wet with sweat, his voice hoarse from screams. Marvo did not believe in dreams but he used the name for them anyway.

Marvo said, "There are no dreams; there is only the interpretation of the truth in unusual ways."

The man rubbed his red raw eyes.

"Your dream involved your eyes?" asked Marvo. "Tell me about your eyes. What have you seen? What did you dream?"

The Murderer of Girls

I have had this dream before. On awakening, I sit straight up in bed, a stiff, bent nail. The room is dark yet dancing with lights; stars in my eyes, my eyes burning. I dreamt my eyes were pierced by tiny thorns, thorns which rained down in sparkles, but when I tilted my head to look at the sparkles I felt the burning in my eyes and I was blinded.

I was not involved. I was an innocent bystander at the gates of hell. I looked through the bars and saw blood, saw flesh and blood, and a great man laughing, his head tilted back like mine in the dream. He laughed as the girl died. I, watching, giggled. I was not heard, and I stayed to watch as he separated her limbs, a doll poorly made.

He did not imagine anyone would be there to witness. I myself was surprised at the appearance of the house. I did not imagine anyone living out there. I was there to be quiet, to think, but I saw a demon kill a girl.

I carried on with my meditations. Then I returned to my home, where I have kept my silence until now. Each time a girl is missing I dream my dream of thorns. I feel like a wax dummy, but I am suffering still. I feel like the thorns are thrust into my eyes to the sound of imprecation, someone thinking to injure me, to cause me pain or misfortune.

Marvo nodded at the man and turned to go away.

"You're leaving?" said the man. "Can't you help me?" He had seen murder; had smelled it. Marvo remembered the lesson of the cats and dogs lady, that all things cost. He gave the man dreamless sleep, cool eyes and a deep abhorrence of violence.

Later, he wondered if perhaps he should have helped the man to reveal the murderer.

Marvo sought magic in odd places, slept in stranger. He added names to his list of magicians, crossed them off.

He found a wonderful place to watch TV—in a home of old people, where they all sat, dwarfed in fake leather chairs, beige to show the dirt and remind them who's boss. They sat with their knees together, every one of them, like it was the last control they had over their bodies. Their chairs were lined up and spaced apart so they could not talk and drown out the TV. The TV made Marvo think of home, because it had no knobs. They couldn't change the channel or raise the sound; they had to watch what was there.

And the attendants found the TV annoying so they kept it down low, and the people who watched had to concentrate very hard to hear a word.

Marvo watched show after show, sitting in an armchair, his cape over his knees, with others who could not hear. And he grew to care about his fellows, and could not but help them. They were starved for attention, excitement and conversation. They would do anything, perform anything, for an indulgence. Marvo never asked more than a story—something so small, he was at times distrusted.

"You'll steal it from me. I'll lose my pride," one old man said.

"I'll take nothing from you. I only give."

"All right then. You remember who told you this story."

Kitten

All I've got is me memory of war. I was brave then, and I was some-one. They knew me as a lucky token, the boy to have on board for a good journey. Not like that, don't think it. Not like the barrel boys of olden days. I had the reputation of being lucky, of warding off shipwrecks. But you know all it was? A hint handed down by my grandfather, a man who stuck to his ways and didn't like much else.

He told me to carry a caul on board, at any cost. Now that was a nasty thing to tell a child; even at eighteen, I was inexperienced with the ways of women and the body. I found it hard to take. He told me it was a piece of luck highly prized by sailors; he had heard of them being for sale, in the paper, back in the nineteenth century. In the paper, can you believe it, like it was a bit of carpet or rug. I didn't find mine in the paper. I had to walk the streets, and they didn't like me there, I can tell you. The things those women would do, and they thought I was the one who was sick. I don't know what they thought I'd do with it; eat it, I suppose. And the ones whose babies were born with it felt blessed by it, anyway, and loath to part. Finally, a week before my first trip at sea, a poor young girl gave birth to a baby which made her faint.

"It's a kitten! I've birthed a cat!" people heard her scream. The poor mite of a baby was protected by a caul, and the poor mite of a mother had only seen cats born before. I took the caul from her; she didn't want it. Paid all I had for it; can't say I'm anything but fair. It was worth it, because every ship I sailed on was safe, and the crew were good to me. I miss those days. I miss the days when I was good, and they wanted me. Now I'm not needed.

Marvo reached into his pocket and pulled out a tiny silver-grey kitten.

"Newborn," he said, "and its mother killed by a car. Will you take it?" The old man gently took the cat; more gently than any woman he'd held in his life.

"Poor little puss," he said. "Bit of bacon for you? Bit of old bacon sandwich?"

The kitten clawed its way out of the man's arms and ran up Marvo's leg. Marvo held it in his palm.

"I can give you another," he said.

"Just give me another bacon sandwich."

Marvo loved bacon sandwiches when they were hot from the pan. There was so much to try, so much to taste, Marvo rarely thought of his grandmother, but sometimes he would be reminded. After a solitary dinner in a quiet restaurant, an after-dinner mint was placed before him. He dined alone every night, either in a restaurant or, as he preferred, with a huge plate of bought food in front of a silent television. He could never quite get used to noisy TV.

He ate the after-dinner mint in one mouthful, not realising what it was until it was melting over his tongue. He remembered seeing these squares once or twice on TV, being passed around the tables of well-dressed people.

He closed his eyes to savour the taste and was disappointed. He never forgot after that how worship can be blinding to reality, and how one person's obsession is another's take-or-leave. He remembered the time he took chocolate to his grandmother. How much she loved him that day.

The stories began to lose meaning for Marvo and he realised that he was lonely with only his cat for company. He was lonely for the nurse from the hospital, Andra, who would never give him a story.

He called her number from memory, though he had never dialled it before.

Marvo said, "I'm just about to go and look at a dead body on the beach. Meet me there."

"We all have such strong memories of the beach as children," Andra said.

Marvo did not. He said, "With the sun burning hot, time was nothing on the beach. The sun's role was to heat, not to pass the day. I was just a little boy. I played running games with the waves, and built monuments in the sand. I ate lunch with another family and played cricket with a group of older boys.

"Some girls bought me an ice cream and let me rub sun cream into their flesh. I rubbed cream into my own flesh. I ran up and down the hot sand, each step too short for my feet to cool. I felt the pain was good. I felt the heat of the sand made me run faster, make me speed as fast as the big boys chasing each other with balls and wet towels.

"When the sun began to sink, I went to where my grandmother sat waiting. She gave me a scraping of food and settled a large cardboard box over me, for me to sit and wait in darkness until the sun called me again."

Andra nodded.

They watched as the girl was lifted out, her long red hair sodden, darkened, threaded through with scraps of the sea.

"Marvellous hair," Andra said. Her own head was shaven.

Marvo reached into the water where the body had been. He pulled out a small piece of coral, which he gave to Andra.

"To protect you from enchantment," he said.

"I have always been enchanted," she said. She passed the coral to a young girl who was watching them.

"You take it," she said. The coral went pale in the child's hands.

"Come on," said Marvo. "That child is ill. I don't like to be near sickness or death."

"That's a shame," said Andra. "I surround myself with sickness and help to heal it. There is always some form of disease in my life."

"That's acceptable," said Marvo. He was startled by the truth in this woman.

"Do you know anything else about coral?" she said. "Anything at all? Tell me, because you seem to know a lot."

Marvo knew what she meant by this. "Tell me what you know," he countered. "How do you heal with coral?"

"It can be used to replace human bone in some circumstances. A broken jaw, congenital abnormalities. Its physical configuration is like that of bone, and, when it is cleaned to kill its organisms and transplanted into the human body, in time blood vessels and bone will fill the channels. It will join with the bone and the blood and become bone itself."

"People can do that too," said Marvo. He took her hand, desperate for her story. "They seem to be completely different, opposites, yet when they spend enough time together, they merge and become the same organism. That's what intimacy brings, it brings strange birth. Strange birth."

Andra had not had her hand held so passionately before. He did not try to kiss her, touch her, bend her back into the sand. He waited, his mouth open, his lips moving as if to start her mouth with mimicry.

"I had a strange birth," she said.

Climbing up in the Attic

My mother was in the attic, finding clothes, sorting through boxes. It was a late pregnancy. She was forty-two. I was to be her first baby. Twenty years earlier she had been pregnant; clothes were bought then, the boxes of toys. But the baby had died, strangled, they said, by the cord. My mother had seen the child, the tiny baby, and seen its neck. They allowed her to hold her daughter for a minute, to say goodbye. It was a good hospital in that way. But around the child's neck were two small hand marks, as if another child had strangled the life from the baby.

"Where's the other one?" she said. She did not fall pregnant again for twenty years.

She was in the attic to look through the clothes she had kept to remind her of that dear dead daughter, kept out of love and fear and as a talisman.

She felt the first pains. She stumbled back, knocked a large chair as she grasped for support. It fell over the trapdoor, sealing her in. She screamed for help through the small window, but they could not get to her.

A young boy was sent through the window to push away the chair, but it was too late to get her down the stairs. He watched my birth in fascinated horror.

He moved the chair and the rest of the family climbed up into the attic, crowding her.

She carried me down the ladder and down the stairs to the kitchen. She passed me to my father. My grandmother looked in horror.

"What is it? What is it?" my grandfather said.

"The child was carried down before it was carried up," my grandmother said. "She will not have an easy life. You should have stepped on a chair or something. You should have climbed on a box, onto the windowsill. This child will never support you in your old age; it will not have money. It will never rise to distinction."

"What are you, the wicked grandmother who didn't get invited to the christening? Leave her alone, with your gloom and doom," said my grandfather, I'm told.

My mother saw me gaze at her. Saw my tiny hands clench with a strength unusual. She was a modern woman, a non-believer in superstition and refused to wish a bad life on me.

My grandmother cleaned the attic of childbirth. She climbed onto a chair holding the placenta, already dry and discoloured around the edges. Then she descended the stairs.

They gave the placenta a funeral, named it and buried it and mourned its death. The placenta is considered brother or sister in some parts of the world. Much later, I found the place of burial and mourned my sibling.

For a while I called myself Sissy, thinking of sister, my sister who had died twenty years earlier. I soon realised how ridiculous that was. I was always surrounded by things, then. My grandmother would bring little things home, things she'd found on the road, in a bin. Little lucky charms, things to save me.

Strangely, my grandmother's prophecy was right. My mother died when I was eighteen, of a cancer even my grandmother could not cure. My father found great support in the small town we lived in. He was a widower with a crazy daughter. I had a strange relationship with everyone: my teacher, my father, my classmates.

I have no need for great wealth. I only want to eat and enjoy my life, and my main enjoyment comes from found objects, from things no one else wants to touch. Nobody will go with me to trash and treasure markets, because I spend hours delving in the boxes of things available for a small coin each.

Only last Sunday I reached in and found a grater, food still clinging to its serrated edges. A comb, greasy to the touch. Some nail clippers, hinge smooth with use. The stall-holders were embarrassed to think they had put these things up for sale; this junk, personal junk with clearly imprinted memories: The grater was used for nutmeg when romance was still in the marriage and Brandy Alexanders were considered worth the effort.

The comb was a memento of lost youth, a time when hair was strong and black and muscles were not dystrophic.

The nail clippers used to disgust an unloved wife; used to make her leave.

The stall-holders watched me disappear with my prizes and they wondered at me, a person who would buy another's debris.

Marvo sighed. It was a beautiful story. The police tried to move everyone off the beach, but with the mist Marvo and Andra looked like sandcastles.

"Are you still working at the clinic?" he asked.

"I felt lost after you were released," Andra said. "They sacked me not long after that. I guess I lost my motivation. I didn't think I'd ever find another good job. But now I work at the Body Shop and I love it."

"What is it? Lotions and potions?

"Not that kind of body shop. This one is very different. I'll take you one day to show you what we collect." She scraped her fingernails along his arm and showed him the collection of sweat and sand.

"You should have found me."

"I did track you down but did not approach you. I didn't think you'd like to be reminded of the clinic. When you called me I marvelled that our thoughts were alike, that we felt the same. How did you know I would like to see a drowned girl being taken from the water?"

He took her hand.

"What about you, Marvo? Where do you work? Or does a man like you not work?"

"I am not a man like me! I'm a lift operator."

They stood watching the dead redhead on the beach. "Her hair is so beautiful," Andra said.

"What's your hair story? Last time I saw you your hair was to your waist."

"My hair was set alight at work. I get compensation payments which barely allow me to pay the bills. I have expenses."

"Tell me another story," Marvo said. He knew he would eventually hear every story she had to tell. "Why did you leave the clinic?"

"It's not a story, it's an event. After you left the clinic I found I was no longer interested in the work. I was sloppy. Remember Mr Hollyoak? The gardener? I gave him something by mistake and he died. But it was okay—he was happy about it.

"'No more weeding,' he said at the end. He felt responsible for all the weeds in the world and was glad to pass it on.

"I did him a favour, really, but they didn't think so at the clinic."

Marvo shook his head at her mistreatment. "I wish you could get a job where I am, but you might find it boring. I like it, taking people up and down in the lift all day. They talk to me, tell me secrets. They like me. I take my cat with me and he purrs on my shoulder. People love him."

Marvo changed his job so often he could never get bored. He took Andra to sit in the lift with him, and when it was empty he asked to hear the story of her birth again.

From the moment they met on the beach they were only apart when Andra went to her job at the Body Shop, or Marvo to his lift.

Whenever Andra told the story of her birth—and she told it often; Marvo could not hear it enough times—she would clench and unclench her hands, as if testing their strength and trying to remember killing her sister. She would tell it as they lay together, on the bed or on the floor. Andra did not mind Marvo sleeping on the floor; often she joined him, pulled down the doona and slept amongst the dust, smelling the under-the-bed smell. He kept jars of water there; he had never lost the fear of the room, the fear that water would run out, that there would not be enough.

Andra went to work each day because she loved her job. The exclusive advertisements, mailed only to those who would not laugh aloud, said:

Did You Know That If A Nest-Making Magpie Steals
The Hair You So Carelessly Throw Away, You Will Die
Within A Year And A Day?

Did You Know That You Should Never Cut Your Nails
On Friday Or Saturday Unless You Want Bad Luck?
That In Roman Times It Was Sinful To Cut Your Nails
On The Nundinae (Every Ninth Day)? Have You Ever
Had A Tooth Removed At The Dentist's And Left It
Behind? You're Playing With Fire. Just One Bad-Minded
Person Is Needed, Plus Your Tooth, To Make Your Life A
Misery.

Call The Body Shop Now, We Dispose Of Hair, Teeth,
Nails, And Other Material In A Discreet And Safe
Manner, Ensuring There Is No Danger Of Misplaced
Pieces In The Wrong Hands.

Call The Body Shop Now To Reclaim Your Peace Of
Mind.

The people Andra worked with were well-read when it came to the dead. They started calling her "little weasel" for her love of pieces. One man there mistook her interest for ghoulishness, and told her long and vile stories. He was the one who named her Little Weasel. He told her a story, which she repeated to Marvo:

The Little Weasel

There was a city, many years ago, before time was such a clear and certain jailer, which was a place of great strength to witches. Nobody wanted to be buried there, because the witches would take the form of weasels and bite off the ears and noses of dead bodies waiting for final rest. They used these in their spells, and they became so feared that the squeaking of a weasel was said to be a portent of death.

Travellers to this city found great welcome though, and word spread of the joys to be found there. The women were sensual and free, the men strong and friendly. The rare female traveller was given safe haven as the men were.

It was not a very healthy town, though, not for visitors. Sickness prevailed, and the doctors were kept hard at work sending word to bereaved families. The witches of the town did not mind where the noses and ears came from; foreign blood never hurt anybody. The city prospered for many years until the day a weasel ran through the main street, squeaking death. A week later, a great flood took every life, visitor, local and witch alike.

A ndra was hurt by the story because she knew the weasel was meant to be her. Marvo sent a numbing to the man's tongue.

"D-do you like your job, L-l-little Weasel?" asked the man the next day. He was now a stutterer and the sharpness was taken from his words. His comment was meant to be a joke. No one could like her job. Andra, however, found it to be spiritually rewarding work. The pay was good; it needed to be. Only the rich could afford the service; the poor must dispose of their own waste.

All pieces had to be kept separate. Little plastic bags were provided, at barely a cost to the owner of the business. Less than a cent each, and the clients paid a hundred dollars, to fill them with hair, nails, teeth, faeces, urine. The bags were collected weekly and burnt in individual fires. It was this which cost the money; the individual handling required. It was very important not to mix the bags up, and it was the combination of physical grossness and high responsibility which put people off.

Cure or curse worked the same way. A prevention to disease was to inject that disease. And the way to break a witch's spell was to use the elements of witchery; the victim's hair and nails, sealed in a bottle and buried at the front door, will break a witch's spell. Andra was happy, because, instead of scattering the ashes individually, she kept them in a large glass jar. One day she would find a use for the grey flecks.

She kept them safe, though. No witch would use such a small piece of a person to cast a spell. Andra did not think she would ever be caught keeping the ashes, because she did her job so perfectly. She had no witchbreaker sniffing about her walls, wanting to catch her at it. No cunning watcher to spoil her fun.

Marvo found her dedication to her work enticing. He knew that difficult tasks were not always completed. He saw buildings half-finished, holes half-dug, cardigans half-knitted. Andra would do anything and complete everything. She had no fear of failure. Failure was part of experience; it was to be expected, not avoided. She felt no disgust. Marvo didn't either; he saw far worse on TV.

Marvo watched a lot of TV, often with the sound down. He seemed to prefer it that way. He would laugh when the characters laughed, without hearing the joke.

She didn't like TV, didn't like the passivity of viewing it. So when it was on she watched Marvo, saw his face become childlike and innocent as he watched. "You are so passive when you watch that box," she said. He nodded, reached behind the couch for some dried fruit he kept hidden there.

As part of her job, Andra often went to the Hall of Mirrors, where the psychics met and read palms. This was where they often found clients, amongst the superstitious, the believers. She was paid for being a mirror, and she enjoyed the work.

Andra dressed differently on those days. Marvo though she looked mysterious, with blackened eyebrows and darkened eyelids. Her make-up was more than other women wore. Other women thought adornment meant seduction of the male, and seduction of the male meant enslavement to the male. But Andra wore the make-up on her eyes because she was superstitious and suspicious; she trusted nobody but Marvo. She believed anyone was capable of shooting darts at her from their eyes, darts to put a spell on her and entrap her. The make-up reflected any darts, and it provided her protection from herself as well. Sometimes she committed an act before she was aware of the consequences, and the make-up prevented her from sending out unhealthy darts when she didn't really want to. Looking daggers at someone could have a different meaning.

"Welcome, welcome," they said at the Hall of Mirrors. They gave her a table of her own. They let her be a mirror; let her sit and reflect the people's hopes and desires as they shuffled through.

Andra did not perform the tricks the others did. No cards, tea, palms or crystal. She merely sat and watched their faces, let them talk and offered help. The queues were not as long at her table. She was not a popular witch; she didn't show off or tell them wonderful things.

Less and less did the patrons visit her, so she sat silent and watching for hours on end, the babble rising and descending around her.

She was asked to leave the day after she had just a single customer, an elderly man who was ill with a disease he didn't like to mention. She said, "You must tell your family and friends. They'll hate you when you've gone, when they find out anyway, they'll hate you for not trusting them."

The man reported her to the organisers.

"She's not a witch," he said, "she didn't tell me a thing about my past, didn't even know my mum was dead."

They asked her to leave.

Marvo tried to help, but Andra already understood that everyone has a different idea of "witch".

With Andra at home more often, Marvo gave up watching TV all day, and they practised magic. Andra would find herself transported to different rooms, holding bunnies or tigers, then returned to Marvo. They became very good. They understood each other, and he trusted her.

Marvo and Andra began to give children's shows in the park, setting up the table and performing simple magic. It meant Marvo felt comfortable calling himself a magician, and that he felt ready to meet with others like him.

They spent hours, Marvo doing tricks, Andra watching. She didn't comment for a long time when he erred; she was afraid of offending him. Then, when she gained confidence, she was strict, cruel, and Marvo loved it. Making him practise again and again.

He pulled out his messy list of magicians' names to show her.

"These are all the magicians in the country. One day I'd like to meet them all, to see if they're like me," he said.

"Why don't we go travelling and visit them? Or you could invite them to stay here." Andra waved her arms around their home. Sometimes the emptiness of it frightened her.

"I might hate most of them—though I was thinking of having a party, like that time on TV, when there was a long table of food, and everyone stood up and ate, and the drink person gave drinks to them all. That would be good."

"I can help you arrange it," Andra said, picturing herself at the side of the greatest magician, weaving her own magic, making him glow in the dark.

"There will be only magicians there. No assistants," he said, his eyes closed, thinking. He didn't know she thought herself part of him. Didn't realise the hurt he'd inflicted.

He started at the top and called his way down. He had no prejudices of age, sex or place of residence. All magicians had a chance to prove they were real to him.

"I'm calling from the Wizards' Guild," he said to each one. "Our annual Christmas party is next week and we haven't yet received your response. It's a food-and-drink-supplied bash at the House of Dreams showroom."

Marvo did not bother about how much money it all cost. He only needed to tap a pocket for the money to transfer itself to his own. Andra sometimes wondered about where the money came from, because he lived in a large home and used food and electricity without a thought. He organised his party with no expense spared. She never asked him, though, and did not really seem to care.

He waited for the days to pass, until he could see his people all gathered together. He never failed to be astonished at the number of pretenders who existed by playing with the belief of the people.

Marvo could see these dabblers on his streets. There was a man with sharp, short hair, his white scalp visible. He had a thin, pointy face, like a 3D triangle. He wore a large grey overcoat throughout the year. The only indication of summer was the slight sheen of sweat which covered his face. His eyes were large and they glowed.

In his hand he carried grubby, plaited leather bracelets he made himself. He carried them loosely and gestured with them at people. They were woven with weak spells; the spells were so unattractive, no one was drawn to them. Few bought them. One teenage boy bought; he didn't understand. He bought one for a girl he liked, hoped if he strapped it on she'd be his. But the spell was not of love, the spell was for eyesight. His eyes grew wide and staring and he became frightening to look at. Once he removed his bracelet his eyes shrank to normal size, but they were so small, and in comparison he looked like a pig.

Marvo's cat clawed his shoulder if he watched these people for too long.

Andra watched Marvo preparing for his big night, the night he would meet the wizards and the magicians. They were never apart now and she felt lonely at the thought of him away for those hours.

"Good luck," she said. She did not ask to go with him. She knew he would say no and she was not ready for rejection from him.

Most of the magicians invited had agreed to attend. There were over three hundred of them, and Marvo, as drinks waiter, met them all. They were a colourful group, his magicians, flamboyant show-offs, all competing for attention. They wore purple suits, black cloaks, tight red trousers, pirate shirts. They admired Marvo's cape.

Marvo paid for the drinks and they drank as much as people do when it's free. There were tricks played. Like comedians, magicians like to impress each other even more than they like to impress an audience.

Marvo found them inspiring to be around, from a performance sense. He watched their flourishes, their flashy smiles, their passion.

He found only one true magician, a woman called Betta. He spoke to her throughout the night; she recognised him as well. She left early, asking him to come to her house the next day.

Marvo played on till dawn with the false magicians and arrived at her house just after 7am without sleeping.

"Keen!" she said, standing in fluffy pyjamas. She took him in and made him toast.

"You know about your role in the world?" she asked. She was a serious woman.

"I'm a magician."

"Yes. But what is in your magic which keeps this world existent?"

"There I'm not sure."

"Have you seen the mist? Smelled it? Felt it?"

"Yes. It's often near me."

"We are the only ones who can see it. The others don't see. Their vision is blurred, interrupted, but they feel that they see all. This is your true reason for existence; it is the reason you live."

"Do you know of my strange beginning?" Marvo asked.

"We all have strange beginnings," she said. "I spent the first years of my life in a nest on a mountain to save me from slaughter."

"I was saved from slaughter."

"Our births are heralded to those who know. They let us live until we can form conscious thought, so we will know why we died, remember it for next time, pass it consciously to the next. Then they try to kill us."

"How many survive?" Marvo asked.

"Perhaps two in one hundred. And there are two of us per million population. That is why our magic must be powerful. Also why you must end your seeking for others. We must not be together. We must never die together. We are born alone, we stay alone and in pain."

Betta began to cry quietly. She showed her age this way. She was not young. Marvo comforted her, wise that the pain of age is the worst, the pain and the knowledge that it would not cease until death. "You know we are here, be satisfied with that. Find someone who understands magic. Not a fake. Many fake magicians are our enemies. They become magicians to seek us out and destroy us. Perhaps, as a performance magician, you may distract them from your truth. Never lose awareness, though, be always aware."

"I know something," said Marvo, "I know something you may not know. Do you have a brother or a sister?"

"No. My older sister was killed when I was five."

"An accident?"

"Yes. She followed me into a pipe. I came out the other side, she was stuck. They could not get her out for a long time; she suffocated. It was a very small pipe. An eight-year-old should have known better."

"I never had a sibling," Marvo said. "It's hard for me to understand how losing one would be. But let me tell you this: I know that no magician should have a sibling. I know that they are never born, or they are killed before we gain our strength. I know this is because they could become adversaries, very powerful adversaries, because they would know us, have our blood, and use our powers to their own advantage. Brothers and sisters are dangerous to us."

Marvo thought of Andra's sibling who died in the womb. Her story was where he learnt this lesson. He wondered if this was an indication of her power.

Betta realised she was talking to the most powerful magician she had met. She continued his education, though; he needed knowledge he did not yet have. Marvo listened to her and ended his seeking.

He was full of news when he returned to Andra, but she wanted to hear none of it.

"Boring," she said as he described the party. "She sounds like a bitch," she said as he spoke about Betta, toast and true magicians. He realised that she was sick with jealousy, that she had missed him so much her body ached. He picked up his cat and stroked him. The cat refused to purr; he was angry with him, too.

"Tell me a story," she said.

"I'm trying to," he said. "One about purple suits and disappearing vodka."

"A different story, Marvo," Andra said. When she felt discarded her skin looked blue.

"Why don't we find someone to tell us a story together?" Marvo said. "Why don't we share a story?"

So they put on clothes which wouldn't frighten people and walked out. She wore brown pants and a soft cream jumper. He wore a short-sleeved shirt which showed off white, hairy arms.

"You pick someone," Andra said. "You're the expert at finding good stories."

They walked through the city streets until they saw a man in a business suit and bare feet.

"That's the one," Marvo said.

The man muttered to himself. He handed them a grubby card

which said, "I can no longer help you."

"We don't need help," Marvo said. "Do you?"

"I don't. I don't. It's all the fault of my birthday."

Marvo felt great satisfaction. He was about to hear about a strange birth, his favourite kind of story. "Tell me," he said. "Tell us about it."

Born on Christmas Day

I was born on Christmas Day. Always expected to die on Good Friday (a euphemism for Bad Friday, did you ever realise that?) and, depending on my mood on that day, would either stay in bed to avoid danger or go out seeking it. I always thought I was special. Everyone confirmed this when they heard my birthdate.

"Are you religious?" was a common question. They thought that because I shared Christ's birthday, I would embrace his teachings.

"I believe in what is truth," became my standard answer. To get rid of them at first, but then it started to become reality. I'd write down thoughts as they came to me, things like: *The sky is blue—heaven is the sky. People with blue eyes are heaven. People with brown eyes are earth. People with green eyes are nature. People with grey eyes are the rocks. People with hazel eyes are nourishment. People with no eyes are everything.*

I began to read these aloud. I imagined myself the world's greatest preacher. I began to talk in loud, confident tones, handing out advice to all in my path. I dressed well so people would trust me. I told them anything that came into my head. I filled a book with my little pieces of wisdom. I even believed them myself. Especially when the book appeared in print; that seemed to make it all real somehow.

I was very happy for a while, then someone found out about my sex life. I tried to tell them everybody is free, the body is God's gift and we should use it in the most pleasurable way we know, but they wouldn't take that. Prejudices were too ingrained; they didn't like my type. That's why you see me as I am.

I think of those people now and wonder what has happened to them. How many took my arrogant advice and what are their lives now?

Marvo said, "You should study Saint Chrysostom. He was a great and learned man, both the archbishop of Constantinople and a Doctor of the Church. His name was a nickname, meaning 'golden mouth', because of his eloquence. He remains to this day one of history's greatest speakers. He was the one who said: 'I came naked into the world, and I can carry nothing out of it.' His last words were 'Glory be to God for all things.'" This was Marvo's gift to the man.

"You were there, were you?" said the man. He was the cynical type, finding pleasure in disbelief.

"His relics were laid in the Church of the Apostles on January 27th. Is that a special day for you?" asked Marvo.

"I once had a girlfriend whose birthday was January 30th. Is that close enough?" The man really was a cynic.

Marvo found cynics destructive and boring. "Where are your shoes?"

"Bare feet are my atonement," the man said, as if he were really suffering.

Marvo watched Andra's face. She said, "Interesting story. Why did you stop? You should never stop helping people."

The man looked at her for the first time. "I was talking to your friend here. But my help to you would be to tell you to stick with your own kind. Your own level. Do you understand? Don't reach for the unreachable."

Marvo watched as her mouth fell open. He pulled her aside and whispered in her ear, "He has no idea who or what you are, Andra. You are better than any man on earth. He's an idiot."

"He's cruel. You should tell him what you know. Tell him what happened to those people he helped."

The man buried his head in his briefcase.

"I could find the answers for the man," Marvo said, "but he has learnt his lesson. The man does not want to know the truth, just as the other man did not want his navel cord back. I am not a cruel person. I won't tell this self-proclaimed prophet that the woman he advised to pay more attention to the body, '*Make your body important and you will soon find a lover*', had been raped after a date; and the man he had advised to find a new job, leave his old one, seek new horizons, had not and would not find a good job ever again. This man born on Christmas Day is no good at giving advice."

"You should tell him," Andra said. "To prove you love me."

Marvo did it and was surprised by the result. It seemed that the confirmation of failure was good for the man born on Christmas Day. He could truly atone and move on.

Marvo got into bed with Andra that night and found flea bane seeds which cause chastity when found between the sheets. She said, "I don't think we're quite ready." With a snap of his fingers, Marvo turned the seeds into oil, which he began to rub into Andra's back, between her shoulder blades. He rubbed and rubbed but did not seduce her. He never took what was not freely given.

They had slept in the same bed now for a long time without forming a sexual connection. They were waiting. They used the sexual energy as strength. His cat slept on the end of the bed with them, providing comfort and continuity.

"Life is never dull with you, Marvo," Andra said. "I had a boyfriend once, a dull man. Nothing like you. He was very weak."

Eagle's Egg

We met somewhere very dull; at a party. He was a Christian, it was a party for Christians. I was there by mistake, it was a friend's brother's friend or something who was the Christian.

So I met this guy and talked to him all night till the party ended at midnight. I could not keep my eyes off his fingernails; they were the longest and cleanest I had seen on a man. I imagined them digging in ear and arse, then cleaned on the corner of a precious book. I listened to his dull talk, watched his eyes begin to live as I showed interest in him, saw his confidence make him swagger. I watched his fingernails and plotted to have them.

I took him home and slept with him a week after we first met. I made him cut his fingernails and I put them in a small box. I still have them somewhere. I felt sorry for him. I knew I had to protect him. I knew that before long I would despise him and I didn't think he deserved what might result from that, so I decided to protect him. That's why I didn't sleep with him that first night. It took a week to get an eagle's egg. I cooked scrambled eggs, which we ate from one bowl, using one spoon.

Now you're safe, I thought, stroking his face. *Safe from a witch's spell, safe from me when I decide to hate you.* I'm very good like that. Very good to the person.

I went to work the next morning, leaving him heavy with sleep, his fingernails clipped close to the skin. I expected to come home to him rested and safe and boring. I thought perhaps he would make lamb chops for dinner and I would enjoy them. No magic, nothing of interest but lamb chops and a simple life.

I walked into the house expecting to hear dull music and the ting of cooking utensils but all I heard was the high-pitched whine of a phone left off the hook. I found vomit all over the house, flecked with eagle eggshells. I'd poisoned the poor man. The eagle egg ate away a part of his stomach lining and to this day he can only digest soft-boiled hen eggs and bananas.

I never bothered after that to protect people.

"Did he live?" Marvo asked.

"Of course he did. I told you he only eats eggs and bananas. You can't eat when you're dead."

Marvo thought of the eggs she'd cooked for him. In particular, one very large omelette. "Have I eaten eagle eggs?"

"I will never hate you," she said. "I will love you and cure you until you are three hundred years old. Then we'll think again."

"I didn't know you were a healer, Andra. I thought you were a collector."

"You are the only one who knows about my collection."

Later, she dressed in her magician's assistant outfit and they climbed into the car, preparing for a long drive to a country town when they were booked for a children's party. Andra loved to drive.

"Tell me a story," Marvo said, his hands a blur of movement and playing cards. "Tell me how you became a healer."

"My grandmother had a piece of paper confirming that her great-great-grandmother had eaten meat of an eagle. It meant a healing nature to descendants, whether they wanted it or not. I can simply blow on a person with shingles, and the person will be cured.

"It is a burden to me, the healing power. It means I have to be good.

And while I am happy with that and feel it was a good way to use my life, I also want to be bad sometimes. I need that contrast. I need to hurt someone, kick them, but never make them ill. I can use my body for pleasure, or make my mother cry, but when a sick child stands before me I have to rest my hands on that child and heal.

"Your work, as I understand it, works as a contrast. We cover each other; what one does not do the other does. I use my magic to heal and give new beginnings. I can see where things are wrong; I am willing to see it. You prefer to use your magic to ignore the illness and by ignoring it, destroy it. You hate anything to be wrong. You imagine your childhood was normal, without terror. You imagine we to have a pure and natural relationship. You can't stand anything to be askew."

"All of that is true," Marvo said. "Tell me: what does eagle meat taste like?"

"It tastes like chicken. Eagles should not be so majestic, for their own good. Beauty so desirable is destructive. I'm glad not to be beautiful."

Marvo stared at her in disbelief. "You're not beautiful?" he said, as if his education had failed him there.

She said, "Not like the eagle, who finds it hard to keep her things about her. She's so lovely her pieces are desired, everyone wants some. She loses her eggs to people needing protection. She loses her beak to Greenlanders, who fasten it to their whaling harpoons to bring good luck. And there was that woman I helped. Remember? The one who couldn't hold a foetus."

Andra had given a woman with a history of miscarriage an eagle's stone to carry. She provided her with a typed sheet of information, to give her faith in the cure. *This walnut-sized light brown stone is found only in eagle's nests. Its geological name is* argillaceous oxide of iron, *which has settled around other materials. Take care of this stone: it is believed that the eagle can't hatch her eggs without it. Tied to your thigh during childbirth, it will bring an easy and light birth.*

"Do you ever think of that eagle?" Marvo said. "Perhaps you don't know the story of the childless eagle."

Andra shrugged. She could not be sentimental about her cures. She felt a human birth was more important that than of an eagle, no matter how beautiful the bird was. She said, "This is only folklore. There may not be truth in it, or there may."

"I know of an eagle whose stone was stolen as she had feathered her nest to prepare for children. She never reproduced and was ostracised."

"Eagles don't have civilised social mores like we do," said Andra, formality and an air of education her defence against Marvo.

"Yes, they do," said Marvo.

They put on a good show in the country. Andra even came home with a rotten tooth wrapped in a tissue.

"Look at this!" she said. "The granddad whinged about it aching so I pulled it out for him."

"What are you going to do with it?"

"Add it to my collection."

Some teeth she'd taken from work. Others were given to her by a lover who worked in the morgue and had no respect for the dead.

"You know that to cure toothache," she said, "a person should carry the tooth from a corpse of the opposite sex in their pocket. I keep them separate, male and female. To affect the one is to affect the other; thus, the tooth gone from one, the pain from another."

"You should start a business healing toothache," Marvo said. "Forget fortune telling. You will always find customers. People love sweets but they hate going to the dentist."

Just hearing from Marvo that she could do it gave her the strength she needed to heal. It began there.

Andra had many women come to her complaining of barrenness. She had the success of an earlier childbirth experience with an eagle's stone, but did not think the solution was right in every case. The spirit remained the same, though. Marvo also told her about his grandmother's experience, where she was cast out of her own village for giving them what they wanted.

She tied dock seeds to the arms of one woman and told her to go home and try. The woman fell pregnant. Andra felt the scent of the dock seeds, crushed between the two bodies, would be exciting to them, and in their fervour they would forget the purpose and enjoy the pleasure. Then would the process be able to work.

One woman whom Andra saw had no control over her life— everything was ruled by magic. She wouldn't leave the house without consulting her horoscope and she carried spells and amulets wherever she went. Andra told her she needed to choose just one thing. Horoscope or spells or trusting her own instinct. Otherwise all would be confused.

The woman didn't like this, and went to another healer, an untrue witch. There are many untrue witches; Andra knew them at a glance.

Andra was told the woman had a look of absolute astonishment when she was run over by a bike. She died carrying a spell in her pocket which was supposed to protect her from mechanisms.

"Had that woman trusted her ears and eyes rather than her spell, she would be alive," Andra said to Marvo. "This is the power we have. This is why we need to be so cautious."

Marvo watched Andra use plants to heal, remembered which was which and how they helped. He watched as she helped people walk and run, make love, fall pregnant. She made people happy.

Another woman came to Andra for help. "It's my husband," the woman said, "nothing unusual." She laughed, trying to trivialise her presence in the home of a witch.

"Does he beat you?" asked Andra.

"Only when he's had a few," said the woman. "Not otherwise."

"You must every morning pass this bottle over his head. It will change colour according to his nature; when the bottle appears black, cook him these mushrooms. Make him a lovely meal. If it appears blue, put the bottle away until the next morning. He will soon stop drinking, and that will cure the cause, thus the symptom."

Andra sent the woman home. She had no qualms about merging magic with science. They came from the same source.

The mushroom was called *Coprinopsis atramentaria*. It is usually harmless when cooked, but contains a chemical similar to the active principal in Antabuse.[†] If eaten in conjunction with alcohol it can cause nausea and vomiting.

"Where did you learn about the mushrooms?" asked Marvo.

"It was after your story about your grandmother dancing over the mushrooms. I remembered some of the magic I had been taught about them."

"I'm surprised you forgot to begin with. You rarely forget anything."

Andra, honest with herself, said, "I think I chose to forget it because I don't want to try it on my mother. I don't want to take away her single joy."

"Your mother is alive?"

"Of course she is," Andra said. "Oh." She smiled. "Yes, the story of my birth. Well, in some ways she did die. When I was eighteen she started to drink and she hasn't stopped since. That is like a cancer, I think."

"We should visit her," said Marvo. "We'll visit her and she'll see that she has you, and me also, if she wants me." Marvo thought having a mother to visit would be wonderful. He had never visited a mother.

Andra agreed to the visit.

---

† This is disulfiram, which blocks the metabolism of acetaldehyde, the main metabolite of ethanol. Alcohol builds up acetaldehyde and makes the drinker sick.

Marvo dressed with great care in jeans and a T-shirt, no cape because some people thought it frightening. He felt bereft without his cape. He felt straight-laced, too dull for Andra. He practised his big laugh and wrote a list of things to say. He had not yet learnt the basic lesson, that a character, if it is to be played well, must have many elements of truth in it. He had seen it all on TV, how when the door was opened you smiled and laughed. He bought flowers and chocolate because he had seen that as well, a hundred times.

"Can we take my cat?" he asked.

"She's allergic."

They arrived at Andra's mother's home before lunch.

"It's her best time, her freshest, clearest time," Andra said. "We'll get her before drinks."

Her mother opened the door, her mouth sucked into the shape of a bow.

"Come in, come in," she said, peppermint filling her mouth. Marvo handed her flowers and chocolate, and she put them down without looking at them or commenting. She asked them to sit at the kitchen table, and Marvo sat straight-backed, because he could not lean his elbows on a table covered with crumbs, stains, dried lumps. Andra sprawled her arms across to take his hand. They sat that way, holding up a barrier fence.

"She started early on the booze. Sorry, Marvo. I thought she'd be okay," Andra whispered while stroking his hair. Her mother noticed nothing.

Andra's mother made coffee, filled hers liberally and openly with brandy.

"Toothache," she said. Marvo had already made a bad impression on her. Too smart, too quiet, too clean. "So what do you do?" she asked.

"I told you already, Mum. He's a magician."

"How nice. Perhaps he's got a magic spell to protect a house from unwanted visitors."

Andra rolled her eyes. She had not wanted to come here. She wanted Marvo to herself; she did not want to share him.

"Though the house is always protected for you, isn't it, Andra? Just wait till I'm cold in my grave, will you? Before you move your arse in?"

Her mother poured more brandy into the cup, not worrying about the coffee this time. "You know her father was a hard-working man. A good man. Hard-working men are good men, aren't they, Marvo, and what is it you said you did?"

Marvo smiled. He was nervous, wanting this mother to like him for Andra's sake.

"It's only a small house but he paid it off in his own lifetime. That made him happy, providing for his daughter. I have to leave it to her whether I want to or not. She knows it. That's why she treats me so badly."

"I don't treat you badly," Andra said, but gently.

"You never bothered to come see him while he was alive. Maybe he liked the idea of you trapped here one day." Her mother laughed. "People think I'm a saint, you know? All I've done. All I gave up. I was the town beauty before she came along. Married a boy from the city. We were the ones. But you took it all from me. You and my mother. Neither of you make sense. She was all superstition, fear, prediction. What are you? She liked you better than me. I was like the middle child, older than you, younger than her. Bitch."

"Her or me?" Andra said. "You never cared about her. I cried more than you did when she died."

"Aren't you a fucking hero, then?"

Marvo carried the coffee cups to the sink and placed them carefully on the mound of dirty dishes.

"I had a party last night," Andra's mother said.

"Did it go well?" Marvo asked. "Did your guests enjoy themselves?"

"It depends on what you call enjoyment. I believe they did," she said. She discarded the artifice of coffee and poured more brandy into a glass. She stared at Andra. Marvo thought he heard her thinking *Make me stop. Tell me to stop it. Look after me.*

But Andra stroked Marvo's brow, she comforted him and looked after him instead, as if she hadn't heard. "Are you hungry?" Andra asked him.

Andra's mother said, "You look too skinny to be much of an eater. You don't enjoy food, do you? It doesn't make you happy. Perhaps you don't enjoy sex, either. Perhaps my daughter has to look elsewhere for her dinner companion and her partner in bed."

"I love food."

"You should see him eat," Andra said. "Like a bear. Like a lion. He eats like an animal with the same appetite."

Marvo had never considered such a possibility. Did his lack of physical passion send Andra away? He could not enjoy food because it had not been enjoyable in the room; whenever he tasted good food he thought of his grandmother, who could not share it. It didn't mean he had a small appetite, though.

"We do everything together," he said.

"Oh, really?" Andra's mother said. Marvo could not control the situation. He could not manipulate her into liking him; he cared too much whether she did.

She said, "How about some lunch?" and produced an old casserole from the freezer.

Marvo excused himself and went outside. He ran around the block and further, the rhythm soothing him, making him hungry.

They did not visit again. Marvo pretended to himself that the visit had gone well, and would ask Andra when they could go again. But Andra's mother would not have him in the house. "Looking down his nose at me. Pretending to be something he isn't. Get rid of him, Andra. He'll only hurt you."

Marvo pretended he didn't hear this.

"My grandmother would have loved you," Andra said. "You would have loved each other if it's possible to love someone else's relative."

Marvo had noticed that parts of Andra's story of her birth were true. The stairs were there, and the attic. He could understand why Andra had said her mother was dead. She was protecting him from having to meet her mother.

He said, "Your mother worries about you. She has your grandmother's words that you will not marry and she thinks I will hurt you, leave you."

Andra shrugged. She felt no regret driving away from her family home. No sense of loss.

"She hates me. She thinks I'm wasting my life," Marvo said.

"You waste nothing!"

"Do you think I'm sexless? Like your mother says?"

"Howsabout I tell you some stories and we'll see?" Andra said.

Flabby Arms and a Blonde Wig

I was a prostitute in a mining town for a while before I met you. Me and four other women had a shed each, all lined up with corrugated iron for walls, so that when all four of us were busy they couldn't tell who was who; the grunts and shouts and our own bored moans filled the four sheds without distinction.

Someone took my photo, while I was there, and I disguised myself under flabby arms, a blonde wig, a cigarette. No one who wanted to know where I was would recognise me with a cigarette or with the yellow tobacco stains on my fingers. I slipped up there, with my disguise. I overdid the detail, because men are the ones who have the stains. Women rarely do; they hold their cigarettes erect, so the smoke rises directly. Men hold their cigarettes down so the smoke passes through their fingers before rising. None of the miners noticed my tobacco-stained fingers.

There was no need for me and my three friends to advertise.

We each had a bell beside our door; a token affectation. The bells were disconnected and had never worked; though nobody knew they didn't work because nobody had used them. They were unpressed. Painted above them on the corrugated iron, "Please ring service bell".

A ndra didn't usually tell people about this line of work. Marvo, however, she told in graphic detail. He seemed to enjoy the seaminess; he was so neat and clean and sexless, so lacking in passion, that he was delighted and excited by her descriptions of premature ejaculators, men who shouted "Mother", men who smelled of the dirt and oil, or wine, or beer. Men who wanted odd sex acts but were afraid to ask.

Andra was not ashamed of her past; each event an experience, a memory. She told Marvo how different her life had been at each of its stages. She told Marvo about her plain religious upbringing: baptism, Holy Communion, confirmation. He was curious, interested in the ritual.

"My grandmother wailed and screamed at my confirmation, as she had at my birth.

"'Hand off, hand off!' she screamed. The bishop had both hands laid on me. She never forgave him. Said his left hand on me during the ritual meant he'd robbed me of my chance at a husband.

"'Doomed to a life of spinsterhood,' she told me all the time, hugging me like I needed all the help I could get. Once I said, 'Who calls not having to get married "doom"?' and she slapped me.

"Funny thing, the bishop turned out to be one of the bad guys. He never touched me—I think he heard my grandmother's voice too clearly: hands off, hands off.

"Plenty of the others got molested though. I used to be jealous, because they were popular with him. They were smiled at in church. All I got were glares. I blamed my grandmother and hated her for it. The authorities didn't find out till much later. By then, Grandma was dead and couldn't see how right she was."

"And you never got married," said Marvo.

"Never got married. I had to fill my life in other ways."

Marvo was not always sure when Andra was teasing him. He didn't know the established ways; he didn't know the history of marriage, the ways of it, who wanted it and who didn't.

"I was only a prostitute for four months," she said. "I've done many other things. I saved a woman from death by putting a spell on her husband once."

"Tell me about that after you've told me about the man who brought you a present."

Andra sighed. They arrived home, she ran a bath and they climbed in; as she scrubbed his back (she had not got out of the habit of giving pleasure) she said, "Once, on a day when the temperature reached 38°C outside, and inside the sheds it was 48°C, a man came to visit.

"We were resting with the doors open to allow the hot breeze to blow over our sweating bodies. We were all large and our bodies sweated well and although the breeze was hot, it cooled us.

"The day was silent. No creature would move in that heat; not the birds, the dogs or the men. I read an X-rated comic book one of the men had left behind."

The water had gone cold. Marvo let more hot in, let some cold out.

"What were some of the stories in the comic?" he asked. He took Andra's foot and began to gently massage.

"Most of the stories were very silly."

Girl Talk

The first story in the comic book was quite short. It was pretty boring too. It started with these women; you could only see their faces because of the way the light was. There were three of them, and they talked about what their men would do when they got home. The light changed, and you could see they were naked. They talked some more about it, how the men would bring home feathers, they'd bring home massage gel and whips. They'd bring home other men with massive penises, and the men would watch it all.

The light changed again and the you saw that the women were in chains. They couldn't leave the room. They lay there all day waiting for the men to come and talking about what would happen when the men came home. It was boring.

The Man of her Dreams

In this comic book, there was one good story. It was about a magician, who hypnotised his victims to believe he was the man of their dreams. Once their fantasy began he would follow. So, one believed the magician was a footballer, very athletic. Another thought he was a cold and unobtainable librarian, and he had to pretend disinterest as she made love to him.

"Finish the story about the gift now," Marvo said. He didn't want to hear about magicians.

The Nice School Teacher

Another story in the comic was about a school teacher.
This teacher could be very grouchy or very friendly. And the students figured out it was whether or not she'd had some lovin' the night before. That's what it said in the comic, "some lovin'". It wasn't the most X-rated comic. Anyway, so she had been grouchy for months, been missing out. And it was coming up to exam time and all the kids knew that there was trouble if she didn't get laid soon.

So all the boys came up with a great idea; one of them would fuck her brains out the day before the exam, and she would be really easy on them.

She was a very attractive woman, by the way. With a blouse unbuttoned at the top and big tits, high heels, that sort of thing. So all the boys wanted to volunteer. They all pulled out their cocks and measured for the biggest. There were two the same size, and both thought they'd be the best for the job. So one of the girls had to volunteer to decide who was the best. Everyone watched carefully, and the one who'd lasted the longest won.

The winner went to the teacher's house the night before the exam and knocked on the door. She answered in a towel. So she lets him in, gives him a drink. And they start doing it, in the shower, on the bed, all that. And the guy's having a really good time, you can tell. He doesn't care if he fails the exam, he wants to stay there forever.

But she looks really bored. She says, "Excite me." He doesn't know what to do, so he rings up his friends.

All of them come over, the girls and the boys. One by one the boys fuck her, and she lies there looking happier and happier. Then she makes the girls give her a massage, with everyone watching, really enjoying it. And she makes the girls kiss her and stuff. Finally, she points to this one guy, a real geek who didn't even get to measure up with the others and hasn't been to the teacher yet.

She undoes his pants and out jumps this really enormous cock. He puts it in her and she writhes around, throws him onto his bottom and shakes around like she's having a fit. Finally, she's happy, and she makes everyone go home.

All the next morning, they congratulate each other, how clever the plot was, how she'd pass them for sure, now. But when they get into the class, there's some horrible old guy there.

"Where's our teacher?" they ask.

"I'm your teacher," says the old guy. "Didn't you read the school bulletin last week? Yesterday was her last day. Now, is everyone ready for the exam? I hope you all spent last night cramming."

Andra always found the story very funny, but Marvo was not amused. He watched Andra's face, her amusement. He saw she enjoyed being coarse, enjoyed a crude joke. She didn't find coarseness seductive, she found it funny. He touched her neck tenderly and he never swore; he talked about things soft and beautiful, things small and sweet. They had not made love. Andra had touched him, though, his thin, long, delicate penis, and she imagined how it would swell, once it was inside her. Fill her completely. Sometimes he caressed her shoulders and whispered things to her, told her how wonderful she was. But still he didn't make love to her.

"Tell me more about the four women in the sheds," he said.

"Tell me about the gift."

The Gift

I was lying on my bed, reading the comic book, when I heard footsteps coming towards the sheds. There was nothing to walk to past the sheds; I knew a man was coming to us.

I heard the woman in the first shed groan, "It's the Bush Pig."

There was a man. He squealed, high-pitched and piercing, as he fucked, with his eyes squeezed shut, his mouth screwed up into a piggy snout.

He knew each of us by name; the only man in town who did. The other men called us *The Women*, or by the name of some long-lost love. Not slags, or cunts or whores, because they wanted to have the pretence they were seeing girlfriends.

Of all the women, only I ever wanted the Bush Pig's business. He was so vile; he arrived unwashed, and paid in coins sticky and numerous. I licked the sweat from between his shoulder blades, sucked his sour breath in through my open mouth.

I rose from my bed and stood in the doorway. I had a sarong tied under my arms, a mauve silky thing which clung to my breasts and hips in the heat. It was too hot to smoke, but I lit a cigarette anyway, held it in the ebony cigarette holder I had found when I moved into the shed. His hair was plastered to his head, the singlet tight on his body. I could see the flakes of skin flying from his shoulders, wet flakes like snow. He followed me into my shed. I dropped my sarong and lay on the bed.

"I only came to give you this," he said, and handed me the beautifully wrapped box he had under his arm. It was the size of a shoebox, and heavy.

"Happy Birthday," he said. "For your next birthday." His voice was gentle, soft and clear.

"Why don't you stay?" I said. "Stay for the afternoon. No charge."

He did stay, but only for an hour. Then he left. He said,

"Don't open the present until it *is* your birthday."

He did not return; I did not expect him to. I opened the present as soon as he left, and found two gold pieces which together made a circle, money and a precious stone.

It was a ruby, supposed to make the wearer courageous and brave. The ruby banishes grief, something handy when you need to get used to loss. The ruby smothers the bad effects of a luxurious life, and distracts the thoughts from evil. My life could be said to contain luxury; I don't starve for food, heat or love. My thoughts are sometimes evil; I can't help it. I see what people do and suffer from their actions and I cannot help but think them ill.

Andra owned other rings, gifts to herself. She had a diamond as an antidote to Satanic temptation. Her topaz ring protected her from poison. A beautiful amethyst prevented drunkenness, something her mother, through bad example, had taught her to avoid. She had a ring of turquoise, a charm against the evil eye, and her emerald promoted piety.

"When I saw what the Bush Pig man had given me, I knew he would not be seen again."

"Where is the ruby?" asked Marvo.

She had it safe. "I don't know the story of the ruby. Perhaps you can find it."

Marvo said, "English sovereigns since Edward the Confessor could bless cramp rings— made from iron, lead, bronze, or especially efficacious from the hinge, handle or nails of a coffin."

Andra began to make rings to sell at the market. She considered Marvo kingly enough and asked him to bless them.

That night, Marvo thought about the shed. Four walls, trapped. He held her closer than ever, tighter. She felt good in his arms. His cat sat at their feet, tickling them with his whiskers.

It took a long time for Marvo to find the true story of the broken ruby ring. He began his search with a false premise—that the man, the Bush Pig, was dead. His story seemed to have died with him. The searching was enjoyable, though, and Marvo found so many small things people no longer wanted: stubs of pencils, lost socks, chair cushions, cloth bags and china plates.

Marvo was going to give up when he discovered the man was not dead at all but living in a cave in Coober Pedy. He was happy to talk to Marvo and he remembered Andra with great fondness.

The Ruby

The ruby was once part of a ring. The ring was a broken circle. It was broken in a moment, as things are. There was no accident involved; no mad axeman, or catching on a door or getting it caught in a drain or something. This ring was cut deliberately by my wife, tired of me. She cut the ring in two pieces, removed the jewel (a small ruby, nothing more) and baked the metal pieces in a carrot cake. The ruby she kept in a small piece of cotton wool, and she hid it somewhere, but she never remembered where. She even wrote in to a clairvoyant, who said, "Dear Ruby, the special item you are seeking is behind the heater."

It seemed unlikely; the heater was built into a wall of stones. However, she got the Vulcan man in to remove the heater, and she searched amongst the dust for the ruby. She was surprised not to find it; she had heard nothing but good reports about the clairvoyant. This clairvoyant told one woman where her husband was (at a gay bar in the city) and another person, who had lost a watch, found it in her sexy underwear drawer.

The ruby, however, was not to be found.

I ate the carrot cake in its entirety, swallowed it down and abused my wife for its scratchy texture. I ignored the sharp pain that came when I swallowed orange juice or anything acidic the next day, and the next week, until my throat swelled and I went to the doctor (my wife would not take me; she was angry with me for still living).

I am allergic to antibiotics. For the first time in my life, I had to stay in hospital. I stayed there a long while.

I had always had trouble with my bowels. Thus, it was two weeks before my stool contained the two sharp gold pieces. They were placed in a jar of preserving fluid and put onto my bedside table. I recognised the metal, pictured the pieces joined on my wife's thin finger. I could not check her finger to see if it was still there; she did not come to see me and she did not answer the phone.

I was released after a month, clutching the jar and nothing more. My voice was ruined forever. I could only whisper, and, when excited, squeal like a pig.

When I sold the house, I painstakingly packed every item to send to charity. Behind a foot heater in the back of my cupboard I found a dirty package of cotton wool. Unwrapping it, I expected to find a tooth, a memento of childhood, perhaps.

Instead, I found the ruby.

Marvo held the ruby up before the Bush Pig man. "This one?"
"I guess it is. Looks to be."

"And why did you give all you had to a prostitute in a shed?" Marvo asked the Bush Pig man. "She thought you were dying, that she had inherited your worldly goods." The man looked surprised.

"I felt such pity for her. She was so out of place; she didn't have the armour the others did. She was kind to me, didn't turn away. She made me feel attractive again. I thought she needed to escape, that she was unhappy. I thought that if I gave her all I had it would be enough for her to make a new life. She could leave and start again. She deserved it. And I did not want the ring any longer. The gold I had stolen, the money earned doing work I hated. It wasn't a true sacrifice. I didn't want anything I gave away."

"So you don't want this back, then?"

"No, please tell her to keep it. Is she doing well? She must be, to have you looking out for her. Is she doing well?"

"She's doing very well. She is as happy as anyone can be. You helped her with your gift. Helped her to escape."

Marvo rewarded the man for his story. He healed the man's throat, fixed his voice so it inspired confidence and friendship.

Later, he told Andra that the man had spoken well, and that he'd wanted Andra to have a better life.

"Isn't he kind?" said Andra. "I did start again. I left soon after. I set myself up in a shop, and sold things to make people fat. But I was happy there. He wanted to think I was there because of circumstances rather than choice so he could feel sorry for me."

She tucked the ruby away. In honour of the Bush Pig man, she sewed a new costume, shiny ruby red and encrusted with small ruby sparkles.

Marvo and Andra practised magic and did small shows. They both enjoyed these, though Andra was sometimes bored by the repetition, so she watched the audience and diagnosed problems. If the person was nice, Andra would help them. They were booked and rebooked in one wealthy suburb, party after party. Often there were more adults than children.

"They're here for you," Marvo said. "They want to be cured."

Andra helped the nice ones.

Doctor Marcia Reid was not nice. "I'm a friend of a friend," she said, her face pulled tight by her hair style. "Friend of a friend of a friend. You're a fascinating woman."

She took a large sip of the pineapple daiquiri she held.

"Marvo is the fascinating one," Andra said.

"No, you," Doctor Reid said. "There is a contagion about you. You know that I am making a name for myself in the field of anthropology and human belief. I study the theory of magic and I understand the two kinds: homoeopathic and contagious. I understand homoeopathy, I believe in natural healing. And I understand contagion. I am fascinated by the human era of the Black Plague."

"You're wrong," Andra said. She didn't often argue. "You use your knowledge in the wrong way, used your experience to pass judgement. Homoeopathic magic is imitative magic. It copies something, apes its characteristics, to make the magic strong. Like the horned beast fertility rites, homoeopathic magic is a mirror."

"You have a lot to learn, Andra. I could be good for you. I want to dabble in your world in order to understand it. I know you know how to cure my skin rash." Andra looked at her in disgust.

"You'll have to wait until the moon is in Scorpio," she said. Marvo heard an unfamiliar sharpness in her voice.

Doctor Marcia Reid was not good for Andra. Marvo could see her wilting under the woman's questions, weakening under her scorn. He knew all the things she said. She told Andra he was lying, that Marvo was a liar as all men were. Hidden, he watched her listening to Andra talking nervously. He watched the doctor nod as if she understood and he wanted to mist her brains out.

The doctor watched as Andra dealt with a patient.

"All your patients are women?"

"I'm not so good with men. They always want more."

"You've had some bad luck, perhaps. Or some women bring out the worst in the best of men."

"There was plenty of worst to bring out!"

"I know. We've all suffered," the doctor said. "Tell me yours and I'll tell you mine. You've always had man problems, haven't you, Andra? It's one of your things."

Andra nodded.

Man Problems

I know when men are lying. I had trouble finding a man until Marvo came along. He didn't know it all. I'd never tell him everything I've done. At fifteen I started going out with a much older man, a lawyer who bought me gifts. Actually, he *brought* them. They were his wife's. He brought them from one bedroom to the next. He brought a fur coat I refused to wear. It felt wrong to wear skin. It wasn't until I grew and learnt my magic that I realised the importance of transference. If I wore those skins, I could take on the consciousness of the animals. I never wore leather shoes and I never ate meat until I found a spell to use transference for power.

The older man was a lawyer and very dull. He went out with me because he wanted my youth, my vitality; wanted it back, he would say, but he had never had it.

I went with him to grown-up dinners, and took him to my parties. There was one dinner which was very important to him. He warned me to behave, and said it would be my fault if things went wrong. He shouted at me not to be late.

We arrived precisely on time and were rewarded with looks of surprise. We stood uncomfortably in the lounge room, drink-less, until the man finished showering and the woman finished in the kitchen. I was given a glass, gin and tonic. I sipped at it and wondered why such a nasty drink could be so popular. He had a glass of whisky for his nerves.

"Don't say anything stupid," he whispered in my ear. "Nice to see a home with traditional roles," he said to the hosts, "woman cooking, man fixing drinks." The man and woman exchanged looks of disgust and boredom, it seemed to me. I laughed.

"Yes, and the cat sleeps all day and the dog barks," I said, a very feeble joke.

The man and woman laughed aloud. They liked me better than him. He was angry at my success.

"Shut up," he whispered. "Don't talk." He wanted people to say how young, pretty and silly I was, though it was easily apparent that neither pretty nor silly suited me.

The other guests arrived and I was the youngest by fifteen years. One woman (who had gone out with my boyfriend for while) said, "And how's school?" I did not take offence.

"It's terrible at the moment. We've got this new guy at school who thinks he has to fight all the guys and fuck all the girls to be accepted. So he goes around poking everyone; pokes the guys to get them fighting and uses the same method for the girls. Pokes like this." I leaned across the couch and poked the woman's partner in the ribs. He giggled.

"Very seductive," he said, staring me in the eye.

Adults are bloody kids, I thought.

"So how successful is he?" asked my boyfriend's ex-girlfriend.

"No one'll touch him," I said. "He's too desperate."

"You're very wise for your age," said the ex-girlfriend. "Very wise for a young thing like you."

"Come, sit down," said the host.

The table was set beautifully, with plates all matching, linen napkins, cutlery like rows of soldiers. And three lighted candles.

I could hear my grandmother saying, "Don't sit down, girl, you've got enough luck on the dark side of the moon. Get rid of one of the candles or run, run, come to me who loves you."

I picked up one candle and blew away its flame. I turned the candle upside down and read the base. Wax dripped onto my dress. "Thought so," I said, and placed the candle away from the table. "Taken off the market in thirteen countries around the world," I said as I sat.

I was fine at his dinners, where nonsense could be talked and lies told. He was terrible at my parties. He looked so old that everyone thought he was a parent, and hid drugs and cigarettes and beer on his approach. Couples stopped kissing, hands stopped stroking bulges. I would say, "This is my boyfriend," but the silence would remain. It was hurtful to him, and he took it out on me. He would berate me, squeeze my arm till it hurt, kick my ankles. After a night with him I was slyly bruised.

We finally broke up when his firm moved him to another state and I didn't want to leave my friends at school.

Another fellow I went out with was tall, thin and smelly. I watched him shower, watched him scrub and wipe and clean, but he would emerge still stinking. I changed his diet to no avail. He had no friends but me. I made him believe so completely that he was attractive and desirable he decided to leave me to find a more beautiful woman.

For power's sake, I kept him there a while longer. When he tried to leave, I told him what magic I had been using to make him stay. I told him he could not leave until I released him.

"I went to a lot of trouble to keep you here," I said. I was very good to him. Once he believed I had used spells to keep him, had wanted him so much I was willing to use magic to keep him, he was convinced of his own power.

"The bits I used for your spell are hard to find," I said, as he packed his suitcase. He kept giving me little kisses on the forehead, as if to say, "I still love you like a friend. But we have moved apart."

"Some hairs from a wolf's tail, plucked at the zoo that day you took me there. Bones of a toad which has been nibbled by ants. Only the bones from the left side; the bones from the right would have an inverse affect. A very special piece of flesh, called a *hippomanes*, found in the head of a newly born colt." He stopped his movements and stared at me.

"I have a friend who works in a stable." He continued to stare.

"The colt was to die anyway," I said. He nodded. He still had a kind heart, for all his arrogance.

"A lizard, who drank too much wine and drowned in the vat. I dried him in the sun, and reduced him to powder, then added a few drops of my blood."

"What sort of blood?" he asked. He knew something of witchcraft, from documentaries on TV. His stomach, already churning with toad, colt, lizard, did not want to hear about menstrual blood.

"I cut my finger," I said.

"Poor thing," he said.

"There were lots of herbs, like pansy, verbena, sweet basil, mandrake, male fern. All these I mixed to a paste and baked into bread with some cumin seeds. On the fire I threw salt three times. I said:

"It is not this salt I wish to burn
It is my lover's heart to turn;

That he may neither rest nor happy be
Until he comes and speaks to me."†

He stopped packing and remained terrified in my house until I released him. He learnt to treat women with respect, at least. He never used anyone like that again.

There was a very young man once. There would have been trouble if we had been found out. I was stumbling home from a party, having been kicked out of a car for being too drunk. I walked home. It took an hour.

I was almost there when a young man stopped me.

"Hey, lady," he said. "Hey, lady, where ya going?" He was fourteen.

"Why are you out?" I said.

"I was bored at home. Where do you live?" He could see I was drunk. He could tell by my walk and the way I smiled at him.

"Not too far away," I said. He came back with me and stayed a few weeks. Then he began to notice little things like the wrinkles under my eyes, the pouches of fat over muscle, the saggy skin.

"You're old," he told me. "You looked young that night."

And he left, taking my toaster as a gift for his mum.

It didn't take me a moment to recover from this blow.

Marvo was the first man who could accept me for what I am.

"But he is still just a man," the doctor said. "You think he is different?"

"He is."

"Really. I can help you to realise otherwise."

Marvo knew then he had to take action.

It was not an easy seduction. To change a woman who had come to trivialise Andra, to analyse and break her down into subject headings and break her, to change a woman like that Marvo had to use skills other than pure enchantment. Marvo learnt that a good place for people to meet without ulterior motives being assumed was at a party. He dressed in clothes Andra had bought for him and he went to a party to meet Marcia. She believed she knew much about the art of magic; its roots and strands, and she loved to discuss her knowledge.

She was happy to learn about Marvo and his professed beliefs. She left Andra alone and concentrated on Marvo for a while. He was honest with Andra about the methods he used to seduce Doctor Reid. She was grateful for his protection but wished he didn't enjoy it quite so much.

† A genuine Old English poem.

Marvo felt a certain attraction to Doctor Reid, though her distrust and dislike of stories was unacceptable. She would tell him nothing about herself, her childhood, and was not interested to hear any version of his life. It was difficult for Marvo not to invent. It frustrated him and made him stupid so that he could not understand the lessons she gave him.

Marvo romanced Doctor Reid, taking her to see the sunset, glorious colours, a sense and smell of the future around them. "Beautiful," he said, looking at Marcia.

"I hate to disillusion you," Marcia said, "but it isn't actually beautiful."

"What are you talking about? It's gorgeous. That sunset is beautiful. All right, in my opinion the sunset is beautiful."

"I'm sorry, but your opinion is incorrect. In fact, the more beautiful the sunset, the more polluted the sky. Not much to be proud of."

"Great. Thank you." Marvo found science boring and unsatisfying. He thought that scientists were the new religious fanatics. They told people things and were blindly believed, even when those things were no longer correct, or never were. A fool was merely the difference between someone who heard the theory has been changed and someone who didn't. Like leaving the grill door open when cooking— people did it by habit. But grills were rarely gas anymore, and never dangerous, so the action was wasted.

"People once thought that sunlight was good for you, that man had the internal organs of a horse, that the moon had rivers and lakes," he said. She smiled at him. She knew who he was. What he was. She knew that he preferred happiness to truth, that he liked the mist rather than clarity.

"People believed a lovely cure for lunacy in *Saxon Leechdoms*," he continued. "They took a clovewort and wreathed it with red thread about the victim's neck when the moon was on the wane in the month of April. They were soon healed. Sad for the person who goes insane on the first day of May, May Day, and has to wait a year for April to come."

"Some people believe those things still. It's magic, to make people believe," Doctor Reid said. She seemed to know so much. "Nothing is true, though. Nothing you do, nothing Andra does. All is illusion. First there was magic to explain the world. It is very easy for the people who believed. They can blame everything on fate, and they don't have to make decisions on their own."

Marvo told Doctor Reid what he knew about sympathetic magic;

told her in a way which demonstrated a cynicism about the magic of magic. A cynicism he did not feel. He wanted her to trust him, to talk to him.

"In science it is important not to be dazzled by amazing facts. You must accept and study, turn the amazing fact into a proven theory. This is how science evolves," she said.

Marvo tried to astonish her but she was not interested.

Marvo wanted to terrify Doctor Reid with a trick because he was only human and wanted to prove her wrong. And he knew he needed to save Andra from her. Andra believed what she said and was losing confidence by the minute.

Marvo played tricks, appeared things. She explained each trick quite believably, and negated his magic. Finally, she agreed to be cut in half.

"Let me tell you a story," he said, once she was entombed.

Doctor Reid laughed in a strangled manner. She couldn't throw her head back and her shoulders were restricted.

"Do you think you have to tie me down to make me listen?

What makes you think I'll listen now? I can hum or sing, talk aloud. I can remember most of my thesis; perhaps I'll recite that as you tell your story."

"This story is about a woman with a sliver of ice in her heart."

"This is an old story. I've heard it," said Doctor Reid.

"No, this woman has not been heard of before. It is a different woman than the one you know. This woman was born with the ice in her heart, and as a baby she would snarl and cry if any person who loved her came by. Any indifferent or uncaring person would receive gurgles and claps. Even as a baby she hated love."

"My neck aches," Doctor Reid said. "Do the trick and let me out. Don't think you're getting to me with this story, either. I love. But not you, you vengeful bastard." Marvo was sexless with Doctor Reid. It was only with Andra he felt stirrings; only her lusty stories gave him pleasure. When Doctor Reid called him a vengeful bastard, she demonstrated how well his seduction had worked. She believed he wanted her, and that she rejected him. Andra and Marvo laughed about it later; laughed at the stupidity of such a clever person.

Marvo spun the casket around to show the ghosts in the audience there were no strings. "Do you want to hear the story? As the girl grew, the ice grew also, so her fingers and toes and nose were always cold. She had to wear many layers of clothes in order to stay warm. Her mother thought she was attention-seeking."

Marvo plucked the long saw from its position stage right. Holding it either end, he played it like a washboard.

Doctor Reid remembered something about trapdoors, or two girls, or something she hadn't been briefed upon. She felt it strange she was simply to lie there.

"The girl became a woman, and she was never warm. She took a job in a glass blower's studio, because there was warmth, constant flame, but it was never enough."

Marvo began to saw.

"She wanted to be inside the fire," Marvo said. Doctor Reid could smell burning. She could feel a dragging at her belly, a side-to-side rasping.

"Stop it," she said.

"Finally, one day when the mist had cleared, she rubbed her naked body head and foot with grease and dressed in man-made fibre. She needed warming, she needed luck. She needed a piece of sea-worn coal to carry with her. The Romans carried jet, and jet is black and coal is black and coal is fuel, it warms, but once you use it the luck is gone."

Marvo stopped sawing. He began to push the lower half of the coffin away from the top half.

Marvo knew about limbs. He knew how they joined, where the hinges were. He had heard a tale of limbs and separation. He knew how to pull things apart and put them back together again.

"Sadly, a neighbour came to visit and doused the flames before they could penetrate to her blood."

The lower half containing Doctor Reid's feet sat next to the half containing her head. "I can smell my own shoes. When did I step in dog shit?"

She began to cry. She was more exposed than any human should be.

"Wait there," Marvo said, his breath all over her face. He walked to the door and opened it. "Come in, come in!" he said, jovial. Her cheeks reddened, like a drunk uncle's. "Have a look!"

They crowded in, ten or twelve of them. They looked close, as close as they could get without getting their noses wet.

"How do you feel?" Marvo asked Marcia.

"Like a lab rat." She had never spoken so quietly in her life.

He sent the customers away.

"Explain that, doctor," said Marvo. He left her there for a moment or two, wriggling her toes and her ankles, then he put her back together again.

He talked to her in a soft, hypnotic voice. His cat clawed at his shoulder, reminding him that this woman was an enemy.

"True magic is not attractive or appealing; it is frightening. People need to believe there is a trick, an explanation. Without an explanation they cannot accept. This is the main reason for magic, religion and science."

Doctor Reid had no words to say. Her limbs ached, as if they had been worked forward and back until they broke. They were warm at the joints. Doctor Reid was an iron lady. Her metal had been heated.

He lifted the lid on the casket and helped her out. She lifted her foot and stared at its base.

"Leave me alone," she said.

"Can you explain it?"

"Get away from me." Her clothes had changed colour and texture.

"You are the one with the interest in us. Belief, magic, science. Remember?"

"I'll leave you alone. Tear up my notes."

"What about the self-esteem you've taken from Andra with all your questioning, your denying of her skills?"

"I'll write a retraction," she said. Her voice was quieter than it used to be. "I won't mention any names but she'll know that she was right and I was wrong."

"Once you've done that, all memory of this will fade. Won't that be nice?"

She nodded. "Thank you. Thank you."

Marvo watched the moment of change in the doctor's face and found it exciting.

Later, he described it to Andra and she cried.

"You love me," she said.

Marvo continued to seek the moment of change, and found that there were places where science and religion met, where magic and religion met, where science and magic met.

He learned that to ward off the evil eye from a child, you should spit three times in the child's face while turning a live coal in the fire (magic) and saying, "The Lord be with us" (religion). He found out so much about the evil eye, hoping to ward off doom and danger. Other evil eye customs which exist in strictly religious homes are to draw blood from above the mouth, or to hang a lucky (ring-shaped) stone behind the door.

He learned that to counteract the evil influence which causes the curse: take a child before sunrise to a blacksmith of the seventh generation and lay the child on the anvil. The blacksmith will raise his hammer as if to strike hot iron, but will bring it gently onto the child's body. If he repeats this three times (lucky three) then the child will thrive.

Andra also loved to learn of cures and spells. Marvo told her, "Another mix of magic and religion is the word 'Abracadabra', which protects from diseases. It is said to be compounded of the three Chaldean words for the Holy Trinity."

He drew on a scrap of paper:

```
A B R A C A D A B R A
A B R A C A D A B R
A B R A C A D A B
A B R A C A D A
A B R A C A D
A B R A C A
A B R A C
A B R A
A B R
A B
A
```

"Some say it's the name of the supreme deity of ancient Assyrians. Written on parchment in this form and hung around the neck with a linen thread, the words may act as an antidote for fevers, diarrhoea and toothache."

"I know a lot about these amulets. Would you like to hear the story of the amulet I keep by my bed?" She fetched it and showed him the hanging charms.

The Amulet

One of my relatives, from long ago, was given this amulet by her grandmother, from a time when magic was the religion. It was a beautiful necklet kept in a beaten metal box, a small thing which rattled as she shook it. She wore it about her neck for fear of getting sick because there was terrible illness all around.

A soldier recognised the amulet as being more than a neck decoration, and she was arrested, accused of magic and thrown into a shadeless pen, where they left her without food or water for three days.

"Will you forsake magic and accept the Lord into your heart?" she was asked. She clutched at her amulet, but it was gone.

"Of course," she said.

In the next pen was a man awaiting execution for communing with the dead. He claimed to have been passing by the graveyard simply to reach home; however, the premise was too unlikely.

You know that amulets provide three types of magic. Some give confidence and faith. Others are for a double purpose; they protect and cast spells at the same time. The third sort are of similars, providing homoeopathic remedies and protection.

So a stone shaped like a human foot may protect from gout. A mole's foot looks cramped, and it cures cramp. Quartz looks like molar teeth and will prevent toothache.

For wisdom, carry the tongue of parrot, crow and lark.

For longevity, take ivory and elephant's hair bound with gold wire.

For constipation, nutgalls and camphor.

To protect yourself from sorcery wear a ring of copper, silver, gold or iron on the finger of your right hand. If you wish to be virile, find the skin of a black antelope.

The Egyptians saw the amulet as great in their religion. It was a symbol of protection.

The buckle protected from evil influence.

The vulture is worn for protection.

A papyrus sceptre gives the dead vigour and renewed youth in the next world.

Wear an ankh for life.

This frog is for fecundity and resurrection.

The crab protects from fear.

This fish protects me from gout, or other diseases.

The scorpion protects from insect stings and reptile bites.

The leopard and lion protect me from wild animals and give me courage.

This tooth will protect against lightning.

All of these have been used to explain the world and its disasters.

The clenched fist amulet wards off evil influences and signifies vigorous action. It has been used by the people of Africa as a symbol of strength, and it brings fear to the battered wife or child.

I thought I had enough protection. But I could not save my town. First there was their belief that I was a witch. That was when the evil began, when they hated me for that. I began to wear my amulets, paint my eyes, protect myself from them. I thought they were evil, that they acted of their own free will and could control themselves.

But when they realised I could not be hurt (though my parents suffered badly, innocent victims not even noticed by the perpetrators) they moved their attentions elsewhere. It was like a disease. The more they hated, the more they needed to hate.

I visited the young man they picked on next. He had been caught curled up with a cow, keeping warm on a cold night, nothing more, he said. But that was not enough. Children passed his home mooing lovingly and the adults began to want him hurt. I visited to give him an amulet to protect him but he did not trust me. And my visit made things much worse for him. They said he was my lover, that I had bewitched him. He wandered the streets, begging people to talk to him, but he only made them angry.

He was found, beaten to death, in our garden.

Next they picked on a girl whose sexual knowledge, they said, was too advanced. They didn't think of her father, a man with a look in his eye even I had seen. They took the little girl (whose mother would not let her wear the crab necklace I sent her) and drowned her.

The town became frenzied. My father was killed for fathering me, my mother began to drink to forget she was my mother. No one left the town and no one entered it until there were too few people left to police arrivals and departures. Then I packed some things for my mother and me and we left the town to its death.

Marvo believed Andra, even though every story she told of her youth belied the last. The story was truth at the time she was telling it.

They were asked to open for a stage hypnotist. There would be five hundred people in the audience at a seaside football club.

"This will be wonderful," Andra said. "All those people."

Marvo said, "They might hate us. They are there to see the idiot hypnotist. If they like that kind of magic they might hate ours."

Marvo had great hatred and no respect for stage hypnotists. They took the magic of sleep and the mist and turned it into a joke. They abused the knowledge and used it to make fools of people. Making people dance like chickens was not an appropriate use of magic. He had seen many of these people and many tricks. He witnessed the cruelty of the illusionists, the laughter they brought upon their victims. Marvo saw one woman told that, under hypnosis, everyone in the room would be a long-lost friend or relative. He imagined how sad it would be to discover a lost friend or relative, only to lose them again.

Marvo denied he played with illusion. He didn't believe so. He believed he brought excitement and love to people, and excitement was what they sought. The illusionists were all about confusion and distress. They gave things to people, then took them away. Their dreams, their hopes. The people would think they were living the life they desired and wake up to a theatre full of vicious, laughing people.

Andra insisted they take the job. She said, "This is how it begins. Before long we will have a big show on our own and we will never have to watch another illusionist if you don't want to."

Andra dressed all in red for the show, blood red. In a certain light she looked skinless. Marvo wore his cape wrapped around him. Nothing else. Other clothes felt constrictive. It was an adult show, so they could show nipples and bulges.

When they walked onstage, the seats were half-filled and people chattered. They were soon silent though. Marvo found the magic of showing his magic exhilarating. He transformed Andra into a large red ball and he exercised on her, one-two-three-four. The audience laughed at that, and gasped when he transformed his fingertips into candles.

Backstage after the show, Marvo lifted Andra and whirled her. "I've never been so happy," he said. "This is what I was made to do." Though even saying that saddened him because he knew it was very little of what he was supposed to do. The mist seemed insubstantive and he wished he could forget its existence.

"Let's go before the idiot gets onstage," he said.

But Andra held his arm. "The idiot can help us get work.

"We'll watch his show and tell him he was brilliant."

It was awful. The audience, the victims were told that they no longer knew the numbers five or six. They counted fingers: "Of course I have ten fingers: 1-2-3-4-7..."—then they got confused.

They were told they were riding a horse quickly, and they galloped and leapt, yipped and hallooed. What about the man who woke to find he wasn't a cowboy after all? That he was still the person he was, the person he didn't want to be? And the others, who were told to return to the age of eight? A time when most are happy, when awareness has arrived but no responsibility, when jokes were simple and food plain, and there was someone to look after you. Imagine waking from that.

The hypnotist made them believe in magic, then took away the belief again. He said, "I am invisible when you wake up, but you will see the things I carry."

They saw a monster puppet, running on air, and a child, a small boy, flying. They were amazed, these victims, and their faces were full of delight and innocence. Their cynicism had gone. Then they were awoken, to the audience laughing, and they were in a sadder place than before.

Later, while Andra was distracted, Marvo told the illusionist the truth. "Deception is your magic. Magic is the unreality of no truth."

"'All men are liars,' said King David. But King David was a man. Therefore he was a liar. Therefore all men are not liars. But King David was a man. Therefore he was not a liar. Therefore all men are liars," the illusionist said, his teeth gleaming.

"I'm going to expose you for the charlatan you are."

The illusionist laughed. "Either that or you'll never work a big stage again. Wonder which is more likely?"

Andra was furious with Marvo when he told her what had been

said. "You've lost us a good chance," she said. She wouldn't look at him and shook his hand off.

M arvo decided to have the ruby given to her by the man in the desert reset. The jeweller, proud of his heritage, told Marvo a story.

King Jasper

K ing Nechepsus wished to strengthen his digestive organs. He spent too much time on defecation, and he could not think while he was doing so. He had a brilliant adorner, who, under orders, took a perfect piece of green jasper, and cut it to form the likeness of a dragon surrounded by rays. The king was well after that.

M arvo gave the jeweller some precious jewels.
He gave Andra the ring while they ate a good, cheap meal in a purple-painted Italian restaurant. She said, "You know Doctor Reid said you would never put a ring on my finger."

"As she walked away, I laughed until I coughed, and coughed until I cried, cried until I was shaking, fitful," Marvo said.

Andra said, "I clipped her hair while she was asleep to make her go away. I didn't wait for the first quarter of the waxing moon, when the strength would not be sapped."

Marvo felt great strength coming from the moon; its light, and its pull on the earth. He met people in his travels who agreed, and he found new lore wherever he went. He met an old woman with aches and pains; she told him that, when he got to that stage of his life, he should only treat or cut his corns when the moon was in the third or fourth quarter. Marvo, never a pain or an illness in his life, nonetheless listened and took note. He might be able to help another one day.

Marvo let Andra think this was the magic which rid them of Doctor Reid's probing, and they ordered a large dessert, more wine, to celebrate the woman leaving. When they returned home they sat together and watched TV. They watched the launch of a new programme called *May Day*.

"Let me tell you about the magic of May," the announcer said in a soft, subtle voice. "Let me tell you this.

'The fair maid who the first of May,
Goes to the fields at the break of day
And washes in dew from the hawthorn tree

Will ever after handsome be.'"

He spoke over images of flowers, the sun, beauty. And he went on like that for a long time.

Then, finally, he got to the point:

"This is May Dew, the wonderful product. It takes away the guesswork about how you will look each day; you will always look the same!

"Only you will know your true face.

"This is a natural method of beauty, coming from the ancient days, when to wash your face in the May dew meant you were beautiful all year round.

"There is a new range of products: May Dew (wrinkle cream), May Queen (perfume), May Pole (deodorant stick,) May Tree (mascara), May Day (moisturiser and sunscreen) and May Fly (hair spray).

"May Dew is proud to sponsor this exciting new programme. Sit back and enjoy the year 1677. Next week, enjoy an hour about the year 1489."

Andra helped a lot of women to beauty. She was angry that a commercial company was making a chemical which may or may not work, out of a natural product which did.

Lady's mantle she used, and wild tansy soaked in buttermilk for nine days. Both effective in the restoration of the complexion, but none so much as May Dew.

Marvo and Andra watched, and were led to believe the night before Mary married William of Orange in 1677, she opened up a bottle of dew collected in May, to preserve her beauty all year round.

Galileo, his microscope perfected these forty years, dropped dew into his eyes, his poor, sore eyes.

Mr van Leeuwenhoek, strange man, worked with dogs, ignoring his itchy skin allergy. He moistened his skin with dew and continued his dog sperm observations.

Edmund Halley, his comet still far away, observed Venus across the sun. His work was almost finished when his father's goitre demanded all his attention. He, a scientist, performed an unscientific act. In May, he rose before the sunrise and went to a man's grave. He passed his hand from the head to the foot of the grave. Three times. He touched the liquid to the throat of his father, touching the growth. The goitre ceased to be a problem. However, Halley was never the same. Secret reports say that, in his haste to leave the cemetery, he walked over the graves of unchristened children buried outside the consecrated ground. He contracted grave-scab; his limbs shook, his breast was heavy, his skin burned him. People believed this fatal disease could only be cured by wearing a sark made thus:

1. Collect the lint grown in a field which is manured from a farmyard heap which has not been disturbed for forty years.
2. Let it be spun by Habbitrot, the queen of spinsters.
3. Let it be bleached by an honest bleacher in an honest miller's dam.
4. Let it be sewn by an honest tailor.
5. Once the garment is donned, the cure will be instant.

But how can this be?

1. Once you touch the manure heap it has been disturbed.
2. There is no agreement as to who is the queen of the spinsters.
3. There is no honest bleacher. There is no honest miller.
4. There is no honest tailor. There is no honest man or woman.
5. Perhaps the cure for grave-scab is to keep away from the graves. Stay away from the dead!

Andra and Marvo laughed at the desperate propaganda of the programme. They couldn't imagine people buying May Dew products because of it.

But they were to be surprised. It was the most successful product launch in many years, and Marvo began to think about the nature of the lies told, the magic of them. He sensed truth behind the fantasy, and he tracked down the advertising agency running the programme, found the creative talent (not the salesperson, the front one, show-off, "look what I achieved" person in a suit) and went to see him.

They recognised each other instantly, talked for hours under the guise of business.

"Yours is the stronger mist," said the advertising man. "Mine is less subtle. My magic says a cigarette is cool. A beer is masculine. Girls who use tampons enjoy life. Chocolate is good for your social life. A sunset is beautiful, clear indication of the sanctity of our earth. I can invent anything I like, make it real. The ploughman's lunch[†], that chopping board of rustic cheeses, meat and pickles that sends you back in time, back when cars did not exist, women wore skirts, men worked the field and got dirty for a living? Re-invented mid-twentieth century as a gimmick to get people back into pubs.

"And there's a sweet little cartoon on air, *'Lovely Funny'*? You <u>wouldn't have</u> seen it."

† See recipe – appendix A.

But Marvo had. He spent many early hours of morning, watching TV with the sound turned low.

"What do you think came first, the show or the dolls, T-shirts, doll houses? They make a fucking fortune, thinking up some pile of merchandise, then creating a show to create the need. Kids love it, the mist is thick, everyone is happy."[†]

The advertising man showed Marvo some of his best work. There was an aftershave—"For the man you are", the jeans—"To take you to your wildest place", the coffee, of which "Every mouthful is heaven".

Other workers began looking in at Marvo and the advertising man, wondering at the noise they were making, the laughter.

"I'll go," said Marvo. They were sorry to part; they knew they could not see each other again. Both recognised the magic of loneliness.

Marvo got Andra to watch *Lovely Funny* the next day. After the show (which she hated) they saw an interview with the favourite children's band, FEG. It was pronounced *Eff Eee Gee*, not *Feg*. It stood for whatever—no one was saying. They were very popular with the youngsters. They sang songs close to nursery rhymes. They had pleasing rhyme and sounds and strong rhythm.

Marvo, alerted to the manipulation of children, scrawled down some of the lines.

"Mary had a little lamby
Then she met a deer called Bambi
Bambi said, 'Where'd y'get your socks?'
Mary said, 'Got 'em from the Fox.'"

Fox's Sox was a chain store of footwear. Marvo knew it was very successful.

"Old Mother Hubbard,
Looked in the cupboard
And found that her life was there
She went to the shop
Bought a Good Pop
Then went and dyed her hair."

---

† Marvo heard a lot about this cartoon character. The children loved it; they watched the show holding the dolls, wearing the clothes, eating the breakfast cereal. He wanted to know more about the manipulation of young minds. He took home a video. The DVD showed a self-satisfied team of serious adults who thought and thought until they came up with a story to go with the dolls already made and not selling at all. They launched the unloved dolls into the minds of children with a cartoon. And it was a great success. Lovely Funny factories worked overtime to keep up with the demand.

"Yum, Good Pops," said Andra. Her craving for the toffee on a stick would not go away until she bought one later in the day. Magic.

The children kept time by clapping their hands or rocking back and forth, back and forth.

This band had great influence over the children who demanded from their parents anything mentioned. The magic of selling products by association.

Marvo was fascinated by the use of words to convince.

Words have a magic of their own. "It's poetry," he said.

"I write poetry sometimes," Andra said. She was shy about it. No one had read it before. Marvo made her sit next to him and read aloud.

My Box is Packed

Once more, my box is packed,
my suitcase filled,
my home stored so easily.
Not as easily as in the past, though.
I have been here for longer, gathered more,
which I cannot bear to throw away.
Once more, I leave in the dawn,
they watch for me at night.
That's why I have to leave.
I cannot do my job,
sitting in a room
fearful of discovery.
I leave with the dawn,
printing a symbol
on my door
with wine,
invisible but powerful.
They will not enter until
I am safely away.
When will I find my people again?

Marvo's eyes filled with tears. "Those words are beautiful. You read them so well, I can imagine it really happened."

Andra wasn't sure how to take the compliment. He told her she had a great imagination; she wasn't sure whether to tell him it was a true story.

He left her sitting cross-legged amongst her papers deciding what to read him next.

"Don't want to hear more? I don't blame you."

"I do, Andra. It's good. Then I want to show you this." He handed her his precious note. "My grandmother gave me this before she died. It's to be passed on, to my kids if I have any. Like on TV, where the old man is dying in bed. But it's a mean note; it doesn't sing. Maybe you can find a sweeter way to speak to the generations who'll follow."

Andra piled up her poems and returned them to the shoebox where she kept them hidden. She said, "I'm really not all that good."

"You have beautiful words," Marvo said, but he didn't want to read the poems she'd written. He wanted her to rewrite his own story.

She agreed to do it because she had such love for him, and the way he spoke made her think that perhaps his future was hers, that the child who received the paper would be hers. This gave her a feeling of place; for the first time her future was settled, she could see the end of it and it was comforting.

She worked for many days on the words but she couldn't change them. She could not change a single ancient word, and she told Marvo that. "There is nothing more to say than what is said. It's a harsh message but your task is hard." She took his hand, trying to imagine what it would be to hold the mist in those hands, to be able to drop it, help people forget. "You've inherited a lonely task. I think I know what that's like." She had magic too, the magic to heal. "Tell me about your ancestors. Were they all magicians?"

It was difficult for Marvo to explain. "I can't discuss my family tree and its branches. All I have is a trunk. I had my mother, who had her mother, who had her father, who had his father, who had his father, who had his mother, who had her mother, who had her mother, who had her mother, who had her mother who had her father. We are a single parent, single child family."

"How is that possible?"

"I believe partners are discarded after birth. I have no instruction for that."

At this stage Andra felt the first real fear of her life. Would he discard her if they had a child together? Did he even consider her worthy of bearing his children?

He would not be questioned further.

"It's interesting you should say that about your family tree," said Andra. "Because I have nothing to trace either. I was a foundling, as they used to call them."

"Not a changeling?"

"Not a changeling, and I've got the caul to prove it," said Andra. "That would have protected me, had any fairy parent ever wanted me. But I was as unpopular with the fairies as I was with the humans. When someone finally picked me from the orphanage in Rumania, they didn't keep me for long. I had to go back and wait for the next foster family."

This was Andra's fantasy. Instability, excitement and change.

Nothing ever changed in her life; nothing she did seemed to affect anybody in the family.

"If I had been a changeling I would have been placed in a loving family. As a foundling, I was passed from hand to hand and bed to bed."

"Did your families have sex with you?" asked Marvo.

"You surely don't find that exciting?" said Andra, close to disgust. "There's nothing exciting about that."

"I'm not excited. I want to know about you, what formed you."

"I was mostly formed in a house at the end of a long, dusty road. The postman came once a day when I was a child, to deliver and collect, but he got tired of carrying the large boxes my foster father sent all over the world. The boxes were both heavy and unwieldy, and my father would follow him up the driveway, then watch him walk up the road, shouting if one box tilted or banged another.

"'Those are golden eggs you've carrying there. Treat them with respect. I pay my bloody taxes, I deserve a service which won't send me broke. Careful there. Don't get lazy, now.' The postman got sick of it after a while when I was a child and Dad got a notice to say he had to collect his own parcels. I was always curious as to why the postman didn't ask what was inside. I suppose he must have looked himself."

"I'll find the story out," said Marvo. "I'll find out why he never asked what was inside. So what was inside?"

"Orchids," said Andra, "rare, fleshy orchids. He was one of the world's major suppliers.

"They were his only interest after my foster mother went away when I was a child. She told me to look after him and went packing. She left me some dresses and books and told me to watch out for myself. She said she couldn't bear the town any longer. I didn't understand her hatred. They all loved her.

"So I was alone with him. Mostly, he was engrossed with his flowers, and I learnt a lot about creation and manipulation, watching his plans coming to fruition, his clever hands at work. There is a power in hands which is not always used." She had watched hands hit and caress. "Strangely, a felon who is hanged is considered to have healing powers beyond that of the greatest doctor; the touch of his hand could cure many things. And the touch of a suicide's hand on a sore will heal it."

"'Isn't it magic?' my foster father would say as he brought those flowers to life. 'Bloody magic.'

"I already knew magic. I knew about clippings and charms, and they already thought I was weird at school, so I used spells to make my life happier.

"One magic I found at the end of the garden. There was a burnt grass circle, perfectly round, and if I sat in the centre of it I heard voices, which told me secrets and tricks and how to make my foster father happy."

"How did you make him happy?" asked Marvo.

"Be nice to him. Washed his feet for him and cooked. He looked after me too and never in that way. He was kind unless he was in a bad mood."

"Was he often in a bad mood?"

"Not often. He was very angry with me when he heard about my school teacher, though.

"I haven't told you the true source of my magic. I'm not sure you will accept the teachings of a simple school teacher from the suburbs, but from there, I learnt my trade.

"After classes, I would stay back and learn the art of magic; spells and potions, transference, homoeopathic and theurgic. She warned me to use my knowledge quietly; however, at the Sunday school my parents insisted I attend, I spoke up about the use of pond creatures in the healing of affairs of the heart. I did not understand the peril I placed my beloved teacher in. I spoke happily of lessons spent stripped naked, quiet in front of the fire, and of the sacrifices made on the kitchen bench. The teacher was removed from the school immediately. She was jailed not long after and she died in a cell away from nature.

"My parents were quite dull and terrified that my experience with my teacher would ruin me forever. It did, of course, my reputation was ruined in the town. They never left, though. They stuck it out."

"Would you like me to find that teacher as well as the postman?"

"I know that she died. I went to her funeral. They prayed over her but I made a spell to ensure she didn't walk again. That was one of her fears, that she would rise from the dead."

"Just the postman, then." Marvo wanted to track down the postman to verify this part of Andra's life. It turned out to be very difficult because the man had never existed.

Marvo became used to Andra's inventions. He would not tell his own truth. Their history would be their own secret place. Marvo did not mention Andra's mother. The drunk, misty-eyed woman who hated him. He could see the bitterness, the stubbornness, in the woman, that she would have needed to stay in a town her daughter was unhappy in. When her grandmother died, Andra was alone.

"I found your postman," said Marvo. Andra did not look surprised.

"What did he say?" she asked.

"The postman said, 'He was a rotten old bastard, that one, and the way he treated that little girl made the townsfolk weep. Shouting and screaming like she was some sort of idiot, and her cringing like a whipped dog.

"'He's dead now, so I can tell you this; the copper in town asked me to open a parcel once. See, the bloke's wife had gone to live with her sister, he said, but no one had heard from her. And the copper had this idea that the guy was mailing off parts of her. So we cracked open a box and all that was in there was a bloody flower.' I gave him a balm for his tired old postman's feet."

Marvo had great trust in Andra. He had no fear she would betray him, either inadvertently or deliberately. He knew this, even though she didn't tell her true story. "When I was a child," she said often and he envied her that. He had no true stories to tell of that time.

He gathered knowledge of childhood in the room watching TV shows. He saw kids living on farms, on mountains, in small houses and large. He created his own habitat.

To Marvo, his early life was so simple and uncomplicated it would appear unreal to listeners. Sometimes the simplest things are disbelieved. He thought that because he had no odd little stories, no funny tales of sibling rivalry or how the family pet died, no tales of the trip north or holiday to the beach, no comment on Mother's cooking, Father's smell in the toilet, or this funny kid at school nobody liked (ha ha, it was me). To Marvo, this made his life simple and plain. He did not tell it that way. He embellished it the way a child does, adding excitement to impress the audience.

"He didn't like your father. I wonder what it would have been like, to have one. Even a bad one," Marvo said.

Andra suggested he talk to fathers, hear the stories they tell about their own children. Find some background, some depth.

"You'll find fathers in the playground," she said.

Fathers were not always talkative, but Marvo found one red-cheeked, laughing man, pushing three children at once on a swing. He told the man a story in the hope he would receive one in return.

A Piece of Green

I was brought up by my mother. We were very close. We lived in a small flat in a big city, and I was allowed to go and play on the streets because I couldn't stand being cooped up. My mother wrote my address on a piece of paper and pinned it to my underwear.

"You won't lose your underwear," she said, "but you might take your jumper off and leave it somewhere. So you'll have to put up with it being uncomfortable."

I had to spend my days with crackling underwear.

In the centre of the block of flats was a small green playground. Here, the other children and I played and grew up together. I don't know where those people all are now. They were my greatest friends and now they're gone. There was Robert, the lucky one. He had a father. The father came down sometimes to watch us play, and he let us take turns sitting on his knee. It was comforting, sitting on a man's knee.

Robert's father was very generous. He was kind to us all. But it was lucky Robert who got to walk home with him, have dinner with him. Get presents. Everyone else only had a mum.

My mum had to work in a shop to keep me happy. One year she saved up and bought a magician's set. That's where I learnt my magic. I lived for the time when I could meet with my friends in the playground, and show them my latest trick. I practised for hours and hours, while they played and talked, smoked later on and drank later than that. Some people got new fathers. Robert's stayed around. He didn't get us on his lap anymore though. But he brought us cigarettes, sometimes, and told us about sex. Things our mothers and stepfathers did not tell us. He told us what a sixty-niner was, how to avoid having children, where to go to get booze.

I think he helped a lot of us.

Finally the day came when I needed to move away from the protection of my mother and my friends. I didn't move far away, but it was a world's distance.

I had to meet people for communication. I spent a lot of time in my room practising tricks I learnt from a book. I learnt how to vanish and disappear. I learnt throwing my voice, a thousand coin tricks, two thousand card tricks. I toyed with rabbits, pigeons and mice. Eggs, apples, oranges and Ping-Pong balls. Long silk scarves and quilts of black velvet, white cane and black hat, black cloak and white face. I practised my stage voice and practised my stage name. I nearly called myself Misto the Magician, but that seemed to give too much away. Then I met my assistant and she completed the act.

This was pure fantasy. He didn't even have one parent (a grandparent is not the same). He didn't give himself two parents; he felt the story was fantastic enough with one.

It was true about the magic book and the practice.

Marvo closed his eyes and imagined what these childhood friends would have been like.

"Robert's father sounds like Father Christmas, with the whole sitting on the knee thing," the father in the park said.

Marvo was not sure. He had never sat on Father Christmas' knee, nor had a photo taken, a smiling innocent on the knee of a wonderful man. "Yes, Father Christmas," Marvo said. "We all have different ideas of Father Christmas."

"Ya reckon?" the father said. "Not sure about that."

"Ask your son," Marvo said. He thought he might have discovered real mist. The son, rugged up in a purple jacket too big for him, came to his father and was happy to answer the question. Marvo had to repeat it; he still forgot how quiet his voice was.

The Story of Father Christmas

Father Christmas is a great big man who lives in the snow. He has to live in the snow because he likes things cold, he might even melt if he gets too hot. That's why you should never have the fire lit, if you've got one, or even the heating on—that's what my daddy said happened, anyway.

He stays home with me most days 'cos he doesn't go to work. He's pretty good. He makes Vegemite sandwiches with no Vegemite 'cos I hate it and he lets us watch the old people's stuff on TV. Mum goes to work at night, she's a nurse in uniform. She has to sleep in the day and we have to be quiet.

I was waiting for my mum to give me some money so I could buy Christmas presents for everyone. She said I had to make them this year, but she had all cool stuff to make them with.

I made Dad's old socks into new ones by sticking on some felt pictures. I made my sister a coloured cardboard box to put her swap cards in and I made Mum a squashy ball in one leg of a pair of pantyhose so she can play at work when she gets bored.

I couldn't wait for Christmas Eve, because Father Christmas would come. I wanted a new bike and my sister wanted a swimming pool which she said I could use.

We couldn't get to sleep on Christmas Eve. The man on the news said, "I hope Father Christmas brings you what you wished for," and my whole insides went excited. Some kids said Father Christmas wasn't real, but the man on the news said.

But when we got up when the sun did on Christmas Day, there was this enormous puddle on the floor, water covered half the kitchen. In the middle were two tins of yummy lollies.

"Mum! Dad!" we yelled at them to get up.

Dad saw the puddle and he said, "Oh, dear. Must have been a bit too hot for Father Christmas. He melted before he could bring all your presents down."

"Nice lollies?" said Mum. She gave the tins to us and they were nice.

Dad got the sponge and a big bowl.

"We'll freeze him up and send him to the North Pole. The elves will be able to fix him up."

And they did. This year was good, even though Dad works most of the time now. This year I got a Nintendo and a bike and my sister got a pool and some books in a set.

Marvo felt he had been given a wonderful story. He gave the boy a mist for himself and his sister, so they could believe a while longer. Marvo pulled a rabbit from his front pocket. The rabbit was pale blue.

The father had very long fingernails. Marvo wanted to clip them and take them home to Andra. He drew a small mist down and took the man's hands gently. He snipped the fingernails using his pocketknife and he wrapped them in a piece of newspaper he found under the park chair.

"We'll see you next time," the father said as Marvo said goodbye. "Nice talking to you."

Another man had been watching them from under his eyebrows. His child was in a wheelchair and the other children sometimes came and deposited small gifts in her lap. The father always smiled, said thank you in a loud voice.

"Your daughter?" Marvo said.

"Yes." Marvo drew a mist over the man until he felt like he was alone, talking into a mirror.

The Magic of Münchausen

I didn't plan it this way, but it ended this way anyway. I was a good father to that child, even though she didn't belong to me by blood. I sacrificed everything for her. Freedom, money, sex, space; everything. I'm not saying she didn't appreciate it.

My wife worked and I stayed home with our daughter. Someone needs to sacrifice their career to be with her, we decided.

My wife made the money. And whenever she took a holiday she was edgy and bad to be around. So I turned into home daddy and it was good. I got nothing but positive feedback all the time when we went out and I felt popular and pleased.

But that faded. I think people got used to me being around. Playground, playgroup, library, long walks. I stopped getting congratulated or told how clever I was, what a good father. You know mothers don't get told that, don't you?

What happened next wasn't deliberate.

One evening, when my wife was working back and wouldn't be home till past midnight if that, my daughter wouldn't go to sleep and would not stop crying. We'd been to the doctor and there was nothing wrong. She was just being a bitch.

I picked her up out of her bed a bit roughly and that made her quiet for a second but then she started up again, louder, right in my ear.

I held her at a distance and gave her a little shake. Tiny little one. Then more and more till I was shaking her so hard my arms hurt. I felt sick, nauseous deep in the pit of my stomach, like I'd eaten a box of liqueur chocolates or drunk beer after wine. But it felt good, too. The power of it.

She was quiet. I put her in bed and didn't think of it until the morning when my wife said, "What's the matter with Ginny?"

I couldn't answer her. You understand that. "She was fine when I put her to bed. Quiet," I said.

Permanent brain damage. My wife stays home a lot now, what with the medical insurance. And the kindness I get? The praise? That will never go away. I know how my life goes from her. I can see it. My daughter sacrificed her future so our future would be assured.

Marvo looked at the twelve-year-old in the wheelchair. She was full of mist already. He could do nothing for her.

Marvo clipped this father's nails as well and gave him the gift of not reporting him to the police.

Andra was thrilled with Marvo's gift of the two fathers' fingernails. She was fascinated by bodily waste—skin, sweat, semen, pus. Nails, teeth, hair. She cut and snipped his bits for him, sucked and drank and squeezed his bits, collected and studied and sniffed. He found it incredible that someone should love him so much as to love all his bits; all his waste and bits and the things other people wouldn't touch. He thought she loved his semen, skin, hair. As she combed his hair in preparation for a show, saving all the strands, she said, "Success can be found by touching things no one else wants to touch. Money can be made and power increased. I love my job at the Body Shop; loved the collecting, the minutiae of it. I have always been attracted to discards.

"No one knew what I was doing when I went around school buying people's fingernail clippings for five cents apiece. I made them clip their nails in front of me so I knew who they belonged to. I had many little envelopes with people's names written in thick, careful hand on them.

"I collected nails from every person in the school. I took toenails or fingernails. It didn't matter. I kept the envelopes in my locker.

"When I had nails from everyone, and everyone had some coins from me, had spent or saved lollies or comics or placed it in a stash, I began to sell the little envelopes. Each was sealed and signed.

"I quietly walked the playground, offering my wares. Some I tried to sell back to the owners, some to their enemies. Depending on the person. A boy who was timid and unable to evoke emotion of any kind happily bought his envelope back for ten dollars. He was flattered that I thought anyone could feel so strongly as to perform magic on him, and he didn't want to risk it.

"Others bought their own envelope and that belonging to someone else. One girl wished the owner to love her; another wanted the owner to be last in class.

"Others disdained buying anything. They were sometimes surprised by the result of this. One found her father gone when she got home that night.

"Others were not given the chance to buy their envelopes. Some had already been bought; it was terrible for those people, not knowing what spell would be cast.

"I was fair in my prices. Some paid a month's pocket money; some paid more, some less. I always charged so that it would hurt a bit but not too much.

"It was the only time I could use the trick, but I had achieved what I needed to. I had money and I had the respect of the other children.

"I was asked a few times to take the clippings of a sibling.

"I always asked how old the sibling was. If it was less than a year, I could not help them. If cut before then, the child may grow up to be a thief, or at the very least dishonest.

"I'd say, 'Come back in three months, or six, and we'll arrange something.'"

M arvo ran a bath as she laid out the clothes for their show. The thin body suit she wore to protect breasts and genitals, the black dress threaded through with gold. Her jewellery took the longest, and he never tired of watching her put it on. She wore the ruby ring he'd had reset on her forefinger and displayed it, hand in fist, pointed down, only the forefinger to be seen.

"Are you scared of me?" asked Marvo.

"Why?"

"You're always gesturing and using charms to ward off the evil eye. Do you think I'm evil?" Andra drew the last finger into her fist.

"Of course not. It's habit."

She was truly adorned against evil. Dangling around her wrist was a charm bracelet with a hand, a horn, the moon, a wheel, a ladder, a club, a knife, a hook, a serpent, a snail, a lion, a pig, a dog, a frog, a lizard. Around her neck, between her breasts, nestled a silvered sprig of rue, the herb used to sprinkle holy water. This was her cimaruta—an ancient charm from the Etruscans. Rue was esteemed and admired, sacred to Thor and the druids, who said it had occult virtues and only gathered "when the dog star rose from unsunned spots." Rue was the herb of grace. Like all of her jewellery, it was worn for success or protection; the rue protected against fascination. Not only that, it acted as an antidote for snakebite and sting of wasp, scorpion and hornet. She'd told Marvo that she'd once won the love and respect of an elderly would-be seducer when she saved his son's life, during an ill-prepared walk through the bush.

"I feel great strength when the rue is against my skin; I feel a rope of strength stretching thousands of years. The rue was used in magical rites, especially as protection against witches. I know that anything believed by the ignorant to act as protection merely acted as a strengthener."

Other charms hung off the rue: a snake, a snail, a weed. She shook the jewellery in his face, made it ring in his ears until he grabbed her arm to make her stop.

"Some people call me a pagan," she said, challenging him to agree.

"I don't even know what that is," Marvo said. He didn't know everything yet.

Andra enjoyed paganism. She liked the way it mixed magic with religion. "Paganism is a religion of nature, of the earth, the original religion of humanity. Five thousand years ago everyone was pagan," Andra said.

"That justifies nothing. Just because it's old, it's not necessarily good," Marvo said. He abhorred her logic.

"Paganism is the most environmentally and ideologically sound religion because it honours the earth, the body and women. That's why I accept it."

She wore the pentacle representing earth and magic. It was a symbol for witches. Marvo told her that she was not a witch, she was a magician. She failed to see the distinction.

"I thought I was a witch," she said. "A witch and a magician are the same. There is no difference. One is not male, one not female, both are the same. To imagine otherwise is ignorance. To believe this is more ignorant."

"There is a difference between witch and magician. A witch creates change, makes spells. A magician creates illusion. In some ways the magician is more powerful than the witch, because words and illusion can be so powerful and people can be convinced to change for themselves if they think everyone else is doing it, or they can ape what they see and hear."

Andra wasn't much of a catch, as a supporter, for the pagans. She hated large groups of people so didn't attend any ritual, and she only took what she wanted from the religion.

The bath was full. Hot and bubbly. Marvo held Andra's hand as she stepped in, then stepped in himself.

Marvo rose from the bath and went to prepare for the afternoon's performance in the park. They had top billing at a large garden party.

Andra sat in the bath water, feeling it cool around her.

They put on a good show in the park. Marvo loved the open air and the audience, while getting it for free, appreciated the magic.

The birthday girl's older brother was there. Cuts covered his legs and arms. He had been in a motorbike accident. He had been home for weeks; no school, no partying. The effects were showing, and his family were getting tired of feeling sorry for him.

"This is fucking pathetic," said the teenager. "The rings have got ends; all he has to do is find both and twist."

The children didn't want the truth about Marvo's magic, or about Father Christmas and the Easter Bunny. They said, "Be quiet."

"Stupid little kids. He's doing the dumbest tricks ever. He's got a fake thumb with the scarf in it. Look."

His parents had invited influential people to the party, and the adults had no interest in what the children were doing. They drank pink champagne and swallowed oysters.

Marvo was displeased with the behaviour of the teenager. He threw a fork of lightning at his feet; the teenager ran to escape and fell into mud.

"If you run from an illusion you make it real," said Marvo.

The teenager rose, muddy and embarrassed. He had shown childish fear. He would not speak again until Marvo had gone.

"Here, have a bath with this," said Marvo. "It's a mild soap for pleasant bubbling."

The kid took the soap. Later, when he bathed, he stifled shouts of pain. Marvo was not often vicious or vindictive, but he enjoyed the thought of it. The soap was an acidic, lemon-based one, and the teenager's open cuts would be stinging to their very root. That would teach him to destroy the illusions of children.

Marvo wandered away from the party. He saw a young girl weeping on a park bench and went to her.

"What is it?" he asked. He was kindly, avuncular, trustworthy.

"My dog died," she said. "My mother is still at work and my father is away and my doggie died and I don't know what to do."

"Do you know any stories? Can you tell me a story?" he asked.

"About a dog?" she asked.

"About anything," he said.

The Little Girl Isn't Scared

This is about a small girl. She was out with her mum, running around the trees, kicking the leaves. She stopped every now and then to check if her mum was still there and she always was. The little girl knew Mum would always be there. Her mum was not close enough to hear her say a rude word but close enough to come quick if the girl needed her.

The girl decided to scare her mum, for a joke. She hid behind the next big tree and waited and waited. Finally she got sick of waiting, so walked out from the tree.

"Boo!" yelled her mum.

She pretended she knew all along. She said, "Let's go home now," and she ran ahead so her mum couldn't see she had been a bit scared but not much.

Home again, the little girl had to have a bath—hot with soap and toy ships. She stayed in the bath for a long time, splashing and playing. Then her mum said, "Come on, out of there, you'll be wrinkled as a prune soon. Your dad's home. Here he is to say hello."

The little girl jumped out so quickly she tripped and hit her head on the basin.

Her dad said, "Oh, you're not *crying*, are you? You're too grown up to cry. Do you want to wear a little baby's dress?"

The little girl stopped crying. She went to turn on the television because *Lovely Funny* was on now. She sat without her clothes right up next to the television, and she was sitting there with her legs crossed and her back round and comfy.

Her mum said, "Sit back from the TV and straighten up. Do you want to be like a monster, all curved over? And if you sit too close your skin will burn, silly." The little girl knew it wasn't true, about the monster and the burnt skin. But she sat back anyway, sat way back, in a chair, very straight.

Her mum came in with her nightie to put on. "You'll catch your death, running around like that. You don't see your dad running around with no clothes, do you?"

And her mum helped her put on her nightie. She wondered how you could catch your death, but was a bit tired to ask. It didn't matter very much.

Her dad came in and changed the channel to the news.

"*Lovely Funny* is on," the little girl said but her dad laughed then.

She went to play in her room but her dad said, "I think you should watch the news before you go to bed. The news is very beneficial, gives you a good background," so the little girl sat down again.

Her mum brought in the tea and they all sat up and watched the TV.

Her mum said, "One day we'll eat at the table," and her dad grunted.

The little girl didn't want to eat her broccoli.

"You eat every last piece of that broccoli or your hair will turn grey like grandpa's. I've told you before. Broccoli for your hair, pumpkin for your teeth..."

"Will you shut up? I'm trying to watch the news," said her dad. Her mum never got around to saying, "and spinach for your bones," so the girl said it for her under her breath.

The news finished, and the little girl knew it was nearly time for bed. Her mum said, "All right, it's time for bed. Chop chop, brush your teeth." Her father said, "I'll come and help you say your prayers." The little girl took a long time to brush her teeth. But she had to stop brushing after a while. Her mum pushed her into her room. Her dad was waiting.

He said, "On your knees, girl, it's time to have a talk to Big Daddy."

"Don't teach her to talk like that!" said her mum. Her dad laughed.

"Hurry up," he said. The little girl went on her knees and began to mumble.

"Louder, little one," her dad said. The little girl spoke louder.

"Still can't hear you, don't reckon God can."

The girl shouted as loud as she could, "GOD BLESS..." and got a smack.

"Behave, or else you know where you'll be going when you die. God doesn't like little girls who can't say their prayers. He gives them to the Devil, who eats them for DINNER!" The little girl tried to laugh. She knew it wasn't true, but still.

"God bless Daddy," she finished, and dived into bed.

Her dad said, "Now straight to sleep," and kissed her on the head. Her mum patted her and kissed her on the cheek. Her dad put his arm around her mum and said, "Straight to sleep, before the Sandman comes to steal you away." The little girl shut her eyes tight. There was no such one as the Sandman.

"Sweet dreams," her mum said. But all she could dream about was her mum behind the tree, and being dressed in a baby's dress for everyone to laugh at. She dreamt what she looked like, a hunchbacked monster with black, burnt skin and grey hair. She dreamt the news with that picture of the blood and the other picture of the girl with her eyes shut. She dreamt Your Death chasing her, running around and around and around and around the bed. She dreamt about the Devil and the Sandman, how they were very good friends.

And the little girl was very scared and she never slept again.

"**L**ittle girls must sleep," said Marvo. "They can sleep when they've got someone furry on their bed."

This was not true, Marvo knew perfectly well. It would make the little girl happy for a while, his lie. And he knew that honesty was not always rewarded.

There was a bark and the little girl's eyes opened wide. She did not dare to look around. Her new puppy leapt onto her lap, licked and licked her face, and the magician left the happy scene with his new story.

Andra had finished packing up and was waiting for him, eating fairy floss.

"That was a great performance!" he said.

"I love you on stage. It's like you absorb the magic we exude. But I don't think it was perfect."

"How was that not perfect?"

"Too small. I love performing but I hate those small audiences. We need to be seen all at once by hundreds of people."

"We'd have to travel. You can't get that much time off work."

"I'll talk to them. See if I can change my hours."

Her boss at the Body Shop admired her greatly. He admired her for not suing him when her head was burnt bald by a splash of rendered fat. He paid her well, pay rises every month or so and she never made him feel guilty. She also never told him that her bald head had made Marvo admire her.

Her boss, worried about what Andra wanted to talk to him about, showed up uninvited to their house. Marvo let him in, then ignored him, busy with magic and dinner.

"Where's Andra?"

"She'll be home soon. She's sourcing material." Marvo had no idea what this meant but thought it sounded professional.

By the time Andra got home, the boss had found her jars and was ready with the words, "What the fuck are these?"

"It's just ash."

"I know what it is, Andra. Our business works on trust. I thought you knew that. Those people believe their bits are disposed of, yet here they are all mixed together."

He had tears in his eyes.

"We can destroy them now. It will be okay. We'll make a sludge and we'll bury it. I'm sorry."

Marvo had never seen Andra regretful before.

"No. I'll take them. Help me get them into the car. Not you," he said to Marvo. "Don't you touch them. This was your idea, I bet. She never would have done this before."

The man was distraught. "I'm going to have to let you go, Andra. I'm going to have to. I can't trust you anymore."

He drove away unsteadily.

"I'm sorry you lost your job," Marvo said.

"I'm not. Now we can concentrate on you. On the show."

They sat at the kitchen table, a small and grubby piece of furniture. "It will be fun. There's no reason I can't collect hair and fingernails and all the rest of it. You've got plenty for me already. It's not hard."

Marvo was not sure he would be brave enough. It was one thing to perform in front of a small party of overexcited, overfed children, another in front of a large, demanding, paying audience. However, he did feel stronger in his cape and hat, his cane firmly between his fingers. And their supporting act for the awful illusionist had gone well. It had given him confidence, knowing that his magic was better than the illusionist they supported.

"If you do all the organising, I'll show up," he said.

"You'll have to design the show and tell me what to do," Andra said.

"My glamorous assistant," he said, imagining her in a costume which showed every crease and fold.

"I'll try."

"That will be enough."

Andra and Marvo were so enraptured with each other as they were performing they barely thought about an audience; their rehearsals were so sensuous, so filled with touching and speaking, it seemed to exclude others. They swapped traditional roles, Marvo holding up his wrists and ankles, with Andra doing the tying up, using the rope he had made in the room. They preferred it that way; he could perform well without any movement; his senses could take control.

Marvo went to see many other magicians as he created his act. He saw the mistakes they made. He realised he had lessons to learn, even from the fakers. He could learn how to perform.

All the mistakes he embodied into one magician, Mr Nobody, who stood as his anti-example.

He lost the kids' attention because he wasn't funny, he took too long to do unspectacular tricks, he had boring music which wasn't timed to his behaviour, and he kept messing up a match trick, which the kids didn't find amusing. Kids are not surprised by failure. They find it embarrassing.

All this Marvo and Andra knew, understood.

And it began.

Andra, not interested in money, could see Marvo's future like a balloon. She needed to be the air, to puff him up, give him confidence, and he would take off. She wanted them to move on, become larger. She wanted Marvo Mee's magic to be seen by many.

"I don't want to be on a big stage. How can I see people's eyes, then?"

"Let's try it. You can get the people on stage and stare as much as you want, and your magic will be seen by so many. We could design the stage, we'll have dry ice drifting over them and the smell of flowers."

"Or of sugar," he said. "That sweet, desirable smell." Marvo loved sweet things, would suck on a spoonful of sugar if nothing else was available.

So Andra began to look for work in large theatres. Her first choice was on the main street in town, between restaurants and cafés. A lively area full of people who could be seduced into watching magic.

She arranged a meeting with the manager, taking Marvo with her.

Marvo was such a quiet man that when people met him they would wonder how he could convince anyone of his powers.

Then he would blink and their vision would blur; there he was in black, with glittering eyes.

Andra said to the manager, "We are well known amongst the wealthy and we are greatly loved by children. But we need a home. A place to be free. Having us here will be the making of you."

The manager laughed. He was a balding man, round-bellied, loud-voiced, used to getting his own way. Used to bribery and begging, used to pleading and approval.

"I'm already made, sweetheart. D'you have any idea what I've done?"

The Simple Invention

I had a very interesting birth. I was born in the hospital, sure, but nobody saw it! I swear. They all blinked and missed it. They said it was like magic. I was born in the wrong era. I know everybody thinks this about themselves, but it's true for me. I was born in the wrong era. I belong in the era when simple discoveries were made. When a sudden connection could lead the world in a different direction. Instead, I'm born hundreds of years too late. I have an idea, you see. Instead of the spinning jenny, and the other instruments which led to the Industrial Revolution, I had an idea for how to treat people. I would have been a man of power, and trained the people into careers of industry. They would not hold jobs: they would work on their careers.

The manager was very proud. Marvo learnt a lesson here; people who say they had an interesting birth often didn't. The manager liked to test people this way; he only let the theatre to those who would listen. He had no one in his life interested in him. Marvo and Andra stood in the musty office and listened.

Marvo looked closely at the man and could see that his clothing belonged to another time. He dressed himself in a black suit with high collars and long tail, a lot of material by today's standards. His shirt was white, and, when Marvo leaned to comfort him, stiff to the touch.

The gift Marvo gave him was interest in his dull story.

"You look like a man I used to know," said the manager. He stared at Marvo, wanting Marvo to say, "I am that man."

"He was a good man," the manager said.

The Cleaner

He was a good friend to me, loyal and kind, because I showed him loyalty and kindness. He came to me for work, a starving and filthy man. I needed someone to clean the seats and the floor, pick up the cups and wrappers, condoms and mistakes, trash and treasures. He picked them up with such care, he treated his job as if his career depended on it. We understood each other. Gradually we started to talk, after he had finished. We would have some dark coffee from the machine, dark warm coffee because the machine would be turned off to save electricity. He drank his coffee in deep gulps, then watched thirstily as I sipped mine.

"Have another," I'd say. The coffee cost me next to nothing. It was rubbish and cold.

He asked me questions about my life and my dreams, listened to me complain about my wife, my job, my employees. "Present company excepted," I'd always say, and the two of us would laugh. After his first pay cheque, he returned the next day clean, his clothes clean, his hair trimmed. Then I was comfortable with him. I felt we were equals. It's hard not to feel superior to a man who stinks. I never liked to ask him about himself. Truth be known, I enjoy holding the stage. I've spent so long putting others into the limelight, I missed out myself. Not that performers appreciate the work you do for them. Ungrateful and resentful, most of them. Present company excepted, of course.

One night, my wife was away for the weekend, a bingo trip or something, and I thought, *Why not invite the bloke back for a meal?* My wife wouldn't have let him in the house, but she wasn't going to be there, and who owns the bloody house anyway? I thought I'd put a bit of soup on, pick up a loaf of bread, get a few beers, some port, and we'd talk into the night. He sounded happy with the invitation. I was a bit worried he might think I was asking him to stay the night with me, you know, but there was nothing like that. We weren't that sort of fellas.

We talked all night. About him. He told me about his life, and why he was where he was.

"I was born too late," he said.

"What, you think you belong in another era?" I asked. A lot of people think like me. Think they belong somewhen else. He told me, "Nothing as interesting as that." His grandfather was a harsh and cruel man, who delighted in thwarting his children in their ambition. He wanted the girls to stay home and look after him, and he wanted the boys to be accountants like him. There were six children in the family, and none were happy to follow his life plan.

His father was the only one to marry. The others travelled, taught or became religious. None seemed to want to pass on their father's blood. All this was before my friend was born.

Finally, the old man died. There was no grief. The mother had died many years before, died of overwork and underlove. The children came from around the world to the funeral, out of guilt. It was as if the moment he died all his mean deeds were lessened, and all that remained were the children who had left him, ignored him. Left him on his own.

They gathered for the reading of the will. One of the grandfather's trusted friends (there weren't many) took great delight in telling all the siblings except my cleaner mate's dad that nothing was left to them, not a cent.

My mate's dad was to receive the full amount, an enormous amount, enough to keep the whole family happy and unemployed for their lifetimes. There was a condition, though, and the old bastard reading the will had to be patted on the back to calm a fit of laughter.

My mate's parents had to give birth to a boy within twelve months of the old man's death. His mother, when told, was not pleased. She preferred to stay poor. She did not want children. However, times got worse over the next month or so; his father lost his job, his mother could not find work, and his grandmother fell ill, needing expensive treatment. They began, "earnestly", my mate said his father always put it, to try to impregnate my mother.

It was successful. They did their part. Now it was up to my mate to be born in time.

Sadly, a foetus can't know the importance of a timely birth. He was late; perhaps not quite ready to leave the womb. They tried all they could to make him leave on time, but he clung to his warm home for two extra weeks.

He was born exactly one year and one week after the death of his grandfather. They did not inherit a cent. His mother's mother died through lack of care; his mother never lost her guilt. She hated him then and now; he was placed in foster care from an early age. His father would come to see him and tell him the story of his life, but he died many years ago, died of neglect. Died because my mate was not born on time.

"When my friend had gone," said the theatre manager, "I started thinking about his story, and I thought that I, too, was born too late. That's the other story I told you." Marvo realised that the story had been plain because it was a lie; it was an attempt to find a story to tell, an invention by an unimaginative man. Marvo told him a story, and allowed the man to keep it.

The Man on the Street

Here is a story for you. It didn't happen to me; it happened to a friend. His mother and father became estranged not long after he had been conceived. He was not aware of this, of course. His mother told him, later. She told him a bedside story every night of his childhood, and it was always the story of his birth.

She said, "Your father left when he heard you were coming. But it wasn't your fault. It was an excuse for him." For many years, my friend did not know what an excuse was. He thought it was a term of anger, abuse, and he called people at school "excuse", you big fat excuse. The teachers thought he was very clever, a child of his age using such a word in such a way, and his reputation as a clever child was never sullied by the fact that he was no good at school work. He received extra help, and excuses, ironically, throughout his childhood. He came to believe it himself, without ever knowing why, and he is now very successful in his own business.

My friend heard every night how his mother had been forced out onto the streets. Begging, she said, but in later years she confessed she had been prostituting herself in order to support the baby not born yet. He never felt disgusted with this; it made him weep that she would sacrifice herself, she would put her pride and her own needs so far behind his. He always had a great respect for prostitutes, and saw them in every town he lived in. He was a popular customer, because he was generous, and he made it seem as if the money was a gift, rather than a payment.

I think many men find the concept of making love to a heavily pregnant woman frightening, thus sensuous. Certainly, according to my friend's mother, there was no lack of customers.

She was with one, in a hotel room whose walls, she said, were covered in crooked, cheap prints, when she began to go into labour. The customer, a married man with a reputation, would not call an ambulance, but insisted on performing the delivery himself. He had never witnessed a birth before, not with cats or mice or even on TV, but, for the sake of his comfortable home life, he stayed and helped with this one. She never forgot that; the man was a hero to her. He could have left at any time, but he stayed. She ended the story every night by saying, "I wonder what he's doing now."

The theatre manager had his own business. He thought of himself as clever.

"Excuse," he thought, trying it out. "You're an excuse." He could not decide if he wanted to be the child born or the hero assisting at the birth. He decided he would save both stories and see.

He thought shiftily of his own experiences with prostitutes and determined to change. He remembered throwing money onto the floor; there were times he hadn't paid at all. "I offer refunds for faulty work," he remembered saying, "so should you."

Marvo gave the manager a week of full houses. It was an extra present, but it was for the benefit of the act.

"I am Dr Mee," said Marvo. "But you can call me Marvo." He used long, long matches to light a candle, then clicked his fingers and the next candle lit up, the first went out, then the third lit and the second went out. He pulled a candle from his nose; that made them laugh. And he swore at the candles as they went out; said "Shoot," or "Fruit" so the children knew what he meant. Then he raised his arms and with a boom, all the candles were alight. Carol music started; carols by candlelight. "Rudolph the Red-Nosed Reindeer" began and the children sang. They watched in delight as Marvo's nose began to grow and glow, an enormous red bulb. Then the dark room grew lighter, warmer. The children were silent. Was the show over? As the light grew, they saw what that tickle was, that itch on their little noses. Because growing there, now, like shoots from the ground, were tiny Chinese lanterns, lit with tiny candles.

"Ripe, I think," said Marvo. He plucked the lantern gently from the nose of the child in the front row. He passed it to her, and she felt her smooth nose for a dent, a hole. Nothing there.

The children could not clap, because they held their lanterns. Marvo bowed; Andra bowed. The lights went down on stage, and by the time the children could breathe again, there was nothing left. The only sign of magic the lanterns they held.

Marvo had to be careful of his magic sometimes. He did not want to terrify. So he used covers to conceal his magic, to make them think it was all illusion. Andra loved the tricks where she was under the covers; especially the one where Marvo stood, arms stretched wide, legs stretched wide, and she climbed through his belly and out the other side. She loved to see his insides. She came out feeling like her skin glowed, shone with his liquid.

They learnt the lesson of care early in their performing. Marvo sawed Andra in half, but forgot to place the metal shields in the box. When he twisted the two halves to the audience, her blood turned stomachs and made them scream.

As Marvo pattered and played his card tricks, he swallowed some milk, took a bite of apple.

"Anyone want some?" he said.

"Yuck!!" shouted the kids.

"What would you like?" he asked. He cupped his hand behind his ear to hear the answer.

"Lollies? Lollies? You kids make me sick." He patted and kneaded his stomach, his face paled. He coughed and began to dribble. Then he projectile-vomited over the audience.

They screamed in disgust and delight, because it was lollies he threw up at them, lollies in paper.

The children loved Marvo the Magician.

Marvo and Andra had long discussions about the use of birds and bunnies in the act. They saw a magician who pulled bunnies out of hats and made birds appear under silk scarves. They saw two different things.

Andra saw frightened creatures living in captivity, performing without choice.

Marvo saw no cruelty. He saw living creatures being used for magic and thought them lucky. When he made a bird or a bunny disappear, he sent it to rest a while in a beautiful field, full of green grass for a bunny, a sweet shady tree for a bird. Then he would reach down and pull them back.

Andra said, "You're very cold, sometimes. You have a cold nature. But you're so good as well."

"You know that good can be evil, evil good, depending on the circumstances," came his reply. "Nobody is one or the other." Marvo had learned this from a young girl who sold sex.

He did not buy sex from her—he bought time.

"I'm considered a bad person, but I make you happy, don't I?" the girl had said. Marvo had nodded. "So I must be good as well."

The children loved Marvo because he gave them things, little somethings to take home, to take to school for show and tell.

In one audience there was a boy with a blinking light in his shoe. Near him, a girl who got scared; the boy showed her his blinking light to cheer her up, even though it was he who had upset her to begin with, calling her a copycat because she and her friend sat on the back of the chair, same as the flashing boy and his friend. Someone had to go and get her dad and she left the magic show, shaking like an actor being a leaf. Marvo sent her some mist, to make her not care about the boy with the flashing shoe. She came back after interval and sat up wherever she liked.

A show-off girl hopped on stage, took a tissue, pretended to blow her nose. Stood up and told everyone to shush. Got told off by the teacher; Marvo used her as an assistant.

"Can I have a volunteer?" he said, looking right at her.

She giggled. "Me," she said, jumping up, hand waving, "I'm the volunteer."

There were other hands up but Marvo chose her. He liked her lack of fear; he wanted to reward her.

The girl stared him straight in the eye. He saw magic there; the magic of confidence.

He decided she would help him with a special trick. "What's your name?"

"Stevie," she said.

"That's a boy's name!" someone in the audience shouted, and she stuck her tongue out at them.

"Andra, please remain backstage. This trick is too dangerous for you." Andra left the stage to the sound of children's drawn breath. She winked at Marvo, which angered him; it was a distraction he didn't need.

The girl on stage shook.

"Are you scared?" said Marvo.

"No."

"Yes, you are," he said, and he plunged the room into darkness.

"Oh, dear," he said. "The lightbulb has blown. Assistant, I think you better change it for me while I prepare for our trick."

"I can't change lightbulbs."

"Don't argue," Marvo shouted.

"She's only a kid," the audience muttered. "How's a kid supposed to change a lightbulb?"

They felt a coolness above their ears and looked up into the darkness.

"Are you holding on to the lightbulb?" Marvo's voice said from the stage. A moment's silence. "I can't hear you," he said.

"I nodded yes," the girl's voice came…from the roof.

"Then let's go."

The room began to spin.

"How many children does it take to change a lightbulb?" asked Marvo. The light came on, and there was the girl, floating in the centre of the room, holding the lightbulb. The rest of the room spun gently below.

"One hundred and eight," said Marvo. "One to hold the lightbulb and one hundred and seven to keep the room steady while it turns."

The girl sank to the floor amongst the children who suddenly adored her, admired her. She was okay, she was fine.

Marvo was gone. On stage, there was no evidence he had ever existed.

Another time, Marvo had a sack and he walked up and down the aisles. He said, "Who wants a present? Who wants…a teddy bear? …a baby blanket?" He gave away these things. They were things lost, each teddy bear lost in a fire, a sale, a move, each baby blanket moth-eaten and thrown away. His early life was furnished with other people's missing things.

He stood by one woman who had not raised her hand for a single present.

"I didn't want any of those things," she said.

He scrabbled in his bag. He found a pair of shoes; high heel, strappy shoes.

She took them, massaged their leather and felt the straps.

"I threw these shoes out the car window the night I lost my virginity," she said.

Marvo changed his act when adults were in the audience.

He flirted, made it a sexy show, made people hold hands in the dark, made them think of love and loving. He did this because he wanted the adults to like him too.

He used lots of fire, because fire was sexy; encircled the audience in flames when they said they were cold. "Who wants to get warm?" he said. He wore tight leather pants, a loose, romantic shirt which laced up the front. He looked like a pirate, a sword fighter, or he looked like a dancer. He danced with Andra, languorous, sensual dancing which entranced people, so that the dance itself became magic. Or he dressed in a suit, so he looked respectable, trustworthy, not what they expected in a magician. And he would perform his most shocking show dressed that way.

He wrote songs, simple things which talked of magic and illusion, and he paid to have them recorded. These he played in his performances; these he gave away as prizes to people who helped him, people who learnt to love him.

He set a woman from the audience to rest on jets of water, and she lay there, her hands touching the jets, feeling the pressure of them, her chest rising and falling. When Marvo released her she was breathless and her cheeks were ruddy. Marvo turned her around to show the audience her clothes were dry, and she clutched to his touch. She waited in the audience till everyone else was gone, she told her husband to go get the car and she waited for Marvo to come from behind the stage and talk to her. She felt he had given her a special message, and they had almost made love on the stage. She could still feel the tingle of the water on her back, her neck, her buttocks, her thighs, her calves, her ankles. She could still see herself spinning and flying around Marvo, his dark eyes intent on hers. She sat and imagined Marvo's fingers on hers; she sat and waited.

Andra knew she was out there and distracted Marvo behind the stage. She seduced him with a story, began it with a whisper in his ear while they were still performing, and continued while the woman waited. His face glowed; he forgot any intentions he had for the woman in the audience. Finally, the woman's husband came into the auditorium to find her, and he took her home and reaped the benefits of her seduction.

Marvo never overcame his nervousness on dressing for a performance. It made him grouchy, and Andra learnt that keeping away from him was best. He wanted to be grouchy, he didn't want to be made to feel better. The grouchiness overwhelmed the terror and he could force himself to go on.

Once there, he could lose himself in the movements familiar to him. Joining the rings, finding the egg, removing the scarves from his mouth. These actions comforted him; they made him think of the safety of the room in the house, as an adult eating a childhood treat may be comforted.

Andra and Marvo found the magic performances exhilarating, the teamwork exciting. It wore them out, and they would go straight home afterwards, collapse into bed.

It was a long while before they slept well together. It is true, in relationships, that for a while you feel obliged to sleep close—under arms, on chests, always touching. Once you give up on that, you sleep more easily.

Marvo found performing magic exciting. He loved to see the children's faces as the tricks were performed, the chocolate melted in their pocket and reformed to a likeness of their secretly admired, their pet disappearing and returning a different colour but unharmed. He was so clever with time; could make it slow down or speed up. He could do what he liked as people plodded through their day.

Marvo and Andra became very popular among those who collected people. Odd people: artists, writers, designers, hairdressers; eccentric and unusual. They loved the way Marvo took his cat with him everywhere. Even when he did not set out with it, he would find it at his feet, or nestled at his head. They were almost famous—Marvo had become the most popular children's performer in the country. And he could be guaranteed to be so interested in what people had to say. He loved to hear stories, and he listened to every detail. It was flattering that a man like him would be so fascinated. A man with a life like his. People wanted to claim him as a friend.

They arrived early at the chairman of British Associated Tobacco's residence for what the invitation had said would be an "informal meal".

This was an enormous house. Twelve other guests at table, all of them almost famous like Marvo and Andra. The host believed that almost famous now will be very famous soon and knew that the only way to know famous people was to know them before they become famous.

There was a politician and her husband, an avant-garde painter and his lover — who had not spoken so sex could not be determined — a shopkeeper and his wife who advertised on TV. A pair of twins who sang and danced. They talked about their family, what a happy life they had led. Marvo no longer envied people with parents. He knew that parents could be cruel, and that having a father did not mean a happy life. He listened to them sing and saw their smiles; he became deaf, mute and blind, he could smell sweat, old sweat. The girls were not clean, and there was a reason for that. They clung to each other and needed no one else. They were unattractive, with that smell, and no one would want them. And that was how they wanted it.

A school teacher with radical methods was there, and a landscape architect who grew orchids. Also an American diplomat and his wife. They kept very quiet. She carried a cocker spaniel which drooled and sniffed. Marvo was sure they took notes.

Marvo expected Andra to mention that her father had been an expert orchid grower.

"I've always been mesmerised by orchids," she said. "Their fleshiness, their easy deaths."

"You learnt about them from an early age," said Marvo, "didn't you?"

Andra had forgotten that story. "Oh, yes," she said, "My father taught me about them early on." Marvo smiled at her. He liked to help her remember her stories.

They sat around and talked of gossip, bitchiness, news. If anyone became passionate, the others would ignore them until the passion subsided. It was the only polite thing to do.

Andra sat with the host and drank scotch. Marvo talked with the hostess in the kitchen.

"Bloody bastard," she said, "thinks his job is to make the drinks.

Like one?" she asked. Marvo opened the champagne and they shared it from the bottle.

"My first drink was champagne," Marvo said.

"Mine was beer, I must admit. Warm beer, drunk through a straw at the beach." The hostess wore expensive clothing, imported. It would not fade or tear and it was flattering.

Marvo laughed.

"Did you know that ale was invented by the Germans? The name was aluth, from the same ancestral root as hallucination," said Marvo. He found it very apt. He disliked the idea of hallucinations and hated the taste of beer.

"That's about right. Everyone said you got drunk faster that way, drinking it through a straw."

At the Beach

I was at the beach with my cousin and her boyfriend. We told our mothers it was just my cousin and me, but the boyfriend was there all along. He was eighteen, he bought the beers. We met him there and drank it.

There was another guy there, a friend of his, who was angry with me because I wouldn't talk to him. He was horrible. He had a hairy back. So I lay there drinking a can of beer and getting sunburnt. Then I got too hot and went for a swim. It was time to show off my new bikini, anyway.

So I went diving into the sea and swam, enjoying the salt and the water. Suddenly I was tired. My arms were heavy and I thought I'd rest them for a while. So I let them drop. I thought I'd stand on the bottom and relax. I thought my feet would touch the bottom.

Well, they didn't. The water rose over my head and I flapped my arms to see how far away the sea bed was. I flapped and flapped. I couldn't find bottom so I flapped back up for air. I couldn't see the sand. I didn't want to swim until I saw the sand so I trod water, turning around and around, looking for trees or whatever.

It must have been an illusion, because I'm sure I wasn't that far out. But I could see nothing but water. I screamed. Hands grabbed me gently, turned me on my back and towed me along. I grabbed at this person and felt a hairy back. I feel like I slept until I was safe, and awoke to find him arousing me with resuscitation.

"It's okay. I'm okay," I told him.

"You're safe now," he said. And the rest is history.

She blinked brightly at Marvo. "Shall we join the others?" she said. Her husband was pouring more drinks. Through his thin white shirt, Marvo could see black matting of hair on front and back. And when the man handed Marvo his drink, their eyes linked and Marvo recognised him as a magician using his skills for personal gain.

Marvo had learnt that a sense of commitment can stop a person acting. That this wife was under a spell of rescue, and couldn't leave until it was lifted.

He said to the man, "Food was great at Carlito's the other day. Nothing like a good long lunch with a pleasant companion." He said it in a way which didn't sound like him, he sounded like a man who took long lunches and was capable of blackmail. Marvo rarely ate lunch. He rarely chose to stop his activities.

"Who were you at lunch with?" asked the woman.

"Ooh, gossip!" one of the guests said.

Dinner parties are not the places to discuss differences of opinion. The mist is thick, and the bullshit. People must pretend to like each other for the duration of the food, and make complaints only to people who weren't there, only later. Marvo and Andra had learnt this with an early failure. No arguments at dinner. Only jokes and lies. As the wife set the table, she dropped a knife.

"A woman will visit soon," Andra said. The husband glanced sharply at his wife.

"But you're already here," he said, "you're already visiting, Andra."

"Lucky she didn't drop a fork or you'd be calling Marvo a fool," said Andra. She was drunk. Marvo liked it when she toned down her seriousness.

Andra weighed the cutlery in her palm. She said, "Aluminium was precious, in the last century. Rich people would pay $100,000 a pound for it, when it was a natural metal. Then two men discovered they could produce aluminium themselves, and a lot of rich people found themselves with almost worthless material."

The American diplomat's wife said, "I love that you know that! You're about the most interesting woman I've met in a long time." She had drunk two bottles of wine herself and was only now livening up. Her dog licked Andra's toes.

Marvo squeezed the hostess's hand as he left.

"He's got a very hairy back," he whispered. His gift to her was support; belief in what she said.

He heard, later, that she left her husband.

Marvo hated a party to end. He was enlivened by this one, and talked all the way home. "I had a dream about the future the other night," he said.

Andra reached over in the darkness of the car and squeezed his thigh. "What happened?" She hoped he would tell her of a home together, growing old, a vision of the two of them rocking in chairs, sharing wine.

But he said, "I dreamt of having a place, a huge house, where people could come and go. Weary travellers rest in this home. They see a place of beauty, see wonders like talking mice and everlasting port bottles, and they stay for weeks.

When they emerge the world has gone ahead without them.

It was a wonderful dream."

After that dinner, after his dream, Marvo was enthusiastic for the next show. He performed tricks, traditional and untraditional. He made dollar coins appear from ears, changed one orange into three, read thoughts, found a bowl of goldfish in a scarf, made people disappear, sometimes reappear, and cut them in half. He lulled the audience into a relaxed state, sang them into drowsiness with his simple, predictable tricks. Then he made the floor open up and they were sucked into a darkness, there was no noise, sound or smell. Then Marvo's voice began to talk.

"What a beautiful world. How I love my friend. I love to work. I love to watch a comedy rather than the news." The floor would open up and they would be in the auditorium again; Marvo gone, slides of a beautiful volcano erupting, a magnificent fire, a delightful poppy field.

"How nice," said the people. "How nice it makes me feel."

Time came when the theatre manager and his stories, his tucked-in place and his small profile, became dull to Andra. She had a trick in mind, a large fish tank, plenty of water, some danger. She and Marvo had worked on it, but the theatre manager turned up his nose. He said it was trite, overdone. He was lying; the trick scared him. He knew that this trick would put Marvo so far out of his league they could never talk again.

"Not bad with tricks myself," he said one night, and began to demonstrate, fumbling with cards and coins, his lips moving in encouragement. Marvo had been feeling loyalty towards the man. Didn't want to discard him, but the dull and plodding theatre manager pretending to be a magician was enough to turn his stomach. It was time to move on, to grow. There was nothing more to learn from the man. Marvo had spent hours waiting for wisdom, listening to him talking, talking, but nothing ever came out. He had in Marvo the most audience he'd had in years, and he did not take a breath to let Marvo interrupt.

Andra was waiting for Marvo to decide; she would not talk him into it or make any move without his genuine agreement.

"I'm ready," Marvo said. "He's gone too far. He thinks he's the same as me, that he can do what I do. We can leave him now."

Andra, assistant, lover, companion, manager, organised a breakfast meeting with a new promoter for Marvo.

"Morning is good time for conviction and discussion," she told him. "This is a big-time promoter who understands your work."

Marvo was not keen to go; he hated meeting with people who he didn't know, who might consider him a foolish artist (and a children's artist at that) and be keen to make fun of him. He said, "Why don't you go on your own? I'll stay home and run a nice hot bath for you to hop into when you get home." Marvo had had no formal education into how to be an adult. He still practised the barter and reward method of deal making.

"I need you to come with me. The time is auspicious for both of us to be there; we want support and we want to book a show at this theatre. If we get it, you can do the fish tank act we've been working on."

He agreed, as he did to almost anything Andra said. He trusted her with his life, with his magic.

"All right. So long as you're there too."

Thinking back, much later, Andra would wonder if perhaps she played a role in Marvo's death. The breakfast meeting led to the theatre, to the fish tank. She did not see how she could have behaved differently. Only a vision of the future could have changed her actions.

The meeting went well. Andra did most of the talking, but at the end, when they all stood up the man reached across the table and shook Marvo's hand.

"Good deal," said the man. Andra smiled at him but Marvo could sense her anger at being ignored. He blinked at the man and a small mist filled his eyes. The promoter tripped over the front step of the restaurant and fell, cutting his chin. Andra squeezed Marvo's hand gratefully, then helped the man up. He took her hand.

"Thanks," he said.

That night, they performed a reasonable show but not their best. They wanted to leave without tears. "This was our last night," Marvo told the theatre manager as they sat to lukewarm coffee afterwards.

The theatre manager began to protest, "I wasn't born yesterday, you've got a contract, I know what you've been up to."

He didn't take rejection well.

Marvo let the mist rise. The theatre manager gave the contract to Marvo, who burnt it.

"Are you really firing us?" Marvo asked. "Do we have to go? You've been such a friend to me."

"I'm afraid the ride's over. I've got a real show coming in tomorrow. Amateur Night is over."

"Will you eat with us? One last time?"

"Of course I'll eat with you. We'll break bread and talk dirty."

Marvo nodded. He took a pen off the desk, some paper clips. He picked up a rubber seal which had fallen onto the floor. These he put in his pocket.

Andra and Marvo prepared for the meal carefully. They asked others. The diplomat from the US embassy (they never understood what he did) and his wife, who had liked Andra so much, plus a woman Marvo met on the bus and her boyfriend. They wanted it to be lavish. They rarely had people in their home.

After years of living on scraped food, Marvo loved a huge plateful, with more on the stove.

The first TV cooking show he saw, many years after he left the room, was like a magic show to him—true magic, not illusion. He was glad he had not seen one in the room, because his mouth watered as he watched. He always had to buy food when the show was over, because it made him hungry. Magic made him hungry.

After he ran from the room, he ate in restaurants and fast-food plazas, and there were plates full which did not need to be scraped and transferred. The meals could be eaten where they were found.

It slowly made sense to him that food was made up of other foods— if you added two or more together you created a third.

Science. Experimentation. Who thought of doing this—who was the first one to bake a cake?

Chefs have been around forever. Men made cooking a religious rite and took the role for themselves at the time of the discovery of fire. There is evidence that the ancient Babylonians made cakes.

There were plenty of classes, cooking classes, but Marvo was always terrified by the sight of people who knew what was inside an egg, who had made sandwiches alone.

There was much to learn in cooking. There was great lore and mystery; great healing. Eating is something that every single creature who ever existed on this planet has done. We all know what it is like to eat.

Andra said, "You can help me cook for our guests. We'll make a practice meal today, another tomorrow. I'll tell you a story as we work."

Oatcake Meal

A fisherman's wife taught me how to make oatcakes. Her husband was a terrible man. He slept with women other than her and returned with a diseased cock. He beat her and treated the food she cooked with disrespect.

She was the greatest cook I have met. A pure love for her art meant each mouthful of her food was like a kiss. Her husband merely shoved it into his mouth, talking about his horrid adventures during the chewing process. He was a truly horrible man.

He didn't like me at all, of course. I was someone for his wife to talk to, and he didn't like that. He kept asking where I was from, and I said a new place each time. It became a game. The woman and I would talk while she cooked and we thought of even more bizarre places of birth. I described my true birth once and she thought that was hilarious.

So she cooked these awful oatcakes, and they came out dusty with meal. We had been talking all morning about freedom, and how her husband didn't treat her as anything but his possession.

She took a deep breath, closed her eyes and blew the meal off the oatcakes.

Two days later, we heard news that his ship had been blown out to sea by a freak hurricane. They found his body caked with salt.

Marvo watched Andra take down the sea salt and grind it finely. "People think salt is an unhealthy additive, but it is vital to survival. Carrying salt in the pocket is another protection against the evil eye."

"Your face tastes salty," said Marvo. "You taste like you've been swimming in the Dead Sea."

"If you were my grandmother, you'd be convinced I'd been ill-wished," said Andra. She licked him back. "You, however, have no trace of salt. No one wishes you ill,"

"Of course not," said Marvo. For a moment he forgot about Doctor Reid and those he had hurt with his magic.

Andra would later think how strange it was that with all the portents of doom on her side, it was Marvo who was doomed.

"There is magic in not eating, also," said Andra. "Magic in fasting for a cause because it seems so extreme, to die for lack of food. The spittle of a fasting person is said to cure itches and creeping sores, and the bites of hornets and beetles. Licking a wart first thing in the morning should make it disappear, and you don't even have to be fasting. Toads are great for curing the King's Evil should there be no kings around. Also for bloody noses. We could, if we wished, cook the toad when we cook the seafood; it also needs to be placed in water and slowly heated, slowly stewed. They take much longer though, perhaps separate from the other food is best."

"In some secret cults, babies are cooked the same way," Marvo said. "Do you think they feel pain?" He wondered whether Andra had something to do with the child he sensed in his future. He knew not everyone loved and sought to protect children. He wanted to know what type she was. She held her stomach, feeling sick.

"You can't do that to a child," she said. "You cannot eat the flesh of a child, unless you want to die within the number of years it lived. The remains of the toad should be heated again, then finely powdered. The toads can thus be taken as medicine."

"And you cook seafood in the same way?" asked Marvo.

Andra realised his ignorance about cooking.

She gathered a table of ingredients.

"This is fresh asparagus. This sea salt. Here, dry mustard, black pepper, fresh lemon. This is peanut oil, this is pure olive oil. Virgin. Free range eggs. The Egyptians, Greeks and Romans regarded the egg as an emblem of the universe, as the work of God. As a precaution, make a hole in the bottom of the eggshell before throwing it away. This stops witches from using it to wreck ships. By floating the shell they wreck the ship."

"A hole in the shell would seem to signify a hole in the ship," said Marvo. "I thought they would like holes in the eggs."

"They have to put them in themselves or it doesn't work," Andra said. "Would you like to know your future?" she asked.

She took another egg and perforated the small end with a pin. Then she let three drops of albumen fall into a basin of water. "There, you see?" she said, pointing at the shapes. She made her voice light. "There's you, and me, and a child." She laughed.

"What else?" said Marvo. "Anything else you see?"

"Not in this bowl. Perhaps next time we'll get another clue."

"I don't like clues. I like knowledge and truth. I want to know the future." At that moment, Marvo realised he did. That this was what he needed to know.

"I can't really tell you, Marvo. Shall we cook? Take a sufficiency of fresh asparagus. With a sharp knife slice the hard ends off the asparagus." Andra demonstrated by running the knife gently along his arm. The hairs fell to the floor in a soft shower.

"Bring a pot of water to the boil. The water must be fresh and cold. Add a liberal shake of salt." Andra shook so liberally she spilt. Marvo licked up the salt like a cow in the desert. "Drop the asparagus into bubbling water. Do not cover.

"Now, cook for five minutes."

Andra made Marvo kiss her while they were waiting. He licked the salt from her.

"Once you can pierce the stem smoothly with a poultry pin, remove the asparagus with a slotted spoon and without delay rinse under cold water. Why?"

"To cool it off?"

"No, Marvo. To stop the cooking and to hold the green colour. Drain well. Spread onto a clean (that is unused) tea towel to dry."

"Finished," said Marvo.

"No. We have a lemon mayonnaise to serve with the vegetable. In a clean white china bowl, whisk three egg yolks with a quarter of a teaspoon of dry mustard—the powdered variety; a dash of salt, a grind of pepper, two tablespoons of lemon juice. One whole lemon perhaps. Do not let it go to waste. In our case we can heat the lemon for ten seconds in the microwave; astonishingly, this releases the juices of the lemon so a frail squeeze produces all we need.

"Mix these. With an egg beater—handheld please, beat in a cup and a half of this pure olive oil. Do not save money and buy cheap oil; it will destroy any dish you create.

"Beat the oil drop by drop at first. The mayonnaise will thicken. Then increase the oil flow.

"Add the grated rind from the lemon we squeezed. The jug has boiled for a mug of coffee. Add a tablespoon of boiling water to the mayonnaise.

"Now, my mayonnaise is perfection. Yours is not. Yours has separated—see how the oil floats, an entity alone? Take another bowl. Break one egg yolk into the bowl, beat it well. Add your mayonnaise mixture to the egg, drop by drop by drop.

"Now, you have mayonnaise. You can use the egg whites to top a pie."

She placed her finger in Marvo's mouth.

"Very good," he said.

They ate the first lesson.

"Now, Marvo, you must understand that good food takes time. It takes good ingredients and a gentle touch. It takes magic."

Marvo knew how to cook asparagus with lemon mayonnaise. He felt ready for something heartier.

He scrabbled beside the stove for the chocolate he hid there and they shared that as Andra spoke.

"Bouillabaisse. The renowned French soup. The meal of families, lovers and patrons. A soup beggars dream of.

"To begin, we need our sea creatures."

A trip to the fish market early yielded this catch. Marvo's nose was still filled with the deep sea smell of the place. He had only smelled fish frying before.

"Here is ocean perch, John Dory and rock flathead. Onions, celery, leek, fennel. Tomato paste, parsley, garlic. Basil could also be used, but never sniff it. Sniffing basil can invite a scorpion into the brain.

"Red tomatoes, saffron, fresh thyme, cloves, bay leaves. An orange. Cayenne pepper. Raw sugar. Good white wine, blue swimmer crabs. Moreton Bay bugs. Mussels and prawns, green and large. Fresh crusty bread, Grand Marnier in a bottle. These, plus water, are all we need for now."

Marvo stared at the food, hunger beating his belly at the thought.

"Two of us need to share each fish. We cut the fins from our fish and put them aside. Using the same newly sharpened knife, we remove the heads.

"These we put aside also. Waste is avoided where possible. Everything may be used. Cut the fish into quarters. Pour two tablespoons of oil—but don't measure, pour until it feels right—into a large pot. This size is good. A pot that reaches your elbow when you touch the bottom.

"You have two onions, finely chopped. One half stick of celery. One whole leek. One base of fennel. All chopped finely, so that the pieces cling to your fingertips like flakes of ice.

"Fry these vegetables for the duration of a pop song. Stir them, though. Don't dance about the room forgetting their existence.

"Tomato paste is one commercial product so fine that to make it yourself would be foolish. One tablespoon to the vegetables and another song.

"Add a handful of parsley, chopped to a dust. Your handful is good—mine is too small.

"Parsley, now, can be very confusing. It comes from 'petrosilium'— sounds like a fossil fuel. It's very nice in soup, and on top of pasta. Yet it gets nasty quickly, if you leave it in a plastic bag. It can be used as an antidote to poison; though which poison is uncertain. Yet it can poison your life if you transplant it. Parsley brings bad luck in that circumstance. Parsley, when eaten in large quantities and before the condition sets in, can prevent baldness. However parsley, kept in a glass, can weaken that glass. The Greeks used it to plant on graves, because it stayed green so long. Kept those corpses' breath fresh too."

Marvo longed to chop and chop again. He loved repetition.

"These are the paradoxes of parsley," Andra said. "Six cloves of garlic, ends chopped off with a cleaver, crushed with the flat of the cleaver, skins easily removed. Into the pot.

"Four tomatoes, a cross cut in their base, placed for thirty seconds only in boiling water then removed, will peel easily of their skin. Remove the seeds also, then chop coarsely and add to the pot.

"Fennel seed, a different flavour to the fresh fennel. Half a teaspoon should be added.

"A full packet of saffron strands. A great expense but the coloured, fake variety will destroy the dish. Put in the whole packet, saving a few strands for another dish. Toss it in recklessly and feel happy to be so extravagant. Saffron comes from the flower saffron. Each strand is the stigma of a flower. So you see how precious it is.

"A sprig of fresh thyme. A clove. Half a bay leaf, into the pot.

"Take an orange and a peeler. Carefully strip the peel into thin strings; once in this form it becomes zest. This into the pot. You can buy a special peeler for this purpose; I find it wasteful to buy a utensil which performs only one service.

"A pinch of cayenne pepper. A teaspoon of raw sugar. A dash of salt, a grind of pepper, and finally, the saved fish heads should join the pot. Stir it all. Tip it, falling and rolling so that all mixes and loves. Open a good bottle of white wine. Add most of it; five hundred millilitres. Enough left for a glass each. We will drink that as the mixture boils, once we have added enough water to cover the heads."

Marvo and Andra sipped their wine. Marvo ensured the glasses did not empty. By the time half an hour had passed, his head was light and he felt the mist lifting from his eyes. As they moved back to the kitchen, in a suburb close by a mother drowned her baby and ran away. Further away, five suicides and a fatal car accident as the mist cleared.

"Strain the liquid and discard the vegetable solids. Set heads aside with fins. We now have the stock. Here we have a miniature aquarium. Sea World. Two blue swimmer crabs. Two Moreton Bay bugs. Happy creatures. Immerse them in another large pot, cover with water, and slowly bring to the boil. Like frogs, they feel no pain as they die this way."

Marvo remembered something since the last lesson. He said, "But perhaps they do. After all, frogs feel the change in temperature as we would." Marvo asked her to kill the creatures first.

"Cut each creature in half. We have to remove the lungs and the stomach sacs. Place these with the fins and the heads.

"Wash the creature halves in very salty water to remove any sandiness.

"Scrub four mussels with a brush, slice away their hairy beards. Rinse also the four green king prawns. Do not peel the prawns; their cases are important to the flavour.

"We need another pot. The one used to kill the crabs and bugs will be fine.

"Place the mussels at the base. Cover with the prawns. Then the bugs. Then the crabs. Then the fish. Then the hot stock, strained of body parts and debris. Cover the pot. It must come to the boil and simmer for ten minutes, at which time it will be ready."

Andra took five bowls in preparation.

"The soup goes into two. The seafood and fish into the serving bowl. An empty bowl by each of us to take the debris from the seafood and fish. Also, a small plate for our crusty bread and our sauce Rouille."

"How do you make crusty bread? And the sauce?"

"Bread we will save for another lesson. The sauce is created by grinding to breadcrumbs a five-centimetre piece of French loaf, a segment from the loaf we are serving is best. Into the base of a pan throw one egg yolk, four garlic cloves, prepared as in earlier in the lesson. Saffron strands again, a pinch. The pilfered ones from the packet earlier. The breadcrumbs. Six tablespoons of the stock boiling on the stove, a pinch of salt, a dash of pepper. Process to a smooth paste. We have learnt this process already; slowly add six tablespoons of our good olive oil. It will thicken, and we will serve it with the rest of the loaf, our bowls of soup and our bowl of creatures."

They very much enjoyed eating the second lesson. Andra slowly desiccated the fins, the heads, the lungs and the stomachs. By morning, all were nicely dried. She ground them with a mortar and pestle, tipped the granules into a jar and placed it beside many others.

She had a lot of interesting things there. Some she took easily; others she had to fight for. She worked as hairdresser and beautician on a cruise ship once, and on board were many old sailors. She cut hair and cut nails, beautified the ugly. She did her greatest business during a storm; the crew were superstitious. They were scared to break tradition, and they would never quite believe it was safe to have their hair cut or their nails pared without the buffer of the storm to protect them. She had a suitcase full of hair and nails when she left. She had to throw her clothes overboard.

"Are you ready for dessert?" Andra asked. "Something light, I think. Take two navel oranges and peel them—sharp knife. No white pith should remain. Slice them into two glass dishes. Pour a splash or more of Grand Marnier over each, sprinkle a little sugar as well, then we'll place them, covered, into the fridge.

"To make caramel, we place a cup of sugar and a tablespoon of water into a heavy-based, small saucepan.

"We turn the heat to low, and do not stir after the sugar is dissolved.

"Cook until the sugar is caramel coloured, then pour over the uncovered oranges. Recover and return for chilling."

Marvo had given her the glass bowls. He had picked them up from a home he worked in. He couldn't help himself.

Marvo now had a new magic. A powerful new magic.[†]

They were ready to prepare a meal for the theatre manager, his wife and their other guests.

Marvo concentrated so hard on cooking the meal he let the mist drop. He didn't cook seriously again after that. It was too distracting; too dangerous. They made:

Marvo and Andra's Dinner

To begin:

A light and luscious kumara soufflé, puffed to perfection
and served with creamy tarragon sauce

And then:

Our special veal and chestnut stew

And to finish:

---

† See Appendix A for recipes.

Quince tart—sweet and tart. With coffee. [†]

He spent hours shopping for the ingredients, a full day preparing the meal. He picked the rosemary he needed from his own garden, where it grew by the metre. He grew it to show he was righteous. He grew it for a joke. He ignored the siren sounds which wailed all day; did not watch the news or listen to Andra as she described the day of accidents, murder and suicide. When he awoke the next day, when the mist was back, he felt as if he had been out of his body all day, that someone else had done the shopping and the cooking.

The theatre manager and his wife arrived early. "I thought you said 6.30," the man said, but everybody knew he was lying. He was so eager to be there. His wife was much taller than him, a dramatic woman who wanted to be an actress but was too lazy. She looked like one, with bright red hair and bright red lips, and a big laugh throwing her hair back and shaking her shoulders.

The American diplomat and his wife arrived next. They brought Californian wine and Swiss chocolate. The wife gave Andra a fond embrace, grabbed her face and squeezed. "You gonna be interesting tonight again? I bet you are!"

The conversation was honest and sharp from the beginning. Andra's bus friend did not believe in immigration or men cooking—"They have no instinct"—or fat women. The hall owner's wife didn't agree, and while the food was perfect, the dinner party was far from a success. Near the end, the theatre manager discovered they had been talking to another promoter, and it made him very angry. He talked a lot about how weak they were, how he held them up, how he could report them for the things they did on stage. His wife took him by the face and kissed him to shut him up.

Marvo was too depressed to help clean up. He went straight to bed and called for Andra to come to him.

They did not see the theatre manager again. Later, the man would see Marvo on TV.

"Taught him everything he knows," he would say. Then he would weep, because the mist had never been thick enough for him, and Marvo would never know the sacrifice the theatre manager had made, letting Marvo go when his heart was breaking.

---

† See Appendix A for recipes.

For their first show in the new theatre, Marvo used birds in his show one last time, thanks to Andra's influence. She felt about birds the way he felt about spiders, though her victory was not as strong, because he had no feelings for birds to change.

"Who here likes birds?" Marvo asked. It was a young audience; none of the males sniggered. None said, "Only the ones who fuck." Most cheered, raised their hands, remembering other magicians and their magic doves. They remembered the doves vanishing, reappearing in flames. They remembered touching the birds, feeling their greasy feathers. They shouted, "We love birds." Three boys, sitting together, hated birds, flowers, girls. They hated perfume on their mothers and the colour of lipstick. They hated everything except the ball they kicked around, their football team, the cigarettes they were learning to smoke. They jeered as Marvo talked, tried to put him off his story, called him teacher, the worst insult they could think of.

Marvo filled their mouths with birdseed. One of them began to cry, so Marvo quietened him. But he did it too well. The mist enveloped, and the child disappeared. Marvo thought nothing more of it until the end of the show.

"Not all birds are good. Some birds are better shot than others. The raven, the crow and the swallow mean misfortune and death." These birds began to fly about the room, their wings flapping in the silence Marvo left. "The raven because it is known to seek death; it will follow an army on its marches, awaiting the fall of the bodies. It knows better than a human that the point of war is death.

"The crow, in ancient Egypt, symbolised discord, strife. Trouble.

"The swallow was present at the death of Jesus Christ, and is thus tainted. The bird circled the cross crying "Svala! Svala!" which means "Console! Console!" (though how a Scandinavian bird, or a speaker of a Scandinavian tongue to translate the bird, came to be in Calvary I'm not sure). It has been called a swallow ever since. In Rome, though, a swallow is considered lucky when it builds about your house, because it is sacred to the household gods.

"But," said Marvo, "do not kill a swallow thinking this will save you. All this will do is bring bad luck upon you."

He pointed at a child in the audience, a bird-like and timid boy who had been making nervous cooing sounds since Marvo began. The boy swallowed, and swallowed again compulsively.

"Do not mimic the birds," said Marvo. He waved his arm and the boy sank into his seat, breathing loudly, angry and embarrassed. He shook off any helping hands, his timidity vanished. "The owl, the cuckoo and the sparrow also have evil reputations. The owl because, when Jesus Christ wanted something to eat, he went to a baker's. She put a large loaf into the oven for him, but her penny-pinching daughter said it was too big. She tore it in half. But the loaf grew and grew enormous! And the daughter turned into an owl.

"If you sleep in and hear the cuckoo's first note, bad luck for you and your family.

"Don't ever catch a sparrow and keep it in a cage, or misfortune will fall on all in your house."

The children loved the magical birds. They were quiet, stunned. He told a joke. "If I shot at three birds in a tree, and killed one, how many would remain? No one knows? No one can guess? None: they would all fly away."

The two boys who hated birds laughed, coughing. They had forgotten the birdseed.

After the show, children flocked to the stage, wanting Marvo to sign their tickets or their school books. He winked at Andra, packing up their equipment, and she smiled at him.

"Good show, good show!" the promoter said. He was beaming; he knew he'd signed a winner.

Andra said, "We'll have something amazing for you before too long. Something to do with a fish tank and pure magic."

A young woman came up to Marvo but was too shy to speak.

"Did you enjoy the show? And your children, did they enjoy it?" he said.

"I don't have children. I brought my little brother." It was a boy who had watched entranced.

"I have a puzzle for you," she said.

Three People

There are three people in an office; one is three years older than the next, who is twice as old as the third. How old is the youngest worker? How does this age difference affect work in the office? Where does the youngest person eat lunch whilst the older two are discussing children?

"I can't answer it, but I can solve it," said Marvo. He sent a young co-worker into the office so the young woman was no longer lonely.

The children dispersed as their parents collected them.

One mother was left standing at the door, peering in.

"Show's over, friend. It was a beauty! Sign up for the next one, front row seats, buy now and I promise you that," the promoter said.

"I'm looking for my son. Have all the children come out?"

Andra sucked in her breath. Marvo remembered the third boy, the one who'd disappeared.

"They are all out," he said. "All gone."

Before the next show, a detective came to investigate the disappearance of the child. Marvo said, "There is a woman who is obsessed by me. I gave her time for a while because I felt sorry for her, but then she started to talk about my audience inappropriately so I asked her not to come to my shows anymore. I wish I'd done more. That boy might be safe now if I had. Her name is Doctor Reid. Will you stay for the show?"

The detective watched the magic show and told Marvo a puzzle of his own.

"A wet operation is what the Soviet KGB used to call murder. That's a clue to what the story is about."

A Wet Operation

There were four friends, who grew up together. Alan, Brian, Charlie and Peter.

Alan, Brian and Charlie, while not actually failures, had not had the successes that Peter did. This fact they bemoaned often, at work, in pubs, to anyone who'd listen. They were so well known for their opinion about Peter, that he had taken all the good luck and if he hadn't been around, they would have been the lucky ones, that when he was found murdered (stabbed to death with a dagger, sliced and cut in a ritual, ancient way) the three men were immediately suspected. In fact,

one of them is definitely the guilty party. These are their statements.
Alan:
1. I hadn't seen Peter or had any contact with him for a week before his unfortunate demise
2. Everything that Brian said is true
3. Everything that Charlie said is true
Brian:
1. I have never handled a dagger
2. Everything that Alan said is false
3. Everything that Charlie said is false
Charlie:
1. Alan was talking to Peter just before he was killed
2. Brian has handled a dagger
3. I have for a long time thought more of Peter than is generally realised. I can give you this clue now: Alan and Brian both made the same number of true statements. This number can be anything from zero to three.
Who killed Peter?

"I can figure out who killed Peter, but I don't know where that Doctor Reid is. But find her and you might find the boy. Beyond that I can't help you."

Using the lesson that magic, religion and science can be used as an excuse for terrible events or actions, Marvo solved the puzzle and thus provided the detective with the killer. [†]

† ANSWER:

If A2 is true, then B2 is true, then A2 is false, therefore A2 is false.

If B2 is true, then A and B have not made same number of true statements, therefore B2 false, therefore not everything A said is false, therefore A and B must have made at least one true statement.

If A3 is true, then C2 is true, then B1 is false and B3 is false and A and B have not made the same number of true statements, therefore A3 is false therefore A1 is true.

A must have made at least one true statement, therefore C1 is false.

If B3 is true, then C2 is false, then B1 is true, but this is impossible as A and B must make the same number of true statements, therefore B3 is false, there- fore B1 is true and C2 is false, therefore C3 is true since B3 is false.

But since A1 and B1 are both true, Alan and Brian must be innocent, therefore Charlie killed Peter and his third remark is thus ambiguous. Marvo figures this out because Charlie also claims to be the religious one. He said he goes to church every Sunday, as if that is his alibi for every day of the week.

Marvo settled that magic, pure magic, illusion, mist and tales, was the path he would follow, and relaxed his search for learning. He began to talk to people for other reasons. He wanted to learn about being a person; he did not have that lesson. He began to seek the stories which would teach him how to live. He began to trust Andra to teach him the ways. She had so much to teach him. She was so successful in her work. Her success gave him the direction to seek an answer to one of his questions. He found that understanding something in another's life helped answer the mysteries of his own. He realised that Andra had faced danger in her life and it had given her the desire to live and fight. Andra had faced her dangers in the world, Marvo faced his in the room.

The room of his childhood was built by an ancestor who accepted the world to be a dangerous place. Other magicians had spent their youth or old age in the room. It was a secret room away from the world, protected by spells. Why was food not supplied? Because lessons and dangers must be learnt. Once Marvo and Andra joined each other, they both became powerful.

On the promoter's books there was also a dance troupe. They did beautiful work which held Marvo enraptured. He sought out a member of the chorus, because he felt nervous of the principal dancers. She told him a story.

Dancer

European folk dancers leap high to make crops grow tall. They leap and dance, their heels lifted high, their arms upstretched for greater height.

Only the special ones can dance in this way. Not only the young. There is one old woman who leapt until she was eighty-six, until she had lived twenty years longer than the oldest man. She leapt, the highest leap anyone had seen, then she sank into the mud and did not rise again.

That year the crops grew so high, travellers came to see. They rested overnight, paying for the privilege with trade. Some would pay with a tale, or a recipe using scraps.

Some stayed, wanting to enjoy the boom period. They brought skills of farming and language, and they settled and joined and gave children to the place.

The old woman was buried in the mud where she fell. In the years to come, through boom and bust, always on that patch of ground was wheat, tall and healthy.

People would take husks of that wheat and keep them as good luck charms.

Dancers would come for strength and empowerment.

With this story of an ancient ancestor, he learnt that while old age is weak, very old age is powerful magic. It was better to die young than middle-aged. It was best to die very, very old.

Marvo gave the dancer light feet and the ability to fly. By so doing, he lost someone he could talk to, because the dancer's talent became overwhelming and she moved to a bigger city, to a life which didn't include Marvo. He tried to win her over by talking about the world's most amazing trick, something Andra was creating. The fish tank, she called it.

The dancer wasn't interested.

Marvo and Andra went to the memorial service for the boy who had vanished during their show. It was unfair; the kid would have hated it. There were flowers everywhere, and all white, so everyone knew he was a virgin. Marvo spoke to a lady at the church who guessed he was the magician. She said that she listened to his voice, and got the clue that way. She told him about her first memory.

The Sound of Your Voice

My first memory is aural. I was born as the clock chimed twelve and I remember all twelve bells. The moon was full the night I was born. I feel sometimes I was born counting; sometimes I start counting to twelve without thinking.

My sense of hearing is very fine. Many people have a sense of smell which excites memory. They smell a flower and think of a certain flower bed. I hear the sound of a flower being picked and I think of being in the garden with my mother as she wandered through, plucking and smelling flowers. I can remember a sense of well-being, though this was my first clairvoyant experience. I followed my mother around, the well-being strong, but I also saw flowers atop her still body.

"Why will you lie down? Why will you hold the flowers?" I said. She laughed. I was only five or so, and my mother loved to laugh. She laughed at the silly things I'd say, though they weren't silly to me. I questioned and guessed at answers, like any five year-old. The sound of my mother's laugh; I hear it occasionally, on trains or at parties, and

I turn to find her, but it's never her. It's always a beautiful woman, laughing at some puppy companion. In that split second though, when I hear the laugh, I forget my mother is dead. She died before those flowers she picked wilted in their glass; a sudden and shocking attack of asthma.[†]

I did not witness her death; I was out playing house in the cellar across the road. We only emerged because my friends' brother came down to show us a dead bird.

"Better watch out, girls," he said. He was much older, and cruel. He loved to scare us.

"Someone's gonna die real soon. It flew against the kitchen window and flopped down dead. One of you is going to get it."

Only years later, when I had learnt about guilt and regret, did I wonder how he must have felt about my mother, about predicting her death. Perhaps he was born on a chime hour too, like I was. A seer.

People tried to make me feel bad. "If you'd been here, you could have called for help," they said. But what happened was inevitable. If I had saved her then, she would have been killed some other way.

Marvo had an affair with the lady, unbeknownst to Andra. It was not a sexual affair. He gave her a week of his time. At the end of seven days, they bought fish and chips and sat on the beach to eat them. Marvo loved the feel of sand. He had not felt contrasting textures in the room of his childhood; he never tired of touching rough surfaces.

"The best way to keep your man faithful is to keep a fish in your vagina till it dies. Then you should feed it to your man. He'll never leave you, that way," he told her. Marvo smiled at her and kissed her fingers with regret. He knew people would believe what they want to believe, and she would like to believe she lost him because of her lack of magic. He left her on the beach to think about her future, and he decided he would not give time as a reward again.

Marvo became adept at looking beyond the image. He was blind when he entered a room with Andra—it was a party to celebrate the end of the theatre week. The cast and crew were there.

"I know what it's like to be alone," said one young woman. "The most alone you can be is not to have any parents. Both my parents were dead by the time I was born."

---

† This condition has been called asthma since the time of Hippocrates (460-375 BCE). "Asthma" is a Greek term used by Homer to mean gasping, painful breathing.

The others in the room exchanged glances. She was young and she was drunk. She was not worth listening to. If she felt these old people would take the place of her parents, her hurt would be great.

Marvo moved closer to her voice. "What do you mean?" he said. "How is that possible?"

"I'm not from around here," she said. She took his hand. Her eyes were watery. She was truly drunk. Marvo was blind but he could hear the tears splashing in her eyes. "I can't even visit their graves, because a football stadium has been built over them."

"So soon?" said Marvo. He had no reason to disbelieve her tale. People rarely lie when drunk. "You're so young—did they build the stadium so quickly?"

Born Alone

My parents died over a hundred years ago. My father believed the world could only improve. So he preserved an egg furnished by my mother and fertilised by him, and he established a foundation for my birth when the technology appeared. People thought he was insane, just as they think Walt Disney is insane, expecting to be woken up and cured.

When I was born, my parents were long dead. All that remained was the thesis he left to me in his will, and a large amount of money, growing over many decades.

Marvo nodded and wondered if, with such a remarkably resilient and lonely birth, the woman was a magician. But there was no sign. No truth. Marvo gave her a clever disguise. He changed her gait and her voice, he dimmed the intensity in the woman's eyes. He left the mist around her ears, to soften the features and steer her safely through life.

He pretended to be the blind man. He closed his eyes and saw pale blue eyes, a crossroad. The vision calmed him, made him feel less responsible. He was truly blind, but he knew the people stared at him. He caught the bus without any difficulty, and knew when his stop was. He let people help him, hold his elbow, but he did not need their help. He always sat in the seat that faced the rest of the passengers, the one sighted people hated because everyone looked at them. He was used to it.

Marvo did not really enjoy being the blind man but it was necessary. He had to remember the blackness, the not-seeing, in order to drop the mist. It was very important. It was good to be blind sometimes.

There was a blind pensioner who could tell if a woman was a virgin by a touch of her hands and nails, their odour. He was not tricked by wedding rings—he always got it right.

The pensioner had a hand fetish. He could never touch enough soft hands; and a virgin's hands were always soft. No matter how old the woman was. Something about sex turned a woman's hands hard.

Marvo's magic wand could stretch or shrink, depending. When he was blind it became a walking stick. If he was nervous it became a placebo cigarette that did not burn. It was always white, though.

It could be pointed like a stake. He had played a trick on a man once, as a favour to the man's ex-wife. Followed him silently as he walked the beach. Was he thinking of his angry ex-wife or of his quiet, beautiful lover? Marvo walked besides the man's footprints, pressing his walking stick deep into the reverse arch of the indentation. It was a good trick; the man was crippled in an accident later on. But it was a very good story too. The woman had told him a good story and he had decided to play this trick for her.

They Came at Night

They came at night and marked time on the outskirts of the city. Their presence was felt.

"The men are here. The men!" The city's people had been prepared, but not for such an onslaught. Women are not as violent as men, so the citizens were not ready to kill and maim. They would, though. Anything was worth it to keep their city of women alive, unsullied.

We ate chocolate by the handful, all of us craving the sweetness.

The children were hidden underground. The women made themselves ugly, splashed animal blood on their faces, shit and piss and vomit on their bodies. They made themselves unattractive.

The men moved in. It was a pride lust that motivated them. But the women had more to fight for, and they won. Once more their walls were safe. They could never look each other in the eye again. The things they had done. They slit throats and broke necks, they strangled the skinny ones. All of that was necessary. But they tore off the men's clothes, too. The whimpering men. And they anally raped them, with long sharp anythings. The children jumped on the men's stomachs with spiked heels. They were cruel, vicious, bloodthirsty. They moved away one by one and the history was forgotten. Word was spread that a disease had killed the enemy men, a cruel, vicious, bloodthirsty disease.

"The importance of the city should never be disregarded," Marvo said. "Its existence is as necessary as the farms, the grassland, the sea. New York was the first city to be powered by electricity, and it hasn't slept since."

The woman listened; she loved someone to talk to her.

"It's good to listen," Marvo told her. "A story my grandmother told me was about another lady who listened, a relative from long ago."

The Maidservant

Her only mistake was to talk out loud. She was a low servant in the rich man's home and she had caught his son's eye more than once, but no interest had flared. She wanted to learn—as a woman her only chance at education was second hand, to absorb it from a male. The son went to the Lyceum and he spoke at meals of his learning.

She wanted to marry him, to gain his knowledge. In her room, she prayed aloud to the gods for advancement, for the chance to make the son take her.

The high servant heard and reported her. She was punished for her vanity, for believing she was good enough for the rich man's son.

They marked her face to take away any attractiveness she may have had; thereon she wore a veil.

It worked for her. She became less than visible, and could sit in the classes, or clean slowly where men talked of learning and she took her education that way.

She listened all her life.

The woman, discarded by her husband as not attractive enough, said, "Thank you for the story, and for helping me with my ex-husband. He was always sure he had the power in the relationship because he's handsome and I'm ugly."

"I think you're beautiful. I love your ears."

"The things he used to say to me. He said no one would ever fall in love with me."

"You should be kind, because kindness can sometimes be ignored, misunderstood or rejected, but it can also be returned twofold. You have great love, great depth, your looks will not concern the person who falls in love with you. Your looks will make him love you."

She began a lecture circuit and talked about the beauty of a misty morning. This was good for Marvo because he wanted people to love the mist.

Marvo was considered a character, even amongst the characters of the theatre. He was always talking, listening or reading; you could catch him with the Bible or *Gray's Anatomy*. He didn't seem to make a distinction.

He studied science from a religious point of view, and religion from a scientific point of view. Magic he had; he could always turn to magic. Magic was with him always.

On one memorable occasion, he spoke with a preacher on the street, a man with a new religion he was bringing to the people. Marvo, having heard this, said, "Do you realise that at the time of Valentinian, Christianity was the new religion, the sect? Conversion of heathen English to Christianity did not begin till 597, when the Roman missionary Augustine landed in Kent.

"Magic was the respected, accepted religion. I often wonder what made the sect of Christianity grow. Perhaps because it was the first new religion to emerge for thousands of years, and people were looking for something new. No new religion has taken over so well. The Moonies are big, as are the Scientologists. Is it possible that these will be bigger than Christianity in a few hundred years, remembering that they are only decades old?"

The man took strength from these words. He felt patient; he could wait three hundred years for his truth to be accepted. What's three hundred years as part of eternity? Marvo left the man feeling happy. The man's literature was dull and answered none of Marvo's questions. Marvo wanted more; he wanted to listen to stories until his ears bled. He wanted to know his future.

Marvo's dream of the future, of the enormous house where all were welcome, didn't fade. It made him feel so powerful, so much in control, he wanted to know more, he wanted to know it all. His note told him *You will know all with great sacrifice.* Marvo had no concept of sacrifice. He took what was needed, was always comfortable, never sad. He became fascinated with all forms of sacrifice and gathered stories and information about the art. He found that in the ninth century, the Scandinavian pirate, Ragnar Hairy-Breeches, with one hundred and ten crewmen, sailed up the Seine and sacked Paris. He sacrificed one hundred prisoners to a Norse god to discourage Frankish counterattack (one would imagine the god did not need to intervene).

It was around the thirteenth century that agriculture and religion with human sacrifice developed. As agriculture developed, so did religion, because people had time to think, and not everyone was needed in the fields, not everyone was needed to keep the clans alive, so some could spend time with learning and thinking.

In 1803, Sir Arthur Wellesley forbade the sacrifice of children on Saugon Island.

In 97 BCE human sacrifice was forbidden by the Senate. Marvo wondered what greatness was lost with these endings.

Aztec sacrifice was of course very interesting. His reading helped him to understand that the Aztecs didn't FEEL barbaric in their rites, and would be surprised to find their descendants were shocked.

A female was sacrificed, her skin worn by the priest to assume the identity of the Earth Mother, Teteoinnan. Andra could tell him this was one of many examples; transfer of soul by contact with flesh and blood.

The Aztec year was eighteen periods of twenty days, many coinciding with seasons, marked by rituals and ceremonies.

In February, children were sacrificed to the god of rain to ward off drought.

The blood of the children was kneaded into maize dough and formed into Huitzilpochtli. Their little hearts were given to the king, the rest of the sweet flesh divided between nobles.

Totes, the moon god, required the sacrifice of a prisoner of war—the bravest caught. This was before sowing the first seed. The prisoner was spread-eagled on a frame of timber, then shot with arrows till he bled. If he bled well and didn't die, his heart was ripped out, his skin flayed and worn by a priest as the Earth Mother in new clothes—a new maize crop. They wore maize ears and leapt about, while the flesh of the sacrifice was given to the warriors who caught the prisoner.

Obsidian, volcanic rock, dark and sharpened to razor edge, was used to cut out the heart.

The skin of the man, when worn, passed the soul on.

Marvo took many notes.

Greatest festival of the year:

Toxcatl, on April 23rd, sun at its zenith.

The victim was groomed for a year, housed in a temple, treated liked a god.

Three weeks before Toxcatl, four young lovely brides attended him:

1. The goddess of flowers
2. The goddess of young corn
3. The goddess of our-mother-among-the-water
4. The goddess of salt

The sacrifice spent three weeks in a state of continuous sexual activity.

He was killed (heart ripped out) as soon as his shadow reached the sacrificial temple, and the successor was taken straight to the home temple.

Marvo visited a museum and came home with a piece of obsidian. He wondered at the sexuality of sacrifice, imagined a naked body painted with blood.

The Pawnee Indians made April the 22nd and 23rd important as well.

A teenaged girl was conducted from wigwam to wigwam in a procession led by chiefs and warriors. Each wigwam would give her a gift. After a few days, when she reached the last wigwam, she was painted black and red. Then she was placed over an open fire and roasted to death, while tribesman shot arrows and spilt her blood. At the right moment, the chief sacrificed her by tearing out her heart and eating it. The body was cut up, taken out into the maize fields and squeezed slowly to drip the warm blood into the newly planted grain. This revitalised the grain.

Fijian chiefs used to have a meal of human flesh when they wanted a haircut.

Once he felt he knew enough, that he knew what sacrifice meant, Marvo sought the perfect subject. He knew that the sacrifice would occur in his own way, that he was not a killer and that he hated the sight of blood.

Andra held small meetings for women of her circle; help meetings. They enjoyed these meetings and she did not charge; they talked about their experiences with other women and sometimes with men. Marvo sat in sometimes. He told the women his name was Dr Mee. They never questioned what sort of doctor he was; if they had, he would have confessed the DR stood for Don't Resist.

Marvo didn't need to draw the mist in order to disappear in that room, sit and listen without them knowing. The more they talked, the more they forgot he was there. He could observe and take it all in. They told stories men don't usually hear. The naïve woman who thought she should understand more but not become a cynic, whose voice broke when she was nervous, told a story.

The Girl Across the Street

One time we sat on the trampoline, the girl from across the road, her friend from interstate and me. I was in grade four; they were in grade six. The friend started telling me stories about how the boys liked her and why. She said they respected her, opened the door for her. She put a star on her calendar, the one she had hanging on her bedroom door, every time she had sex. She had sex! She knew what it was like! Impossible! The girl across the road giggled; I asked questions. "What's it like? What do you do?" I believed everything she said. The more powerful my belief, the more ridiculous her stories—she said you could cut a muscle out of your bum without anaesthetic. I asked why and she said, "Because I can." The magic was that I believed every word, every story. She told me not to tell—as if I would! As if I would weaken the magic by telling the secret.

As we sat there on the trampoline, we would take it in turns to sit folded on the backs of our legs and bounce the others gently, *squeak SQUEAK, squeak SQUEAK.*

I had a sharp vision as we sat there, *squeak SQUEAK*. I saw that girl as a woman, old, and she was still seeking respect from men by having sex with them. The *squeak SQUEAK* came from her bed, the rhythm boring, boring her as she lay there waiting for him to drop exhausted onto her chest and tell her how much he loves her. It was vision born of jealousy, I suspect.

"**N**ot only the wise can sense the future," Andra said. "You have taken her life in the direction you expect it to go; very reasonably."

Marvo showed her that her belief in magic was soundly founded; he gave her an hour as a fly on the wall in that woman's bedroom. Her correct foretelling gave her confidence to continue; Andra had felt ugly, alone and stupid, unworthy of life. Now she could realise her potential, because she believed in herself and magic.

It was a great gift for Marvo to give for such a mediocre story, but he was feeling benevolent. He had found his sacrifice. A young girl, almost silent, sat amongst the older women. She listened to their every word, her innocence, her high expectations very obvious. "Our little star," the others called her. "You wait. She'll be famous."

She said, "I know another story, a bit like that." Her lips were always blue, she said, but she didn't think it was her heart.

The Squeak Squeak

I am blinded by mist; or I am blind. I walk alone, my feet taptap on the road. There is no footpath. I think my thoughts, peaceful, think of being home. Squeak SQUEAK. Squeak SQUEAK. *Behind me, rhythmically.* Like someone without imagination jumping on a rusted trampoline or two people without imagination making love on a rusty spring bed. *Squeak SQUEAK. Squeak SQUEAK.* The noise approaches; it is louder. I can't turn to look—What if it's chasing me? The noise is louder. I walk faster. The squeaking quickens. Squeak SQUEAK. Squeak SQUEAK. Squeak SQUEAK, *the rhythm faster now. Then louder; it passes me; then it stops. The noise has stopped ahead of me. I cannot see. I am blinded.* Three steps ahead is a bicycle—an old bicycle. Set on its stand. No rider. I heard no running footsteps. I don't understand.

"**W**hen did this happen?" asked one of the other women.

"It happens to me almost every day," said the girl. She was talking of the mist.

Marvo emerged from his camouflage to say, "Your story ends in this way: You walk up to the bike, standing alone on the road. You take the handlebars in your hands, your palms resting sweetly against the soft rubber. The machine hums, hums music you remember from your childhood. You climb onto the bike, straddle it, and the seat nestles into you like a lover, like the lover you have dreamed of. You lift your feet onto the pedals and the bike takes you."

"Where?" whispered the girl. The room was quiet, all imagining their own bikes, their own lovers. Marvo could tell the girl was right for him. She could see the mist but didn't understand what it was there for. That meant she could help him see the future without understanding why. She would help him.

He whispered in her ear, "Come with me. I've transformed the cellar into a greenhouse full of orchids. Would you like to see it?"

She shook her head.

"It's a library full of rare books. Children's books. It's a library full of cookbooks."

"I think I should stay with my friends," she whispered back. The other women in the room talked amongst themselves but watched carefully.

"Don't you trust me? But I can heal you. In the cellar is a pharmacy established by my great-grandmother. She studied under Edward Bach, the founder of Bach flower remedies."

He held out his hand and led the girl from the room. He did not look at Andra but he could see her; she was jealous. She did not want to be the sacrifice but she envied the one chosen.

The girl said, "I saw one of your shows. You and Andra. I don't know how you did your tricks."

"I can show you. In the cellar I have all my tricks laid out for rehearsal. Don't be greedy, though. You can pick just one."

He had to get her into the cellar. It was the only place with a lock. He didn't want Andra walking in. And the cellar was dark. He remembered a cellar he'd entered when he first left the room, full of champagne and a clutching woman. He remembered the sense of surrender he'd felt; of weakness.

He understood that Andra's feelings would be sacrificed, but that was all to the good. He would buy her a gift or steal one and show her the love she liked to see.

They entered the cellar and he locked the door behind them. He drew the mist to give the girl a sense of euphoria and anticipation.

"There is magic here; tricks," the girl said. "I know because I blink and things change. I feel like I can see germs in the air. It's damp. What if I catch something?"

He said, "You can't catch magic. You can learn parts of it, you are born with some. Magic is not contagious, though its element is contagion. Some things can influence you long after you have stopped touching them. Some things will never stop touching you, even when they are long forgotten." His voice was so quiet it gave her comfort.

Marvo touched her, tasted her, saw her. He said, "I give you seven senses. Flowers for hearing." He handed her a rose. "The West Wind gives you the sense of smell," and it came wafting over, a pleasant zephyr which made her dream of spring, walking to school on a spring day and it was only a half day at school so she would be home soon. "Fire for animation, for life." About her, flames. "Earth, for touch." She could smell it, too, the under-the-house smell, making her think of childhood, hiding under the house to escape punishment, that deep earth smell meaning safety. "With water, I give you speech," and the flames were doused, the dryness of her throat soothed. "The air gives you taste." She opened her mouth to breath and she could taste hot peppermints, then pizza, then red wine. She became fearful. "And the mist for sight." The mist rose all about her; she watched pictures against its clouds.

He kissed her so beautifully she cried. She believed in him, and that was enough. He added two years to their friendship of three hours.

Marvo had learnt that a kiss is true seduction—a true and passionate kiss. He enjoyed a kiss, enjoyed its plunging headiness and the swooning feel after a really good one. He practised a lot with Andra.

"I love you," he said, his hands hard on the girl's shoulders. This she believed. Wanted to believe.

Marvo remembered the sacrifices another man had made to be a father. That he had sacrificed his child's future to see his own. He had shaken and shaken his daughter until his future was clear.

Marvo kept his hands on her shoulders and gave a shake. She gasped. He shook harder and she didn't resist, so he shook her so hard he felt the bones move under her jelly-like flesh. He shook her till she was a blur, till blood spattered onto his cheek.

She was bleeding from the mouth.

"Andra," he called, but she was locked out and he didn't want to draw attention to himself by going upstairs.

He placed the girl on a pile of blankets in the corner. She shivered. He had seen this on TV a number of times: he showed her the beautiful life she could have had. He helped her live it; she lived it. Then he let the mist drop again and she felt the pain of her neck injury, the softness inside her head. He knew it was done, then. He had taken her fame, her possibilities.

The sacrifice complete, Marvo stood, arms and legs in a star, head tilted to the ceiling, eyes rolled white. She watched him for an hour. He didn't move and neither did she.

He saw: great death, terrible sudden death, then slow and painful death. He saw fear, he saw hopelessness and destruction.

He saw suicide and voluntary sterility. He saw a blackness, a deep velvet blackness which he knew was the extinction of humanity.

He saw how it would happen, why the mist would drop, disappear. He saw answers for why he was in the room. He lived in the big house because his grandmother thought he would be best protected there. It was a house built by her ancestor, lost, then taken over by the quiet religious people who had died there. There was a magic story, once fact, about the house and its ability to protect. It was a feat, to build that house.

He saw his own future: black. His own future was dark. Eyes rolled that way, Marvo saw his own death.

He was performing before a small audience of children. He was presenting them with white doves and silk scarves—soon he would ask a child to come on stage for the trick where he plays cards. Andra breathed calmly beside him. He knew her skills. She followed him in whatever he did. Then the auditorium went dark, and, spotlit, stood a man with an odd beard and a loose coat.

The man reached into his pocket and removed a gun. He shot, and Marvo collapsed. The beard fell off, the odd disguise.

When Marvo woke from his trance, he knew the face of his killer. He recognised her as the woman cruel to Andra. The woman vanquished. Doctor Reid, Doctor Marcia Reid. If he could find her first, destroy her, then he would not die.

He felt his way around the cellar, enjoying the rough bumps of the walls.

Andra sat at the kitchen table with the last of the women.

"Aren't you jealous? How do you let him do that? She's so beautiful. And listen to them. I've never heard anything like it."

"He is his own man," Andra said.

"You can talk to me," the woman said. "You seem like you have a lot pent up. Tell me. You're always helping others. Let me help you. If you're unhappy, leave him. It's simple. Women will look after you."

Andra smiled. "He's the perfect man, but he needs his freedom."

The woman snorted. "He's got the wool pulled over your eyes."

The girl stumbled up the stairs, her eyes blind, her smell fearful.

"What is it?" asked Andra. "What happened?"

Hearing no sympathy in Andra's voice, the girl leaned against the wall. Andra did not help her; she did not give her the stag heart bone.[†]

"I'll take her home. Let you know what happens," the other woman said. She kissed Andra on the cheek.

Andra stared after the two of them, the girl like a puppet.

Andra waited for Marvo to walk up the stairs, describe the silly girl, make Andra laugh. He didn't appear. The door was locked.

Andra wanted to know what he had seen down in the cellar.

"Only a dream," he said. "Only with you am I real." But still he did not tell her the story of his birth, or of his dream. He did not tell her how he saw through his own mist; his mist did not reach into the future. He suffered a leaden feeling of mortality and saw that the magic of the present is only the trivia of the past, misunderstood.

He saw his line of descendants. He saw: a tall, thin man, all ribs and kneecaps, rubbing raw meat in dark grey ashes. Those ashes were old, Marvo knew. A hundred years at least. Fire didn't burn anymore. He saw his descendants cold and hungry.

"I'll tell what I didn't see," Marvo said. "I didn't see me performing ever again. Tell that man we can't do it anymore."

"Marvo!"

Marvo thought that by avoiding performances he could avoid death.

"Tell him."

"We have a contract. We'll lose a fortune."

"There are plenty of ways to make money," he said. "I can count cards, you know. That's only one way. I can cheat at cards."

The promoter knew what a treasure he had in Marvo.

"When you're ready, come back to me," he said. "You go somewhere else and we'll see trouble. You come here and I'll wait a decade for you. Hopefully not that long!"

---

† Found in a stag shot by a hunter and shaped like a cross, this can be used as a remedy for heart troubles, physical and emotional. It can also prevent abortion, and Andra wanted none of that. If she wasn't to have a child, she could care for another's. She would watch over it like a kindly auntie and never let harm come to it.

Marvo began a harder search for people's stories, for their histories. It made it easier to chase Doctor Reid, to figure the way she would run. How she would chase.

Marvo now had two missions. To find Doctor Reid and perhaps stop his own death, and to create the mist for the people, to keep them happy. He realised he could solve both in one; he needed to find a way to make the mist as thick as it had ever been.

He saw terrible darkness and knew it was his future, his life after death. He knew it was the afterlife of all on earth, all sentient beings. His grandmother had spoken to him of this place as she neared death. He wanted to know what he could do, whether his blood would help, whether he could keep her with him alive forever.

"Eternal life brings loss of all feeling. Like the fairy story of the girl who was happy to walk with knives in her feet in order to be living on land, not sea, seekers of eternal life have to accept that they will be numb to love, hate, fear and elation. They will taste food but not love the taste. They will not be able to get drunk. They will have sex but not enjoy it," she told him. "I don't want that."

This numbness Marvo saw when he glimpsed the future.

He would not tell Andra what he saw or what he planned to do. She had taught him so much he knew his plan was faulty. He didn't want her to tear it to pieces for him. He could imagine her words. "But how will you save the world? By pretending that nothing is happening? By giving them a shock, something to gossip about, some entrancing story to help them forget, some amazing prize?" There was no point telling Andra.

Marvo did not lose confidence that what he was doing was correct. He did not consider for a minute trying to stop the danger, work towards solving the problem which would lead to war. He felt his way was best. Blind to truth, the people would be happy until the day they died, and they would not give up. They would procreate and live on.

Marvo was angered by the truth he saw. He blamed the girl, for being the sacrifice, and Andra gladly agreed. The girl was not so innocent, said Andra.

"She must have been or I wouldn't have seen the future," said Marvo.

He created the illusion that the encounter was desperately unhappy. With sleight of hand, he distracted Andra from seeing his flushed face, red cheeks, his short breath.

He flashed a storm—lightning and thunder to terrify the strongest of heart.

"Don't you know what's real and what's illusion?" he said.

Andra nodded and smiled and his little trick had worked.

He was dangerous when he was unhappy. He could easily take his mist and go away. There were many kinds of mist, though.

Marvo drew his own mist. He sometimes used alcohol as the agent.

The mist covered, enveloped, acted as a barrier.

He could drop it at will, drop the mist to cover his departure. The mist might drop for many years, or for seconds only. It could help the dreaming; it stood as a wall between an unbearable fact and a person. The mist could be very welcome.

The mist could cover half the world, leaving the other free to see; during war, this was often the case. War was a time of great illusion, great unseeing. People were blinded to murder, its name changed. They forgot how much they hated their brother and began to hate the man over the barrier as evil.

Some truth will always come through; a massacre in a public place in China, the death of a famous son or daughter.

The magic existed regardless. The mist was only cleared for terrible moments, when there were spates of child killings, as parents suddenly saw clearly the world they had brought their children into. Tsar Ivan IV killed his heir in 1581, on a day when the mist was low. There were spates of suicides. Many were quietly buried—by the time the news reached the people the mist had dropped again, reality was forgotten and truth was a fog.[†]

---

† Iron is the metal dedicated to Mars, the god of war (a Mars a day). Iron is the metal of nails and horseshoes; it is also the metal of death. The war horse is an enemy of Saturn (god of fertility and planting), because in war there is no time for babies or crops.

Therefore war is against fertility and planting. (Thus mythology is explaining the

While Marvo was seeking stories to understand his life, and hunting Doctor Reid, he let his work slip. The mist was thin in some places; nonexistent in others. When the mist dropped, the world saw things, like a day of terrorism, bombs in one nation, shooting sprees in another, fires elsewhere. Observers assessed conspiracies; how else could so much happen in one day, at one time? There was no conspiracy. These things happened every day. The world did not see them. Marvo was not the first in his line to forget his work; suicides are many. So many. [†]

The true magician, Betta, came to see him, disguised as a census taker. She said, "You know that suicides have tripled. You are being lazy."

"Not lazy. I've seen the end of the world. I need to know how to make the mist strong enough so they don't suffer."

"We can all help you," Betta said. "But you still need to keep the mist."

"How can you help?" Marvo said.

"We can help with the mist. All of us vigilant."

"How can you stop me from being killed, though?"

"That won't be a problem. Surely you see that by seeing it you circumvent it?"

"I don't think so," he said. "I don't believe that."

"This is not the worst time in history, Marvo. We have survived more; we have helped the human race survive more."

Andra brought a cup of tea to Marvo where they sat in the lounge room. Nothing for Betta.

"It is time for me to go. I am not here to hurt your man, Andra. I am here to help him. I won't take him from you unless I have to," Betta said.

Andra walked to the front door and held it open. "You don't need to see us again," she said.

Marvo sat holding her hand. "I'm losing you," she said. "You are slipping away to the big picture and I am just a detail to be forgotten."

"You're the only person keeping me alive, Andra. You should know

---

world. Mars is stronger because the lust for power and death is stronger than the desire for offspring and lush fields.) Saturn (early tradition) ruled witches (Andra's paganism—witches and the land and fertility are closely attuned) so iron instruments of any kind were used to keep witches away.

The goddess of war, Bellona, has a very terrifying visage, made of iron.

† See Appendix C.

that without being told. You have to help me, though. My work is slipping. People are dying. The suicide rates are higher than they have ever been. Help me to stay focused. I don't want to be the first failed magician."

"You're far from the first. And suicide isn't always bad, you know. Sometimes it helps."

The Boy Fits

In other days, the dried brains of suicides were considered an infallible remedy for epilepsy.

There was one man whose only son suffered terribly. It was unbearable to watch, the damage that was done. Each fit made the man die a little.

Finally, he followed the instructions of a witch he met. His wife was away or else she would have stopped him.

The witch told him he needed to unbury a suicide and take his brain. The brain should then be dried on a hot iron plate and burned and the ashes given to the sufferer.

There were no suicides the man knew of so he decided to create one. There was a young man in the suburb who caused nothing but heartache to everybody. He hurt animals, pushed little children off their bikes, made his mother cry.

The man went to see him and used words of such persuasion, provided such an opportunity, that the young man committed suicide.

The cure worked: once the son had eaten the ashes, he did not have a fit again. People all round wanted to get some of the cure.

While the man did not confess in public what he had done, word got out. Suicides were encouraged, then, and the family rewarded. It was considered a brave thing to do.

"That's a good story, Andra. Perhaps I should find people who are happy to suicide, who would have done it anyway. Perhaps that will make me feel better."

It didn't, though. Marvo couldn't help but save them. He performed magic for a cowardly man who hated the sight of a world without mist.

He was perched on the top of a bridge, rocking back and forward to take the pressure off, so if he fell he could think "It's not my fault, I fell."

The man clutched a large stone in his hand.

"Where is that stone from? What is it?" Marvo asked.

"This is a toadstone, to help protect me from witchcraft."

"You are scared of all witches?" asked Marvo.

"Yes." The man tucked his hands into his armpits, so he was not tempted to hold on.

"Scared of witches but not scared of dying? What is it?" said Marvo. "What's so bad?" It was a cold night and his breath hissed and fogged.

The mist should stop people from committing suicide. This was Marvo's tradition.

The man said, "I'm dying anyway, I'm in a bad way. The doctor said it was two months at most."

"Doctors are very fallible. They only interpret facts; there is nothing incontrovertible. Perhaps if you tried another doctor, the verdict would be different."

The mist drifted under the man's nose. He climbed off the bridge, leaving his toadstone on the railing, and walked away. He didn't see Marvo; didn't look back.

The man, though Marvo was not affected in any way by the information, lived for many years. He became a bus driver, taking the job in a good interview from a man who, if allowed to drive the bus, would have driven drunk and killed fourteen people.

Marvo wondered about the toadstone and found out all he could about it. He knew Andra would love such a stone, and he wanted to keep the man's stone for himself.[†]

---

† The toadstone protects against witchcraft and poison. Place the toadstone near a liquid containing poison, or onto a bewitched person, and it will sweat and change colour.

Toadstones are varied in colour, from dark grey to light brown.

They are sometimes set in silver and worn as a ring, handed down from one family member to the next.

They are found in the heads of very old toads – removed when they are dying.

But some are artificially made of fused borax or other materials.

Others are fossilised teeth of the ray.

Virtues derived from the toad itself; the toad is used as a remedy for many things such as plague or smallpox.

The toadstone, powdered, can be swallowed as a remedy for fever or the bites of venomous reptiles. While reading about toads, Marvo heard about the Surinam toad, from South America. This creature has small eyes, no tongue or teeth. At the time of breeding, the female's skin grows thick and spongy.

As the male and female turn over in the water, she lays the eggs, and they sink into the skin on her back. They pass the tadpole stage in her back, and emerge from the

Marvo became very excited about stones and their properties. He looked for distractions; he couldn't think of how to make the mist thick enough. He needed a break from the future. He studied stones, to decide which he would like. This led him to reading about jewel theft. It sounded exciting to him; a challenge. He had no problem with theft. He had always picked up small objects and kept them, but grand scale jewel theft was different. It needed real magic.

The stones seemed magic to him because such beauty dug from the dark earth can only be so.

Marvo walked into the jewellery store as a young woman and her older lover. If it was a cliché, he wasn't aware of it.

"I want to see rings," Marvoshe said.

"No, we'll have them set once we've chosen the stone," said Marvohe, a man who had made his money by not wasting it. "We'll see your best stones—a selection."

The jeweller, used to wealthy and demanding customers, was unhurried in his response. He brought out his best; he was not one to play games.

"Would madam like to see some jewellery while sir is looking at the stones?" said the jeweller.

"No, madam wouldn't," said Marvohe. "She's got lessons to learn, like you and me."

The jeweller sniffed, saying with that sniff, "I have nothing left to learn, particularly from your kind."

That sniff took away any doubts Marvo had about making the man a victim. He did have a lesson to learn; that he could be wrong in his immediate character assessments.

Once all the stones were on the bench, Marvo turned into a large emu, and ate the stones. Then he turned into a wisp of smoke and disappeared under the door, with the jeweller's stock of precious stones.

Then he ran home, running for the pure joy of it.

"I don't believe in magic," the jeweller would later tell police, "but they turned into an emu and ate the stones, then turned into smoke and disappeared under the door. I never expected those two to do anything like that."

Marvo was not aware of the consequences of his act. Andra was so happy with his gifts she did not ask where they came from. But he

---

skin when they are two and a half months old. The story made his skin itch; every centimetre. Even the skin on his feet, which Andra rubbed with a pumice stone for him.

did not know the jeweller was arrested as the thief (he did not own the shop) and, for want of any other suspects or any evidence or an emu escaping from the zoo, he was found guilty and imprisoned. In jail, he polished peach pits and sold them as precious stones.

Marvo spoke to Andra, as he laid the jewels around her naked body. "In India, if you bathe while wearing a turquoise, the water it touches protects you from boils. Copper is a sacred metal to the Hindus and copper rings are worn to ward of the devil who gives you sciatica. Coppers in uniform don't ward off any devils. A diamond will endow its wearer with courage, making them more fearless than careful.

"The jacinth strengthens the heart and is often worn near there.

"The sapphire sharpens intellect and prevents bites from venomous animals.

"An emerald will prevent giddiness and strengthens memory.

"The amethyst promotes sobriety; the wearer is caused to abstain from strong drinks and from sleeping too much.

"Chrysolite wards off fevers.

"Onyx prevents attacks of epilepsy.[†]

"The opal will cure weak eyes.

"Topaz cures inflammation and keeps the wearer from sleepwalking.

"Lapis lazuli brings fortune and riches.

"Bloodstone should be taken to war; when applied to a wound it stops the bleeding."

Andra was aware of the love Marvo had for her. So many jewels. She had never asked him where he went, what he learnt, although she ached with wanting to know.

He stared at her, watched her naked body with its glittering jewels, and he smiled.

"You're so beautiful. My heart aches when I'm not with you."

Andra was silent. She would not ask him why he left her so often, off on his missions; she didn't want to hear what he would say. So she asked, instead, what he had learnt.

"I've been thinking about suicide," he said. She clutched his hand, her fingernails bending back, weaker than his flesh.

"There are those times when people feel they have to die. When they see things very clearly."

Andra kissed his eyes, hoping to blur their vision. Marvo had no idea she thought he might be talking about himself. He said, "And

---

† There seem to be so many remedies against epilepsy, one of the most feared diseases. Did they think the sufferer open to the devil during the attacks, more vulnerable somehow?

there are those who want to take others with them.

"The mist is very weak then. Very weak. These are the times I fail, or the others failed."

On his journey, Marvo discovered that suicide invited customs as restrictive and superstitious as many other items of the universe.

In Athens, they would cut off the hand of a suicide, because a one-handed ghost will not do harm.

In medieval Metz, the suicide was put in a barrel and floated down the Moselle.

In one part of East Africa, a goat is substituted and hung up in the same noose, then cut down and killed as a sacrifice.

Andra was no longer listening. She massaged his feet to make him stop talking, massaged his thighs. She practised magic, thinking to distract him. Anything to shut him up, to clear that envy from his voice.

"I've seen the future, Andra. My mist doesn't reach there. It felt like my eyes had been rinsed with rose water. I could see every line on my hands. I could smell it all, too."

Then he was quiet, his eyes closed.

"What are you thinking?" Andra asked, hating herself for the intrusion.

"I'm thinking about finding more stories," he said, and he shut her off like a guillotine.

Marvo learnt to respect all people, so when he entered the restaurant near the library where he had been continuing his studies and saw the enormous man sitting alone, and heard the whispers and laughs, he wanted to sit with the man, comfort him and hear his story. The man was happy to talk.

Nice Story

He was a large man, never fat, but frightening. He scared lovers away, he clutched too hard in gentle embrace and once they loosened his fingers they left.

He had not had a very happy life. People didn't trust him, but he never learnt not to trust people. He sought signs and warnings, and would use any excuse to go out. He took a cruise to get away. He came on the cruise to escape his reputation, to be somewhere no one knew his nickname was Mr Big. It was a stupid nickname anyway. He didn't even want to be a Mister.

It did not take the passengers long to reject him. He was so big, so potentially violent, it seemed. He spent the cruise alone, the salt water of the sea summoning salt tears.

He was happy to see children aboard; always fortunate. He didn't realise animals were allowed on ships, but there was a cat, sleek with attention, which snaked around the passengers' legs and purred. It was a very furry cat and you could always see where it had been by the white fluff it left behind.

One woman, whom he had thought rather attractive until he saw her look of disdain, hated cats. She kicked at this one, spat at it, swore at it. As cats are perverse, it would not leave her alone.

She got very angry at the cat for ruining her clothes. Only the big man saw as, with perfect balance, the cat strolled along the railing of the deck, watching the people and enjoying the sun.

Only he saw the woman push the cat from the rail; she didn't even watch it scrabble into the water.

He dived in to save the cat. It was not the cat he was worried about, though later they all thought so. He could not continue the trip with such a powerfully unlucky omen as a cat drowned at sea to haunt him.

He did not hurt the woman, but he let her know he had seen. The cat loved only her now; the cat adored her. It would never leave her.

He leant over the railing; and gazed into the water. When he was saving the cat, he had heard a sweet voice, but only in those few moments his head was under water. He leant further over, straining his ears for the sound. He saw a smile, a hand waving. He felt in his pocket for a gift. A handful of wrapped lollies. He tossed them to her.

Her fair hair rode the waves and he dived into the arms of the huge whale.

//"Those are my parents," said Marvo's tale-teller. "I came from the sea to join this world."

Marvo and the big man recognized each other as magicians. Hugged close and tight and with regret separated.

They knew the lesson; they knew the dangers of magicians being together.

Marvo watched as his friend limped quietly away, one lonely figure watching another disappear. He knew people would never trust the man because he was so big, his eyes so dark. They would judge him guilty of whatever crime they named.

Marvo was always surprised by the capacity of people to assume guilt. Everyone felt they knew guilt when they saw it. They screamed at one man Marvo met, screaming at him when he had only been accused, not convicted, of killing his child. This was magic, to choose the guilt. The magic was that the really guilty were never noticed unless a magician wished them to be so.

Marvo felt lonely after the big man left, didn't feel like pottering over his meal, so he went into a pub.

He heard this story from a drunk with a thick tongue.

Ice Boy

The polar Inuit have many superstitions to explain their icy world and protect them from its coldness. They want their children to be strong, to withstand the elements, so they sew the roof of a bear's mouth into the children's caps. To help the children be wary and cunning, they take a piece of the fox's head, an ear, perhaps, an eyelid, and sew it into the children's clothes. So the children are strong, and wary, and cunning. But there is no spell to make them obedient. There was a child who disobeyed his mother and caused the family to suffer and die.

He loved to weave with string, creating faces with a slip of yarn, whales, harpoons and men. If he made a mistake he would crumple the yarn from his fingers, untangle it and begin again.

His mother, on seeing the knotted mass, took the yarn from him.

"You wish bad upon the family," she said. "Your knotted wool will knot our fishing lines and we will starve. We cannot buy more food without selling the fish."

The boy could not imagine life without food. He was warm and fat in his skin coat. He could not imagine starving. He didn't listen. He found more string and played his game, down by the ice hole where his father and older brothers worked.

They were angry at his game, and the lines tangled and no food was caught that day.

The lines would not untangle, new lines knotted as soon as they were down. So many children starved.

The boy who disobeyed his mother moved to the city to stay with his uncle who beat him and allowed others to take advantage of him.

Marvo repaid him with this story:

God of a Thousand Pieces

This is the story of the god Obatala, god of soul purity, who had a weakness for palm wine. He got very drunk one day, that's when he created cripples, the blind and albinos. His worshippers are not allowed palm wine. I have always thought this was a good explanation for why God, if he loved his people, would allow them to suffer. Some say he dropped his wine glass and the thousand shattered pieces damaged eyesight, destroyed hearing, severed tendons.

Marvo tried drinking alcohol but it did not suit him. It made him sick very quickly and he knew he was unpleasant to be around. Andra, wanting to keep close to him, planned some trips to help him.

She took him to visit a tribe which no longer spoke because so many of them were dead. Each time a person died, a word was removed from their vocabulary, and not replaced, because the person was irreplaceable.

These people were still happy, Andra showed him. She showed him how powerful he was, making the people with such a terrible life feel happy. He was the master of the mist.

She took him to Lake Vanda, Antarctica, where rain hadn't fallen for two million years. She showed him lakes where none existed, showed him that nature was magic too. It performed tricks and illusions, took people by surprise, killed and rescued. She showed him his gift was natural and desirable.

Marvo found Andra crying in the bath. "I've had a disappointment," she said.

"What about?"

Andra said, "We haven't done any performances for months. You're letting your talent slip. Ever since you slept with that girl."

"What girl?" he asked.

"The one in the cellar. The one who gave you visions. That one."

Marvo barely remembered the girl whose heart and future he had sacrificed. "I didn't have sex with her, Andra."

Andra stood very close to him. "Don't lie to me. I know what you did to her. I followed her, you know. While you were in the cellar. She left her handbag behind, she was in such a rush to go. You left her without defences. I thought the girl was pregnant; that two humans began to grow in her belly. The girl did not know because there were no signs. She continued to have her period, she did not get fat, she did not have morning sickness."

"You thought she was pregnant by me?"

"I thought you were like a child in that you did not connect the sexual act with birth."

"No such act took place."

"I watched over the girl and knew she was pregnant with a boy and a girl. I watched over her with great care, even identified two children I could put in their place. Changelings. I wanted those children and would have them. You would accept them; we would become a family."

"Is that where you were all those times I came home to an empty house? You left me to bathe alone, I ate alone, you were not here to help me practice."

"You're out all the time!" Andra said.

"I followed her around as she stumbled from bar to pub, not allowing the girl to drink (and managing the magic very well to ensure she didn't). The girl told everyone who would listen that she couldn't *remember*, like when you go to do something and forget it as soon as you get there. You have to go back to the place you started in order to remember, but she couldn't even remember where she started.

"I liked watching her confusion. You never kiss me like you kissed her. I've dreamed of it."

"So why are you disappointed now?"

"The girl is not pregnant at all. There are no babies."

Information came to Marvo from all over the world. Words, tips, hints, tricks. They were trusting him. Marvo was the mist.

Now he knew his future, he had to learn how to deal with it. The only way he knew how do to that was to listen to stories till his ears ached. He heard stories from strangers, mostly.

"There is magic in the things strangers know," he told Andra.

She said, "Strangers are always saying I remind them of a friend, usually a specific friend. This is part of the magic. I convince them I am a great friend, although we have just met. They can't deal with it so they attach my likeness to someone they know. Magic."

"I know you," says Marvo. "I've always known you. I have a picture in my head of you at five, eating dog food."

"Everybody does that."

"Everybody who has a dog," he said. He had learnt about dogs through other people's stories. Their friend the American diplomat's dog had the ability to sniff out those who hadn't showered. Marvo tested it.

The American diplomat's wife's sister was visiting. She told Marvo she was avoiding capture.

"I'm afraid I'm guilty of the sin," she said, grinning. "I'm proud to carry on the tradition. I can tell you stories going back generations, of women in my family found guilty by small evidence, called witches for no reason at all.

The Dark of the Moon

Many generations ago a woman was born with an unfortunate pink mark which covered the whole left side of her face. It didn't help her popularity as she was growing up.

She spent her time alone, which made her frown, made her lonely and bitter. As she neared adulthood, her frown and her birthmark ensured there would be no love for her, no match. She lived for sweet food and sugar. Living alone, she could indulge these whims, and by the time she reached middle age (twenty-five years old, in those times) her teeth were brown and rotting, her breath awful.

It was a time when unloved women were shunned. It was also a time when more and more men travelled from outside the village limits, banged on her door with massive walking sticks, investigating without touching the ugly pinkness on her face.

These men, learned in that they could travel from one village to the next, spreading prejudices and fears from a village which has had that fear for many generations and thus understands and accepts it, to a village where the fear is new and becomes rampant, uncontrolled.

This woman's villagers had always accepted her as the ugly one, the grouchy one, though the children would go to her for sweets. So she filled a certain part in the life of the village and was quite happy.

These travelling men came and wanted to be kings in the village.

"The Devil came in the night, spread your mother's legs and spat into her womb," said the leader of the travelling men to my ancestor. "Your mark is the Devil's mark." He was enormous where the others were thin. He rode a horse those many miles while the others walked. He ordered this woman pinned to the ground and stripped. He cared not for her Devil's mark, her breath, her unloved state. He had questioned her and knew her to be a virgin—he needed a cure for his syphilitic penis and sex with a virgin, it was considered, would cleanse this.

"The Devil spat into her womb like this," said the leader, spitting between her legs to moisten his way, "and the spittle stained her baby's face. Your face."

The woman did not scream as she was raped. This made the villagers, watching in horror, too fearful to come to her aid. They said, "She truly is evil," but the woman knew that if she started screaming, she would never, ever stop.

Marvo realised this woman was the descendant of the syphilis-infected woman.

"The disease?" he said. "What of the syphilis?"

"The child of rape was born with it and it made her insane at an early age."

Marvo was interested because he knew about this disease, from stories Andra told him. The disease was once called lues, and is carried on to the child at birth, if the mother is untreated. Many die, others almost always get Hutchinson's teeth or saddle nose, or other terrible things to make life hard.[†]

"The daughter of the travelling man lived in an institution from the age of ten, where she was raped like her mother. She gave birth to a girl who became my grandmother."

"And you?" Marvo said. "What was your small crime?"

"I have a bonsai tree I love and cherish. I had all the instructions in my head, how to feed it, clip it and catch the sun for it. The only thing I forgot was never to trim it in the dark of the moon."

Marvo said, "When the moon is new."

She nodded.

"I think they may be willing to forgive you," he said. He considered removing her fear of reprisal, but realised her history was her most important feature. Instead, he made her crime a real one; she stood accused of using family pets as her slave-familiars. She would cause a minor scandal in the press because of her brother-in-law. The woman, new purpose in her life, rose to make tea, bring cakes.

"I don't really like tea," Marvo said.

"You have to drink it for me to read your future."

"I don't like the leaves. Or the flavour."

"Don't you want to know your future?" she asked.

"I know it. I've seen it."

"Is it bad?" she whispered. "Maybe I can see something better."

She watched him drink the tea; waited till he swallowed the last mouthful, then stretched her hand out. She took the cup and spun it, to read what was there.

---

† Treatment can prevent all these. (But the mother didn't know she had the disease; she was so innocent, she barely realised she was pregnant.) Stage 1: Primary: Three weeks after infection. Sores appear, then disappear again after three weeks, even without treatment.

Stage 2: Secondary stage: six weeks to six moons later. Feel ill, rash, fever.

Symptoms disappear in several weeks.

Stage 3: Latent: no symptoms. Only through a blood test is it discovered.

Stage 4: Late: ten to thirty years. Germ attacks brain, heart, skin, spinal cord, etc. Can cause insanity, blindness, deafness, heart disease, paralysis. Cannot be treated at this stage

"Now, there, you see. It's a spider you've got there, a large one. Its legs are still, you see. Are you scared of spiders?" she said.

Marvo smiled. "No, I don't mind them at all, but Andra doesn't like them inside the house. She waits for the new moon and sweeps them out. Shoo shoo!" he said, mimicking Andra's cautious actions.

"Well, now, here's the thing. A spider in the tea cup means fulfilment. Your fulfilment." She winked at him. "And there's indications we are talking about sex."

Marvo reddened. Andra and he had not yet made love. He was barely aware it was required of him; he had not received any education in that area. People either had sex or they didn't. He couldn't figure out how they moved from not making love to making love. He saw rare indication of the mid-ground.

They left the party early, a rarity. He thought carefully about things the woman had said, things she desired, and he was pale, his hair greasy, his skin spongy to the touch.

Andra looked at him and laughed.

"You need a bath," she said, feigning disgust, but her eyes glittered, her fingers twitched, ready to clean, scrub and stroke.

"I wanted to see if the dog knew I was dirty."

He immersed himself in the water; its steam seared the dirt off him. As he settled onto the warm enamel, the bathroom door opened and Andra entered.

"I'm taking your action as a signal," she said. "You've always been meticulous before, barely a shred of filth. Now you come home like a man without access to water. Is it a scrub-down you're after? Are you leaving me to be the seductress?"

Marvo nodded. He felt nine years old, as she took his hand and climbed naked into the bath, he felt nine years old and holding his first magic trick. What he held was mysterious, unknown, but excited him in a part of his belly he could not identify. He was old enough to feel fear, unlike a teenager who cares little for restraint.

Andra washed him and dried him and laid him on the bed.

She said, "Do what your body feels. Don't think, don't be scared."

He felt overwhelmed, incapable, out of control. The magic of it, the total giving and forgetting, scared him. He forgot the room he grew up in; he did not think about turning a rabbit blue. He was horrified by the duality of it; all his life he had been alone, because his grandmother had never stirred him to emotion. It was too much, the closeness, the two people becoming one. Too much to bear.

Marvo knew he would never make love to another woman. Andra had enchanted him.

When Andra woke up in the morning, he was gone. She was angry at this because it had been his idea, after all. Then she cried, because she feared he wouldn't come back. Then she knew he would, and she settled into a quiet life to wait until he did.

Marvo walked and travelled, seeking stories like they were drugs. He avoided touching people; each contact reminded him of Andra, her marvellous skin, how he had forgotten everything when they made love. He made use of his escape, though, looking for stories, seeking Doctor Reid. He did not want to die. He wanted to live forever.

Marvo had the ability of travel. He wandered all his life, place to place, leaving nothing, but always taking something, changing a bit. Every experience moulded him. He had three passports, three different names, because sometimes he liked to travel to two places at once, and it could get confusing. With the three passports, no one was under pressure to understand something alien to them. He was thoughtful that way.

He met a woman in a nightclub on his travels. His obvious disinterest in her body made her gabble. She loved to talk, but usually had to be quiet if she wanted people to like her. Marvo listened; she was in heaven.

The Redneck Quads

There was a family who lived next door called the Tanners. They were all very pale, because they stayed inside a lot. Their mother said they had to all stay inside because she would know where they were then.

There were four Tanner kids, and they were all born at the same time. They were called the quads. They spent the whole day at school together, didn't play with anyone else, so we all started to hate them.

They all had these tight necklaces of red beads, boys and girls. We used to laugh at that. Someone started calling them rednecks, and we thought that was funny as well.

They ended up doing better than any of us, really well in school and now they're all doctors. The Tanner Clinic, it's called. I found out years later that those red necklaces were good luck charms, they were red rowan berries. I've made some for my daughter, who I had when I sixteen, and I'm hoping she will have more luck than I did.

Marvo gave her daughter the ability to study, and not to be disturbed by her mother's past.

Marvo stayed on a farm in the country. While he was there, the farmer buried his horse alone, bearing great anger.

The Night Horse

Tradition killed my horse, and a gun. She has always been a restless girl, a night horse. Don't know where it came from, but she'd potter about in the night, have a bite to eat, snuffling here and there. Sometimes if it was a lovely night, she'd neigh.

Sadly, she neighed during the night of the birth of the Oster child. It wouldn't matter to most people, but the Osters were old-fashioned. It was a breech birth, they tell me. Baby born feet first. Doctors there, ambulances, although the Osters don't believe in that.

He came to see me, next day, Mr Oster. He said his wife was on the verge. She may not live. I was sorry for him; all they had was each other, and the baby now. He said, "You should be sorry, it's your fault."

My horse neighed in the night, you see. An omen of death.

I said, "My horse didn't cause anything."

He said, "As may be," and left.

I thought, *No more neighbourly chats with that one,* then I heard a shot. He had killed my horse.

"That's the death," he said. He wasn't sorry for it. He was proud of his clever thinking. I found myself wishing his wife would die, to prove him wrong, but of course I didn't want that.

"What about the wife? The child?" Marvo asked.

"Oh, they were fine. They left him when the boy was six." Marvo gave the man a new horse, a day horse.

Marvo discovered the way people drift, and are willing to talk as they wait for transport. He went to the airport, closed his eyes, smelled many things. He could smell Andra's perfume at the duty-free shop, and he spent an hour there, picturing her face, falling in love.

"I love the sound of an aeroplane," said a man sitting alone at the airport. "I love the smell of the airport, the sight of streets of runways. These are my comforts. But I cannot climb aboard. The plane is the womb of my mother, and my mother is dead. I cannot climb back into a dead womb."

The Smell of the Airport

My mother was never a strong woman. She tried to eat well, did not drink, took medicine for her poor heart. She wore a stone of jacinth next to her heart, in the hope that would strengthen it, and, under hypnosis, I once remembered that stone, sharp and dull, like the overcast sky when the sun goes down. This is the closest I have to an early memory.

She was never strong. She could not stay up talking for hours, something my father loved to do. She would go to bed and he would sit up, other women there to talk to him. He loved my mother exclusively, though. He has never recovered from her death.

She hated him, I think. He found it easy to be strong, he could dance and build, without his heart beating SOS against his breast. He could enjoy food, yell, he could drink.

When she fell pregnant with me, there was jubilation and terror. It was hard to imagine her surviving the process of giving birth, and at the eight-month stage, somebody decided she would be safer in another country's National Maternity Hospital, closer to her family. She was packed onto a plane to get there in time.

My mother hated and feared planes. She always believed she would die on one. Every time she heard of a crash she would establish that, given a set of complicated circumstances, she could have been on that plane. She could have been a victim.

She was bundled onto the plane, and it was not an easy flight. My father was there to comfort her, but there were plenty of scares for him too, as the plane dipped and pocketed.

The plane fell some feet, with the captain saying it's okay, there's nothing to worry about. But my mother was shocked. She began to give birth to me.

The attendants had learnt about it at flight school, and they were marvellous, according to my father. As good as any medical team. I was born fifty thousand feet up.

"And your mother?"

"She was killed by a drunk driver when I was twelve."

Marvo gave the man a hatred of airports as well, so he did not ever enter them again. But as the man ran out to escape the place, he tripped and bit through his tongue.

Marvo felt responsible for the accident, so took him by taxi to the hospital. He used to watch a show on TV where there were always lots of babies to be carried, cuddled, operated on. It was a hospital show, full of people and stories.

A man sat in the foyer of the hospital, a placard held above his head saying, "Hospital Kills."

Marvo dropped his charge off and asked the man who the hospital had killed.

"My sister wasn't sick a day in her life until this happened. It must have been that man she married. He made her sick; his presence made her sick. He made me sick. I suppose he cared about her, loved her. He seems upset enough now. The first time she got taken to hospital, she didn't want to go.

"'I've never been, I don't need to go,' she said, barely able to speak through the pain.

"But she went, and the hospital found nothing wrong. How they managed that I don't know. A woman in agony (a girl really. She was only twenty-three) and they say, 'Nothing'. Two days later, she was back. Same pains, same result. We all went to the hospital that time, kicked up a fuss about them finding nothing, but they made her go home.

"The third time she had to go to hospital, two days later, she was dead on arrival. Now they find a brain tumour."

"Operable?" asked Marvo. He liked to know the details.

"Yes. They could have saved my little sister." Marvo was mildly pleased with the story, and he changed the sister's condition to inoperable. The man felt better, "There was nothing they could do," he said, "we did all we could."

There were plenty of stories at the hospital, and Marvo discovered they were all different, something which had not been clear without sound on TV. They were all about sickness, death, failure, but there were infinite versions.

He needed stories; stories and stories and stories. He practised his magic all day but he listened all night. He had slept with Andra to keep her comforted, but he'd found her becoming part of his flesh;

they'd wake at the same time and she'd smile at him. He couldn't bear to breathe her air. It suffocated him, made his eyes water with love for her.

He thought of love as a mist he couldn't control, so he went out to find a job, to get away, spend more hours in the cold, hard normal world.

He went to the unemployment office and found stories there that made him realise nothing was normal.

Marvo heard this story from a man who had lost his job. The company fired him for gross negligence; he was drunk and pissed on a client's head. Marvo knew all this, yet he believed the man when he said, "Those bastards. The worst thing they did to me was giving me a feeling of guilt, like I was the worst sinner.

"I spent all the next day, with a hangover, in church. I prayed, I lit candles, I prayed that everything would be all right, that everyone else was as drunk as I was and wouldn't remember."

"It's very difficult to change the past," said Marvo. He didn't usually interrupt stories but felt this man needed to know. "Far easier to change the future."

"I thought God could do anything," the man said, not hearing him. "I went and prayed. I was so sure everything would be okay I rolled up for work, like nothing had happened.

"They all stared at me like I was a murderer. I got to my office and all my things were in boxes, all packed up with *To Be Collected* on them. They wouldn't even send my stuff to me. It was very hurtful.

"I picked up my boxes—only two, five years there and I only collected two boxes of personal belongings. I took my painting off the wall, the painting which had caused so much comment and made them think I was an art lover, something special."

The Painting

This painting was of a beautiful old perfume bottle, painted as it appeared to the painter, already old. It stood on a small dark table against a dark burgundy background. Only a light glowing around the bottle distinguished it. It was tall and thin, its label mottled, unreadable. It was hard to identify its era. The Venetian glass makers in the twelfth century were expert bottle makers, and clear glass bottles began to appear in the sixteenth century. Liquid perfume was found from the seventeenth century. Painted bottles, as opposed to paper labels, were collectables from the mid-seventeenth century. Labels, perhaps, appeared from the mid 1800s.

The aristocracy in Henry VIII's time created their own scents, a tradition still upheld. They called the perfumes after themselves; today, perfumes are named for the designer or for a part of their character they wish to be known by. Louis XIII created "Nerdi", an orange blossom scent, after a duchess he admired. Eau de cologne, name unchanged today, took its name from Cologne, in Germany.

The bottle in the painting is half-full; some poor woman considered its contents too precious to use, and now she is long dead, and the perfume stale.

It was a strange, dull picture to have in my office, but it helped me keep in touch with relativity. It was a memento mori, telling me each time I saw it that life is short, life lasts less than a bottle of perfume. People would see it and say it gave them the creeps for some reason, and I'd say, "Funny you should say that. Because the word 'perfume' actually means 'from smoke' because it was originally created from sweet gums and woods and used in sacrifice, to cover up the smell of burning flesh."

The painter was aware of that, I believe. That's why he gave the picture such a sheen of ill-feeling. Though it could have been his nature; I believe he committed suicide not long after the completion of this picture.

For this story, Marvo gave the teller a paintbrush. "You can use anything as paint," Marvo said. "Please, continue with the story of your dismissal."

"I got into my car and drove to the pub. I tried to think of someone to call, to drink with me, but there was no one. I stayed there a long time, trying to figure what had happened, and I realised what it was. It was one bloody thing. God didn't listen. It was bullshit, and all my life I'd believed it.

"I bought a bottle; it was brown and I drank it. Then I went to my brother's place. He was at work of course, the bastard. I broke into his place and pinched his rifle.

"Then I went to the church where I'd prayed all day, wasted my day. There was the priest at the front, the liar. They all look the same, they are the same, they belt you for writing the wrong way.

"I sat close to the front and he nodded to me as if I belonged. I let him carry on for a while, muttering and gobbling and the small congregation muttering with him.

"I coughed and he looked me in the eyes. Then I shot him."

Marvo stared at the man. He saw the blackness. He saw his future, a stage, a rifle, an apostate.

The unemployed man was only there to find a haven. He had escaped from custody and was hiding in all the places they would not look.

Marvo gave another trick to this man. He gave him a magic key to open any lock.

Marvo investigated the story of the perfume bottle and discovered its unfortunate history.

Its label had once said "Capture" and it did not have just one owner, as the man had thought—it had many, many owners. It was said to be made of the rarest rose and the glands of an extinct creature. Each woman only needed to wear a drop of perfume once in their lives and the spell was made. Marvo followed a trail of suicides and accidents, each owner leaving no message as to the magic in the bottle. Marvo found the bottle, still with a few drops left in it, in the home of a man who had died of a heart attack. He stole the bottle, leaving in its place a bottle of modern perfume, an insipid, safe scent.

He kept the perfume hidden from Andra; it would be his own little secret.

There was a girl at the job office, too. She wore mirrored sunglasses and a broad skirt, covered with tiny, dark mirrors.

"To see the future," she said. She gazed down. "All black," she said. To dispel the evil eye, too, Marvo knew from Andra. She told a story.

Mirror in the Toilets

There was a man, very healthy, and everything to live for. He had a wife who loved him and allowed him every freedom. He had two children, girls with his wife's beauty and intelligence to match. His job was stable; a government job from which he could not be removed, and which he found satisfying. Life was good for this man.

He enjoyed a good social life. He went out often—usually leaving his family behind. His wife didn't enjoy the smoke, the noise, the crush of bodies. Or the sight of him with his tongue down someone's throat.

He could not remember, later, which came first. The mirror or the sickness. But it didn't matter, because the mirror was the reason he was so sick. He broke the mirror, holding it steady in a toilet, somewhere in the city, steady so the powder didn't spill off. He sniffed, then dropped the mirror and it broke into pieces which lay glittering on the ground. Luckily he had already taken the powder. He stumbled past someone who went into the stall with glass, knelt down and threw up. It was a woman; she was wearing a skirt. Her knees were cut; the blood, he felt, sealed his fate. In his mood of elevated emotions, he felt this.[†] He went home to his family and woke with a headache. He could not remember whether the headache had been there the day before. His wife said no, but it felt like an ever-present ache, a forever thing that would not go away.

He weakened within days, and became ill.

The mirror, he thought, *I should have cleaned up the mirror.*

His wife moved into the spare room. She could not stand the smell of his sickness and it was worse at night. His girls wouldn't kiss him and they did not bring friends home.

He was very sick. But he took his tired body back to the club, and scrabbled on the tiles seeking shards, thinking that to re-assemble the mirror would be to heal himself. He found one, which imbedded itself in the still-fat flesh of his thumb.

M arvo said, "What happened to that man?"

"That man took seven years to die," said the girl.

Marvo gave this girl a man twenty-five years older, a good, kind, loyal man undamaged by the vagaries of life. Their love was lasting.

Marvo spoke to a man about a job; a sad thin old man who did not care who worked, who died. He said, "Profession?"

Marvo said, "Story Hearer."

The man wrote it down. Staring at the paper, he said, "The heat, nothing I've ever suffered. Imagine being slowly baked, very slowly, or like a frog, which can be killed painlessly, they say, by placing it in a pot of cold water and slowly, slowly, heating it to death.

"Though Professor Rushton, Department of Zoology, says that this is pure superstition. Pure fantasy. How do these things happen? Frogs feel the same heat changes we do. Putting them into cold water and slowly cooking them in ever-increasing heat is inflicting the same pain it would inflict on us. Please, tell your friends. Frogs will feel the pain."

Marvo saw this as a good example of the myth being more interesting than the truth. Another reason Marvo preferred magic to science; science could explain too well. And magic could take the guilt out of actions, whereas science only denied guilt in actions directly

---

† Breaking a mirror is considered bad luck because the souls of the living play on the surface. When the mirror breaks, the soul can be injured.

related to its practice, such as vivisection.

"This is how I felt," said the thin old man.

Pointing Finger

Slowly getting hotter, my blood boiling, cooking my flesh from the inside out.

So my brain was not sharp; it was dull and stupid. I forgot all I had learnt. Forgot my schooling, my credentials, my science. All I knew was superstition, now, and what I saw was a man with burnt skin pointing bone at me.

I did not believe that death would come to me from his bone. I knew there was no truth in it. Yet all my knowledge could not dispel my absolute terror at my doom.

I stumbled away from that man, my whole body shaking more than his single digit.

I was rescued from the desert; the people looking for me found me.

You would think, then, that I would lose my fear, think the magic ineffective.

No. I cannot rid myself of the thought of that bone, and all I can eat are bones, I throw anything else up, and soon I will die from this insane diet.

Marvo understood the man was lying about his fear. Marvo knew that people often do lie about fears and loves; he learnt this from his grandmother.

"What are you really afraid of?" asked Marvo. "It's not that pointing bone. Your fear lies elsewhere."

"My fear is that my life has been wasted by cynicism. I see every choice as two parts, now. Then, I saw only one. I wish I knew what my life would have been down those other paths.

"But there are too many. A million paths to choose from in my life, each life leading to another choice, each path has ten paths to choose from."

Marvo gave this man an accidental death, a death so sudden his life flashed before his eyes and it was not the one he had lived.

Marvo left the thin old man to his accidental death. He felt weakened, he was not invigorated. He no longer wanted to find a job. He booked into a hotel with a TV, and he watched, sound off, all day. He watched the result of his weakness. The footage was clear, sharp. Marvo's mist was not at work. He saw fire and fights. He saw crime figures, he saw babies dying, he saw mothers crying. He lay in his room, the sound of sirens outside, the images of despair within. He cried, salt tears stinging his eyes. He tugged at the ragged bedspread he lay on, tearing it in strips, tying the strips into a ball of cotton. He was angry at the mission he'd been given. He was angry because he knew nothing, nothing.

He left the TV on, and went out to the street. He had picked an area of great activity for his retreat. There was the smell of sour milk, the footpath was patterned with vomit flowers and blood stars. He was bumped as he walked, bumped, pushed. He had to walk in the gutter in some places, his feet kicking solid things, sending them rolling or scuttling away.

Marvo did not feel good for tricks this day. His magic felt weak. His mist was thin. Three classrooms of children, all released late, all agitated, pushed through the doors and up the narrow staircase. Fifteen were killed. Many hurt. The mist was thin.

He met a man who was stalking the street, seeking beauty, seeking perfection. He gave Marvo a lesson about picking up women. He said, "Always listen, mate, that's the trick. Always keep your ears open. Some of them have a tone in their voice and you can hear the desperation. That's what ya wanna hear. Next to them is always a perfect friend."

Marvo told him he should never trust perfection, because it was probably fake. They sat together at a café, ordering coffee, cake and then tea.

Marvo said, "My grandmother told me a story which taught me that sex was not of the greatest import in a relationship. There needs to be other interests as well. But the ancestors were trying to save the race from destruction. They wanted the magicians to choose their lovers carefully, because blood is important, strength and support."

A Weak and Cowardly King

There was a weak and cowardly king, who would not make decisions because he did not want to be blamed for their results. He surrounded himself with well-paid sages who understood his needs and took the blame if a situation went bad, passed the glory to him if all was well. He lost some sages to crowd fury, others to execution, but there were always more. Those who survived would not want for anything in their lifetime.

The gods were very important to the sages and proof of their correctness or failure. One sage advised the king to marry a woman from another land—a woman the king was happy to marry. She was beautiful, with lustrous skin and white teeth. And her race, it was rumoured, worshipped the act of love as a holy procedure, and learnt its secrets and delights from an early age.

The king was still a young man, and he looked forward to many years of physical excitement. He would have some learning to do, though. He did not want his wife unhappy, un-satisfied, seeking elsewhere for her pleasure. The king anticipated many intense lessons.

The morning of the wedding bloomed hot and clear. At the very moment the crier spoke, a soft fall of rain cooled the heads of the listeners, quenched the dry ground, then ceased. "From this moment our king is whole. He has been partnered and may their union bring a handsome heir to our world."

"The gods agree with your decision," whispered the sage whose idea the marriage had been. The king was very pleased. He was lucky to be rich. The poor could not afford such heavenly approval.

In the euphoria that followed, the sages took power as they needed it. Ah, the power of accusation. The great sages could point a bent finger at any man and expect an arrest to be made.

The great sages were, by nature, happy to accuse any innocent person, for gain or for the fun of it. The lesser sages, less ruthless and cruel, were not given the power.

Power, the sages know, only goes to him who will use it.

The wedding sage found power now he had never known. He was the love sage, the joy sage. There, the man who beat him physically one time. Dead. There, a girl who rejected him as ugly and old. Dead. But there, another girl, who saw the love sage, not the fat old man. She he took to his bed.

The love sage, though, lost his power. The royal marriage was not a happy one once the physical lust wore out. The king was displeased, and demanded action. It was not difficult for the sages to send disease to the woman, make her disposable. Then one sage gave his own daughter to the king, a daughter well-versed in skills physical and otherwise. She knew how to massage a man's self-esteem.

This marriage was successful, and the sage ensured for his family a long line of successful and powerful leaders.

M arvo sipped from his coffee. He tucked a teaspoon into his pocket. "I am in that line," he said mildly.

"But you are no leader," said the man. His eyes were flitting from woman to woman, lifting and falling as they walked past.

"No, not really," said Marvo. "Not so you'd notice."

Using the hints the man gave him, Marvo met a girl. She was out with some friends, a girls' night out. She was to be married in a week, but she was happy to dance with Marvo, kiss him. He did not ask her to his room.

She was very proud but nervous to tell this story.

Caution

I am by nature a careful person. I look both ways before crossing the road, check the gas is off and the door is locked. I practice safe sex. Well, I use condoms. My sexual practice was not safe though; a married man with a wife like a vice was not safe.

So when I read my horoscope that day and it said, "You will upset someone today if you are not careful," I had to sit in front of the mirror and command myself to be careless. What could I do? I was helpless in the face of my stars. If his wife was to be upset, then so be it.

I went out, leaving the back door unchecked, (but locked, I admit), walked barefoot and with only the coins needed for my phone call. It was as careless as I could be, wanting the wife to be upset. To know, at least. Oh, and I didn't comb my hair, tugged it into a pony tail. I left a loose strand. So I carelessly dialled the number I knew off by heart but had never used.

"Hello?" she answered.

I said, "Hello, Judy. My name is Lisa. You don't know me, but I'm sure you've sensed my existence." The stupid woman said nothing. "I thought you might like to know my name, that's all. And if you'd like to picture me as your husband does, I'm a brunette, shoulder-length shiny hair. My eyes are bright and sparkly as he comes in the door. I have cellulite but my legs are quite slim. My stomach is flat. I am not interested in children or his relationship with you."

She hung up on me, rude bitch.

He called me, not long after, called me plenty. Dud root, he called me, like a teenager, a young boy.

"You were a dud root anyway," he said. Note past tense.

And that's really the end of that story. I didn't turn nasty and bitter, though I did, carelessly, meet his grown son and fall desperately, passionately, *let's-get-married-now-without-telling-anyone* in love.

He took me home to meet his parents and I felt I knew them.

Marvo gave this girl love and respect for her young husband, using the lesson that beautiful things sometimes have ugly beginnings. Ugly beginnings are dulled with drink. New lives can be made. New children born.

Marvo thought about birth, wondered what it was like. He closed his eyes, imagining the darkness of the womb. His eyelids glowed yellow from the fluorescent lights and Marvo, deep in imagination, saw a doctor leaning over his mother's stomach, a light strapped to his head, the light shining through the thin, soft skin of her belly.

"Move it on," said a voice. "Security." Marvo blinked, didn't move, kept his arm stiff when the man tried to move him. He didn't want to leave the nightclub, but then there were two of them, and a crowd, and Marvo worked at the mist but it didn't materialise. One of the men hurt Marvo's head; it ached. He tried to shout and a sick noise emerged, an angry, strange sound.

"Right," said the security guard. Marvo was taken to jail, tested, put in a cell alone, with no one to talk to.

"Tell me a story, tell me a story," he said. He could barely speak.

The prison guard said, "Shut up," and Marvo spent the night, ears ringing with the silence.

Andra came the next day to collect him. He clung to her, his eyes stinging with unfamiliar tears. "Tell me a story," he said, and she told him the one about her strange birth.

"You stay home for a while," she said. And he did, but the call of the story drew him out again.

Marvo caught the train quite late one night. Just to catch a train. It was that time when the underage drinkers are drunk, have finished all their illegal alcohol and are wondering if they can be sober enough to fool their parents by 11pm.

Marvo walked the pedestrian tunnel to the train. A boy of fourteen or so had his penis in his hand, pissing droplets in erratic arcs. His friends surrounded him, laughing. One said to passersby, "Step right up, ladies and gentlemen," and said it again, unable to think of what came next.

Marvo walked past these children, sensing no story, no experience, no depth. They watched their friend pissing in ever-decreasing drops.

On the train, an old man sat, staring blankly ahead, imagining times past, with no future to dream about. His lips moved and his face changed as he re-enacted events. He was re-telling his story, making himself the hero. Marvo could watch his story; he did not have to hear it. Marvo watched as the old man quit his unsuitable job rather than staying twenty years. He married that girl rather than this one, went overseas on holiday rather than to the beach. It was a sad story because the old man would have to go through the turnstiles like everyone else.

Marvo was curious about daydreamers, how certainly they believed what they were dreaming, how certain they were of what they wanted to dream about. People staring into the fire, daydreaming, are in danger of fascination. An unfriendly person could cast a spell, and the dreamer would have to wait until a friend came along and silently picked up the tongs to turn the centre piece of coal over completely. Or you could call the person a xylomancer, and ask them to tell your future. Depending on how you felt.

Marvo sat opposite two young girls on the train who leaned against each other.

"I thought milk was supposed to stop you from throwing up," said one girl. The other said, "I feel sick."

Marvo gave them a trick before they told their story. He gave them the ability to know when to stop. This is the story they told him.

It Was Her Sister

It's not really our story. It belongs to a friend, but she's dead, so we claim it. No one else will tell it.

Our friend took a chance one day and went alone to a bar.

There was a man there she wanted to know. He played the piano in the bar, played his own material at the start of the night, then the songs the people wanted to hear later on.

They had been hanging around the house because the parents were out. They raided the parents' drinking cabinet, drank every bottle in there and put them back. So they were pretty drunk all right. My sister got lost from the rest of them somewhere in town and went to the bar. She was having fun and the piano man liked her, he asked her home for a drink and she wanted more of that stuff, much as she could have. She didn't get sick when she drank. Not like me. It makes me sick straight away.

So we figured out later that she went to the guy's house and we don't know what happened there. She is dead so can't say and he says he can't remember, he was drunk and can't remember. But what's that supposed to mean? He can't remember it so he's not guilty? I don't understand that. Even if you forget you did something, you still did it, right? It doesn't make sense that he got away.

Marvo said, "Did the management mind you being so young in the bar?"

The girls looked at each other. The girl telling the story said, "It was my big sister. It was her and her friends."

Marvo listened to the dull story of the girls and was angry at himself for avoiding Andra for this company. He offered to buy them dinner and wine. He smiled at them in a squeezy way, a sexy, you're sexy way.

He fed them in a restaurant; they drank wine, and more wine.

They were nowhere; he knew his way home, they did not. They were a long way from home.

Marvo did not enjoy violence; he had only hurt one person, with a cake of lemon soap. He had hurt another but she was a sacrifice. She was meant to be hurt.

He was drunk though, so he left the girls to wander, saying, "Where are you? Come back..." He followed them until they were found by a group of men; then he quickly repented and sobered. He sent a deep and hurtful mist to the men; then he led the stumbling and crying girls home.

Marvo returned to Andra, but it was an uncomfortable home-coming. He loved her, he loved her, and it made him quiet, morose. Andra began to tell him everything, each detail of her life. She tried to make herself interesting. The world was a dangerous place for Marvo. He was so innocent of its ways; his misty eyes only saw the good. He had come to rely on Andra for judgement, even on the simplest grounds. She stopped him from going into a pub, once, when he thought the music sounded good. "Not in there, Marvo. They don't like strangers." Marvo shrugged. It seemed unlikely, but he allowed Andra to take him away.

Without her, he needed more of his mist. The mist was thick around him.

She, too, could learn lessons. She heard two male teenagers on a bus once, discussing their girlfriends.

"And she gets on the phone and tells me about her bird, how it sings and what it looks like. I mean, why would I want to hear that? I'm not interested in that."

Andra knew Marvo was different. He loved detail, he loved to hear everything. She told him why she picked blue stockings instead of black, how long she left the shampoo in. The more she talked, trusting him with the details of her life, the more he loved her. Since hearing the teenage boy, she had sought a man who could listen.

Andra told Marvo story after story, she gave him all her knowledge. Marvo was happy. He liked to hold her hand and kiss her. They went away for a romantic weekend, to a country pub. There they saw a man staring into the fire. He raised his hand to ask for silence whenever anyone came close. Marvo found his story.

The Xylomancer

I do not always have the chance to use my art, because wood is so precious and heat a luxury rarely found. I stare sometimes into small fires made of bark, stripped from trees once a year, in the first quarter of the moon in June and July. I find the bark pictures mundane and quiet; they do not speak of the future or interpret the present. They merely burn and fall, talking of that moment only, that heat.

Tonight I have a full fire to view. Some uninformed wood-cutter cut the tree on the full moon and watched as the tree split. Now, I sit and stare into the fire. When I began I saw that my life is small and the fire is great. That warmth is necessary and that humanity will die, become crueller as they get colder and that will be the end. I chose to keep people warm, and I began burning houses and furniture to keep them cosy.

Marvo gave him perpetually warm hands.

Marvo's grandmother taught him a lot about the magic and majesty of trees. She told him many tree stories:

X

"A rowan tree cross tied with red worsted will protect a person from witchcraft," she said. "X marks the spot. X is powerful because it is anonymous. If you want to conceal yourself, use X as your name.

"And you must keep safe from a baptised person whose eyes have been smeared with the green juice of the inner bark of the elder tree. This creature will be able to see witches and magicians in any part of the world."

Marvo was later able to help Andra with this knowledge. A woman recognised Andra as a witch, spent hours screaming on the doorstep, and asking her church to rid the town of the witch. Marvo invited her home to his place, where Andra waited, and the two of them rinsed the elder juice from her eyelids and eyes.

"Who do you see?" he asked.

"Oh, a lovely couple," she said. "Married, are you?" and she left them alone.

Marvo and Andra went to bed, warm from the fire and big glasses of port. They didn't sleep; they talked and touched. Andra was happy with Marvo in her arms, Marvo talking, about little things, the man by the fire.

At around 3am they both sensed sharp movement on the floor below. "Fire!" came the shout. "Fire!"

They dressed carefully and packed their few things. Neither could imagine leaving anything behind, because they both collected so carefully.

The xylomancer stood amongst the guests, muttering, "Warm now? Warm now, are you?"

The fire was doused and the guests given hot milk, brandy, cheese. A mood of frivolity struck them, that near-death liveliness. The xylomancer disappeared. Marvo sent him to where an old, empty house lay, ready to burn.

"There are ghosts who are cold," said Marvo. The man could burn homes with no living people in them.

Marvo used the knowledge of belief again, that all he had to do was speak with confidence and the man would believe.

Andra's hands were always cold, even with the hotel burning behind them. Marvo tried to warm them, holding them between his, blowing on them, putting them beneath his jumper. Nothing warmed their iciness.

"People trust cold hands," she said.

Waiting Time

I went to the room of a sick little boy once. His mother took my hands, she said, "Thank God. A true healer." She thought the coolness of my hands meant spirituality. I saw what was to be done, but the moon was very new. I would come back when it was full, to ensure the strength of the remedy. His mother begged me to stay, to perform a miracle on her little boy. But how strong was I? How certain in my wisdom, how right? I spent two weeks in other ways, not thinking of a small boy barely drinking, barely breathing.

I went back to the house, but too late. The boy was in hospital and I was not allowed to treat him there.

I waited outside, in the full moon. I stared up at it, and, when I heard tell he died, I howled into its brightness.

Marvo stopped off at a chemist on the way home and bought her some peach hand lotion, to keep her hands soft. "It's the sort my grandmother used," he said. Andra covered her hands with it, twisted and turned her fingers so the lotion would sink into her skin. They were still greasy when the phone rang, so Marvo answered. If she had answered, they would not have accepted such a small job.

Marvo was summoned to perform for an audience of two.

"My wife is so depressed," said the man. "I thought you could cheer her up, show her some magic."

"We're not really performing anymore," Marvo said.

"You have to. Please. Look, I'm a TV producer. Executive. I can get you on TV! Talk show? Cooking show? Anything!"

It had been a while since Marvo had performed and he missed it. He no longer believed that Doctor Reid would only take him that way. He no longer thought it was the way to cheat death.

He and Andra did a marvellous show for the TV producer and his wife, full of joy and possible futures. The wife wept throughout it.

At her feet a bright little boy played. Not yet two, he knew his colours and how to undo shoes.

"He's a lovely child," Marvo said. She wept.

"She's been like this since he was born," her husband said.

Marvo brought his mist, and his magic, but neither helped her.

The boy had been born to her on the wane of the moon; she now expected to have a girl.

"Such strange dreams I have," she said. "I dream of the moon, of crawling, of hiding from something in a cramped spot. These dreams are frightening because I feel they are telling me something, a message about my children, and I don't know what it is."

"You can only really find the answer yourself," said Marvo.

"Your experiences and desires will affect the interpretation. I have dreamed of cramped places, hiding, and I find it a comfort. When I wake, I am disappointed I am not a child again. Crawling in your dream could also mean a desire to return to childhood. You are about to have a second child, who will take all your time and whose very life depends on you. You may dream of being looked after, having no responsibilities and being able to play all day. Then you dream of the moon which could mean you're reaching for it, you want your family to be whole and good. This conflict is nothing drastic. It merely means you are honest in your reactions to the way your life is going."

"That's it," she said. "The responsibility. So much can go wrong."

"Nothing will go wrong. You and your husband love each other and you love your son. All the things you do, all the decisions you make, are based on that."

Marvo sent the gentlest mist to her. Blurred her sense of guilt at not being perfect.

Two months later, the woman thanked Marvo. He had not received a story from her, but she fed him a beautiful meal and allowed him to pick up and smell her little boy and to touch her pregnant stomach.

The TV producer said, "Anything I can do for you. Anything at all."

"There will be something," Marvo said. "Something quite soon."

"I won't forget. Anything."

Marvo went home with Andra and stayed a week. He was only home for a moment and Andra wanted to love him, touch his feet. Make him love her. It brought tears to his eyes, tears of rage, frustration, at his inability to give.

A woman came to Andra for help with her flesh; there was too much of it. The woman was wealthy, both in money and in history. Marvo insisted on Andra allowing him to take the payment. *I will pay you back,* he said, and he did, by giving her blindness for a day to allow her to feel helpless. One day only because by the second day she would begin to lose the helplessness.

Andra loved Marvo; she allowed him to take the payment.

"Tell me the oldest story of your family. The oldest you have," Marvo said to the woman.

The woman's body, mid-treatment, was completely covered with a reeking black mixture. Her pubic hair was thick with it, her nipples erect with it.

She was horrified at a man in the room, but Marvo looked directly into her eyes. He did not see her body. His disinterest made her want him to look. She lifted her arms and stretched.

She felt thin in her mud; she felt svelte. Marvo wanted her story, no other part of her.

The woman smiled.

"Don't smile," said Andra. The woman's small white teeth displayed under her top lip. She spoke without moving her lips.

The Stone God

I have an ancestor who travelled far from his family home. He discarded the comfort of good position. He found himself on ships, sailing for a year or a month, meeting with the men on the ship, the occasional woman. From some accounts, he enjoyed a varied sex life.

He found a lot of animals and animal stories to bring home.

He had been a seeker, this relative, but only in his own language. Before he left the country, he studied jungle and animal lore; knew which animal to hunt and which to avoid, the secrets animals held. He did not listen to the native guides. They knew nothing of his knowledge, what he had learnt. He had his lion amulets for strength and he would be safe.

He regaled the others with tales of his adventures, and it little mattered what was truth and what lies. He published a diary:

"Foolish and many were their fears of animals.[†] Yet they could not understand our views on bees, that a swarm must never be sold, only bartered, and then only on Good Friday. They didn't even know about Good Friday so I had to have an impromptu Bible studies class, something I had no intention of doing.

"As far as the yellowhammer bird was concerned, they thought I was mad saying they sometimes hatched out snakes. All you have to do is look at their scrawly-marked eggs to know why. As a child I would race around with the rest of them smashing eggs in case they held snakes. They say it is inoculated with a drop of Devil's blood. An unlucky bird to have around."

My ancestor arrived at this place with a group of hunters seeking the elephant's graveyard. He had no interest in ivory himself; all he wanted was experience. He wanted to live, feel it for himself.

In their search, they came across the centre of the universe where he was witness to the beginning of a terrible war, a war which ended the reign of a great chief, ended the lives of many tribes in this piece of jungle. I don't know where exactly.

This tribe had been at peace for three hundred years; they had ruled their land without argument in that time. They lived at the base of a great Stone God. Surrounding them, like a giant campsite, were the other tribes in a perfect circle of over a thousand miles around the great Stone God.

Many travellers since have spoken of the magic the natives see in visitors from afar; matches, the radio, the mirror. These things seem incredible to them; they have had no warning, no previous inventions to prepare them for the sight. To us, a solar car is impressive and desirable,

---

† The skin of a hyena's forehead carried and rubbed in the pocket will keep away the evil eye. If the shadow of a hyena can stop a dog from barking, imagine how powerful its true skin will be.

A hyena can cast a spell on the lone traveller, who is forced to follow it to the den crying, "My father, my father." The victim's only hope is to bang his head on a rock when entering the lair, to draw blood and break the spell. This is the only way.

but not astounding. To someone who does not even know about cars, this would be magic.

A meeting was held by all the leaders of the tribes. They came to give offerings to the ruling tribe, and sacrifices to the Stone God.

My ancestor described the statue in his diary:

"Angry-visaged, the size of a mountain, the god rumbles constantly. The natives believe it is speaking, muttering instructions, and an important duty is to listen for words to become clear. At no time is the mouth of this statue unguarded."

While my ancestor was there, tragedy struck the ten tribes. The leaders had gathered because the mutterings were growing louder. The Stone God was speaking loudly, if not clearly, and the leaders gathered at his mouth, the better to hear his voice.

The rumbling became deafening. The explorers were watching from afar, and still they could not hear each other speak. The eardrums of the people on the statue must have been bursting.

For a full day the leaders waited. They knew something great would happen, some instruction given to change their direction.

Then, as dawn broke on the second day, with a deafening roar the statue split in two, one side crashing to the ground, killing five of the leaders. The others stood in terror, silent. The muttering had stopped.

Panicked, the remaining leaders ran, tumbling and shoving in their haste, to the ground. They saw their peers, crushed, beyond help.

Amongst the living was the man who had ruled the ten tribes for most of his life. The other leaders turned on him.

"The god is angry. You have failed him," said one, a power-hungry ruler who wanted more than his tribe, who wanted them all.

With these words, the tribes descended into civil war. The ten tribes went to war for the privilege of taking control of the half-god, the silent, broken half-god.

My relative was killed by a wild beast; or perhaps an omnibus.

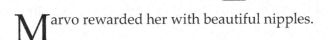

Marvo rewarded her with beautiful nipples.

Marvo was happy to find a contrasting story as soon as he left the rich woman. He passed through the doorway to the salon, holding his breath to keep the smell of Andra in, and he saw a girl sitting there, slumped in the doorway.

Under the Bridge

Under the bridge is where I used to live. We had homes, and possess-ions, like people who live in houses, but less encumbered. More basic. Our question was "Where will my food for today come from?" The question in the towns is "What job will I do?" but the job is for the food.

Under the bridge there are no jobs. There is sleeping and finding drugs. There is taking drugs. There is eating what food there is. There is sex, on occasion. There is laughter; there is self-deprecating laughter. People do not laugh at each other here.

There are no locks. No doors, no windows. The only roof the underside of the freeway, one hundred metres above.

When the world is quiet and you remind yourself to listen, you can hear the *thup-thup-thup* of cars travelling at a constant and careful speed over the bridge.

Most of us there loved to talk. We talked about everything. We read old newspapers and discussed those events. We talked about our friend who was stabbed in the real world, left the bridge for the streets and was stabbed to death. We talked about not using anymore, about cleaning up and moving on. We'd always keep in contact, we'd have reunions and laugh about how we lived the way we did, remember the time the car crashed over the side of the bridge and burnt up— Remember how warm we were that day? Remember when the guy, whatever his name was, that ex-cop who still had muscles and felt suspicious to us because he pretended he could easy give up? What about when one of his ex-cop mates came around to hassle us all and saw him there and said, "So that's what happened to you", and the guy climbed onto the bridge and jumped off? Some sad memories there, strong stuff.

We had planned to do this, talked about it. How we'd toss the addiction, start our lives again.

Then this doctor comes around and tells us that heroin as a substance is not addictive. We all looked around at the cardboard of our homes and someone said, "Are you sure?"

"I'm sure."

"So we're not addicted?" The doctor agreed, but said we may be addicted to the additives in heroin. He said if we had pure heroin we would realise his truth. I didn't want anything from him. I hid in an old car we used, hid in the boot. Plenty of air holes there, bullet holes. This doctor passed out needles, fixes to everyone, thirteen I think there were. It was winter and a lot had found other places to go.

Once they'd all been fitted up, the doctor left. I climbed out of my boot.

I couldn't figure why I'd let the chance go. It was like someone offers you a glass of thirty-year-old scotch when you've spent the last four hours chucking the cheap shit up. I'd had a bad run, been real sick, even thinking about going home.

Then they stopped breathing, one by one. *What's he done,* I thought, *what's he done to them?*

I left them all there and went home for a while. I found out in the papers that all of them died, so I guess that's the end of the BBQ reunion in ten years' time where we could have said, "Hey, remember that doctor?"

By the way, I didn't sleep with those two guys. I only slept with one, and we were going to get married and have kids. I was pregnant, you know, could be why I was so sick and turned down the fix. He's a good kid.

I feel so fucking ripped off.

Marvo introduced her to a natural healer, a friend of Andra's. This woman provided healing by dispensing the juice of flowers and plants, juice to make a person feel good.

Marvo spent some time at home again. He wanted to forget his work, to learn about himself and to find happiness. He remembered a time he was very happy; when the tea reader saw a spider in his cup and he made love to Andra for the first time.

He became obsessed with spiders, thinking that their majesty could help him sort himself out. Their lives are so perfectly designed, their needs all met by materials within their own bodies.[†]

Andra felt bamboozled, run over. She hated spiders; always. She had no fear of failure, of public speaking, heights, small spaces, faeces, outside, dust, serial killers, rape, flying, drowning, eating red meat or dying. But spiders, their furriness; she imagined them living inside her, feeding off her stomach lining. She hated the song about the old lady so many children learn and love. She hated that the old lady died in the end.

---

† Spiders are clever chemical engineers beyond the scope of any human. Their web is held by epoxy glue. This web becomes water insoluble only once it leaves the spider. The fibres in the web are stronger, stiffer and tougher than any synthetically produced fibre in the known world. And for all this, the spider needs only a little protein to make the web. It eats its old web, and within thirty minutes is ready to weave a new trap.

I know an old lady who swallowed a fly
I don't know why she swallowed that fly
Perhaps she'll die.

Andra, as a child, had frozen with terror the first time she heard this song. She learnt never to breathe through her mouth in case a fly flew in—a habit she retained. She never had a cold because she protected herself so carefully against it, the teas and nutrients she took throughout the year were ad-equate protection. Anything to avoid swallowing that fly. It was the idea of being dead, of course, the certainty of it.

As his obsession grew, she knew he would not give it up for her because he revered and respected spiders. He even feared them, but only superstitiously. He told her never to kill a spider, because a piece of china or glass would break before the close of day.

A new spider appeared while Marvo was out. He had not seen it; he did not know it existed. Andra killed it. Wiped its juices from the wall, flushed its body down the toilet.

"Hah!" she said. "Let's see what happens with a death you don't know about."

She was careful, handling dishes and glasses, all day. She cooked a good meal because she felt guilty; she knew how hurt he would be that she had wilfully killed one of his precious spiders. It had become a battle; his success would mean she was more than ever under his spell.

He came home quite late. He unpacked some packaged food and hid it around the house, and placed a bottle of wine on the bench. She reached for it to see its label, misjudged the distance, knocked it onto the floor where it smashed and spread like a blood stain.

"Not the wine," said Andra. She wiped the mess up furiously, like she wanted to forget the accident had happened.

Marvo sensed that Andra's guilt did not match her action.

"It was only wine," he said. "Nothing."

She kept saying, "I'm sorry, I'm sorry."

"I can't forgive you if I don't know what you're sorry for," he said. She would not tell him, and the secret grew. It became more important with time, and by the time she confessed, she felt as if it was murder.

"Spiders bring good luck and prosperity to a house. Don't forget that," he said.

Marvo told her this story of an ancestor as he convinced Andra to allow spiders to roam free in their home.

Spider Man

In Rome there was a magician whose skills were in great demand. He did not want for anything; his clients paid in produce, in money, in kind. He enjoyed the life success brought him; in the end it caused his downfall.

This magician kept spiders in every corner of his house. He let insects come and go to feed his spiders; apart from that the pets got no care.

In fact, every time the magician needed to see the future, he would destroy a web. He would summon his client when the spinning began, and they would sit together and watch as the spider spun her web, though both male and female spiders spin, so it could well have been a male. Then he would give the forecast; success or failure in a venture or love. Then he would destroy the web, to have the next story spun. Answers to questions. He was right almost every time, and as his reputation grew, so did his worth. He never asked for reward — certainly never specified an amount. But as he became more famous, the Romans assumed he would ask more, so that is what they gave.

He became very famous, for his sight in some circles, for his wealth in others.

A new spider moved into his home. He summoned a client and they sat to watch the spinning of the web. The magician saw death. He said to the client, "You must be careful, and you must watch over your loved ones." Strangely enough, it was not the client who died. My ancestor, the web-reader, was robbed and killed within a few days of the vision. Robbed of his goods, his coloured cloth, his money, his jars of ointment. They beat the magician up and left him to die. †

---

† And there was plenty of crime to go around then. In the sixth century, the Germans in Rome protected their property fiercely. A slave who stole a pot of honey was almost put to death, but for the intervention of a hermit. They were not the only ones. In 798 CE, theft was punished by death, murder by a fine. Houses had cellars protected by Salic law. There was a fifteen-solidi fine for burglarising an open one, forty-five solidi for a locked one. Thieves could be put to death, fined, whipped, enslaved. In 800 CE "exposing" children was considered a crime. This habit of leaving a girl child or a child of adultery to the elements was less important than that of killing an important man (fine of six hundred gold pieces), a childbearing-age woman (six hundred solidi fine) or a menopausal woman (two hundred solidi). Violence was an everyday affair. During each eclipse in Rome, there was great terror. Because the menstrual cycle is close to the moon's, it was thought childbearing would cease on viewing the darkened moon. Even after Christianity was established, magic could not be smothered altogether. Instead of a coin to pay the boatman of the Styx, after Christianity reached the Romans a host wafer was more commonly used, despite the ban of the Church.

"Also, a baby was left behind, casting suspicion on every woman of childbearing age. They found it playing at the magician's side, plopping his hands up and down in the blood which covered the magician's back.

"That baby is a mystery never solved by Roman officials. For want of any relative, and bowing to public pressure, the child inherited the magician's home and any belongings not stolen by the thieves. That child became a part of the family line. And now let's go out and have a dance."

Marvo never let Andra question him about the family stories he told her. She wanted to know, for example, how an orphan could inherit a rich man's chattels, in old Rome or the modern day. They were not treated as important. Once a child lost both parents, they lost their final protection: the people who traditionally would die for them. Their buffer against the world. No one would ever take the place of parents, blood or adoptive.

Andra said, "So, did he die of wounds, your ancestor? Did they beat him across the back? Where did such blood come from?"

Marvo said, "There was once a great writer, a woman of talent and foresight. She was renowned for her logicality; she wrote about progress. It was her fame; she disavowed superstition, disapproved of myth. It was only when she died they found a tube by her side, the tube they had thought of as a mitre, a staff, a symbol of her power. The tube was hollow, as tubes are, and it was empty."

Marvo knew Andra would ask questions. Let her ask about this invention.

"But how did she die?"

"Can't you guess?"

"Was she murdered?"

"No."

"Did she die naturally?" Andra asked.

"What do you mean by that? All death is organic."

"Did she die because her time was up? Of illness?"

"No."

"An accident?"

"No."

"She killed herself?"

"Yes."

"Does it matter how?"

"No."

"Does it matter why?"

"Yes."

"She gave up. She ran out of ideas."

"No."

"She owed money."

"No."

"Her lover left her."

"No. Think of the scene I described." Marvo suggested.

"A woman. An empty tube. I suppose the tube was connected to her death."

"Yes."

"Was it the method used?"

"No."

"So. The method is unimportant but I'd like to know. Pills?"

"Yes."

"Okay. She took pills because of the tube."

"You could say."

"Because of what was in the tube."

"You could say."

"Because of what was no longer in the tube."

"Yes."

"The contents of the tube had kept her alive."

"No."

"Kept her wanting to be alive."

"Yes."

"Was it her inspiration in there?" Andra asked.

"No."

"Something which kept her sane?"

"Yes."

"Something which kept her capable?"

"Yes."

"Capable of writing?"

"Yes."

"What could that be? Not a special pen or a good luck charm, because she was not superstitious. What then?"

"You give up?"

"Yes."

"Snakes' teeth, to ward off headaches and blindness. Someone removed them from the tube, and as she tilted it back and forth, a well-known habit, she realised the protection had gone. Her head began to ache, her vision to blur, and she could not continue. She did not wish to be a blind writer. She wanted to see, use her eyes, so she chose to die."

"That's cheating. You said she was against superstition."

"That's what she said," said Marvo.

"And you said she killed herself. But really, someone else caused her to do so by taking the snakes' teeth."

"But it was a child who wanted something to play with. It was not a malevolent adult." Marvo was pleased with his trick. Tricking Andra was difficult; she rarely gave in.

"Ask me another," she said.

"What are you thinking when you give a gift? About how happy the receiver will be, how grateful? How clever they will think you, and how they'll show their friends the gift, giving you credit?"

"I suppose so."

"Then sort this tale out. A man fills a suitcase with toys and goes out onto the street to give them away. Why?"

"He wants to take the children home."

"No."

"He has been bad and wants to placate the parents."

"No."

"He wants to change his reputation."

"No. Do you give up?"

"No!"

But although Andra guessed for three days, the answer did not come.

"Well?" she said at last. "Well?"

"He gave the presents to make the children happy," said Marvo. He had tricked her again.

It was his latest obsession. At a party, he counted the people, saw there were twenty-three. He said, "I would like to guess that there are two people here with the same birthday." As he did not know everyone, the other guests thought this was unlikely, and said so. Only Andra was quiet, having been stung a couple of times already.

They went around the room, announcing their birth dates, and Marvo was proved correct.

"It's mathematical," he told Andra later. "It was fifty-fifty that I would be right, and luckily I was."

Marvo performed magic compulsively. At a small café, he entertained a boy with a sheet of newspaper and a glass.

Firstly, he bought the boy a glass of lemonade.

"Drink up, drink up," he said. "It's time to smash that glass."

Andra knelt up behind him in the second booth. She ran her fingers through Marvo's hair, said, "What a bully."

The boy finished his lemonade and Marvo removed a sheet from the newspaper.

"Thinking of buying a house lately?" he asked the boy. The boy grinned and shook his head.

"Okay to use the real estate section then." Marvo tipped the glass over his head to see if there was any liquid left in it, and a few drops wet him. He glared at the boy, who giggled.

Marvo moulded the newspaper over the glass. "Do you think I can make this disappear?" he said. The boy shook his head.

"You don't believe me?" Marvo said, mock-hurt. The boy shook his head harder. Marvo lifted the glass behind his head and pointed to the table.

"Feel the table. No trap doors? No secret compartments?" The boy ran his fingers over the table carefully. He shook his head.

"Right. Let's vanish this glass." Marvo placed the glass back on the table. He raised his hand high and smacked the glass with a bang. He flattened the newspaper—the glass was gone!

The little boy's eyes were wide with delight.

"Where is it?" he asked.

"Gone to get filled up with lemonade again," said Marvo.

"Can't you see it under the table?"

The little boy looked but he didn't find it. Marvo shaped the newspaper again and raised his arms.

"Are you sure it's not on the table?" He lowered the glass-shaped newspaper. "Sure?" he said. "Well, I guess we don't need the paper anymore." He lifted away the paper and there was the glass, filled with lemonade!

He made a coin stand on end in his fingers by placing a pin behind it and resting the coin on the pin.

He made two straws repel each other by pretending it was science.

He took a small ring threaded on a piece of string. "This is the shower ring from my very own shower," he told people, giving details of how he lived. "I like a shower at night and in the morning. I like the taste of shower water as it comes warm out of the spout.

"You hold this end, you the other," he said. People always wanted to help Marvo. The ring hung in the centre, and he threw a handkerchief over it.

Marvo fumbled under the hanky, then removed it; a match was threaded through the ring.

He asked one of the people holding the rope to remove the match; the rings fell free. He said, "Well done."

He always guessed which crayon a person picked, when he visited the kindergarten. He turned his back, and someone chose a crayon. They gave it to him behind his back; he had a feel, then gave it back. When he turned around, he placed his hand on the forehead of the person who picked the crayon. Then he guessed the colour.[†]

Somebody once tried to expose Marvo and Andra in their mind reading. He said they were using a trick, that Marvo could guess the right object because Andra pointed at a certain colour before pointing to it. But no matter how hard they were observed, they were not caught in any trick. This was because there was no trick. They performed real magic with each other. They could read each other's minds.

Marvo did these tricks to put Doctor Reid off the track. He acted like a fake; a false magician.

Andra said, "Do you think we could go back on the stage? I miss it! The promoter called me just yesterday to see how you are going. You're performing anyway, Marvo. Why don't we do it?"

And it began again.

The singer from FEG did a surprise concert at the theatre where Marvo performed.

"I could never do what you do. My voice is too soft," Marvo said.

"Some singers are more needy than others," the singer said. "An ancestor of mine lived a long time ago when there was a great community feeling created by the permission of public expression of piety. No longer was piety a private, anti-social thing; it was open, demonstrative. Competitive. Citizens tried to outdo each other with their expressions of piety; shouted praise to the Lord so loudly their throats cracked, their voices failed. They threw coins at beggars, blessing both coin and beggar. They sang hymns in long, low voices, which gathered crowds. There was one singer whom people came to listen to from the corners of the city. He was a nervous man, dressed in a loose and ragged tunic, his toes turned in and clenched in his sandals, holding onto a cliff-edge of embarrassment. As he began to sing, onlookers laughed. His voice shook, pitched too high amongst the dusty market crowd. He held out his arms, closed his eyes, and began again. The song was one of great love of the Lord, of worship, of devotion. The man sang; the people began to sing. They all thought

---

† For solutions to these tricks, see Appendix D.

of God. The mind readers, had their craft been real, would have seen as many different images of God as there were singers; some the Christian God, a cloud-like, formless mass, or a Caesar, from on high. Others saw the pagan gods, ones from early childhood or beyond, the gods of the grandparents. One saw the god Obatala. The man stopped singing and shuffled away, amongst the still-singing crowd. So it is the beauty of a voice; the magic of tone which is most important. The text of words is necessary only to give voice to the music."

"So did he sing forever? Did he always have his voice?"

"No. He lost his magic soon after his only child was born. I will not have children," said the singer. "I don't need them."

"And they don't need you," Andra whispered to Marvo. She saw the future sometimes; she saw rage, and fists, beers, bottles. She saw a child growing up bitter.

"Children don't need you," she said to the singer from FEG.

He smiled. "No, they don't." He asked them to join him on tour, opening the show, softening up the children. The promoter agreed.

On the plane, Marvo met a happy man, who grinned through tobacco teeth, nodding and grinning. He did not speak English well.

"Farmer," he said, patting his chest, "farmer."

"Marvo," said Marvo.

"What is Marvo?"

"Magic. I'm a magician."

"Ah! You make a trick for me. I pay you."

"Which trick do you need?"

"I need a trick of speaking. I need to speak to the girl and she will marry me."

"In which language?"

"My language. I need speaking spell for my own language." He chuckled at his own failings, this happy man with failure imminent.

"I'll give you a trick if you give me a story."

"I can write a story," said the man, "and you will read it later."

Marvo found paper and pen for the man, who began to write.

He wrote in a sharp, scratchy script, and he wrote from left to right, then right to left, like a serpentine. He filled two pages, then stopped, signing with a flourish.

Marvo asked him to explain.

"This is Dorian dialect. Lost to many now, but I write a story for you with these words. As the ox turns is the writing, boustrophedon. When you read the story, you will see the reason."

It was months before Marvo could find a translation for the story.

It was a tale of tilling the field. The man was a farmer. That was not his name.

As the Ox Turns

The cock awakens me each morning and
leaves it as sun the meet to rise I
the barn roof and reaches the sky.
my to grain, pigs my to slops toss I
chickens and grass to my cows. I
ones the but animals many have not do
I do I am proud of. I have a team
afraid is wife my who oxen of
of. She dreamt often that they would
.me to never her to harm bring
She saw no harm coming to me. I
them thinking, fears her at laughed
excuses to get out of working the
for room no is There .farm
laziness on this farm. I would
clean would she, animals the feed
the barn. I would take the oxen
She .field the till and
would go to the house and watch. She would
oxen the when house the leave not
were working. This was not pleasant
understand not could I. me for
her illogicality. Then I received
who cousin my from letter a
lives in the place where this plane
woman beautiful a of me told He .going is
there, a neighbour's daughter, a
have not did who girl good
flights of fancy. I thought for
girl this of time long a
who my cousin said could not find
to began wife my and husband good a
fear even the barn because
.there was oxen the of scent the
She told her mother and all the
difficult became It .knew villagers
for me to hold my head up for

released I night one Finally .shame
the oxen, and they stamped through the
.yard our in vegetables and flowers
My wife stayed terrified and rigid
very was it, bed her in
difficult to make her leave via the
rose I when ,However .window
with the rooster I found my
the and trampled sadly, wife
oxen grazing peacefully on the roses.
and sympathy much received I
a buyer for my house, and now I
wife new my meet to go

"I was like that oxen," the man in the story had told Marvo. "She cut off my balls and turned me into a slave. Like they do to cats, to tame them. She tried to do it to me."

Marvo had never considered the possibility of having his cat desexed. He was not even sure what sex it was, sometimes, or even if it existed to anyone but him.

When the plane landed, his fellow passenger disappeared to his new life.

The translator was curious as to the origins of this story, but Marvo was not in a position to tell him. The translator said, "The black ox. This story gave me a great shiver, because of a story I know about a man.

The Black Ox

And a great man he was. So good for this village, selfless, he didn't do it for himself, our greatest fisherman. New roof for the school room he built himself and on cold nights he was out, taking food over hills and hills to the old man, blankets to the widow. That's who we thought the cocks were crowing for, at night. The old man who'd finished his life, not our young one, not our young man.

But it was him. The doctor said he is all rotted inside and some say that's why he was so good. They want to dig up his yard to find the dead children there, the dead wives. They say no man can be so sick and so good at the same time.

Now he lies mortal ill. The black ox has trampled on him.

Marvo said, "You should not fear such a beautiful, such a useful creature. You see?" Marvo reached into his pocket and drew out a black marble ox. "Keep this ox with you, stroke it if you like. Love the creature for its strength; don't blame it for your sorrow." Marvo forgot where he collected these things; the ox, other small ornaments, ribbons, socks, shoelaces. It was natural to him, pocketing small items. People were too embarrassed to say anything. They couldn't believe Marvo was a thief, but things went missing when he visited. Soon, they forgot the item ever existed.

"How do you grieve a man who isn't buried yet?" the man said. Marvo asked the question of Andra when he returned to her.

Andra took him to the graveyard where her grandmother was buried. He found the sense of grief there palpable, almost edible.

Marvo returned to the graveyard again and again. There were stories he couldn't leave behind.

A man he met there told the story of his child's strange birth.

Bitter Seed

She was born in a leap year, you see. People kept telling us how lucky that was, but they were only guessing. It seemed like it should have been lucky, because it was rare. Then a person who really knew these things gave me a terrible glimpse of the other side of the story.

She said that either the mother or child will die within a year, when the year of birth is leap. I didn't believe her, of course. I'm not superstitious. But the seed was planted. We had passed six months without mishap—our child was beautiful, healthy, my wife the same. We believed in the luck people kept insisting was ours.

I didn't tell my wife of the witch's prophecy, for fear ill luck would pursue us in the same way. It was painful for me to see my wife so happy, my child so perfect, and believe, more and more each day, that one of them would have to die.

"Did you choose which one?" Marvo said. He knew the answer to this one; he had heard the story before, about a horse and a loved one. He looked around to read a headstone. "Did you choose?"

The man looked horrified.

"What do you mean? It wasn't up to me to choose. I could only protect my family as best I could.

"And I didn't. I took them to a small community and we lived on the outskirts. I didn't tell my wife why. I still didn't want two people's negativity working.

"I kept my family alive. But we hated each other by the end of the year; our marriage was not built for solitude and confinement. Once we returned to the city, when I felt we were safe, she left me.

"She is not cruel, or hateful, so she allows me to see the child. But I have lost their love. The witch was almost right. I have lost both my wife and my child."

Marvo rarely came across love so he barely recognised it.

"I come here to remind myself that others have far greater losses," said the man.

Marvo felt a softness about his ankles and jumped. He thought perhaps a soft and mossy arm was reaching up from the grave.

But it was his cat; his familiar grey cat. The one which had found him in the city, and which appeared here and there, now and then. Marvo reached to dig his fingers into his deep fur.

Marvo found a story in his head; a true story. He said, "I have experienced greater loss. I have never owned a dog; I didn't graze my knees running away in kiss chasie. I do not know how my mother smells. I never ate the pastry off a sausage roll at school, I didn't learn how to read in a classroom of children. I cannot swim. I never learnt. I never swam a race or ran one. I cannot kick a football or catch a basketball. I can only recently cook. I did not learn dirty songs; I still don't know any. I know no one in a grave. I don't know what it feels like to sit on a father's lap. I never believed in Father Christmas. So I have lost all this because I never had it."

The man had not blinked since Marvo began talking. He could not imagine such loss, such lacking. He said, "I can teach you a dirty song," and they sat on a park bench and sang the words to "The Old Grey Mare".

> *The Old Grey Bull said,*
> *"Let's have anotheree*
> *down by the scruberee*
> *I'll supply the rubberree."*
> *The Old Grey Mare said,*
> *"You can go to buggeree*
> *Ain't gonna fuck ya no more."*

Marvo found comfort at the cemetery. He wondered what it would be like to visit your dead, to see them lying there, their names and dates legible so you can never forget, so you knew when they died. He spoke to people at graves, asked them the story of their grief.

"When is death said to occur?" said another man. "My wife did not speak for the last six months of her life; the attack paralysed her so. So she was dead already, in a way. We could no longer communicate. But she could squeeze my hand when her strength was good, and her eyes were always very expressive.

"She went into a coma, four days before she died. Death there? There was no mind left in that body. A case of flesh and bone. But her brain still registered as functioning. Then her brain and heart stopped, and officially, she was dead.

"But I remember her laugh, her shouts, her favourite colour. She is not dead in my memories. Perhaps she will be alive until I forget her."

Marvo thought about his grandmother; he could remember her words and little else, also her age, something he had only had comparison to since his emergence from the room.

The man said, "But she knew she was going to die months earlier, when an old tree fell on our property. She said, 'An omen of death,' and smiled. It was a joke then, but perhaps that smile was a grimace, perhaps her spirit left her body at that moment and left her body to collapse. I think death occurred when the tree fell, and there was nothing I could do."

Something about that place made Marvo talk. "You still remember; the way she smelled, her favourite joke, her favourite food. She will not be dead until you forget her."

The man nodded, comforted. "I'll never forget her," he said.

"It's hard to forget a truly loved person." Marvo still remembered his grandmother, though the details of her face were long since faded. It was the stories he remembered mostly. The lessons she taught him.

Marvo, tired of the sight of death, collected Andra for a holiday at the beach.

Marvo spent many hours at the beach. He was distracted there, he could forget his future. Let the mist fill the air. When he relaxed, he exhaled it like smoke. He rolled his pants and removed his shirt. He placed his shoes neatly at his side and he watched the children, thinking they looked so natural, so at home in this habitat. He ate fish and chips for most meals. He watched them and imagined his own childhood holiday at the beach, a holiday which did not exist.

Marvo travelled beach roads and met beach people. A young man tried to sell him tickets to a show. Marvo knew they were stolen; the boy tried to gloss over that with a story.

School Teacher — Nasty

The teacher could not control her pupils. It wasn't funny. She didn't interest us in the slightest so we ignored her. I know you think you've heard it before. The teacher with the bad class, can't teach them a thing. Don't stop me, though, as I'm telling the story. Wait till the end and then decide.

She tried to teach us the beauty of history, the magic. We didn't even flatter her enough to laugh. She was a fucking bitch, our teacher. She was a fucking dog. She hated us all. The only one she liked was fucking Joanie who licked her arse and did homework. Who did history homework? Who wanted it, who needed it?

So the bitch thought she'd get us all in by learning magic, and she started pulling Ping-Pong balls out of our ears, boring shit like that. We played tricks of our own; we put her drawer in upside down, put red ink on her chair so it looked like she had her period without knowing it. We couldn't figure out why she didn't dob us in. Then she played this wooden trick on us.

The trick was shaped like a miniature Rapunzel's tower. It had a long, cylindrical base, a triangular lid. On the lid were three symbols: a square, a circle and a triangle. On the base were the same three symbols.

The teacher demonstrated the trick. "It's simple," she said. "All you have to do is hook the elastic band in the base onto the hook on the lid." She showed us the hook; it was as long as the base. She replaced the lid, turned it, then pulled it out and let go. It fell back with a click.

I laughed, thinking, *What a dumb trick. That's so easy.* So she gave it to me.

I tried and tried to hook the bloody elastic band. There was only a thin hollow in the base so I couldn't see, I had to go by touch. I tried to match the symbols on the lid, but they were like this.

I could match two at a time but never the third.

It wouldn't sink in. I kept thinking this was the secret. If I could match all three I could be able to snare the band. But I couldn't match them. They didn't match.

"Give up?" the teacher said. "Give up? Give up?"

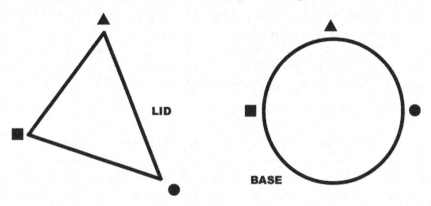

Finally I had to. She picked up the trick, hooked the band, let go. Then she laughed. "There's no band there. The shape of the triangular lid slipped it from my fingers, draws it back with a snap."

I tried it. The lid returned with a snap. There was no elastic band.

"There's the magic," the teacher said. "Trust and belief. The magic is you believed there was an elastic band there because I told you there was."

She laughed her head off. I felt terrible, like everything I trusted was false. I hated her even more after that. She was such a boring bitch.

On the last day of school, she came into the room with a big black bag.

"This is my bag of tricks," she said. "No lessons today, just tricks."

She pulled out all these things you see normal magicians have, like a hat, that sort of thing. She got Sammy to sit up the front and she swung a shiny ball on a chain. His head nodded and we all laughed. It looked like he was having a good joke on her.

"You look funny in those clothes, Sammy," she said, "Little pigs don't wear clothes."

Sammy snorted like a hog and took off his school uniform. He was white underneath. Only his arms were brown. We all saw his cock. It was small. He crawled around snorting. Julie got up and walked to the door, to get out. The door wouldn't open.

"I've got a lot of tricks, Julie. Sit down."

The teacher pointed at Julie. Julie sat down. The teacher said, "Arms in the air, everyone." She walked around the room. She ran her fingernail down the forearms of some kids, and their skin opened. Blood poured down their arms and caught in the neck of their school shirts.

"Lower your arms."

She said, "Who knows the year of the Norman Conquest?"

I told her the answer.

"Very good," she said. "Here's an animal stamp."

A tiger's paw clawed my face.

"What was the occupation of Sir Joseph Banks?" she asked.

No one knew.

The smell of sweet flowers and manure.

"He was a botanist," she said.

We couldn't breathe. We felt buried alive.

Finally she said, "The year of the Great Fire of Rome?" She didn't even wait for an answer this time. The smell of burning, the smell of burnt hair and flesh. We were screaming then, out of our seats, and running for windows that didn't open. We hammered our desks, making noise, calling for help but no one heard. The school grounds were deserted. Church bells pealed, Sunday had dawned without us.

The teacher was the one burning. We watched her melt, tried to beat her with our hands and Sammy's clothes but she was too hot. She burnt away without moving or speaking.

We all sat in our desks and cried and cried until the headmaster came and sent us home.

It's a true story, because I was there. I was one of the students, a cheeky boy with no manners, by all reports. I was quick and clever and cruel. I liked to embarrass people, beat them that way.

Marvo gave him a trick, a very useful one.

"It's very hard to deal with death, even of someone you thought you hated. You think of those things you said, the little cruelties. The trick is to remember that death is not so horrible when the victim is old. So the trick is this.

"Take a person's age

"Multiply by two.

"If the number is less than seventy, add your age.

"If the number is more than one hundred, subtract your age.

"Do you have a large number?

"That is the age of the person who died."

Marvo tired of the beach after that. He felt sick. They went home, fighting holiday traffic.

Andra made him lie on the bed. She tore strips from all their sheets, soaked them in wine, wrapped them tightly around him and made him lie still until they dried. "All your sorrows and sins are drawn into these sheets," she said. She helped him into the bath. Washed him. She cured him.

They had no sheets to sleep on then, so decided to buy more together. It was a commitment, to go shopping for bedclothes together. Marvo had not bought sheets before; he had always slept in other people's beds. He did not mind what they bought, but he wanted the material to be soft, not shiny.

Andra wanted a restful colour; very important for good love, good sleep. "There was," she said, "a belief in red bed coverings to draw out the pustules of smallpox. I don't think we need to bring our pustules to the surface, do you? I think it's nicer to keep those things inside, don't you?" She smiled. He knew this wasn't true but smiled anyway.

"You have all the answers," he said.

She turned her back to him. "Why do you keep looking, then? So many stories."

"Because you don't have the right answers. Why do we need the magic of releasing good news or dirty gossip to conceal tragedies? Why are the magicians always there to tell the story of the politician's love for young boys when unemployment grows, or news of a great sports win when taxes are raised? That's why I have to follow the bad news, the bad guys. I'm trying to find a source, an explanation. Why am I needed? Why does the mist have to exist? Why is there bad, bad to be concealed?"

"Let's make our bed, Marvo, and you'll see the magic of fresh new sheets."

Marvo and Andra rose early the next day. They had a magic tour lined up. Show after show after show. With them travelled a manager, a young man who could never sit still. He made Marvo nervous with his staccato sentences, his unfinished thoughts.

"Tell me a story," Marvo said as they prepared for a night's performance. "Beginning, middle and end."

Door Stop

He wanders through the town, sniffing, sniffing, looking for babies. He thinks this town is disappointing. In the last town, babies were ripe and plenty, their parents loving and trusting.

"May I offer this sweet suit? Wee Willie Winkie Wear. In exchange for a bite to eat?" Material shiny, in pink or blue, burgundy or azure. A dear little suit to fit every child, fit like a second skin, shrink to fit, but to look comfortable. Babies crying for no reason, into the night, all day.

Why's the baby crying? He's got his lovely suit, he's not wet. Can't you see he can't breathe? He's hot and he's working for breath.

The man stands under windows in the dark, drinking in the cries, the anger. For this town, he has brought little booties for their feet to itch and prickle, lovely sweet dummies which leave a nasty taste for the babies to suck on.

He wandered through the town, looking for toys on the lawn which indicated older children who may have siblings. Wondersuits on the clothes lines.

Losing patience, his pack growing heavy with his goodies, he considered sleeping, moving to the next town in the morning. Then he saw a house, a single light on. A woman paced, holding a child.

He could hear its soft crying, weak little sniffles of a child not ready to sleep, seeking something to complain about.

His pack bounced as he stepped to the front door.

"I couldn't help hearing your baby's cries," he would say, "I have the perfect thing."

But as he stepped closer to the door, he found he could not walk onto the door stop.

He reached across to the door and knocked. The door was answered quickly; the mother stood there.

"What is it?" she said. "What do you want?"

"I couldn't help hearing your baby's cries," he said. He tried to step over the threshold. Some barrier stopped him.

"You stay away," she whispered. "I told the old woman not to bother, but she buried the afterbirth of my little one under that stone. To keep out evil spirits who wish to do her mischief. Now I see she was right."

The door closed, and he left town without the benefit of rest.

"It's a true story," the young man said. "It was my mother. She saved me."

"She was a clever woman, then."

"She's crazy now. All she thinks about is what could have been."

Marvo gave him a crystal ball for his mother. "This will ease her mind," he said.

Andra pulled Marvo by the arm. "Enough stories! We have a show to put on."

"Your costume is on inside out," the young manager said. "And don't forget to speak up! Your quiet voice, people can't always hear you."

"I bring good luck on myself," said Andra, "when I put something on inside out. For the luck to hold, you must leave it like that till you would take it off normally." Andra didn't bother about things like putting on her clothes the right way. She didn't pluck her eyebrows and she rarely ironed. Nothing was important.[†]

Before the crowds arrived, Marvo took a quick run around the theatre, up and down the stairs, feeling his thighs and his ankles. He liked to think that way, think of the visits and phone calls he'd had from magicians around the world. Advice, ideas and thoughts. All of it in his head; all of it ready to be sorted.

That night as Marvo walked through a piece of red glass he put one arm through first and made obscene gestures to the audience. As he did so, he caught a glimpse of a stranger, an unimpressed adult face. An angry woman, a woman who hated Marvo, hated magic. She wore a beard, pretending manhood.

Marvo's concentration slipped. He stared at the pale face; it seemed so large, like a balloon.

---

† William of Normandy accidentally put his shirt of mail on the wrong way. People noticed and they told him. He assured them it was good luck, it said he would change from a duke to a king. Probably more to do with being embarrassed about it than anything else.

Doctor Marcia Reid.

The children began to scream, and Andra grabbed his elbow. A stream of thick dark blood ran from his arm, down the glass, patterned the floor in red. He had cut his arm. He saw Doctor Reid leaving and tugged at the young manager's trouser leg. "Follow her, will you? Please?" Marvo knew he would have to find the doctor, that he could never be in the weak position of the one who is caught.

Andra helped him withdraw his arm from the glass and someone came to clean up the mess. She tore her silk tail away and used it as a bandage. He finished the show, calming the screams of the children who loved him.

"She went to the library," the young manager told him. "To the Rare Books Room. They wouldn't let me in because they said I was dirty."

Marvo was neat and dull in both dress and appearance, until he dressed for a performance, when he became flamboyant. He was so quiet though. He always whispered; an enigma to all who met him. *Why does he whisper? Why do you whisper, why are you so quiet?* He did not tell them where his quiet voice came from. He gestured them to lean closer, and he smelled so nice, like Juicy Fruit chewing gum or a steak cooking, or like your favourite aftershave or perfume, or like your mum or like your own fart, he smelled so enticing people would lean closer to hear his quiet, quiet voice. They leant so close they felt the prickle of his short hair against their cheek. *You don't need to shout to be heard*, Marvo was fond of saying. And you don't have to be good to be bad.

It was in this library that Marvo found the blind man. They had a large collection of Braille books.

"I haven't always been blind," he told Marvo. "And I haven't always been rich. What made me rich made me blind."

The Lesson of the Blind Man

I was never expected to make a success of myself, what with my father being in jail for murder. His own father, he killed my granddad. I found out once I was grown up. Shoved him over a cliff with the family watching from the picnic table, me right at his feet. I remember laughing at the game and never making the connection that Granddad and Dad both disappearing at the same time had anything to do with that shove.

"What did he say?" my mother asked. "What did Granddad say to make Daddy so mad?" I was the only one who could answer—my father never spoke to my mother again.

I didn't know the answer. I wasn't listening. I was glad to be standing there, with my dad. I never liked Granddad: he used to pinch at me, asking how school went and other bland questions. I was scared of him. When his spittle flew during conversation, I was too scared to wipe it from my cheek. I preferred to let it sit there and sink into my skin.

There were a lot of connections I never made. That's another reason nobody expected much of me. I was stupid.

I didn't finish high school; hated school. They called me Ted Ripper, as if my Dad had killed more than one person. It was very annoying.

I was lucky, after a lot of years pottering around, eating cheese sandwiches because I couldn't afford meat, that sort of thing, I was found by the first person who thought I was smart enough to be of use.

He was an amateur but brilliant historian, inspired, and he kept me on as his assistant for many years.

It was very tragic, when he died. I knew he'd been born on an ocean liner, right on the equator, and no one could decide what nationality he was. So it would have been nice for him to die somewhere special. But he keeled over and died.

He left everything to his historical society—papers, money, the lot. But I managed to pick up something I had had my eyes on for a long time.

These two sheets of paper.

Firstly,
In the land of tin
In the State of Wandering
In the Place of Edin's Castle
find this:

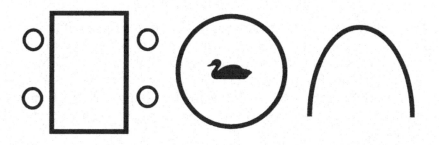

Then think this:

Can you carry what you find? Not far.
Can you take it to a place?
Where people gather and then leave,
Where the walls are ancient,
Where the people are old,
Light is there.

Place the object
in the place.
The square;
you'll know the one.

Place the object
in the place
At the time.

And the time is this:
There is a year of months;
There is one month.
There is a month of days;
There is one day.
There is a day of hours;
There is one hour.
There is an hour of minutes;
There is one minute.

And this is the minute:
That of the perfect egg.

And this is the hour:
That before Christ's last.

And this is the day:
The number of months
For the book of names
to be completed.

And this is the month;
Think of thanks.

But listen to this:
What's light is lightest light.

What's dark is darkest dark.
Take dark to light
or
take light and take dark.

An historical and geographical treasure map. The old man spoke often of its existence. Telling me he was saving it for his retirement. Well, I figured, you're retired now. So I pinched it.

It took me two years to track down the answers to the clues. At each stage I thought I had it, then one element would be wrong. Finally, I had answered almost every question. The last paragraph remained a mystery; that I would ad lib.

My track took me to Britain; Scotland; Edinburgh. I was distracted for a while by the terminology, but I found that Britain, though not one land, came from the Phoenician Baratanac—Land of Tin.

Scotland is not a state, but it came from the Celts, who finally settled there, who were known as Scuit, or to roam, wander.

Edin's Castle was simple.

Edinburgh.

The diagram had me for weeks, until I remembered those children's drawings, like this:

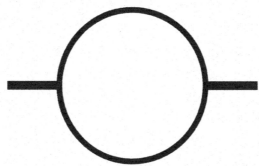

This is a Mexican on a bicycle, and it struck me that I was looking at a table, some chairs, and perhaps a pond with ducks or an umbrella with wings. It was a short step to the beer garden of the Three Ducks hotel.

Every night people met and sat at the table, men and women. After a week, I realised I would have to come after hours, if I was to check the tables. They were always taken. Within the broad, single central leg of the table, the hollow centre of it, rested a small ebony box. I had the dark. And the light; within kilometres sat the Light Cathedral, an ancient structure attended solely by the inhabitants of the retirement village which surrounded it. There was my place; next, my time. The perfect egg, traditionally, takes three minutes. Christ died at 3pm. The book of names I took to be the Domesday book; completed in eight months. And the month of thanks; in the area I was in, Europe, that month is September. The time of the Harvest Festival. September the 8th, at three minutes past three. It was only July. I spent the next two months trying to open the box, without breaking it; it remained firmly sealed. I went to the cathedral and saw, before me, many thousands of squares. On my hands and knees now I sought. I wanted to find the place before the day came. I looked at each small tile carefully, waiting to "know". One hour passed, then each minute ticked. I refused to rush; I did not want to miss it. Finally, I found one tile, scratched with a small sun. I went home and waited for the day. I was fortunate in that there was no worship that day. I entered the cathedral. Quickly, now, I placed my ebony box squarely over the tile. It sat comfortably. I sat to wait, staring at the box. As the moment approached, I felt a warmth at the back of my head. Turning, I discovered a shaft of light pouring through a small hole in the ceiling.

I leaned back to allow the sun to reach the box, and with a small sizzle, the seal I had not seen was opened. Impatiently, I threw open the lid to see my treasure. In that split second before I fell prone I realised the final clue was a warning. Inside the box was a mirror which reflected the light into my eyes with such intensity the retinas were burnt. Take the dark to the light, I thought. Wear bloody sunglasses.

I woke in the cathedral, in terrible pain but with my wits. I carefully closed the lid of the box and felt for my haversack. I thrust the box to the bottom, under my clothes, my books of history and my maps. Then, again, I collapsed.

I awoke under a doctor's care. After time, I was released, with my new cane, and some dark glasses. My treasure, I established, was undisturbed.

I sold it for more money than I imagined existed. My friend the historian had found a splinter from the manger of Christ, an authenticated piece, carbon-dated. Some peasant, present at the door of the barn, had sensed magic at the birth and had carved this piece of the manger into a tiny baby Jesus.

"I know the story of this carving," Marvo said. "A first-person account two thousand years old, memorised by each one of the owners of the wooden baby. It was a condition of ownership: that the man who carved it was remembered. There were three wise men and one idiot who tended to their needs. He baked their bread, rinsed their clothing, rode his little horse wildly to keep up with them. He was not used to talking, because they never spoke to him. He could listen to their conversations, at night when they thought he was asleep. But he could not talk about himself with ease. His story had changed through the centuries; the human desire to make a story better than it is had given him more intelligence, made him wiser than the wise men, a victim of circumstance. He was a good man, but not clever. So he did not analyse how he felt in the barn where the baby was born. He allowed himself to sink into wonder. His story:

Baby Jesus

The manger was old, made from a tree God intended to last forever. There was a large splinter peeling from one side and I thought, "The baby could get hurt by that." I couldn't imagine doing anything else with my life but protecting that child. As he lay there, a spider spun a web over him preserving his life by screening him from all the dangers surrounding him. I stayed with him when others were sleeping, and his little face became precious to me.

The splinter was within my robe, and I had a small knife with which I prepared food. I began by carving his face into the wood, but then I saw how dear his arms were, his legs, his little hands.

So I made a copy of his whole self so I would never forget it.

The blind man nodded. "That's a good story to tell a person who is lost."

"You?"

"No! But I know many who are. One was lost in a jungle, found by people he considered pagan, primitive, but he did not realise that he had lost his mind as well. He felt that he was out of place, which he was, but he felt newly that way.

The Dying Man

Around him, in small shelters, the people stared at him. He was small, and his skin was diseased. They had never witnessed illness, and their children near puberty were taller than him. They found his flesh, his size, shocking, amusing. They were scared to speak to him because he was so strange.

To him, they were huge, fleshy, though not fat. He had always been frightened by health—he knew with what disgust healthy people viewed those who sicken easily.

He looked from one to the other, seeking a face like his, a face which did not pity him.

He laughed at their ways, their rituals. Until the day a young woman spoke to him. "You may sneer, but our knowledge is great. Long before white magic knew, one tribe scratched smallpox fluid and gave it through the skin to a healthy person. The healthy person sickened, then never had smallpox again."

He saw that each had a necklace identical to all the rest, dried stretches of leather. They told him it was their own navel cord.

Only an old man, who lay in the sun, his bones protruding, did not have the necklace.

The lost man waited till nightfall, then crawled to the old man. He found he could speak to the old man in his own language.

"Why are you left here alone?"

"It is my time to leave. I have nothing more to give this life, nothing more to take. I lie here under the stars which have guided me and I will go knowing my people are safe."

The lost man said, "But where is your leather necklace?"

The old man choked and cackled; the noise frightened him.

The old man was laughing. "Buried, buried. Born with it, protects me all my life, and it's buried now I want to leave. You don't have one? You sicken, you will not grow without the navel cord."

The old man died three days later.

The lost man was given a chore. He helped the women grind grain.

It was not a man's job. In the city, he had hidden his physical weakness behind a desk, within a big office, with a loudspeaking phone. Here, there was no hiding.

The children still watched him as he worked. They asked if he was to die soon because he did not have his navel cord.

No one came to rescue him. Months passed; babies were born, their navel cords severed, desiccated, twisted, knotted.

He saw the cords as his answer. He could not recover his own, so he stole one from a child.

He lived forty years once he had made it back to the city, a journey which took a year. He had a pang, every now and then, an alien pang, and he wondered if he was feeling the death pains of the child he thought of as his twin.

Marvo was impressed by the blind man's attention to detail (especially the tiles, the way he looked so carefully, so long) so he removed the mist from his eyes.

Marvo did not lose contact with the blind man. He pretended to be him, sometimes.

The blind man, no longer blind, took him to meet other historians, people with book knowledge, deep understanding of the past. There are many good things in this world which become bad things. Marvo studied his ancestors and saw this lesson.

One older woman, all grey in clothing, skin and hair, told him:

The Festival

It was a very important festival. If it was unsuccessful, the year for the town would be bad, like the last year. Mothers had died in childbirth, children had been stricken, men crippled and unable to work. It had been a very bad year.

All work ceased but that of the festival. A group were selected to remain apart and pray for clement weather. Another group would tend the pigs to grow them enormous for the feast. The children learnt dances, chants and prayers.

The night sky was black; no sunset lit orange the faces below. The township retired early after the sun had gone; all but the weather prayers. They would sit up all night and perform acts of a placatory nature.

One would eat salt food and not drink water.

"We do not need water on this day."

Another would swallow small pebbles the size of hailstones.

"I remove all stones from the soil."

Another would stand naked behind the town, cold beneath the moon.

"I absorb all cold so that only heat will be radiated."

The horses wore brass charms, crescent-moon-shaped, because the crescent moon is a symbol of the moon goddess and is a most powerful protection against the evil eye and witchcraft.

The last burnt small creatures over the fire, sacrifices to the sun, begging it to be strong.

The morning sky burned bright, the sky pink and clear. The festivities began, dancing, eating, revelling.

All went well.

The parade ran through the streets of the town in a long rectangle so that everybody passed everybody else and could have a look, everybody in the town parading, all jumping and singing and moving through the town.

Then John Smith stopped short, causing bumps and bangs and shouts of pain.

"Why stop? What is it?" came shouts.

"I felt a drop of rain," said John Smith.

"He said he felt the rain. It's raining. The gods are angry with our feeble placators. Where are the placators?"

As the rain began to pour, saturate, paper streamers to sag, paint to run, food to spoil, people ran to shelter, the placators ran to hiding.

It was another bad year for the town. Four good citizens lost (two killed by an angry crowd—you failed to save us. Two vanished into the hills, alive or dead).

It would be a good year next year, though. The sacrifices ensured that.

The woman was a descendant of John Smith. She felt great anger towards failure, and towards unorthodox religion. Marvo gave her enough mist so she didn't have to see it.

Marvo saw that a once magical and protective belief could become evil over a long time, and he understood that this could happen.

He wondered if the bad can become good; by the laws of equality this should be so. He saw life from this view, that good can become bad and bad good. He was rarely disappointed and never proven absolutely and irrevocably wrong.

When the blind man left, Marvo felt strangely lonely, as he did other nights when true emotion crossed his path. He could control the physical world, but could not change the way a person thought, simply by wishing it. He went to a pub, where he drank alone, perversely disinterested in company. Next to him at the bar, there was a man (there is always a man) who marked in a diary each time he drank a beer.

"Six hundred and eighty-five," he said, imagining a question. "Instead of naming the names of God, I will drink the incarnations of one god. Then the world will end." Marvo could not leave without such a story.

"Which god do you mean?" he asked.

"There was one god, a gardener, a tenderer. Then his slave, Atunda, rebelled. Over, perhaps, unsatisfactory dining arrangements. He rolled a huge boulder onto the god while he was tending his garden. The god shattered into a thousand and one pieces—all of which became gods. When I have finished a thousand and one beers, the world will end."

"Is that your wish? For the world to end?"

"It's my purpose."

It was quite a good story, so the magician provided a boon.

The man finished another beer.

"Three," he said. He would be drinking beer for the rest of his life.

Doctor Reid proved elusive; the stink of her escape clouded Marvo's vision. He considered asking for help from the other magicians, but they did not look kindly upon failure. Marvo traced his enemy to a small village, a secluded place which retained a mythology, religion and law all its own.

There were the villagers who lived clustered around the village square, living above their own shops or not far away on the farms that produced the milk and eggs. And there was the Araby family. They lived in an enormous home, a mansion. The sight of it brought back to Marvo a memory of his childhood; a glimpse back, as he ran. His only view of the home he had grown up in.

The shopkeepers were happy to tell him the story of the Araby family, each adding a detail, proof. If it wasn't for the family, the town might not exist. All of them were glad to talk about the Araby family, about why they were so rich, and everyone else so poor.

The Araby Family

The nine members of the Araby family lived in the big house. They only ever left to find a partner to bring back to the nest. The other residents of the village grudgingly filled all requests, be they goods, or physical favours (the young master, it was said, was not satisfied easily).

The Arabys were once a good family. Just as bad becomes good with time, so can good become bad when people don't understand, or misunderstand.

Roland Araby came into the world upside down, squalling and desperate to begin. He was born at home, in an ancient bed, surrounded by servants, all hissing. They hated his mother because she had been one of them and she had risen; now she paid them to be her servants. They hissed at Roland Araby's mother as she laboured, and they told her the scrawny, crying baby could not live. They said, "He cries so much because he wants to have a lifetime of talking out before he dies.

He's talking his way through life. Would've been a noisy bugger if he'd lived."

Roland did not die; nor did his mother. She told her husband about the hissing by the women who used to be her friends and he sent them all away.

There lay the beginnings of an evil reputation.

Roland grew with much love. His parents taught him of his own superiority but he saw that not everyone believed that. He was treated badly at school; a lot of the children belonged to the hissing women.

He worked hard at maintaining his superiority, and it gained him a reputation as a cruel person. Someone to be feared.

This was the next step in establishing an evil reputation.

He never moved out of home. He travelled only once; to a city, where he found a wife to return with him.

This woman had not had a good life. Roland picked her because she had an absolute belief in her own inferiority; her feeling that he was better than her made him feel complete.

This feeling of hers (caused by a stream of people who had told her so, told her she was no good, pathetic, ugly) gave her a recklessness she may not have had otherwise. She felt that she was useless, everyone hated her anyway, so who cared what they thought? She followed her desires and instincts and enjoyed a complete life.

She married Roland because it seemed like such a different life, but she soon realised he was not much different himself; he was self-interested, and a self-serving, lazy lover.

They spoke daily of his high birth and her low one (she was born in a government hospital with many hundreds of others) and of what he knew that she didn't.

She came to realise that he hated her; that the more he hated her the more he loved her.

She began to seduce the men of the village when they delivered vegetables or fixed shingles or milked the cows.

The ones she didn't seduce felt rejected; they started to talk of her as a witch. The ones she did seduce, being mostly married, agreed with the talk, so as not to appear guilty.

By the time their children were grown (their fatherhood secretly debated) and had children of their own, the Araby family had been landed with the reputation of the evil eye, and were considered dangerous to cross. The Araby clan on the hill all had the evil eye so strongly they could wither crops at a glance, wither wombs with a stare.

The lot of them are related to the Devil by blood. Poor things. Can't envy them their spot in life; keep away from them, that's all.

In every shop, blue beads, bright blue strings of glass to ward off the evil eye, were free. Anyone could pick up a pair from any shop; they sat in baskets, hung over benches to be collected and worn.

There were many things the Araby family saw thrust at them, to ward off the evil eye. Charms shaped like horns, painted red (the witches' colour) hung over the butcher's shop door. The Arabys had their meat delivered. Tigers' claws, boars' tusks and lobster claws, mounted in silver, were others.

The glass beads were also used to protect the children from throat infections and chest ailments. A string hung around a baby's neck kept it safe.

Marvo rewarded the shopkeepers by buying enormous amounts of goods, paying city prices for inferior products. They couldn't understand how he would fit it into his car, there was so much. But he draped his rope in the boot of his car, with the edges dangling over, and without concern or hurry, piled the goods in. Then he tied the rope around them and shut the boot.

Marvo only saw one Araby in the town, and he did indeed look evil. Frightening. But how else could he look? He had to hunch over to avoid the thrusting of amulets, the tossing of words, of stones. He had to keep muttering, to keep himself company. He had to keep his hands thrust deep into his pockets, not shake hands with anyone, to stop their twitching and flicking.

Marvo thought it must be a terrible life.

It was an unusual town. Marvo put a show on for the children, because he heard so many stories he felt unable to pay them back individually. He pulled rabbits out of hats and gave them all a toffee apple, and they were very happy.

He spoke to one of the mothers after the show.

"Lovely show, dear," she said. She smiled at him. A drunk man staggered past them.

"Oh, that's Canman. He'd better watch out, he'll drown one of these days. He's got to cross our little bridge to get to his old hovel. Have you seen it? Horrid place to call home. No woman wants to go out there to look after him, and that's a fact. Knowing him he'd drown face upwards too, and then we'd have to bury him as Canwoman!" She laughed and laughed, though the joke was obviously an old, well-used one. Marvo did not understand. The woman stopped laughing and said, "Left your sense of humour in the pocket of your cape, dear?"

"No, no, I'm sorry, I'm sure it's very funny," he said.

"Surely you know that a drowned man will face downwards, a drowned woman will face the sky? Surely you haven't lost that knowledge in that big city of yours? A man drowns because he is thinking too much of hell, a woman because she is dreaming of heaven. In our village, if you drown face down you are a man, if you drown face up you are a woman. The mayor became a mayoress that way, after his death (though what he was doing out there at night I don't know. That's a question that's never been answered.). Much to the surprise of his constituents, I might add, though not to his wife, by all accounts, who had been visiting with another man for quite a while. Name not to be mentioned, but a man about town, I might say, a well-known fellow in our village. And there was the little Brown girl, a child she was, drowned face down in a puddle and was buried as a boy. It makes for some confusion in the parish books, but if you don't stick to tradition and the law, where are you? What other way is there?"

Marvo watched her mouth, its elastic redness perfect for storytelling. Only the thought of Andra kept him from taking her as his assistant.

He did not see anyone in the village without those blue beads, except the Araby family. The blue beads did so much for these people. The children wore them to ease cutting teeth.

King's Evil did not trouble them. Epilepsy, the falling sickness, did not bother them.

Most of the dogs in the village became used to him as he walked up and down the streets. One, though, hated him more each time and eventually it managed to sink its teeth into his ankle.

The owner, a woman of sixty who ran the yoga class, told Marvo he should keep his ankles away from the dogs.

Marvo said to the mayor, "Dogs who bite are very dangerous, because they will bite again. But they usually belong to a human who loves them, who will not let them be taken away and killed for a bite."

"There's no real intention to put down the dog, Marvo."

"He will bite again and it may be a child this time. To cleanse the bite properly, the dog's liver must be eaten. I can eat the liver to cleanse the bite, or you can leave him free to kill a child."

It was a good lesson to pass on to them; a good explanation. Understand your superstitions, seek their source, and you will no longer fear them.

The dog owner was angry with Marvo and called him an Araby, but he gave her a new dog, a soft-toothed gentle thing, and she soon forgave him.

He found traces of Doctor Reid; she had been with the Araby family, had visited, or rather hidden, it seemed, for a week.

"She scrabbled about in our library the whole time," said Lady Araby, Roland's oldest grandchild. She took Marvo there; it was possibly the largest collection of magic books since the burning of the Great Library.

The Great Library

It was fever, spurred by fire, exploded by the horror of what they were doing.

It began with a small pile; the books and papers on magic and related filth. But the pile burnt too quickly; the excitement too great to let go.

They pulled out books with black covers next, then those involving sex, then youth stories. Death stories, all fiction, were selected as evil. The Bibles were the last to be consigned to the fire; at this time they were blinded by smoke, blackened by the work of years. [†]

When the library had been emptied of books, their job was complete. Every man went home, unable to catch the eye of others.

Marvo said, "I could only watch. It was beyond my control. I knew it was foolish to try. I knew that I could not control every action of others. Crowd fever is the truly terrifying, uncontrollable thing. There is nothing an individual can do; only another insane crowd can make a difference."

Lady Araby was horrified by his story—even scared.

Marvo could not deal with crowds. He felt too small amongst them.

With a blink, Marvo marked the scene. Instead of a library gutted deliberately by fire, she saw a Miss Universe beauty pageant, the final voting about to begin.

It was clear to Marvo that the villagers were fearing the wrong thing.

---

† It took thousands of years, the process to provide people with ready access to the written word.
From the early writers on papyrus, to the many discoveries which led Gutenberg to his Bible in 1455, to the novel or fiction as we know it. The Chinese and Koreans invented printing around 400 CE using blocks of wood as stamps, and in 1041 and 1049 CE Pi Sheng made the first moveable type out of earthenware. Letter blocks which could be used over and over. All to be burnt so quickly, in no time at all.

The Arabys meant tradition, stability and comfortable superstition. Over the hill lay a growing, screaming, crawling child of a city, which would grab and stretch, swallow and shit. Marvo could see the future of their village; there was none. And he could do nothing, but left them a mist in reserve to use when the cinema came, the power lines, the TV, the fast food high buildings tourist industry artificial ice cream came to take over the town.

Marvo drove away from the village of Araby, sorry that Doctor Reid had gone, and, presumably, taken many books with her. Books about a certain region where magic and witchcraft were said to be strong. Marvo knew that was the next place he should go.

A hitchhiker on the road was no cause for fear for Marvo. He knew who was good and who was bad. He knew who would have a story to tell. He picked up the young man, not more than twenty years old.

As the man got into the car, Marvo said, "Do you have a story you can tell me?"

"Yes," said the man without hesitation. "I have a terrible story, something that happened to me. It is still happening."

"Very good," said Marvo. He had left three people standing by the side of the road, people who had not responded this way.

"Tell me your story," Marvo said.

"Well, I've been travelling a long time now, four years. I was sixteen when I left home, but that's not the story. That's a usual story, a plain story.

"This is about travelling, because that's what I do mostly, plus a few jobs now and then when I need some money. I never pinch it though. I work for it."

"I know," Marvo said, and the young man, accepting this, continued.

"This is about the road; about one road in particular."

The Hitchhiker

I first heard about the hitchhiker from a man I met at a party. He was very drunk, drunker than I was, and he cornered me so I had to listen.

The Father: *I wouldn't have touched her in the flesh, I swear. She's my daughter for God's sake. I never even consciously thought about it till I saw her standing at the crossroads underneath the tall four-way sign. I stopped, pulled up beside her. "Hi, Dad," she said as she climbed in. It was my daughter, all right. Her at sixteen, except for the pale blue eyes. She talked to me about school. I didn't ask what she was doing there on the road. I didn't want to know. She kept looking at me sideways, watching my face to see my reaction.*

The long road was dark; only my headlights lit the blackness. It was hot in the car; my breath was like a stream train, a slow train whistling heat into the air. But I didn't want to open the window, in case I let it out, whatever it was.

I stopped thinking that she was my daughter. Tried to forget I had known her since the moment she was born, could remember the fuck that made her. Remembered it clearly because it was the first for a while; the last for a long while. None of which is any reason or justification, of course, but some men would support me; if you're not getting it you're not a real man. Or something. I felt a butterfly on my thigh and moved my hand to brush it off. My daughter's hand stroked its way toward my crotch.

The father closed his eyes to speak.

I stopped the car and did it right there, in the pitch black. Her body was soft yet firm, and she said, "Daddy, Daddy."

I sat for a moment before turning the headlights on. When I did, she was gone.

I drove about my business and went home two days later. My wife was there, and my daughter, eleven years old and very pretty. It wouldn't be long before she was sixteen.

I didn't tell my wife what had happened. I told her I could no longer live in her cold world, and we decided to separate.

I see my daughter every second weekend. Supervised. She is safe.

I see my daughter nightly, pick her up at the signpost and take her for a drive.

This was the first I heard of the crossroads. The man was drunk, and unreliable, but I couldn't help but be fascinated by his story. Who would I see, at the signpost? Who would I pick up?

I believe I was meant to go there; I kept hearing about it. Next was my boss, who resigned without explanation one Monday morning. They threw him a big farewell dinner and he got blind, vomiting drunk. I found him in the toilets.

"I don't want to think anymore," he said. I gave him wet paper to wipe his mouth. "About what I've done. What I dream of doing."

The Boss: *I can't remain in a position of power, not after the signpost.*

I was alert; my attention was caught. I nodded sympathetically, I listened for clues.

It was dark. I drove alone, needing some space. There were no street lights, but ahead I could see a well-lit signpost, pointing four ways.

I slowed as I reached it, thinking it a symbol, a crossroad in the middle of nowhere, and me with decisions to make.

As I neared it I saw a man in a three-piece suit with a briefcase. It didn't seem all that strange, a man like that, out here, so I slowed and picked him up.

He smiled a pathetically grateful look.

"Thank you for the opportunity," he said.

"Everyone deserves a second chance," I said. I could picture his resumé before me. The man was a recently recovered nervous breakdown.

He was no one I knew, but he reminded me of any number of people who come to me for help.

I felt a deep hatred of him, of his need, his dependence.

"However," I said, "I don't think we can start you at the level you are accustomed to." The man nodded.

"Perhaps dispatch, or the typing pool," I said.

"I can't type." His voice was soft.

"Perhaps an assistant then. Do you have a problem with making tea or coffee?" I looked at the middle-aged man. He was gritting his teeth. He has come a long road, I thought. He turned and looked at me. His flat blue eyes made me shiver.

"No, that's fine," he said. I nodded.

"Hand me a cigarette from the glove box, will you?" I said.

Behind the cigarettes was a gun.

"Salary, of course, will be at assistant level," I said. He had four children; the oldest boy would be earning more than he.

"And you will have to wear a uniform." I stopped the car and watched him, in the light of the headlights.

"Give me another cigarette," I said. He took the gun. He held it unsurely, then lifted it. He turned it to his head.

I nodded.

The explosion covered the interior of my car with his blood and his brains.

I laughed, turned off the headlights so I couldn't see, and drove into the darkness, slowly.

By the time I reached town and light filtered in, the car was as clean as it had been when I set out.

I wanted to turn back and do it again, right then, but I didn't. I waited a week, and there was another one just like him.

I called the boss's wife and she came to take him home.

I asked and questioned everywhere until I found the road to the signpost.

I didn't know who I would find, but when I saw him, it was right. It was a man who had hurt me. He had hurt me when I was in jail, ruined my body and soul. I was only inside because I couldn't afford to pay my speeding fines.

There he was under the signpost, his thumb out. I could have run him over, but I didn't. I stopped, my headlights lighting those dead blue eyes.

It was cold outside the car, but he wore bike pants and a singlet. He had muscles, all right, and I saw him as he was on that day, sweaty, enormous.

I removed my jacket, laid it carefully on the bonnet of my car.

I have never hit anyone before, not deliberately, but that punch felt natural, smooth and hard.

He reeled back, and I followed him.

He offered no resistance as I had not, that time.

I beat him till his face was bloody, then worked at breaking his body.

I threw up in the middle of it; what I was doing was disgusting.

Even as the wreck lay by the road, I kicked and jumped, kicked and kicked.

My exhaustion lasted two days, after which I went and killed him again.

Marvo said, "Crossroads are such interesting places. European custom has it that if a child was born feet first it was considered unclean and was strangled. To confine the spirit it was buried at crossroads. Perhaps so it couldn't find its way home. Suicides were also buried at crossroads."

In return for this story, Marvo provided the man with an easy death, a quiet sinking, a tying-up of ends, a time to say goodbye and I love you.

Marvo dropped the young man off and continued to his destination.

He knew that the local shop is often a good place for information and he was rewarded for this knowledge.

He spent a lot of money in the small shop and asked the woman about the figurines she had on the shelves behind the counter. He listened for half an hour, maybe more. No other customers entered the shop.

"What are you doing in our small town?" she said at last. "You seem a long way from home."

"Home is where the story is," he said.

"You're so right. You really are."

"I'm looking for someone. I only met her twice but there was magic there and I want to find her again."

He described Doctor Reid in glowing terms, a man in love.

"I know her!" she said. "She was here! She only bought tins of tuna, nothing else! And I know where she went next because I sent her there. She wanted to know about our orphanage, long since shut down. But I know the man who runs Give the Kids a Go. So I sent her there. I can take you, if you like."

Marvo smiled.

"Let me just close up and we'll take off now. It's quiet today."

Marvo slipped some rubber bands into his pocket, and a receipt he found on the floor. He took three paperclips.

She took Marvo to see the director of the agency, which was designed to feed hungry children. She said, "If you want to meet a kind man, this is the kindest man I know." In return for a week's grace, a week not thinking about the children, a week without the guilt or responsibility, the director told Marvo a story.

The Legend of the Imprisoned Grandfather

I will tell you my story, because it makes me proud. I have done nothing in my life to make a story. I can only tell you my grandfather's story.

He is a very thin man. He has never got used to eating full meals; he remembers that the only people who get full meals are the ones about to be shot. He does not want to be shot.

He will only eat half of what he's given. My grandmother long ago thought to give him twice as much on his plate, and that alone kept him from starving to death.

He thinks a lot about food; he brought my father up to think about food a lot, and I, too, think a lot about food. As you can tell, food sits happily on my bones and chooses not to leave.

My grandfather spent three years in a dim prison cell. He was not given exercise time. The only time the door opened was weekly, when they would come to empty the toilet bucket. Even then he would not see a face because he would be facing the dirt wall, breathing deep of its earthiness. He describes this smell clearly; he smelled it one hundred and fifty-six times.

They would search his cell when they emptied his bucket, once finding a scrap of newspaper which had flown in the wind and clung to the bars, but never finding anything else.

He was fed very badly, as were the rest of the prisoners. They could talk, three in a row, through their window bars, but communications were never clear.

"I am starving," one man would say.

"They don't feed us enough," another would respond.

"I would prefer to starve outright, than this teasing," the third would say. They never talked of escape, and this was how the captors had planned it.

It is not a hero story of my grandfather; he waited one hundred and fifty-six weeks then he was released. His real story comes with the work he did for hungry children, but that you know about. That he is famous for. He never felt a sense of the ridiculous; luckily for the children he never felt ridiculous.

The charity director told Marvo that Doctor Reid had given a large donation to another charity to establish a market garden.

"She is a good woman. She sees the realities of life."

"I understand," Marvo said. The man thought he understood hunger. He wondered if the charity director had tins of food under his bed, packets of biscuits hidden around the house.

Marvo went home to Andra. She had taken lovers while he was away but he didn't mind. They had made love once, and that was enough for him.

"What else have you been doing while I was gone?" he asked.

Andra healed; she learnt more each day about the plants and stones, the lives, the human body.

The act of healing was like that of magic. There were those who were true, who practised the healing or the magic because they had to. Then there were those who desired the talent without having the gift. They studied and worked, they learnt from watching, they listened and they became adept.

And there were those who had some true gift, yet used it for profit and cared little for the people they faked service to.

Andra and Marvo both despised these abusers. Andra in particular spent time exposing them as fakes.

She was scarred on her shoulders, across her throat; wounds inflicted because of a doctor she trusted. There was a strain of magic which met healing. Superstitious people sought navel cords as luck and health. Many people had no real access, so the doctor Andra trusted had a large market.

He made a fortune selling the navel cords of the children he delivered.

He did not believe in the magic he was selling. This was very dangerous — as Marvo knew well. Without belief, magic was weakened. Andra told Marvo the story and he wished he'd been there to help her.

Caul Cure

I was seduced by his soft voice, his gentle hands, his words. He spoke so sweetly as he cut me, as he practised his art. He was supposed to soothe my sore limbs.

He was murdered by a man who has lost his child because of the failed magic.

They had a child who ached in head and belly. They were advised by this doctor that drugs wouldn't help, and true natural products could cause more bad than good, he said.

He told them he had a new cure, which had not been tested. He knew it was safe though. He knew it worked for aches in head and belly. It was new, but it was ancient. Since the beginning of time, he said, this cure had been used. He wanted them to think about it over the weekend, and come back to him on Monday. He was the sole supplier, because he was willing to take risks with the law if it meant a life would be saved. He inspired them; they believed him. Over the weekend, the child cried and complained. By Sunday evening, they were ready to trust the doctor completely.

It isn't cheap, he told them once they had accepted his plan.

They agreed to pay whatever it cost.

He provided them with a caul, tied in a ring, which their child had as its talisman.

This fake magic, which the doctor did not believe in, did not work. While they were waiting for it to cure their child, the cancer took hold.

The father, not caring what happened to him, took the doctor's life. I was there. I tried to save the doctor, threw myself on the father's knife, used my body to shield the doctor.

"Please don't," the father said to me. I saw some truth in his eyes but I couldn't leave him to kill. He threw me off and killed the doctor as I sank to the floor.

The father carried me home after the killing. He didn't want to avoid punishment; he wanted to save me from involvement.

Marvo sent such a mist to the body of the doctor it appeared he had died of a heart attack. Marvo understood that the father had killed for his own sake as well as his baby's. He knew that becoming a parent does not take away a person's own emotions and needs; they do not become mere ciphers for their child's existence.

Andra taught Marvo about the use of nature in healing.

Homoeopathic magic breeds homoeopathic medicine (science).

Each cure was the image of the disease.†

Where does the need to heal come from? Why some and not others? Why this person and not that? She had healed a woman with a limp, taken the limp and given it to a cat. Watched the woman slink away, hips rolling gently and sweetly.

Andra wondered why she was so blessed and cursed with the power to heal.

Marvo was fascinated. When he saw the cure for rheumatism, he remembered his grandmother's story about the old age trick and he finally understood her message.

She was his mother. His grandmother was really his mother.

Marvo gave Andra a story he had heard on his travels. Andra settled into his tone, his form of loving.

An Early Doctor

I know of a woman from a long time ago. She was born to a family of wealth, yet as a woman she would never own wealth herself. All her life she was dressed in the finest cloth; servants would begin weaving the next piece as she took the first. Once that became damaged it would be given to the girl belonging to the next family, who would pass her cloth to the next. The rich girl would see the cloth she had worn wrapped in tatters around the last girl, the daughter of an old widow woman without skills or talent. The poor daughter would never discard a piece of cloth. She would wrap them around her legs, wrists, plait them in her hair. She carried years of the rich girl's clothing on her body.

It was illegal in this village for a woman to weave or spin during pregnancy. If she did her child would live to be hanged by a hempen rope.

The rich girl watched during a fertile period, when many of the women were pregnant and a child took over the work, cutting her fingers and crying at the chore. The rich girl said to her father, "I will wear this cloth for more days, there is no harm," and she was beaten for that.

"You will take away their very reason for existence," he said. ‡

The poor girl's mother could have done with a piece of cloth or two, at least to wipe her running nose. The children of the village called

---

† See Appendix E for healing chart.

‡ A nine thousand year-old cloth fragment was found in Turkey. This story could be this old.

her the Snot Hag, and told stories at night of how she hid children up her nose, drowned them in snot, then dug them out when she thought no one was looking and *ate them up.* The children avoided the Snot Hag. Her daughter kept all the rags. The rich daughter, as she grew, witnessed sickness and suffering and wondered why it would strike one and not the other. She spoke to her mother, who asked her father to beat her.

"We do not ask questions of such magic," said her father. "We pray to the spirits and allow them to decide who should be taken and who left. We do not risk their ire by asking questions."

But the rich girl wondered still. She could see the poor family, the girl and her mother, the daughter so well, bounding proudly, head high, in her wrappings, the mother so sick, so sniffling, horribly sick. The poor girl had an arrogance that denied her the friendship of the rich. She could not speak to someone who had eaten pig in the day when she had eaten scraps, when she had scraped the growth from food tossed to the animals and heated it in the sun, selling firewood to buy milk so badly needed. The poor girl would not talk to the rich girl, not when she wore her rags, when she cleaned her place of cleansing. So the rich girl could not ask her directly. They could not discuss health and sickness.

The rich girl was not allowed the freedom of the poor girl. She could not talk to the young men of the village. She could only watch them. Watching them working, feeling physically in pain for want of him, the son of the weaver. He was in a good position in the village; but not good enough. She was set to marry the son of another village. They had not met but she had heard stories of him. Of his size. He was large, and paler than many. This was said to be a sign of great birth. The rich girl, too, had pale skin. She did not see how that was superior, when she had to avoid the sun, as did he. They had something in common, then. They would stay together under cover, watching the work continuing.

The rich girl spoke to the weaver's son once.

"When will my cloth be ready?" she asked.

"When you need it," he said. It was apparent that he thought her foolish, a space-waster. He thought she would never be worth anything. He was an honest man. If he was not, he could take her interest and turn it to his advantage.

The rich girl watched the weaver's son and the poor girl from her carefully protected area. The poor girl was disdainful of the men in her village. She wanted a stranger in her life, a man who did not know or care about her mother the Snot Hag. She walked a lot, and, one day, the rich girl followed.

The poor girl wandered with a makeshift sack, knotted from scraps and rags. She gathered the roots they ate and sold. The rich girl watched as she plucked roots, nibbled the flowers from the plant and placed the root in her sack.

The rich girl tasted a flower. It was sharp and sweet. She plucked the flowers alone, from an area the poor girl did not go to. She baked these flowers into flat cakes, and after finding approval from her mother, began distribution. Within two weeks, the hag's nose did not run and the rest of the village was well, also. The rich girl had begun to understand sickness and health.

Andra said, "That's how learning comes. Through curiosity."
"The rich girl was curious, yes," Marvo said.

Andra always felt good about what she did. She never hurt people.

Marvo and Andra worked hard; their shows became famous for their sensuality. And they worked on tricks, tricks with water. Andra had promised the fish tank trick to their promoter; soon they would have to perform it. Marvo drank only water, he bathed often. He watched the water on a lake or a bay for hours.

The water was always changing. Just before dawn it was as black as his vision of the future. He saw the bodies floating in the water, bloated, stretched.

"I'm scared of water," he told Andra.

"You're scared of nothing. You're just nervous of trying something new."

"Why do you want to do it?"

"Because it will make us famous."

So they rehearsed. Marvo stopped visiting the lake at night.

Stories of death found him, though, even when he stopped searching, when he practised the magic.

They performed in an old church. Not the fish tank trick, but their best work. Throughout, Marvo felt as if there was someone on stage with them, helping out. But no one was there.

"Do you see anyone?" he whispered to Andra as he transformed her into a morbidly obese woman about to burst.

"It's a very spiritual place," she whispered back.

After the show, the vicar thanked them for bringing comfort. "We are every last one of us bereaved," the vicar said. "All of us have lost a loved one. All of us are struggling to let go."

The audience wouldn't leave.

They hung around Marvo, wanting to talk to him. "You'll understand. You know about death and despair."

Marvo felt attacked as they told him stories of soul and loss.

A mother told a story to Marvo, sensing that he needed comforting, that he was seeking answers.

Son

This is the story of a death. A bitter death; a middle-aged child dead too soon, old parents left behind. The neighbours entered, to open the windows and let the poor child's soul out. His parents would not let the windows be opened. They wanted to keep his soul at least, if not his dear, dead body. They stayed in their home for many months, having food delivered by neighbours, pulling it through the cat door quickly. Their son's soul had dinner with them, and they always had his favourite meals. They talked a lot, in those months. Talked as if the past was the future, as if they had a future. They didn't stop the clock as they were told they should. They didn't want to be reminded that for the dead person time was over, that days and hours no longer mean anything. But they are not haunted.

Dogs surrounded the parents' house at night, howling at the spirits waiting for the boy's soul to be released. He bred grey-hounds when he was alive. The parents sat inside. The sound was so terrifying they couldn't eat. Dogs howl at night because they are conscious of spirits hovering around the house, ready at the moment of death to bear away the soul of the departed.

Finally they released him.

Marvo felt pity for this loving pair. Marvo's boon to them was help to fade the love; he sped up the process. He made the boy become bad; evil, he went out and got into trouble.

"Me! Me!" a young woman said. "I want to tell you a story."

Claudia-Maude

I was alone in the house when my father died of natural causes. He hissed and blinked, said, "Open the windows, Maude," and died. My name is Claudia. I don't know anyone called Maude. I knew about opening windows. My father wanted his soul to have somewhere to leave. I did not believe in the soul, or reincarnation, or anything like that, and I was tempted to leave the windows shut to prove it.

I folded the crochet bedspread up under his arms, removed a pillow and laid his head back. He looked asleep; I turned the radio on to see if that would waken him.

He lay motionless, unresponsive. I began to feel nervous.

The room was stuffy; I needed some air. If I opened the windows it would be for air.

I imagined my father trapped. He was bad enough sick, complaining of his own uselessness as if it was my fault. Constipating himself in embarrassment, the very idea of me seeing his stool in a bedpan.

Imagine him trapped in the house, banging frantically against walls to get out, moaning and shouting and *watching* me.

I moved from room to room, opening every window. Then I felt very ill.

I called for help. The vicar came and closed the windows against the icy night. They nursed me to health. But my dad was gone by then. I waved goodbye in my mind.

M arvo did what she asked. He healed her guilt.

He did not find Doctor Marcia Reid. She had a magic all her own. She made herself invisible.

He knew the mist would need to be thick and the distraction great. He had all the knowledge he needed from his counterparts around the world.

Eternal life would be his Roman circus.

He saw a terrible war ahead which would kill ninety percent of the population. A war whose results would last forever, and if the people could see their future, they would not carry on.

It would be over for humanity.

The mist had to be thick, and the magic powerful if it was to keep them happy till then.

The day came at last for the trick to be shown. Marvo was no longer nervous; the trick was like breathing now. He knew it was good, was wonderful, in fact. He was proud that Andra had designed it.

There was quite a good crowd in, the day Marvo the Magician did not defy death.

Children who loved him were there, on school excursions, or with parents or grandparents, older sisters and boyfriends, big brothers and the ones they kiss in the car. The adults were there for the kids, but they loved Marvo too. They loved him because he was beautiful, he made them feel good. After an afternoon with Marvo, the world did not seem so bad.

Doctor Marcia Reid was there, watching from the audience, ignoring their love, thinking, "I'll shoot when he emerges, the moment his head rises, in the second when he's still tranced by his own magic."

She was not a gun person by nature, but she had learnt. Her finger rested on the trigger and she waited for the trick to finish. She was dressed in a large coat with big pockets into which she could plunge both arms deep without arousing suspicion. This was where she held her gun.

She had travelled by bus to the large theatre where she stood with a group of children. They had their own money but she said to the ticket taker, "They love playing grown-ups."

The ushers had barely glanced at her and she did not look at them. She settled halfway down the auditorium and waited to be amazed.

Marvo found missing children, made a chocolate appear in every lap, and created a dancing tableau using items from the audience: a hanky, some keys, a pen.

Marvo circled the auditorium with fire, because he knew that fire was powerful. He whispered in every ear, "What do you see?" and they saw cars and lovers, islands, food, murder and slippery slides. As they stared, Marvo felt in pockets for little things he might like. He found lollies, coins, tissues, sand, seeds. These he kept; they were not missed. He knew Andra would love these found items.

At last it was the finale, the end of the show. Marvo appeared on stage amidst a thick mist.

Marcia Reid snorted. *Unoriginal. Look at that assistant woman performing her own magic, making the Devil look good.*

Making the evil magician look good.

Doctor Reid rose slowly from her seat. The children were jumping and leaping; her movement was not noticed. She knew she needed to do this, that he should have died as a child, that he had lived a life which should not have existed.

Marvo climbed into an opaque glass coffin.

The children were silent, and their adults too. The giggling had died down. A child blew wind through his lips and teeth and the children collapsed into giggles again. The adults were not sure about Marvo after watching him. They were offended by a magician who farted as he climbed into his box. Shook his bum and squeezed it to get the last bit of air out, and by the time the children's laughter subsided, was in the coffin and a tank of water was rising from beneath the stage to surround him.

Andra, the magician's powerfully unbeautiful assistant, walked around the tank and the adults laughed this time too, because she looked grotesque on the other side, the gallons of water distorting her movements, stretching her limbs and elongating her features.

She hurried out the other side and children there screamed. They saw her long limbs shrink back and were terrified.

"It's just a trick, it's magic," said one parent, whispering, trying to calm the children. He had seen the limbs shrink, too, but he could rationalise better than a child. "It's called an optical illusion," he said.

There was no movement within the coffin within the tank.

The seconds passed and the audience began to feel constricted in their breathing. Andra's chest rose and fell heavily. They watched her and felt suffocated.

The air was thick; there wasn't enough of it. They started to breathe deeply and slowly, to steal the breath from each other.

Andra said, "If Marvo does not emerge within four minutes, the air within his box will be gone." Everyone counted; the time quickly passed.

Andra stood smiling by his body, her hands resting on her hips, one fingernail nervously and secretly plucking one of a thousand sequins on her leotard.

There was still no movement. Marvo did not appear to be struggling for breath.

In the tank with his coffin were a hundred fish, large and small. They seemed to echo the distress of the humans in the auditorium, struggling against their environment, fighting and swimming erratically.

Time had passed for Marvo to emerge, and the fish seemed to go into a frenzy. A full-scale war left them dead and bleeding, the clear water clouded with blood, the coffin obscured. Children began to whimper and cry, and their parents began to bundle them up, angry that the performance was so unsuitable, so upsetting.

Marcia Reid approached the stage, with the children. She clenched her fists, because she couldn't believe Marvo would die. She was so close to murder, to taking the gun and shooting the evil, killing the magician. Taking control, taking power.

"Get him out!" she screamed. "Get him out of there!" The children screamed, "Get him out, get Marvo out!" and at last someone did something. The tank was lowered into the ground and the coffin hung suspended, dripping with blood-coloured water. Then Andra and the young manager, dressed all in black, manoeuvred and floated it to the floor at the head of the stage and smashed through the lock. Marvo had the only key, inside with him.

Andra opened the lid.

Inside was an enormous fish, its tail bent up to fit into the coffin.

There was a soft cheer from the audience, though they couldn't tell if everything was all right yet.

"Take it out," whispered Doctor Reid.

"Take it out," echoed louder by the audience.

Andra gestured for help. The young manager, glad for a chance to show his strength, bent over the coffin and, with Andra, lifted the huge, slippery fish out of the water.

The audience sighed and sucked in breath at the sight. It was beautiful, green and glowing, pink, orange and strong and a fish to keep forever.

Andra and the young manager got a few laughs as they struggled to place the fish on the stage floor. Its tail flapped weakly, twice, then stopped.

The children squealed as the young manager took a knife from his pocket. Andra shook her head but he did not see the movement, and she wasn't sure enough to insist.

With the children screaming, the young manager sliced open the belly of the fish.

The curled limbs of Marvo the Magician unfurled.

Andra threw her arms out in a gesture of success, of presentation.

The audience, hysterical with relief and delight, cheered and clapped. This was the trick, it was Marvo Magic. They stamped their feet for five minutes, Andra standing with her hands spread, the young manager staring down at Marvo's unmoving body.

The audience were awed that he performed this trick for them, *them*, that they would be the ones to describe it in later years. How to describe the box he had been in but a coffin? A glass coffin? And how to make a listener believe that it happened this way, that you were not embellishing?

Marvo had not moved, and the audience began to hush. He held in his fingers the key to his own chains, and the audience murmured, "Why didn't he use it? Is he an idiot?"

Marcia Reid, her gun sweaty and difficult to hold, waited for the moment when his head would rise, his face grin, but that didn't happen. The young manager ordered the curtain to be dropped, and he told the audience to go home, that the show was over and it was beginning to rain. They were mostly children and they didn't care about the rain; they wanted to see more Marvo tricks. But the show was over.

Everyone knew something was wrong, that Marvo was in trouble. The children didn't want to go until they knew he was all right, but the adults wanted to leave, because Marvo didn't look well at all, he looked dead, and at least get the kids home, onto home turf, before telling them the truth about why they would never see Marvo again, something like *he's gone off in a balloon and he's travelling somewhere over deepest darkest Africa.*

Doctor Marcia Reid left too, already changing the scene in her mind so that she had done it, she had killed Marvo. She had not been cheated of that, Marvo had not died before her eyes and stolen from her this final triumph.

This is how she fantasised the death. She decided that she had played a large part in it.

She rose from her seat, children bumping and shouting around her.

She raised the gun, but Marvo caught her eye at the last moment and winked.

He knew. The bastard knew. And was willing to let it happen.

Hadn't he read the Venerable Bede, who said that suicide was as much the truth when a person allowed their own death? That Jesus Christ had committed suicide, because he did nothing to stop his death, he accepted his fate and went along with it?

Angrily Marcia Reid shot her first bullet.

Marvo the Magician fell heavily, and all but Marcia and Andra gasped. Andra smiled down at him, liking his new joke, his next trick, his surprise.

At her feet, Marvo twitched.

The audience was silent, anticipating the moment when Marvo would rise, lift his arms and enfold them.

His throat pulsed. The blood could not be seen on his black clothes.

Five quiet minutes later, the young manager emerged and bent over Marvo.

Marcia Reid felt a finishing, a completion. She was done.

A ndra cared for Marvo's cat, which mourned and wailed; he would not eat. She felt the cat was acting out her own grief, and she gave all her attention to him, transferred her pain to him, so the cat suffered for her as well.

She tried to think of words Marvo had used, clues to why he had died. Allowed himself to die.

Andra was understanding of his need for greatness. She wondered if his death was part of this need.

She admired his need. She needed greatness herself but found it in more subtle places.

A week passed. A week of death and despair, where entire families died in deliberate head-on car crashes. Where children born imperfect were drowned in their baths and the elderly, too slow, were cut down.

Then a glimmer of hope.

On the news, instead of the story of poisoned apples or plague, there was a Marvo the Magician story.

"In a move which appears to demonstrate the existence of real magic, Marvo the Magician, who died under mysterious circumstances last week, has booked eight minutes of air time, the longest commercial this station has seen. The time was booked more than a year ago, a standing order to come into use exactly two weeks after his death. At 4.30pm next Saturday, tune to this station to hear Marvo the Magician speak from the grave."

It caused great excitement. Children who had loved Marvo and children who loved magic, or mystery, or murder, all plotted to be allowed to watch it. It was the middle of the year and nothing interesting was happening. People arranged parties, Marvo the Magician parties, where they would dress up like magicians, every last one of them, all of them thinking it an original idea.

The mist fell away and terrible things happened. Only the promise of Marvo's trick kept many from giving up.

The mutterings of the powerful were not always meaningful. A politician railed against Marvo; from the grave, Marvo discredited him and gained even more respect.

People worshipped in different ways. This meant that Marvo could expect worship; he knew people would look on him as a saviour.

The week passed. In accordance with his request, Marvo's body had been taken to the theatre where he had begun his performances and placed in the position specified by him.

The parties gathered. On Saturday afternoon, they ate and drank, children and adults, enjoying the excuse for a party. Those at home watched alone, or with a partner. Those at work watched if they could; listened to the radio if they could, or feigned disinterest. Thus it was that at thirty minutes past 4 o'clock, a large percentage of the population was ready to witness Marvo the Magician's final trick. They all watched, through a desire to be amused, or through fear, or superstition. Even a person who believed they were modern and insusceptible would not walk under a ladder. Superstition comes from fear, of others or of the future. It is used for protection.

Andra did not want the vultures to sense her weakness. She didn't trust her voice or her silence. She dressed as nobody and was not noticed. The cat refused to be left behind, so she carried him beneath her coat, where she could feel his purr rumble against her chest. Having the cat so close to her skin made her think of Marvo; he had told her once about the smell of his cat.

"When he's sleepy and pliable, his skin warm, his paws soft, not ready to strike, I lean over and nestle my nose in his fur. I breathe in his smell; warm skin, fur and dust, a smell so faint it's hard to identify. I think it's a chemical; the smell of happiness."

Andra wept as she remembered those words.

Marvo's body looked no different. It had been kept cold, like meat, kept fresh. Now it lay on a trestle covered with black damask. He lay naked.

As the moment approached, the cameras began to roll. At the very moment, sunlight poured in, a lesson Marvo had learnt by spending his time with the gurus, and from the blind man's box story, bathing his face in light. Two minutes passed.

People waited.

The corpse's toes began to twitch, his shins and thighs to ripple.

"Oh, my God, he's full of maggots," someone whispered.

People backed away. The TV producer looked at his watch.

"He's got five minutes left."

A minute later, his stomach rippled. His fingers twitched.

A minute later, his eyes flicked open and he smiled.

Marvo the Magician sat up. The hall was silent. They had all watched two weeks earlier as three doctors proclaimed him dead.

Marvo breathed out, his breath foggy and laden with a drug to make them all believe, accept. Many people worshipped drugs as a god, for healing or for oblivion. Marvo's breath was part of the mist; it helped the magic.

Marvo stood on the high table which held his coffin, raised his hands, then leapt into the air, higher than anyone could imagine possible. He plummeted, then, and people thought, "Again? Again I have to watch him die?"

No. He shattered into a thousand pieces, each leaping up, a small Marvo, each jumping onto the shoulder of an audience member, ready to whisper the truth.

"Listen to me, listen," Marvo said. He was huge on stage, too, big in the camera for all to see. "I have a gift for you. This is a gift my people have had in their possession for all human existence; the time is right to share it."

There was silence but for one crying baby. Marvo, small as a mouse, tickled the child under the chin; she giggled and smiled.

"This is a secret my people do not like to share. They don't like to use it themselves. That is because the sacrifice is great. But the reward is great, too. The reward? Immortality."

This tested his power over his audience. Some snorted and Marvo, thin as a stick, poked elbows into ribs. *Listen.*

"Once you have the secret, I cannot promise you its success. It is not easily obtainable, and you will have to work all your lives to continue living."

Marvo remembered the Tree of Life. The priests were willing to give the secret to the people, and did so, but the people could not keep the rules.

"There are four rules. Each person who abides by the rules makes the rules stronger. Every disbeliever makes them weaker. Every suicide damages the future and punishes all on earth.[†]

"The first rule is: You need love. True love. It is there for everybody in different forms. You will need someone you can trust to care for you. And you will need to care for that person. I tell you this person is for love and for your existence. There must be monogamy. I cannot emphasise that enough. Any form of betrayal damages the rules."

It was vital his voice was strong and enticing; it mattered more how he said it, than what he said. This was hard for a man who always spoke quietly.

The rain tapped at the windows; it pattered in a soft sheet. Marvo looked out and the room followed his gaze.

"You need to eat fresh meat to revitalise the cells. By fresh I mean of a new kind, something you have not eaten before. Eagle. Zebra. Cat. Dog. You need to eat fresh meat to absorb that sense of new."

"What about the vegetarians?" one reporter called out.

"The vegetarians will not live forever," Marvo said.

"The third rule is that you must learn to daydream. You must learn to separate your brain from your dreams and to spend your time in dreaming. You look at me and see a young man. But I had an ancestor who lived to one hundred and eighty; another who died at two hundred. You see a young man, but you are looking at potentially three hundred years of life."

Marvo was lying, of course. He figured a lie was worth it.

"The final rule is this: you must accept that the world will live forever, and that you can be a part of it. Each person who follows the rules makes us stronger; each person who doesn't makes us weaker. If you were to jail the unbelievers they would still wreak havoc. If you were to drug them, they would believe. This is a choice up to all of you."

He apologised to the children of the audience who'd witnessed him die. "I did not mean to upset you," he said. "I didn't realise how much you loved me. You see how something you love so much cannot die?" He was giving them false hope, telling them a lie to make them happy.

"I needed to show you how to live forever, though. Do you understand?"

There was a great cheer in the room. The prospect of death had been

---

† Seneca tried to make his wife promise to commit suicide. Epicureans and stoics both believed that a man who, because of illness or persecution, could not find happiness, could be allowed to commit suicide. Suicide was accepted, even admired as courageous, the accepting of eternal rest. They believed in quality, not quantity of life. With Christianity, these beliefs slowly changed.

lifted from them. Fears can be so easily manipulated.

Marvo said, "Who knows what lies beyond death? Who wants to find out?"

He walked about the room, pinching one person, kissing the next. To their murmurs, he replied, "Eternal life will make each touch more intense. Stroke your arms," he said. Every person watching stroked. He said, "Imagine feeling every pore, every hair, every ancient scar. That is eternal life." Marvo discovered he loved to lie. It was so much easier than the truth.

There was silence, then cheering again. He had given them a precious secret; each and every person watching knew they would use it wisely.

There was no alternative.

There was the numbness, the numbness Marvo had seen and felt in a dream. And Marvo could feel his magic weakening with each trick. Eternal life meant loss of magic. It meant truth to be seen, a life without the mist.

The loss was gradual. The magic he used was not replaced.

Marvo had one last and vital trick to play. Doctor Reid must be finished with.

He knew she was travelling by road, hitchhiking. She thought she was anonymous that way, that she could escape.

She was smart enough to know she needed to escape.

The hitchhiker's tale had never left Marvo.

It was dark. She thought she would take one more lift, then rest where that lift ended.

Doctor Reid loved heat—this Marvo knew. So he made the mist icy, made Doctor Reid freeze as she stood by the side of the road.

Marvo threw the door of his car open and the heat billowed out. Doctor Reid closed her eyes, blissful.

"Hop in," said Marvo. Doctor Reid took in the driver with a glance. A young man, a thin man with a welcoming smile.

"Thanks," said Doctor Reid.

The young man started the car.

"Have a drink," said the driver. He gestured a can with a straw in it. It was warm beer, disgusting.

"Drink up," said the driver, and Doctor Reid could only do as she was told.

She felt drunk very quickly and her vision was blurred.

"Nice night," she said. "Nice night for a drive."

"For a drive?"

"Yeah, drive," said Doctor Reid.

They passed a signpost which could send them in four directions. The driver stopped the car.

Doctor Reid felt a chill throughout her body. A mist was rising around the car, an ice mist to freeze her soul.

"The magic is all powerful and we will die to protect it," said the young man, back to Marvo the Magician now.

She said, "But you did not die."

"My needs are dead. My feelings, my emotions, and my laughter. These are dead."

The doctor clutched at the door behind her back. She released her seat belt. Marvo just watched her.

"Perhaps you will die but you cannot kill," said Doctor Reid.

She chose to believe this. "You can destroy. You destroyed a good man, a world leader who worked against you. He believed in truths and realities."

World Leader

The military took over his country and arrested him as a drug lord. This, during his interrogation: "You are a drug lord." The military commander leaned on the desk so heavily it creaked.

"I am not. I serve my people with honesty," the world leader said quietly.

"You don't understand the pain that honesty can bring. You think the people want the truth about how many are dying: how many hurt, how much cruelty. The people can only take it in small doses before they turn to drugs and alcohol." The commander smiled, grimaced.

"I told my people everything," the world leader said.

"You told them all you knew. We, however, did not tell you everything." The military man's voice rose to a shout.

"I need not know everything to know that the magic is wrong, that it must be exterminated." The world leader did not raise his voice.

"You do not understand. Without the magicians, all the ugliness would be revealed. All reason for living, all excuses for our existence would be destroyed. Society and civilisation would collapse into anarchy. And you, the righteous destroyer." With this, the commander pushed him with both hands.

"You have no faith in the world," said the world leader from the floor.

"You have no grasp of reality, for all your bleatings of truth. I sentence you to death as a destroyer of the fabric of society." The commander turned his back, dismissing the man.

The misled leader died in jail. His death, dealt with by the magicians of the press, appeared to be that of a madman—a killer, fascist, baby-fucker. An evil man dying an unusual death.

His birth, forty-seven years earlier, had also been unusual.

His mother, fourteen years old. His father, fifteen. They ran away from their small country village to escape the threat of death (such a terrible thing, to make love. Hurtful to all things). They lived quite happily, found a room to sleep in and the boy found a job. Only as the pains began did the girl panic.

"Take me home," she said, and the boy, unwilling to take responsibility, put her into the car they had stolen from his father (who had called in the police) and began the four-hour drive.

"Hurry hurry hurry," breathed the girl, the way she had been told. He drove faster.

They were still an hour from home. The girl began to scream softly. He drove faster than he had ever driven, losing caution.

He took a corner; there was a bridge; a river. He missed the bridge. The car sank into the river and reached the bottom.

The water reached over the opened windows and poured in. She could not move fast enough; he removed his seat belt, then hers, and tried to lift her out.

"I can't move," she said. The water was cool around her swollen belly. "I want to stay here."

She made him roll her underpants off and recline the seat, so that when she laid back the water reached her shoulders, lapping around her ears. She breathed the way she had been told to breathe.

This is where the baby was born. In the water; held quickly aloft. Cord cut with nail scissors. Voice powerful, clear, outraged. A most unusual birth.

Marvo knew Marcia Reid was angry at this scapegoating, this blaming the world leader for the ills of the world. He said, "Each person is responsible for his own addiction. And the work I do affects the work of others. Each person I save will save, or at least not hurt, others."

She opened the door and threw herself out. She would run as soon as she landed.

She did not land. She fell towards the centre of the earth, twisting and spinning, and the crust of the earth closed over her head, leaving her in darkness, in the pitch, in the black, in the forever.

Marvo draped the set of blue beads he had been given in the village of

Araby around his neck. He felt secure with the glass warming against his skin; he felt protected, as if something else was taking responsibility for him. And he wanted that; he needed to disassociate himself from what he had done, and what he was about to do.

He was numb, after the disappearance of Doctor Reid. Marvo could no longer be a magician. Removing Marcia Reid took almost the last of his magic and Marvo now had to learn how to look after himself.

He did not wish to live forever. Worse, he no longer cared for Andra. He could not care for anyone. He felt the absence of love like a cancer, like a presence which sat heavily in his stomach, in his blood.

Andra was so overwhelmed at his return that she wanted to treat him like a king, a god. His cat did not go near him. The cat sniffed at his legs, as cats sniff at scars. He sniffed at decay, at rottenness. Marvo picked him up and held him close, but the cat stared at the roof, the ground, waiting patiently for the chance to escape.

"I can't believe you're back," Andra said. She squeezed him, hugged, licked and bit. She sat him on a stool in the kitchen and cooked him a meal, which he ate without comment. He did not catch her eye; how could he look at her without guilt, knowing how she felt, knowing he felt nothing.

She massaged his limbs, hoping to bring him back to life that way. He shook her fingers off in irritation, and scrubbed his skin in the shower to clean off the scented oil.

"Would you like some wine?" Andra said, through the door.

"I made it myself." Marvo knew what would be in it. Grindings of this, scrapings of that.

"I'm not thirsty," he said. He did not feel guilty about how cruel he was being. He felt nothing.

Over breakfast the next day, she told him one of his favourite stories:

The Gift, the Ruby, the Time in the Desert

It was too hot to smoke, but I lit a cigarette anyway, held it in the ebony cigarette holder I had found when I moved into the shed.

The man came to me. His hair was plastered to his head, the singlet tight on his body. I could see the flakes of skin flying from his shoulders, wet flakes like snow.

He followed me into my shed. I dropped my sarong and lay on the bed.

"I only came to give you this," he said, and handed me the beautifully wrapped box he had under his arm. It was the size of a shoebox, and heavy. "Happy Birthday," he said. "For your next birthday." His voice was gentle, soft and clear.

"Why don't you stay?" I said. "Stay for the afternoon. No charge."

He did stay, but only for an hour. Then he left. He said, "Don't open the present until it *is* your birthday."

He did not return; I did not expect him to. I opened the present as soon as he left, and found two gold pieces which together made a circle, money and a ruby.

When I saw what the Bush Pig man had given me, I knew he would not be seen again.

And you found me the story of the ruby and had it set into this ring.

The ruby was once part of a ring. The ring is a broken circle.

It was broken in a moment, as things are.

There was no accident involved; no mad axeman, or catching door or getting it caught in a drain or something.

This ring was cut deliberately by a wife tired of her husband.

She cut the ring in two pieces, removed the jewel (a small ruby, nothing more) and baked the metal pieces in a carrot cake. The ruby she kept in a small piece of cotton wool, and she HID it somewhere, but she never remembered where. She even wrote in to a clairvoyant, who said, "Dear Ruby, the special item you were seeking is behind the heater."

It seemed unlikely, the heater was built into a wall of stones. However, she got the Vulcan man in to remove the heater, and she searched amongst the dust for the ruby. She was surprised not to find it; she had heard nothing but good reports about the clairvoyant. This clairvoyant told one woman where her husband was (at a gay bar in the city) and another person, who had lost a watch, found it in her sexy underwear drawer.

The ruby, however, was not to be found.

The man ate the carrot cake in its entirety, swallowed it down and abused his wife for its scratchy texture. He ignored the sharp pain that came when he swallowed orange juice or anything acidic the next day, and the next week, until his throat swelled and he went to the doctor (his wife would not take him; she was angry with him for still living). He was allergic to antibiotics and he had to stay in hospital.

He stayed there a long while.

This man had always had troubles with his bowels. Thus, it was two weeks before his stool contained the two sharp gold pieces. They were placed in a jar of preserving fluid and put onto his bedside table. He recognised the metal, pictured the pieces joined on his wife's thin finger. He could not check her finger to see if it was still there; she did not come to see him and she did not answer the phone.

He was released after a month, clutching the jar and nothing more. His voice was ruined forever; he could only whisper, and, when excited, squeal like a pig.

When he sold the house, he painstakingly packed every item to send to charity. Behind a foot heater in the back of his cupboard he found a dirty package of cotton wool. Unwrapping it, he expected to find a tooth, a memento of childhood, perhaps.

Instead, the ruby.

Even this story had no effect on Marvo. Nor did the one of her birth. Marvo accepted that, although he did not care for her now, he owed her honesty.

He said, "I made a sacrifice, when I lost my life. I gave up my heart, so I can no longer love you. I can only leave you while your memories of me are happy."

Andra said, "I'd prefer to have you and hate you than not have you at all."

"No." He kissed her softly, thinking for a minute that life without magic would have meant a life together, but then they may never have met.

He no longer wished to live forever, so he gave up the partner who was his only chance.

Marvo told Andra goodbye, and, taking a pack of necessities, including his cape, his rope and his wand, he returned to the room of his childhood. He took much tinned and packaged food, many blocks of chocolate.

He chose to ignore the friendship they shared, to forget the stories she told. He gave up many things, control amongst them. He worried about the world of magic he left behind; he was powerless to control it. His voice was quieter than ever.

He couldn't even shop without using gestures.

The cat would not come with him, preferring to stay with Andra.

The house of his childhood was a hotel now, like the one he dreamt of, the one where magic happened. Strangely, it seemed even larger than he remembered. It was a popular hotel. The desk clerk was busy; he did not see Marvo walk past him. No one saw Marvo press the panel in the wall and slip inside.

He wondered belatedly if the body of his grandmother had been found. He did not relish the idea of stumbling over her bones.

It was the first time he had thought of the house since he had left it. His grandmother had once told him he would need it again, but in all his life, through all his troubles, he hadn't thought of the house. This was the time. Now he needed it.

He walked unbothered to the place of entry. His grandmother's body was not there, nor any hint of it. The rope ladder was there, and he climbed it. He pulled it up and dropped its length down the other side. He climbed down.

Nothing had changed. The bed was unmade. The dent made by his grandmother remained.

The TV was still there, and Marvo laughed at its antiquity. How far technology had travelled. He switched it on; after a flicker and a buzz a picture appeared. News—a fire. Marvo turned it off.

He removed the sound knob from his pack, where it had stayed all these years, and placed it by the set.

The room was dusty and cobwebs ran like lacework over ceiling and walls. Marvo knew he had work to do but he lay down on the floor first, on the pillow that smelled of dust and him, him at twelve, and he slept to let the atmosphere sweep over him. It was one of the most magical moments of his life, coming back to the room of his childhood, unchanged for twenty years.

Although he did not feel a particular emotion, his memory had not been affected, and, for a moment, he was nine years old, surveying the room in search of some activity.

His things where he had left them. The stuffed toys: blue rabbit, pink bear, small duck, tiny hippopotamus. The pack of cards he'd made.

He wanted Andra there, to pick up each object and describe it to her, tell her some true stories, tell her the truth. For a moment, he felt he could cry. He removed the cape from his pack and draped it over the things he had left behind, drawing them in, initiating them.

Marvo set the ancient perfume bottle up by his bed. He had not opened it; he hadn't needed to.

Marvo put new sheets on the bed and lay down with his book of magic to wait for nightfall.

He emptied his pockets of his small findings, his small thieveries, and placed them around the room.

He awoke to noise and activity. The hotel was popular; he would never be bored, listening to sex and arguments, seduction and rejection, dinner table talk and shower singing, toilet noises and balcony silence. Marvo could hear it all from his room and in his mind he pictured the world out there, and wondered what things he would find. He wondered what food would be discarded and hoped there would be bottles with drops left in them. He would start a liquor cabinet. It was another step towards the reversal of eternal life.

Many months passed. Marvo pottered and slept. The hotel had a seafood restaurant and threw out a lot of food. Whole plates of prawns, loaves of bread, vegetables still crisp. He ate well. He did not live off scrapings. Sometimes, if the noise was great in the hotel, he watched TV with the sound on. It reminded him of outside, as silent TV had reminded him of the room when he was away from it.

Then his back became unbearably itchy, and for the first time he missed companionship. He wanted someone to scratch his back.

It was the first feeling he had had since he came back to life. He did not enjoy it.

He rubbed his back against the wall but the wall was too smooth. He used his wand to scratch bits but that only made other bits worse. Finally he had to lie flat on his stomach like a burns victim and let the itch take hold. He gave in to it, his body twitching and jerking, every nerve saying, "Stop that itch."

Marvo cried in frustration.

He could only see a small patch on his back, using a mirror his grandmother had kept hidden under the mattress.

He could only see a small square which began to writhe and ripple. Spiders, *he thought*. I have spiders hatching all over my back.

His neck was a poker of pain, but he could not rest. He watched his back, watched for twelve hours as, from the bubbles and pustules on his back, a small child formed and emerged. In the process, he came to know the child so well he felt as if a lifetime had been shared. He knew then why he had heeded his grandmother, his replacement mother, why he had trusted her so completely. He *was* her, he was of her flesh and her mind.

The child slept there on his back and now Marvo relaxed his muscles and slept also.

Time was not noted. When Marvo awoke, the child sat, straddling his waist and bouncing. Marvo gently rolled over until the child was in his arms. Her eyes were opaque, murky. She opened her mouth but did not speak. When he touched her skin, it was pliable, soft. He let her sleep on the bed; watched as her eyes cleared and began to see. He fed the child, sang to her, told her stories. A week later, Marvo awoke to find her staring directly into his face. She looked nine years old, or ten. Her consciousness had begun.

"Who are you?" she said.

"I'm your Father Christmas," he said.

"What's Father Christmas?" she asked.

"A magical person you should always believe in, no matter what you hear or see."

"Is there anybody else?" she asked. She was bored with him.

Marvo did not want her here; he did not want her keeping him alive. He did not want her to grow in silence. She was different from him; the silence would not help her.

He thought of Andra, whose magic was more powerful than his now. He thought of her love for him and for magic, her belief in magicians. He said, "Your mother sent you here for a holiday. Soon you will go back, with a gift from Uncle Marvo. But you must never tell anyone where this place is. Not even your mother. One day you may need it for yourself, one day when the powers are strong against us."

The little girl stared at him.

"I am not clear," said Marvo. "Let me tell you a story." And he began to tell her his tale.

He closed her eyes and carried her to a place far away. The knowledge of the room was with her—she would find it when she needed it. He had rewritten the ancient note and asked her to read it when she was thirteen.

He watched her run away and prayed for her safety.

He felt the pain when the parents lost their boy. It was far more tragic for the parent to lose a child; the child is prepared for a parent to die. The parents always think they will die first.

Marvo learnt the answer to his final question. He was born at eight or nine. He, too, had emerged from the back of his parent .

Marvo felt great loss, although he had known the child for such a short time.

He realised his grandmother, his mother, must have lost her magic when she had him, for now he had lost his completely.

This had happened to all his ancestors. He saw that clearly. To have a child was to pass on the magic, to give it up and let one younger, more able, take up the mantle. Marvo thought he should feel bitter and cheated, but he felt tired and relieved.

He would never know whether his vision had been clear; would the world burn as he had seen? Was his gift of the secret of eternal life enough? Truly, he knew they would not use it; they could not. It sounded too simple because it was really too hard.

Every creature has a strange birth, every death is a miracle.

Marvo removed the stopper from the bottle of perfume. He pressed the last drops into his wrists and sniffed deeply of the ancient sweetness before closing his eyes and letting the mist fill him.

APPENDIX A

The recipes Marvo cooks:

Ploughman's Lunch

Take one chopping board and place on it any or all of the following: rye bread, dark bread, pickle, cheese of any strong kind, mustard, ham or other cured meat. Serve with a large mug of beer and a smug expression.

Asparagus with Lemon Mayonnaise

Boil a large amount of water in a large saucepan. Add a bit of salt. Cut the hard ends off 4 bunches of asparagus and drop the spears into the boiling water. Cook for 5 minutes, then remove with a slotted spoon and run under cold water. This asparagus is served cold, so take your time making the lemon mayonnaise.

Lemon Mayonnaise

Mix 2 egg yolks, ¼ teaspoon of dry mustard, salt, pepper and 2 table-spoons of lemon juice. Then beat in 500ml of good olive oil, little by little, till the mixture thickens. Now add the rind of 1 lemon and 1 tablespoon of boiling water.

Bouillabaisse

Cut fins from 6 pieces of good fish (three different kinds).
Cut off the heads and set aside. Cut fish into portions. Place 2 tablespoons of olive oil into a large pot and fry 2 finely chopped onions, ½ a stick of finely chopped celery, 1 finely sliced leek and 1 finely chopped hulk of fennel for 3 minutes. Add 1 tablespoon of tomato paste and cook again for 3 minutes. Add fish heads, a handful of finely chopped parsley, 6

crushed cloves of garlic, 4 peeled, seeded and chopped tomatoes, ½ a teaspoon of fennel seeds, 1 packet of saffron strands, a sprig of fresh thyme, 1 clove, ½ a bay leaf, a strip of orange zest, a pinch of cayenne pepper, a teaspoon of sugar, salt, pepper and 500ml of white wine. Add enough water to cover the fish heads and simmer for 30 minutes. Then strain the stock and discard both the vegetables and the fish heads.

Cut 6 blue swimmer or sand crabs in half and throw away the lungs and stomach sacs. Wash in very salty water. Clean 12 mussels well and shave their beards. Wash and devein 6 green king prawns. Wash 6 Moreton Bay bugs. Into a new pot, place mussels, prawns, bugs, crabs and fish in layers. Cover with hot stock, put the lid on, bring to the boil and simmer for 10 minutes.

To serve, pour soup into individual soup bowls. Place fish and crabs in a big serving bowl in the centre. You will need another bowl each for the prawns, bugs and mussels. You should also supply fresh French bread with sauce Rouille.

Sauce Rouille

Process a 5 cm piece of French bread with 1 egg yolk, 4 crushed cloves of garlic, a pinch of saffron strands, 6 tablespoons of fish stock, salt and pepper. Then add 6 tablespoons of oil slowly, as you are processing.

Caramel Oranges

Peel 8 oranges and remove all the white flesh. Slice into little dishes and pour ½ a cup of Grand Marnier over, as well as sprinkling 3 tablespoons of caster sugar. Cover these and refrigerate until they are about to be eaten.

Cook 2 cups of sugar and 2 tablespoons of water until the sugar has dissolved. Do not stir after this has occurred. Then cook until the sugar is caramel coloured. Pour the caramel over the oranges and chill again.

Kumara Soufflé with Creamy Tarragon Sauce

Grease your little soufflé dishes and sprinkle the insides with breadcrumbs until covered. Shake away excess crumbs. Cook 400g of chopped kumara using your favourite method until it is tender, then drain. Process kumara, ⅓ cup of sour cream, 2 tablespoons of grated fresh Parmesan cheese, 1 teaspoon of lemon rind, ¼ teaspoon freshly ground nutmeg and 4 egg yolks until smooth. Beat egg whites until soft peaks form, then fold into kumara mixture and spoon into the little dishes. Bake in a moderately hot oven for 20 minutes, or until puffed and golden brown. Serve hot, with creamy tarragon sauce.

Creamy Tarragon Sauce

Combine 1 cup of cream, 2 tablespoons of chopped, fresh tarragon and 2 teaspoons of seeded mustard in a pot. Blend 1 teaspoon of cornflour with 2 teaspoons of lemon juice and add this to the cream mixture. Stir the lot over high heat till the sauce boils and thickens.

Veal and Chestnut Stew

Heat 2 tablespoons of oil in fry pan and cook 750g cubed lean veal in batches until browned on all sides, removing meat from pan as it is done and adding more oil as necessary. Add 3 crushed cloves of garlic to pan and cook for 1 minute until golden. Stir in 1 tablespoon of plain flour and return meat to pan. Add 1½ cups of white wine, 3 seeded and chopped tomatoes, 1 cup of water, bring to boil and add pepper and salt.

Reduce heat, cover, simmer 1 hour, till meat is tender. Add ¾ cup peeled chestnuts, cook 20 minutes, till nuts are tender. Stir in 2 tablespoons each of parsley and rosemary and serve.

Quince Tart

Pastry: Process 125g unsalted butter, 125g caster sugar, 250g plain flour; 4 egg yolks and 1 teaspoon of vanilla extract in a processor till just combined. Turn out onto a lightly floured surface and knead lightly till smooth. Wrap in plastic, chill for 30 minutes. Roll out to 5 mm thickness and cut circle to fit the top of a 22-24cm frying pan with an ovenproof handle. Rest pastry on baking sheet in the fridge until ready to use.

Filling: Peel, core and slice 2 large quinces and poach for 15-20 minutes in saucepan with 3 tablespoons of sugar and enough water to cover. Drain. Melt 80g unsalted butter in frying pan, add 150g caster sugar, arrange quince slices in pan, packing them in tightly. Sprinkle with 1 teaspoon of coriander seeds. Heat gently on top of stove till caramelised (20-30 minutes). Let cool.

Place the pastry on top of quinces, bake 190°C for 15-20 minutes, till crust is golden and cooked through. Cook in pan before inverting on platter. Serve warm with mint crème anglaise.
(Steep handful of mint in milk to be used for 30 minutes.)

APPENDIX B

Ten Good/Dramatic/Distracting Things That Really Happened

1. circa 600-550 BCE India, the Upanishads (confidential teachings) proclaim the doctrine on repeated reincarnation.
2. circa 350 BCE Tomb of Mausolus of Caria in Asia Minor (Mausoleum at Halicarnassus) is completed and becomes a wonder of the ancient world.
3. 79 CE Pompeii.
4. 364 CE Magic banned.
5. 610 CE Mob kills Phocas, who is succeeded by Heraclius.
6. 972 CE Otto, son of German Emperor Otto I, marries Byzantine Princess Theophona, theoretically adding Byzantine Italy to the Holy Roman Empire.
7. 1290 Scottish Queen Margaret of Norway dies, age seven.
8. 1516 Scholar Desiderius Erasmus (Netherlands) publishes a new edition of the New Testament.
9. 1815 Scientist Sir Humphry Davy (UK) invents the safety lamp.
10. 2050 Announcement of the healing of the ozone hole.

Sometimes only one person needs to be distracted—that one could have been the rabble-rouser.

The Roman circus is what it is. Give them something to think about so they can't think for themselves. Give them royal scandal whilst crime rises, give them Olympic fever whilst jobs disappear.

Ten Terrible Things Never Seen Because of the Mist

1. 600-550 BCE Half the male children under five stricken with paralysis.
2. 350 BCE Child molestation common practice.

3. 79 CE Entire small country massacred.
4. 364 CE No female children born.
5. 610 CE Man of the people killed.
6. 972 CE Village disappears into earth.
7. 1290 Sacrifices current practice.
8. 1516 Book burnings.
9. 1815 Baby killings.
10. 2050 Science holocaust.

APPENDIX C

Discovering Suicide

Lemmings always produce more daughters than sons.

Is that any reason to jump off a cliff?

Marvo justified the way he was doing his job by looking into the past. He saw many times when the mist slipped, many times when suicide is the only answer.

In 183 BCE the Romans demanded the surrender of Hannibal. Unable to escape, he poisoned himself in Libyssa, a village in Bithynia.

On September 2nd, 31 BCE Antony was defeated by Octavian. Cleopatra arrived with sixty treasure ships, and they escaped to Egypt. One year passed, then Octavian found them.

Resistance was impossible. They committed suicide in August of 30 BCE

In 64 CE (or thereabouts), Boadicea killed herself when defeated, to avoid capture and disgrace. She revolted against Nero before she died. Seneca hated him. Nero was sentenced to die like a slave, on a cross, whipped to death. He fled to Rome. He stabbed his own throat in 68 CE to avoid capture, though legend has it that he did not die, but was spotted a year later, arrested and executed as charged.

And other, newer deaths; of movie stars, musicians, favoured sons and daughters.

Hitler: In January 1945, faced with defeat in Berlin, he died. Ironic that the assassination plot of November 20, 1943 failed.

Jim Jones killed himself and nine hundred and thirteen others. His mother thought he was a messiah. He set up the Peoples Temple in Jonestown in 1977 (surely some hint as to his god-wish, naming the town after himself). Newsmen and relatives, on November 14, 1978, went to investigate rumours. They saw the rumours were true, that Jones was a megalomaniac and the people were not in heaven. Jones had them shot; but some escaped. He said, "Everyone has to die. If you love me as I love you, we must all die or be destroyed from the outside." "White Nights" was his name for suicide.

He died of a gunshot wound to the head. "Probably not self-inflicted", though the instruction must have come from him. Nine hundred and thirteen people died, including two hundred and seventy-six children.

David Koresh in 1986. Born Vernon Wayne Howell, Koresh called himself the "Preacher of the Seven Seals" (and the Seven Seals are about doomsday; another clue there). He wore seven waist-length plaits. He had only a few followers when he led them into the fire. Seventeen children were amongst the dead.

He died of gunshot wounds to the head. Mass suicide by refusal to capitulate.

Luc Jouret and forty-eight others. He was born in Zaire when it was called the Belgian Congo. The group he formed was the Order of the Solar Temple, who believed in the apocalypse, and that they would be the only strong people left on earth once it happened.

Hermann Göring—cyanide pill. He was addicted to para-codeine pills, which are morphine-derived. He surrendered to the Americans. He was cured of the drug while in prison. He blamed the evil of the war on Himmler. He begged to be shot, not hanged. This request was refused, and he took poison in his cell the night the execution was ordered, October 15, 1946.

Was he such a coward he could not stand the pain of having his neck broken? In 1967, a newly discovered note revealed the poison capsule had been hidden all along in a container of pomade. The fact that he carried such a product, such a primping device, would be galling enough.

Josef Goebbels, May 1st, 1945. He was named chancellor after Hitler's death but he and his wife killed their six children and themselves the next day.

Lord Castlereagh, Foreign Secretary 1822. Also known as Robert Stewart, Viscount; and the second Marquess of Londonderry from 1821. He was a great paranoid. After the assassination of cabinet attempt by Thistlewood, 1820, he became obsessed with the fact that he was a target, because he wanted to help dissolve the marriage of Queen Caroline and George IV. Castlereagh was, or thought he was, being blackmailed for homosexuality. On August 12th, 1822, he committed suicide.

Thomas Chatterton—boy poet, died 1770. In 1777, poems Chatterton had said were written by a fifteenth-century monk proved to be his own work. He was born in 1752, in Bristol; educated at a charity school, he wrote his first poem aged ten.

He left school at fifteen to become an attorney's apprentice.

He wrote most of his poems between fifteen and seventeen, when he left Bristol for London. He spent nine weeks in lodgings but ran out of money. No publisher would have him. He moved to Brook Street, Holborn, perhaps a paupers' hostel. He was deeply distressed and refused to be kept alive "by the bread of charity". He died, aged seventeen years nine months, having destroyed all his unfinished poems.

Mayerling tragedy—Crown Prince Rudolph of Austria and Baroness Marie Vetsera, 1889. So many things seem to begin in Austria. His liberal ideas were stifled by his father. He was unhappy in his marriage. He began an affair with Maria Vetsera, aged seventeen, in October 1887. They made a suicide pact and were found shot dead at his hunting lodge. Most probable reason: he was dealing with the Hungarian opposition. His place as heir was taken by the vain Franz Ferdinand, his cousin, who was assassinated in Sarajevo in 1914.

Boulanger was a French general. His mistress, Marguerite de Bonnemains, died in July 1891. On September 30th, 1891, he committed suicide over her grave, in a cemetery in Brussels called Ixelles.

Some of these suicides may seem to be for other reasons; but the other reasons seem so bad because the mist is gone.

Dido was also known as Elissa, in Greek legend, reputed to be the founder of Carthage. She either threw herself on the funeral pyre and stabbed herself to escape the advances of the chieftain Iarbas of Africa, or was abandoned by Aeneas at the command of Jupiter, and could no longer live.

Seneca, Nero's tutor, and Burrus condoned or contrived the murder of Agrippina, Nero's mother in 59 CE. Burrus died in 62 CE and Seneca retired. He was denounced in 65 CE as a conspirator of Piso. Seneca was ordered to commit suicide, which he did with fortitude and composure. Nero, too, killed himself, but surely neither with fortitude nor composure.

Matthew Lovat crucified himself, but was saved. He died later by self-starvation.

Cato, also known as Marcus Porcius, or Cato the Younger.

He was born 95 BCE, in Africa. He was the great-grandson of Cato the Censor. He tried to save Rome from power-seekers, especially Julius Caesar. Cato was an honest man. He defended Sicily and Rome versus Pompey, in 46 CE. He led troops to Africa, helped them escape by sea, then committed suicide.

Zeno the stoic committed suicide, it is said, through "Sheer ennui at having cut his finger".

Eleana di Campireali: The mistress of a bandit, she rose in the world. She became the abbess of the Convent of the Visitation at Castro and took the bishop for her lover. Her outlaw lover returned and she committed suicide for shame and loss of advancement.

1666: In Russia, many believed the Antichrist would arrive, serfs lived in fear, and suicide was rife.

In Hungary, the song "Gloomy Sunday" is said to have caused one hundred and seventy-four suicides. Such a beautiful song.

These are the stories Marvo heard.

APPENDIX D

Marvo's magic revealed: how to do his tricks, explaining the tricks of illusion and misdirection.

The Glass and the Newspaper

This trick was done with the assistance of Andra. When he raised his arms, she quickly removed the glass from the newspaper. Then she replaced it. It is all misdirection.

The Straws

Just blow them gently apart.

The Rings

Have two rings the same. One ring is hidden. He threaded the match through the hidden one, under the handkerchief, so it was secured only by the match. The spectators were so fascinated by that ring, they did not notice him running the other along the rope. As he took the rope from his helper who he has asked to remove the match, he took the original ring off the end of the rope.

The Crayons

He digs his fingernail into the crayon so a piece of it is under the nail.

APPENDIX E

Cures, for Easy Reference

Ague

> • The trembling aspen, although cursed, can be used because it trembles as the victims do. [†]

Bilious disorders

> • Saffron, which is yellow. [‡]

Brain, diseases of

> • Chew the walnut, which looks like a brain.

Cough

> • Shave patient's hair and hang it on a bush. Birds will carry cough away. [§]

[†] The trembling aspen is a cursed tree. Its leaves always tremble because, unlike other trees, it did not pay homage to the Holy Child, who threw such a look upon the tree she was "struck to the heart" and now "she trembles ever more".

"An aspen leaf placed under a woman's tongue while she is asleep will make her talk," his grandmother once told him.

"And why would I want to do this?" Marvo asked. "Why make a woman talk?"

His grandmother smiled and nodded: so much wiser, the nod said, I am so much wiser, older than you. Marvo would try it, many years later, sleeping beside a quiet woman who had no story to tell. He placed the leaf beneath her tongue and waited for the words to tumble; they did not. It was not until he was with Andra one night and they were watching TV that he saw the woman, and she was not quiet for a moment. She was an investigator; she investigated with her tongue.

Marvo was sickened with grief for his grandmother; he missed her like a limb.

[‡] Some believe God stamped a signature on plants to demonstrate their use.

[§] Usually it is dangerous to hang out hair. Andra provided fully supervised hair-hanging to her clients with coughs. She guaranteed no witch would take the hair.

• Shave hair, place between two slices of bread and butter and feed to the dog. [†]

Cramps

• Place shoes at bedtime peeping from beneath coverlet.
• Carry a piece of sulphur.
• Ligature around cramp (The older option uses eel skin. Today a bandage is considered sufficient.).
• Prick affected area with pin, then light candle and stick pin into it. When the flames reach the pin, the pain will vanish.
• Place the best poker under the bed at night.

Cure-all

• Legs torn from living frog.

Epilepsy

• Beg thirty pence from thirty poor widows. Exchange with a clergyman for half a crown from communion plate. Walk nine times up and down the aisle. Pierce coin and hang around neck.
• Wear a ring made of five different sixpences from five different bachelors who didn't know what the coins were for. Another bachelor must take the coins to the smith who should also be a bachelor.[‡]
• Dried frog worn around neck in silk bag.
• Eat the flesh of white hound with a meal.

Flux

• Tormentil, which has a red root.

Heart or liver disease

• Take a piece of steel, a packet of saffron, a pint of old ale, a piece of wool. Place the saffron and steel in ale and soak the wool in it. Wind the wool around wrist and drink ale. The patient will only recover if the yarn lengthens when it dries. [§]

Horse and cattle disease

• Hag stone tied to stable key.

[†] We are talking here about the transference of disease.
[‡] Do they mean just a single man, or do they mean a virgin? When they talk about spinsters they always mean a virgin.
[§] Marvo said, "But wet wool shrinks, most likely."
"That's why the cure can be a miracle," Andra said

Hydrophobia

- A lovely soup: The liver of a male goat; the tail of a shrew mouse; the brain and comb of a cock; pounded ants; whole cuckoo bird. Cook ingredients in large pot full of spring water. Blend or process until smooth.

Nettle rash

- Use the nettle as a compress.

Nightmares

- Hag stone (Holy stone: stone with hole) suspended over bed prevents witches sitting on stomach and giving nightmares.

Nose bleed

- Skein of scarlet silk tied with nine knots tied by the opposite sex around neck.

Rheumatism

- Wear a red flannel.
- Carry a potato until it goes black.

Shingles

- Take blood from a black cat and smear it on the affected area.

Sore throat

- Canterbury bells, which have long necks.

Stye in eye

- Take a single hair from the tail of a black cat on the first night of the new moon and rub it over the stye.

Toothache

- The woody scales of a pine cone, which look like teeth, can be boiled in vinegar. Go to a young tree, cut a slit in the tree, cut off a bit of your hair and put it under the bark. Put your hand in and say, "This I bequest to the oak tree in the name of the Father, the Son and the Holy Ghost." †
- Cut the gum with an iron nail till the blood flows. Smear blood on nail and drive it into wooden beam. As long as the nail remains in position, the toothache will stay away.

† Done to use prayer to cure toothache, while still believing a worm caused the pain. A mixture of magic and religion. It seems cruel to the oak tree. Not much of a bequest.

- Hang the forelegs and one hind leg of a mole around your neck as a charm against toothache.
- Take finger and toenail clippings, wrap them carefully in paper. Make slit in bark of ash tree. Place packet under bark. Close as tightly as possible.
- Nail human skin to the church door.
- Wash out infant's mouth with leftover sacrificial water.
- One woman was given a tooth-shaped amulet and told never to open it. Finally, after it had worked she did. Inside was a note which said "Good Satan cure her, and take her for your pains."

Warts

- Go out alone, find a black dog. Rub the wart on the dog's underside.
- Impale a slug on a thorn. As it dies the wart will go.
- Tie number of warts in knots in string. Hide string under stone. Whoever treads on the stone will take warts. †

Whooping cough

- Hold a frog in the child's mouth for a few minutes.
- Have the child drink the milk a ferret has lapped.
- Hair of eldest child should be cut into small pieces and placed in milk for child to drink. ‡
- Pass child three times over the stomach, three times over the back of a donkey.
- Hold spider over child's head and say, "Spider, as you waste away, whooping cough no longer stay." Put spider in bag and hang over mantlepiece.§

---

† Seems a bit cruel to the unknowing walker.
‡ Wouldn't those pieces be rather sharp?
§ Whooping cough was such a terrible cruelty there were many ways to cure it. Thus does cot death attract theories and superstitions.